BLIND SITE

ANDREW VAN WEY

BLIND SITE

ANDREW VAN WEY

GREYWOOD BAY

Copyright © 2021 by **Andrew Van Wey**

Cover Design: Stuart Bache | Books Covered UK
ISBN-13: 978-1-956050-01-1 (hardcover)
ISBN-13: 978-1-956050-00-4 (paperback)

V.21.9.4

Visit the author online: andrewvanwey.com

TRIGGER WARNING

The millions of listeners and viewers who tune in to my daily show know that I am a trusted voice in these strange and frightening times.

My publisher, however, has insisted that I include this warning for those of a more delicate nature.

So, if bad words bother you, if violence and suspense knot your stomach, if discomforting facts unsettle your mind, then consider yourself warned. Put this book back on the shelf. Point yourself in a more soothing direction. Perhaps the bookstore staff can lead you to that colorful section with its stickers and children's books and promises of happy endings. You won't find that here.

But you will find the truth.

—Sam Stephens
The Conspiracy Isn't a Theory: Your Prepbook for the Next Revolution

I<small>T BEGAN IN A DEEP PLACE OF FORGED METAL AND STONE</small>, <small>WITH AN</small>
alarm's blinking red light and a man who thought, *This better be good.*

Security guard Roger Fenton regarded the console as experience had taught him. Another government drill, no doubt, and paperwork to follow. His vision shifted, past the winking red light, past the framed photo of his wife, to the TV's blue hue and the news from the edge of the Iron Curtain. East Germans onscreen, taking hammers to the wall, shattering concrete and bending rebar; West Germans gathering at the Brandenburg Gate, welcoming the fall. President Bush's face filled all nine inches of the portable TV.

Then static consumed it.

Roger smacked the old Sony. This was breaking news, dammit. The alarm could wait.

Then the TV screen exploded.

Roger's annoyance vanished. So did his hearing, along with half his left ear. Lips that had sneered at the alarm seconds ago were now speckled with glass. His front teeth were crimson shards, holes he wouldn't notice for minutes. Now, he tasted the tang of adrenaline. Now, the alarm had his full attention.

Roger pulled himself off the floor. With a flick, he depressed the red lockdown switch. Then he was on his feet, limping down the hall. Klaxons wailed along the concrete walls. Machinery rumbled deep in the facility, emergency systems now coming online.

As he inserted his keycard in the reader at the RESTRICTED end of the hall, he felt—no, he *knew*—something was behind him. A frigid glare bloomed upon the nape of his neck.

Impossible. He was the only guard on duty. For an eight-hour shift, this corridor was his. Three hundred feet of metal and concrete, two magnetically locked doors, one at each end. His employers had given him these tools: a thermos and a gun, a new IBM computer and an old Sony TV. And they had given him orders: in case of emergency, guard the far door.

Trembling, he tongued the shards of his front teeth. Needles pierced his jaw as he plucked glass from his face. He was wounded, yes. He needed medical attention. To hell with this job.

Then he heard the voice.

"Help..."

He spun. The hallway—*his* hallway—bathed in flickering red light. Color-coded piping threaded the walls: blue for compressed air, green for steam, orange for chemicals. His TV, splayed open and sparking.

But it wasn't the dying Sony that loosened Roger's bladder. Nor the acrid fumes of burnt circuits, the whining of his burst eardrum, the alarms crying, *Eee-ooo, eee-ooo.*

It was the woman floating in the hallway.

Or rather, it was half of her.

A glistening form, nude and wreathed in smoke, hung in the air with arms outstretched. Wet hair clung to her breasts, curtains over a heaving chest. Her stomach was translucent. Where hips should have met thighs, flickering ribbons swayed, like kelp in gray water.

Warmth dribbled down Roger's leg, his courage pooling in his size eleven boot.

"Help me, please!" cried the fractured woman. She was twenty feet away, yet her words enveloped him, wet echoes bristling every hair on his skin. "Make them stop!"

In a blossom of red glass, the lockdown lights burst. Shadows swallowed the halls. The wailing klaxons sighed as the electrical systems fell offline. Darkness, and silence. Only the ambient groan of the mountains above these subterranean halls.

Roger's left hand crossed his hip, grasped his flashlight. His right hand fumbled for his service revolver. With two snaps of a leather clasp, he had his .38 Special in one hand, his Maglite in the other, wrists crossed in the Harries technique. Funny how fast his training came back.

What wasn't funny was the hallway before him.

One hundred yards of dark concrete. The sprinkler system and colored pipes and vast shadows. His guard station, far off. The dying television, smoldering and hissing.

And no legless woman. No floating torso. No trace she had ever been there. Deep machines were coming back to life, drowning out the *eeeeeeeee* of his damaged ear. He could feel his Maglite rattling against his revolver, feel his heart hammering in the back of his throat: *lub dub, lub dub*.

Bulb by bulb, the hallway flickered red, and the wailing klaxons returned. *What if I'm concussed and not thinking straight?* Roger thought. *Or worse, what if I'm losing my mind?* No half-formed woman had floated there. Such a thing was illogical, impossible, insane.

Behind him, the RESTRICTED door whirred open. In nine months he'd never seen a soul step through. Emerging now was proof there were others here, deep beneath this mountain.

"Damn, you're on backup power too," the man said. Roger placed him in his late twenties, hairline receding. A pale face behind shattered glasses and a torn lab coat. "Did they get to your fuses yet?"

"What fu-fu-futhes?" Roger stammered. Hard to make S and Z

sounds with broken teeth. He cleared his throat, spoke slow: "What's happening?"

"Never mind that," the man said. "Now listen to me: what's important is what happens next." His voice trembled yet his words had an academic locution, trained and precise.

"I don't underst... sta... follow." Roger stole a glance past the scientist. Beyond the RESTRICTED door lay the unknown. A blank, even on the evacuation maps. But there it was. A short hallway and an open chamber. Loose lights swaying above what might be an auditorium.

"We've had a cascade, a real proper fuck-up," the scientist said. Roger caught the echo of a British accent. "Now, Roger, I need you to listen. Can you do that, Roger?"

Roger blinked; this man knew his name. "I... Yes, I can."

"Good. At the other end of the hall, past your station, there's an override console. You've seen it, yes?"

Sixty yards down the hall: twelve buttons and a steel grill set into the wall. Roger had passed it each shift, given it no more notice than the water fountain. Now, he truly saw it for the first time.

"You put your security code in, then press star, then input the following: seven, seven, three. Star, star." Roger glimpsed an ID on the lab coat: *F. Linamore, MD.* "Seven, seven, three, star, star. Roger, say that back."

"Theven, theven, three." Roger cleared the blood, enunciated. "Star, star."

"Your code first, then star," Linamore said.

"Then the numbers."

"Good man."

"What about you?"

"We've got to secure our lab," Linamore said. "But you need to secure this facility. Roger, this is what you've been hired for."

"It is?" Roger swallowed.

"Indeed. Now go. Run!"

What Roger lacked in speed he made up in momentum.

Twenty lumbering steps, and he came to a sliding halt. The red shadows unfolded. A torso appeared, followed by two silvery eyes and hair over a face twisted in pain.

"Help us!" cried the woman. "Please!"

Her voice came from everywhere. A shriek off concrete, a cry drowning out the klaxons, a whisper behind and piped right into his mind.

Roger, frozen mid-step. Wanting to run, to scurry backward. Away from the override console. Away from responsibility. Away from this impossible task.

Then he noticed the woman's arm. Just a subtle motion, a flicker. The edge of her shimmering arm grazed the wall...

... and slid right through it.

These halls were poured concrete and beams. A million tons of metal and earth formed this facility. And her arm simply passed through.

If she couldn't touch stone, Roger supposed, then maybe, just maybe, she couldn't touch him. It was a trick, like at Disneyland. A hologram made with lasers or mirrors.

So Roger found his footing. Found his courage. Wiped sweat from his brow and found himself charging.

"No!" she cried. "Please help us! Please!"

Shoulders down, Roger drove toward the floating figure. Closer. Closer. Then he drove through her. There was no impact, no stumble. Just a chill and a shifting breeze. Glancing back, he saw a vague torso fading, like ash in the wind.

Fifty yards now.

Forty yards.

Thirty.

The override console neared, a gleaming protrusion, all stainless steel and rubber.

Twenty yards.

The hallway erupted in shapes.

Legs. Arms. Fingers and eyes. Hands unfurled from the walls. A leg kicked down from the ceiling. A headless body, two shimmering balls of mercury where eyes should be, hoisted itself out of the floor. Something pale crab-walked along the ceiling, reaching out with sinuous hands.

"No! Please!" screeched the chorus. "Help us! You have to listen! Don't do this!"

Roger plugged his ears but the voices were too loud. He sensed nothing could silence them. If he tore out his eardrums, he'd still hear their cries. Feet pounding, ankles wobbling, piss-filled boot squish-squishing, his heart drumming and his lungs burning and—

Then he was at the override console. Punched his code in. Seven, seven, three, star, star.

A deep tremor as machinery rumbled into action. The klaxons died mid-cry. And the bodies were gone.

"Challenge red," said a woman's voice over the PA system. "Response omega. Challenge red."

To Roger, it was meaningless. Just a calm mantra in this now empty hall. He was closer to the exit now, yes. Closer to clocking out, once and for all.

And the deep tremor grew.

"Challenge red. Response omega."

Klaxons returned, now above the exit. With a click, metal descended, sealing the exit behind a steel barrier wall. Roger lurched forward, an instinct for immediate escape. Logic halted his feet. This was eighteen inches of plate steel, strong enough to shrug off a nuclear blast. No way out.

And the tremor didn't stop. It shifted, like a great snake meandering through ductwork.

Pop! The sprinkler above the barrier burst, raining gray mist. *That's not water*, he realized. Water didn't rise and swirl. Didn't reek of chlorine and stick to the tongue.

Pop! Another sprinkler burst like a bottle of champagne, fog coating the floor and rolling off the walls.

"Challenge red," the pleasant voice said. "Response omega."

Pop! Another sprinkler, closer, dimming the halls behind chemical curtains.

Roger didn't consider himself smart. He slept through his community college lectures, skated by on low C's. But he didn't need a degree to read this situation. His muscles coiled and tensed. Frigid adrenaline shoved him forward. His feet followed the orders his brainstem spat out. Go! Run! Faster and faster!

He ran past his guard station. Past his shameful puddle of piss. Twenty yards to the RESTRICTED door and the klaxons caught up. He prayed Dr. Linamore hadn't locked it.

"Challenge red," said the voice, so calm, so serene. "Response omega."

The pipes above rattled. The RESTRICTED door was ready to seal. Roger tightened his thighs and strained his ankles. Pushed off against the industrial floor. Ten yards. Seven. Five.

"Challenge red. Response omega."

The klaxon let out a final warning. Three yards away and Roger threw himself into the door. A click above and six holding bolts retracted. Gravity did the rest. Two tons of steel descended with a shattering clang. The barrier sealed Roger's hall and all within.

But not Roger.

He lay on the other side, deeper in this facility than he'd ever stepped.

Here, the concrete walls widened. Here, the ceiling rose to a geodesic dome, all wires and smoldering lights. That scientist, Linamore, he had called this a lab. Like calling the Sistine Chapel a church. Fear became awe as Roger staggered up to the balcony.

To his right, a box platform loomed behind mirrored glass. To his left, a metal catwalk curved on, a perfect half circle to observe the chamber below. From this top deck, he looked down upon an open auditorium, three concrete terraces lined with machines. There were tape drives clicking and spinning. Computer terminals flickering green. Some were functional, others reduced to cracked plastic and glass.

Thumbing damp hair from his eyes, Roger studied the floor of the chamber. Around it, like notches lining a clock, sat twelve ovoid objects, egg-shaped and smooth, nested upon wires and pipes. They looked, Roger thought, like iron lungs. Or seed pods, every edge and angle sanded down to a curve.

Two pods were bent and distended, as if something had tried to hammer its way out. Another half dozen lay open, gull-wing doors exposing dark waters within. Three pods sputtered and hissed steam, doors unfolding.

A wet mass hit the concrete, flopped, and rolled. A fish? No, that was an arm. And there was another. He stared down at the chamber, seeing but not believing. A face wreathed in smoke, eyes made of mirrors. A latex-wrapped body, threaded with tubes. That was a mask on its face, Roger realized, squeezing the rail to keep steady.

The form hoisted itself from the pod at seven o'clock. Damp and gasping, it pried the rebreather from its face. It was a *he*, red-haired and no older than eighteen. He collapsed to the floor, steam wafting off in silvery threads.

Legs emerged from the pod at eleven o'clock, then a plump body. Another man, older, bearded. He slipped to the floor, rolled over, and vomited.

A shape tumbled out of the five o'clock pod. Sent a medical tray spinning and scattered syringes.

Roger didn't notice the needles. Didn't notice the gurney, the stained restraints. All he noticed was the woman's form that heaved with each breath. His stomach tightened when she tore off the rebreather. He'd seen her before, minutes ago. Then, she had been floating in the hallway. Then, she had been missing her legs.

She looked up from the chamber, looked right into Roger's eyes. Two words left her lips. "Help us."

"Challenge red," said the calm recording. "Response omega."

From a distant place, Roger realized the alarm was now sounding in here. From a distant memory, he recalled omega meant "end."

Then it came: the rumble, the click, the hiss of sprinklers filling the chamber with clouds of gas thirty feet below. The machinery, the pods, the wet people and their cries: all swallowed by fog. And it rose, reaching up in fingers of gray.

The way back was sealed. To Roger's left: the metal catwalk in the chemical mist. To his right: the box platform behind mirrored glass. The scientist—Linamore—had to be taking refuge within.

Roger tugged on the door but the handle was firm. He banged on the mirror but it just jostled and warped. Pressed his eyes to the glass. Dim shapes beyond, perhaps another way out. Behind him: mist swallowed the chamber. Twenty seconds. Perhaps thirty, if he held his breath.

So Roger raised his revolver and fired.

The first slug scarred the mirrored glass. The second ricocheted, striking the steel door with a *pling*. Roger remembered his training, what the range instructor had once said. Glass is strongest at the center and weakest at—

He aimed for the edge. Squeezed the trigger three times. The klaxons were screaming but his Smith & Wesson screamed louder.

The hammer hit on empty and a cry left his lips. There was only a crack.

Fifteen seconds...

So Roger grabbed his flashlight. Raised that pound of anodized aluminum and three D batteries. Brought it down on the glass. Each blow grew more desperate, each strike less precise.

This shouldn't be happening, Roger cursed. The wall was crumbling in Europe. There, the Iron Curtain had collapsed. Here, in the homeland, Americans shouldn't be gassed by their own government. He had a life, a wife, a future unfolding. He wasn't... going... to... *die!*

The crack became a crevice. The fractures expanded. A buckling strike and the mirrored surface came apart. Roger drove his boot heel—and two hundred and fifty pounds of American desperation—straight into the mirror.

In a glistening shower, eight feet of glass collapsed.

Momentum carried him through. Shards tore his sweat-filled uniform, grated his skin.

Then he felt himself rising inside the box platform. Felt his heart collapsing.

It wasn't the computer systems. Or the klaxons and red lights or the gas pouring in on both sides of this mirror.

It was the people within the room, a dozen at least. Their lab coats, their chalkboards and charts. The clinical walls and their clinical stares. Eyes behind plastic as their respirators clicked.

They were all wearing gas masks.

"Jolly good show, Roger," said Linamore's familiar voice. "Now we'll take it from here."

Roger met their dispassionate gaze. Heard the wheeze of their respirators, their amusement, their laughter. Watched their features fade, fog swallowing the scientists one by one by one.

Then it was Roger's turn. The chemical mists embraced him, dampened the klaxons and dimmed the red lights until only gray remained, bitter and blinding and endless.

[PART 1]

As the future ripens in the past,
   so the past rots in the future —
   a terrible festival of dead leaves.

— Anna Akhmatova, *Poems of Akhmatova*

NOW

THE PHOTO IS POSTCARD PERFECT: A BLOOD-RED SUNSET SMEARED beneath a tangerine haze. The distant silhouette of an acacia tree rising above amber grasslands and migrating giraffes.

Caitlyn drops the photo and opens her eyes. A near match between picture and place; only the details differ.

Here, now, a nocturnal world unfolds before her. Dust drifts across the dark savanna. Scrub brush leans in the breeze. Wide umbrella thorn trees rustle, lonely canopies over islands of quiet. No sun burns above, just the pale moon in solemn watch over this ancient heart of Africa. Night in the Maasai Mara, yet nothing truly sleeps.

A bat-eared fox meanders through the scrub, tail swaying. Far off, an elephant romps among crackling deadfall. At Caitlyn's feet, a belt of ants swarms past her toes.

Squatting, she studies the colony. Army ants, or *siafu* in Swahili. Blind and bulbous, they form a marching column as wide as her arm.

Limping, a young Maasai tribesman drags a dead warthog through the ocher insects and settles against a tree. He hikes his *shuka* cloth up past his knee, revealing a gashed calf, the wound tusk-deep and crimson. He plucks an ant from the swarm, presses its furious head to his wound. A squeeze, and the pincers sink in. With a twist and a flick, he tears the body off.

Another ant plucked, another pair of pincers pressed into flesh. In this way, he sutures his wound.

The tribesman takes in his work, pleased. Takes in the midnight savanna. He does not take in Caitlyn, who's watching nearby. Does not see how her body glows beyond her youthful complexion, moonlight made flesh.

The ants march on. The wounded warrior rests beside his game. The umbrella thorns rustle and lean as the dust drifts westward.

Yes, a beautiful place, Caitlyn thinks. Visiting the Great Rift Valley is like returning home.

But this isn't right for her client.

So she imagines the next photograph. Visualizes its frozen shapes. Ridges and crags and ice-covered spines. A tail of snow off a great mountain, like a pennant on a castle spire.

Caitlyn blinks...

And now she is there.

White blades pierce a cerulean dawn. Nuptse and Lhotse peaks, seven thousand meters of rock and ice. This is the Khumbu region, the heart of the Himalayas, the crown of the world.

Behind Caitlyn, down trail, a group of German climbers approaches. They move with a confident swagger, hellbent and headstrong. Canteens clang against the frames of three-season backpacks. Gloved hands pass protein bars as chattering teeth tear at foil.

Caitlyn has known climbers like these, has a few clients just as crazy. Weekend warriors with seven-figure salaries and twenty-five years of climbing the corporate ladder. Twenty-five years of momentum.

And when fifty looms on the horizon, a part of them snaps. Private health clubs are swapped for private trainers. Home gyms become trips up the Matterhorn and December in New Zealand, climbing Mount Cook. Then comes the big one, and Caitlyn always advises her clients the same.

"Go home," she says. "Your life isn't worth this cruel rock."

The slowest German pauses, glances back in her direction. He squints, taking in the trail. Perhaps he feels her gaze. Perhaps he hears her whisper. Perhaps he wonders how this tattooed young woman can stand here in yoga shorts.

He sees only empty trail. Then his eyes rise, tracing the cold ridges, settling on colorful prayer flags fluttering in the dawn. He raises a camera and snaps a photo.

Perhaps he will make it home, Caitlyn hopes. Perhaps he will share that photo with someone worth turning back for.

A whistle, a shout. The leader calls out, "Hurry up!" The climber lowers his camera and moves on.

Caitlyn strolls the narrow path, climbs an icy boulder. Her bare feet feel no cold, no warmth. She is the perfect hiker; she leaves almost no tracks.

Leaning out over the glacial valley, she can just see the peak of Everest: 8848 meters, each step promising nature's indifference.

No good. Her client requested something unique, not a cold death.

She thinks of the photos, shuffles them in her mind. An image of five rivers converging. An ashen lake and a wall of torrential falls. Jungled banks lining whitecap rapids where a million gallons crash down through arboreal cliffs.

She blinks...

And now she is there.

A tour helicopter buzzes overhead, carving a spray of downwash across this wide river. Caitlyn's toes touch the surface, undisturbed. Below, curious fish follow her heels. Their eyes are different, she supposes. More attuned to the bending of light. Do they wonder, *How does this liminal woman walk upon water?*

The roar of another tour helicopter chases them off.

Today, Brazil and Argentina share the Iguazú River, but these are just names on a map. This gnarled shore whispers of history more ancient than helicopters or hotels. Only the jungle owns this dance of water and mist.

Caitlyn surveys this 360-degree view from the waterline. Yes, this is good. A good enough start. There, at the shore's edge, an old trail nearly devoured by vines.

She focuses on it, blinks.

And now she is there.

Walking among the banana trees and strangler figs. Surrounded by brambles. Caitlyn lets the dappled path guide her. Drifts among a grove of cockspur coral. Past a vine-choked Jeep and down a trail untrodden for years. Along the rim of a sinkhole where roots cling to an earthen maw churning with currents.

And then the trail ends. A hidden grotto unfolds before her, moss-soaked and crowned in orchids and begonias and bromeliads, fiery and blooming with life.

Caitlyn has seen daylight paint the dunes copper where the Namibian desert meets the azure Atlantic. She has watched the sun crest the brick ghats of Varanasi. Witnessed it dip beyond the sandstone spires of Angkor Wat.

But here, somehow, light thins and frays until only a dozen golden threads weave the shade of this time-lost glade. Tourists and hotels, the helicopters and tour boats, all so close by. Yet the jungle has kept this grotto to itself.

For now.

Her watch vibrates, slow at first, an echo shaking the jungle, root to canopy. Time's up.

Twenty seconds.

Caitlyn steps over a log and stops at the edge of the sinkhole. Vines descend into the glistening depths. Caitlyn takes a deep breath.

Ten seconds.

Then she throws herself into the maw.

Seven seconds.

Falling, falling, down into the earth, where ancient rivers roar.

A squeaking colony of bats at the edge of light's reach. Mushrooms and lichen and the rot of deep rivers rising now, rising fast.

Five...

Four...

Three...

Wet rocks rush her. The inner sanctum of the falls, churning waters and rending death, furious and final and black.

Two...

One...

WITH A SIGH, Caitlyn opens her eyes. She reaches out, tracing the edge of the space before her. A coffee table. A stack of photographs. A joint, half-ashed and skunky. She feels this all, home. Her fingers find her smartphone, unlocking it.

"Alarm," the voice assistant says. "Alarm cancel button."

Her finger slides over the button.

"Alarm canceled," the smartphone chirps. "Home screen."

Her finger skims the display. The voice assistant reads off the apps, arranged from most used to least. Still, sometimes Caitlyn loses sense of which screen she is in. And when she returns to her body, she still thinks in colors and shapes and sights to behold.

"Music player," the phone chirps. "Email. Phonebook."

She presses *phonebook*. The haptic feedback clicks in response. A downward swipe and the phonebook reads off names: I, J, K.

"Kim, Phillip J. Kingsley, Jamira. Kissinger, C. Howard."

She narrows in. The phone confirms the name. Her earbud informs her the call is in progress. Dialing... Dialing...

A firetruck's lowly howl drifts in through the bay window. Outside, four to five blocks away, Caitlyn estimates, southbound down 19th Street. Further off, she smells the Pacific. Cool salt and minty yerba buena. Evening soon to come.

With a hiss of overseas switches, the call connects. "Caitlyn," a man's voice crackles over the hum of a jet engine. "Great timing. We were just talking about you."

"Goodness, nothing bad, I hope."

"No, no, the opposite actually. One sec. I'll switch to the in-flight line."

The engine hiss cuts off; the line holds.

Caitlyn fights the grin curling her lips, but the trip's afterglow lingers. She stands up, stretching her legs. It is ten paces to the bay window and the joint has left her unbalanced, woozy. She follows the sofa, feeling her way there. Then she feels the sunlight wash over her. Six blocks away, the firetruck is now honking at traffic.

Howard Kissinger, her client, is both forever busy and unfathomably wealthy. Forbes estimated he works sixteen hours a day. Bloomberg claimed the alimony from his previous marriages could fund a mid-sized American city. And still he is a romantic at heart.

"Caitlyn?" he asks, clearer now from the line in his jet's bedroom. "Still there?"

"Yeah, sure," she says. "You know, I've got Mark Zuckerberg on the other line, so…"

A polite laugh. "Tell Zuck he owes me. That shitbird poached the head of my R&D."

"Absolutely, he'll get an earful. If, you know, I ever talk to him."

"So listen, I have to say you were right: sailing up from Rio was the best decision, hands down. Nikki and I spent the week circling Fernando de Noronha. We were tempted to retire on the spot."

"Well, it's a marine park. That's a problem." Though for him, she suspects, not insurmountable. "But I'm glad you enjoyed it. Actually, that's why I'm calling. I don't mean to pry, but are you still, you know… planning on popping the question?"

"I wanted to. I mean…" She senses him cupping the phone, whispering, "I keep waiting for the perfect moment, the right place. Set and setting, you know? I've had this damn ring in my pocket for days. Christ, I went scuba diving with it. Feels like a grenade."

The diamond's the size of one too, Caitlyn muses. Sure, Mr. Kissinger is just another rich CEO; it's easy to mock his champagne problems. But when it comes to women, Howard is as confident as a boy at a middle school dance, all elbows and knees. To Caitlyn, it's endearing.

"You're still in Brazil, right?"

"About to fly out. Nikki has a photoshoot in Belize. Figured I'd drop her off."

"With respect, Mr. Kissinger, I suggest you reconsider."

"The jet's already fueled, Caitlyn. I'm not sure—"

"I've found your perfect setting."

There is a pause. A whisper. "Really? Where?"

"Iguazú, north of the falls."

"Never been there."

"I'll send the airport code and have a guide waiting. This'll put you a day behind, but trust me: if Nikki doesn't say yes, she never will."

"How..." She hears him clicking his tongue. "Caitlyn, are you sure?"

Caitlyn isn't sure about a lot of things. Like being a billionaire twenty times over. Or running a fintech company with half a million employees. Or cruising the Brazilian coast, a former UFC champ turned bikini model on your arm, and a ring once worn by the duchess of Windsor in your pocket. Caitlyn isn't even sure what hue the light is that now falls on her face. If the oranges and reds she sees in her travels exist beyond this persistent midnight.

But she is damn sure of that hidden glade and its sun-threaded orchids.

"How do you know?" Mr. Kissinger asks. "How can you be sure?"

"Because I just got back."

2

TAMPA, FLORIDA
TUESDAY, 11:30 P.M.

THE AUTOPSY SUITE IS A CRISP SIXTY-FIVE DEGREES. NEXT TO A stainless steel cadaver rack is a wooden stake mounted behind glass that reads, *BREAK IN CASE OF VAMPIRES*. It is this curio that catches the investigator's eye, allowing him a moment to collect his thoughts and harden his stomach.

"Okay, tell me about Deborah Anderson," Michaels says and returns to the business before them.

"Sure, you read the report," the medical examiner says and unzips the body bag. "But seeing is believing."

Michaels studies the corpse, mind fighting to reconcile the diagrams on the page with the body before him. "Yeah. Nothing like water from the well."

"You can say that again." A screech as the examiner pulls a stool up to the table. "Jesus, just look at her."

He is an older man, this pathologist. Soft in that way men often go on the downslope of fifty. *Diabetic?* Michaels wonders. Or trying to hold it together. Tampa has its fair share of crime, sure, but it isn't statistically violent. Certainly not *this* violent.

"I'd like to take a crack," Michaels says. "Helps me keep things objective. Just tell me when I start coloring outside the lines."

With a stretch and a snap, they don nitrile gloves. "Have at it, Special Agent."

Technically, Michaels is a field agent, not a special agent. His job makes no distinction, preferring any title that opens a door.

And technically, his job doesn't exist.

The Foundation, the agency he works for, is a line item on yearly budget appropriations, buried several thousand pages deep, listed as *MISC SPENDING – DISCRETIONARY*, and rubber-stamped by a senator, a congresswoman, and a federal judge. His badge, his credentials, his concealed carry, they all trace back to an LLC in Spokane. In eight hours Michaels will need to brief his coordinator. Yet the corpse is still briefing him.

A deep breath. Old meat, rust, damp salt that sticks to his throat.

"Victim is a female, late fifties, seventy inches tall, and in good physical shape. Frequent swimmer, I'm guessing, from the tan lines and developed shoulders."

"Debbie was fond of the laps."

Michaels eyes the examiner. "You knew the deceased?"

"It's a small county, small field. We crossed paths from time to time."

This man's demeanor makes sense now. A stranger on the table is one thing. A colleague, that pierces that veil of professional detachment. Especially one that met this end.

"Cause of death is hard to assess," Michaels says. "Violent, obviously. There are multiple signs of trauma. Her left hand is fractured at the wrist, perhaps defensively. No signs of tissue beneath fingernails. Her right arm is just…"

"Looks like a noodle, don't it?"

Michaels swallows. A noodle left out to dry. "No signs of sexual assault. Her left hip, however, is dislocated. There's bruising near the socket."

"Her spine, actually." The examiner points to where tan buttocks merge with the pale base of her back. "L4 and L5, where the lumbar meets the sacrum."

"Those are big vertebrae, aren't they?"

"Big and strong as they come. They bear the heavy lifting."

"And they were dislocated prior to death?" Michaels asks, leaning in close to the woman's skin. Purple and blue colors her hip.

"Dislocated?" the examiner asks. "No, these were fractured. Shattered, really. Like glass. See, if you press here…" He takes Michaels's fingers and pushes up the spine, from buttocks to lower back. "Feels like a sock full of tacks, don't it?"

Rigor mortis has long since dissipated, so the sensation is undeniable. Like rubber against gravel.

"No signs of osteoporosis?"

"No, not that bad."

"Mild osteogenesis imperfecta?"

"Brittle bone disease," the examiner says. "Would be a thought, but her spinal curvature doesn't suggest it. X-rays reveal normal skeletal growth. And her eyes… Well, most OI patients exhibit a bluing of the sclera. Like a tint, right? Hers are white. Well, they were until…"

"The left one burst," Michaels says.

"Globe rupture, technically," the examiner says. "Like squeezing a grape."

"Hence her sunken temple." Michaels points to the cave beside her ear. "Her cheek was shattered."

"Takes tremendous pressure to fracture the zygomatic bone. Saw it in a baseball game once. Pitcher took a line drive to the face. Most of the time it's the skin that lacerates first."

"Like a boxer getting his cheek split."

"Yep, yep," the examiner agrees. "Then you have petechial hemorrhaging. Here, it's just straight to the bone."

"Meaning?"

"Meaning there's no cutaneous trauma. Skin around her eye's not showing signs of impact. Which is… unusual."

Michaels takes a step back, takes in the woman's remaining eye. Within it dwells lost photons, the last flashes of forty-eight hours ago. If only he could harvest that dead light, wind time backward, and look out at whoever did this. To tell them, *Justice is coming.*

The only way to do that is to continue forward. He asks, "What about her jaw?"

The examiner clears his throat. They had to get to this part eventually. "What about it?"

"How much force would that take?" Michaels asks, adding, "To pull her jaw from her face?"

THE OFFICE of the Hillsborough Medical Examiner sits at the residential edge of Terrace Park, Tampa. Dim lights, empty roads, narrow sidewalks. A cicada hums from an oak, its song too early in the season to find a chorus or mate.

Michaels lets the bay breeze wash over him. Hopes it might wash off the smell of clinical death. Hopes this cool night will settle his mind.

A few blocks of walking, and he comes to a softball park, well-lit and silent. Finds a seat upon the metal benches. Pulls out a toothpick and chews the bamboo, savoring the cinnamon sting.

The brain is a three-dimensional organ. It synthesizes reality through spatial locations, strengthened by senses. It uses ritual to build mental connections. Some investigators smoke, if only to step away and reset the ruts of the day. Michaels chews toothpicks and counts prime numbers.

Deborah Anderson, fifty-eight, Caucasian, female. Found face-down in the shower room of the YMCA. Red waters when the first responders arrived. Witnesses: none. Video footage confirmed she was the only one to enter the locker room.

Who could do this?

No, no. Ask, Why do this? Calm the waters before stirring the pot.

And so he sits. Studies the baseball field. Studies the grass. Chews his toothpick and lets his brain seek out patterns.

The big secret is there's rarely a eureka moment. Cases are

built first from chaos, then the interweaving of clues. Confluence and flashes of—

Anger. Yes, he senses a flash of anger. And more. A loss of control.

Another toothpick. The wounds: imprecise and clumsy. And yet, what absolute strength. Deborah Anderson had been ravaged, violated, broken. Her death a tableau of contradictions.

Another flash: a famous case. A college kid, a tiger pit, and too much tequila bravado. Michaels didn't blame the tiger; it had done what nature instructed.

But Deborah Anderson didn't bear any sharp-force trauma. No incised wounds. No abraded tissue. A total avulsion of the mandible was a contributing factor. Cause of death: drowning from blood aspirated into the lungs.

Whoever did this walked through the YMCA doors and the camera caught nothing.

Michaels spits onto the bleacher, switches to a new toothpick. Far off, the sprinklers spritz the softball field. In a few hours, these bleachers will warm with bodies, and the home plate will echo with the crack of bats.

And Deborah Anderson will forever be cold. *Think, think.*

Internally, she was a map of contradictions. Her ribs had been split, her trachea torn, and her heart crushed like an old can of pop. Plane crash victims end up in better shape.

And yet, plane crashes leave evidence. Streaks in the earth, broken trees, and burnt brush. The only footprints in the YMCA shower had come from her New Balance shoes. The only hand that had touched the door had been that of the teenage worker. A girl who had come to collect towels and left with a head full of horror.

The toothpick bends between his teeth. He imagines the crime scene as it existed a few days ago.

The shower room, one entrance and exit. Unless there had been a maintenance door. Had the killer lain in wait? Perhaps hiding in a bathroom stall or a locker. Biding their time, then coming out and—

No. That's speculation. *Focus on facts.*

Another toothpick, another angle. *Rewind Deborah's day, reverse the events.*

The gym at 7:30 p.m. Picked up dry cleaning at 7:00. Thirty minutes on the freeway. Left the hospital at 6:25. Her day spent culling research in the Department of Clinical Neurophysiology at Tampa General Hospital. A thousand people in and out. Had someone she worked with wanted her dead? A professional rival, a scorned—

No. More speculation. Stick to the data. The truth is in the trauma, etched in flesh, written in a language unique to the killer. Now, how to read it?

Another toothpick. Dawn, an orange glow to the east. And his thoughts race as his fingers begin to twitch. Begging to let out a little spastic tic, the clap that offers relief in times of mental stress. He holds it, fumbles for another toothpick now. Yes, he needs it—

It snaps between his thumb and index finger. Just bends in half like a kid with a dry stick. *Shit. That's it.*

Whoever did this, Michaels thinks, *they lost control*. Not of their intention but of their strength. The first wounds were targeted; the rest had grown sloppy. A piñata, spilling candy. A blindfolded kid still swinging away.

Deborah Anderson speaks to him now. Her one eye. Within it, those dead rods and cones tell part of her story. This isn't random. This kind of violence came from vengeance, retribution, wrath.

Michaels unlocks his phone and auto-dials the first saved number.

"Thank you for calling Wong's Fine Chinese Dining," says a voice in a perfect Cantonese accent. "We are currently closed. Please leave a message."

"Field Agent Michaels, badge ID seven, seven, three, beta, zulu," Michaels says, removing the last of his toothpicks. "I need a full ViCAP scan flagging for two or more of the following external and internal wounds. Are you ready?"

There is a pause, then: "Affirmative, go ahead, Field Agent."

Michaels lists Deborah's traumas in alphabetical order, external and internal. ViCAP, the Violent Criminals Apprehension Program, is a shared database for law enforcement agencies nationwide. Written in legacy code and patched together over the years, ViCAP isn't perfect, and for Michaels it often casts a net too wide. But when you're searching for a needle in a haystack, first you need to find all the farms.

"Multiple hits," the operator says in nonregional diction. "They're coming to your phone now."

Michaels hangs up.

The fence rattles as the groundskeeper unlocks the batting cage and starts setting up a pitching machine. Knees popping, Michaels stands. At his feet lie seventeen toothpicks. Six and a half hours of reflection. And now a hunch based on one data point.

What he sees on his phone confirms it. Deborah Anderson isn't the first.

3

CALIFORNIA STATE UNIVERSITY, MARIN
LOFTUS HALL OF SCIENCE, 10TH FLOOR - FRIDAY - 10:30 P.M.

EYES HEAVY, KEMBO LEANS AGAINST HIS MOP AND LOOKS BACK ON HIS work. He has dust-mopped the floor, vacuumed the carpets in each office. To the sultry hum of Ella Fitzgerald, he damp-mopped each hall from end to end. Rinse and repeat, twelve floors in all.

Now, he wonders, what will his wife be making for breakfast? He also wonders, how much longer can he stand?

This had been a good job, once. A university salary and fair overtime. Now, Kembo is a contract employee on a staffing agency payroll where time is pliable. The overtime Kembo worked overnight will be pushed to next week.

And if he complains?

They will pay overtime, of course. Then they will reduce his hours to zero for a month. He has seen it before.

Still, Kembo takes pride in his work. Shiny doorknobs, a smooth floor. These are the joys of diligent labor.

Which is why the scuff in the middle of the hall bothers him.

There it is, past the WET FLOOR sign, not fifty feet away. A faint blemish upon the drying linoleum. Kembo turns back, pushes the bucket and mop down the hall. He truly is tired.

A chill passes through him as he nears the rogue spot. The

halls seem to constrict like a tightening throat. Impossibly, he senses he is no longer alone.

And he isn't. At the end of the hall, the elevator dings. The hairs on his neck rise. In the elevator, something small and dark crouches, a shivering mass of fur and fang.

Then it bounds out, followed by a pair of tennis shoes. The dog is more toy than a proper companion. Still, Kembo recognizes it and the man in the tennis shoes.

"A good morning to you, Professor Moore," Kembo says.

"Morning, Kembo," the man says, keys jostling as he unlocks his office. "Have they had you here all night?"

"No, sir, just early to rise," Kembo says. He finds lying distasteful, especially to Professor Moore. He is one of the good ones. One who speaks to him as a human and not an immigrant janitor. Still, a terse word to facilities by a well-meaning professor could cause Kembo trouble. Best to smile and move on. "You know how they say, early rising for birds hunting worms."

"First in the field, fresh for the fight," Professor Moore says. "Sun Tzu, I think."

"I take your word for it."

Professor Moore smiles, his eyes two friendly diamonds behind glass. There is a calm regality to the man that Kembo admires. An intellect, sharp at times, soft at others. Perhaps his own son may have such a future.

"Well, Kembo, you have a great morning."

The professor opens the office. The little dog follows him in. It is then that Kembo realizes the professor knew he was lying. After all, he's still wearing the same clothes.

Ah, work to do. Kembo wets the mop, runs it over the scuff. Yet the scuff doesn't come off. He squats, studying the floor. Broken linoleum tile. As if some hammer has struck in five places, all clumped together. Strange. He doesn't recall feeling it beneath his mop.

An echo down the long hall now. A buckling and a snap. Kembo rises to his feet, eyes widening.

There is another dent in the floor, a few feet away. The tile folds in on itself, as if a handful is being pried up. No. As if something has fallen upon his freshly mopped floor.

A third crack. And a fourth. These are larger now, bigger. Each spaced a few feet apart. And for a moment, Kembo worries they might fire him for this. Whatever *this* is.

A pair of indentations form parallel to each other. Speckled gray linoleum dents, splits. Five curious ruts run past each indentation, and he thinks, oddly enough, of a cat scratching the floor. Or a bear, coming down off its hind legs. Paws flexing and—

A low, concussive hum. The air pressure changes. With a furious crack, fresh indentations race across the floor, away from Kembo. Faster and faster. There is nothing there, no shape or form, yet a damp wind scatters letters from faculty drop boxes. The WET FLOOR sign teeters and falls.

And now it is gone. Less than ten seconds, and all that is left is seventy feet of broken linoleum and loose papers drifting down this silent hall. Kembo studies the mess, pacing the length of the floor. Who should he call? And what to say? Most of all, who will believe him?

A new noise cuts into his thoughts. The dog, barking. A furious howl, again and again. And behind it, something new. A meaty smack, followed by a rattle. Like furniture moving.

Thump! Crack... Thump! Crack...

Kembo nears Professor Moore's office. The scuffs on the floor didn't stop, he realizes. They had turned near the door.

Thump! Crack... Thump! Crack...

"Professor Moore?" Kembo taps the door. He can hear the dog's frantic yaps, senses commotion inside. He reaches for his keys—

Then the door buckles outward.

Kembo is knocked off his feet, bounced off the opposite wall, and comes to lying sideways. Cheeks stinging, ears ringing, for one calm moment Kembo wants nothing more than to shut his eyes and rest on this cool floor.

But he can't. The door to Professor Moore's office is twisted, folded outward by an internal blast. The little dog squeezes out through a bent gap at the bottom, takes off down the hall, barking the whole way.

Thump! Crack... Thump! Crack... Louder and louder until—

Kembo seizes the door, trying to open it. The latch is still engaged, but the top half is bent. A glimpse inside: an overturned desk, a tilted shelf. And there is Professor Moore, pirouetting and spinning, twirling and screaming. The wet *thump* is his body against the walls. That *crack* is the breaking of bones.

"Hold on, Professor!" Kembo cries out. His fingers find the master key. Now he is shaking the door open. He must help this poor man. Yes, he will carry him out.

Instead, he stops dead in his tracks.

Professor Moore clutches his chest, as if in the throes of a heart attack. But it is not this fact that holds Kembo back. It is the professor's feet.

They are six inches off the ground.

"Dear God..." Kembo whispers.

Deep notches bloom upon the man's neck. His left leg twitches, two more joints than there should be. His right hand flails as if swatting off flies. Then two of his fingers snap back.

With a rattling cry, Professor Moore mutters three final words: "Help me... please." His eyes go wide. Too wide. A burst of plum shatters his glasses.

The professor's body hits the floor, lifeless and broken. Kembo doesn't hear the wet thump. He doesn't hear the dog barking. Doesn't hear the cry of the security alarm as he runs down the stairs and out the emergency exit. Nor the cars honking at him, the shouting students, the birds chirping. He hears nothing of this calm spring morning, just his own frantic screams.

[4]

UNIVERSITY OF CALIFORNIA, BERKELEY
MONDAY - 9:00 A.M.

DENISE CARRUTHERS, FIFTY-ONE, HAS A STRONG POSTURE, AN authoritative frame, and a smile that shouts of furloughed dreams. It is this presence that snaps the student assistant from his smartphone. He does not know that she is carrying a firearm. Or that she is a special agent with the Federal Bureau of Investigation. What he senses on an instinctual level—more than anyone who has walked into the Bursar's Office this morning—is that this interaction will demand his attention.

"Morning," she says. "I need to pay my daughter's tuition deposit."

With a quick tap of the keys, the student brings up the forms. "What's her CalNet ID?"

"I don't know. She's a freshman. Will be a freshman. She was accepted last month."

"Congratulations. So I'll need to verify if she gave parental permissions to access her records."

"I just want to pay the deposit."

"Right. 'Cause often parents want access to, like, grades and stuff and I have to tell them, 'No, this isn't high school.'"

Carruthers smiles. "No, this isn't."

"Name?"

"Carruthers-Letova, Jade. Date of birth—"

"Got it right here." A double click. "Says you don't owe a thing."

"That's not possible. It's the fall deposit, next—"

"Right. Except it says she declined her enrollment. Filed two days ago."

Carruthers was expecting a lot of things when visiting her alma mater this morning. Sticker shock at thirty-three years of tuition hikes. The nightmare that is parking in Berkeley. Even the administrative hoops that come with the bureaucracy of a big state school.

But she wasn't expecting this.

"I JUST DON'T UNDERSTAND why you wouldn't discuss this with me," Carruthers says into her phone, into the ear of her daughter, who's some three thousand miles away. "Jade, we talked about this. High school with your mom, college here in California."

"Mom, you talked about it," her daughter says, and Carruthers can hear the school bell ringing, the hallway humming with students in the final weeks before summer. "You never asked me, like, about the other places I applied."

"I thought those were fallbacks. You always talked about Cal—"

"Yeah, 'cause you always did, and it's where you and Mindy met and it's like you always assumed it was the default."

"Well, wasn't it? You went to science camp here."

"Two summers ago. Mom, you should totally be happy. UVA gave me a full scholarship so you don't have to pay a thing."

Virginia, Carruthers thinks. Might as well be another country. At least then Jade could learn a new language. Game face now.

"No, no, sweetie, I'm proud of you, really. And it's not the money, you know that. It's just, well, I was looking forward to being a part of all this—"

The phone buzzes. Incoming call: *SF FBI OUTREACH*.

"Sweetie, can you hold?"

"Mom, I'm between classes—"

"Thanks." Carruthers clicks over. "Special Agent Carruthers."

For two minutes she listens, first nodding, then uncapping her pen to jot down the address, the details. A long-limbed skateboarder walking his pit bull zooms past her and circles back. A flick of his eyes to her phone, to her purse.

Carruthers shifts to her left side, shoulders between them. *Don't try it, kid. Not today.*

Off he skates, thinking better. Or perhaps he never had his eyes on her purse. Years of working for a three-letter agency have worn down more than her trust. She has to remind herself not everything is suspicious.

She finishes taking notes, takes in the Berkeley students, the morning sun warming the trees, the grass still damp in the breeze. Pauses before switching back to Jade. She is losing her daughter. Each passing month, each disappointed sigh that leaves Carruthers's lips and poisons Jade's ear. She wants to tell her so much, things there aren't words for. To rewind the divorce and the cross-country move back to a time before Denise Carruthers became the stern mom, the one who only calls with bad news.

"Honey, listen, I'm not mad. I'm just… hurt. I guess we had divergent expectations and I thought—"

"Wait, *you're* hurt? Mom, you never even asked my opinion."

"That's not true, I—"

"Shit. I gotta go to class. We'll talk soon. Loves."

"I love you—"

The call ends. And it occurs to Carruthers, here in the shadow of Sproul Hall, not far from the fountain and the trees she passed as a graduate student decades ago, that the bedroom she keeps for her daughter will continue to stay empty.

5

SAN FRANCISCO
WEDNESDAY – 3:00 P.M.

EIGHT DAYS AGO, CAITLYN SENT OUT HOWARD KISSINGER'S REVISED itinerary. The private jet filed a new plan and she tracked it via FlightAware to Cataratas del Iguazú airport. There, the local liaison was waiting on the runway.

His name is Tiago, a trilingual Argentinian expatriate who oversees a small network of boutique properties around Central and South America. Keanu Reeves has him on speed dial. Caitlyn does too. And though they have never met face to face, Caitlyn and Tiago trust each other. He runs a professional operation; she has seen it firsthand.

What she didn't see but trusted to occur was the following.

Tiago would lead Mr. Kissinger and Nikki to the falls, and then they would take a boat beyond, upriver, into El Parque Nacional Iguazú. Tiago would tell Nikki this was Señor Kissinger's idea. Tiago would tie the boat up on shore at the GPS coordinates Caitlyn sent. He'd provide them with a basket of meats and cheeses, a bottle of wine and a satellite phone. Then Tiago would point to the old trail, and he would wait at the boat until the guests came back, hours later, giddy and smiling and engaged to be married.

Caitlyn is not psychic or a clairvoyant. She is, in her own little way, a classic romantic.

Which is why when the doorbell chimes, a good feeling guides her feet across the soft carpet. Tuesday and Saturday are for groceries. Monday is for dry goods. Friday is her cheat meal, a movie, and a nice bottle of wine. Every day is for Amazon Prime, yet she's not expecting anything.

"Delivery for Caitlyn Grey?" the courier shouts as she follows the banister to the base of the stairs.

"Yep, that's me." She tries to sense his location, perhaps to the left of the mailboxes. Beyond: the whir of traffic, the hum of buses, the rumble of a motorcycle, its exhaust modified and blasting past *bzbzbzbz*.

Her toes curl. Her neck stiffens. Every inch closer to the gate and her muscles tighten and tense.

"I just need your, uh... need you to sign, if that's okay."

His hesitation tells her everything. He is hurrying; it's only now he has noticed she is blind.

"Of course." Caitlyn holds out her hand, hoping it's close enough. He presses the tablet against it. Her fingers find the bezel. Then she swipes and circles. "I hope I didn't just delete everything."

"What? Oh, no, not at all," he says. His accent is interesting. A twang that reminds her of childhood abroad. She listens to the crinkling of paper, the rustling of leaves. A hollow thud, like thin wood or a box. "Um... where do you want it?"

"Well, I'm not sure," she says. "What is it?"

"You... want me to open it?"

"Do you mind?"

"No, ma'am. No, I don't."

Caitlyn almost laughs at the *ma'am*. She will be twenty-seven in three months. Her hair is short, a tight bob under-shaved on her right with a peacock feather tattooed behind the ear. She is blessed with a dozen freckles. The baby fat never quite left her cheeks, balancing the soft smile she inherited from her mother with her father's sharp eyes.

Caitlyn goes light on the makeup these days, not because she is blind—a common misconception, she has long since developed a mirrorless routine—but because it has been one year, six months, and seventeen days since she has left her apartment building.

As the courier opens the package, a garbage truck rumbles down the street. Sweat sprouts across her back.

"So there's a bottle of wine," the courier says, tapping on glass. "And a lot of flowers."

"Are they pretty?"

"Oh hell yeah," he says, then clears his throat. "I mean, they're really nice."

"What are they?"

"Um... there's, like, pink roses and purple hydrangeas. They're all wrapped in this big leaf thingy. The vase is beautiful. Crystal, maybe? And there's orchids too, I think. Like a lavender color, or... Shit, I'm saying all these colors."

"No, no, it's fine. I understand." Caitlyn smiles. He sounds cute. And she is aware that her blindness is often disarming. Some see disability and mistake it for vulnerability. Some want to save her. Objectively, she knows she isn't bad on the eyes. After all, she can step out and look back.

"Oh, there's an envelope and a note," the courier says. "It says, 'She said yes.' And there's something else, a... Jesus."

Caitlyn grins. "They fit him in there too?"

"Come again?"

"Jesus? In the envelope." Her cheeks flush. Bad joke.

"Right. No, it's just... There's a check for fifty grand."

"Oh," Caitlyn says. "Jesus."

. . .

SEVEN HUNDRED AND fifty square feet isn't much, but it is enough for Caitlyn. A Goldilocks zone. Any more space and it feels overwhelming. Any less, and it's cramped.

Feels is the key word. Caitlyn's relationship with her apartment is through her sense of touch and memory. It is twelve paces across the bedroom. Five across the bathroom. Seven to the kitchenette. Thirty paces from one end of the apartment to the other, passing the bedroom, through the foyer, the living room, and into the T-shaped office at the north end. Six paces to the left, and her fingers fall upon her computer station, her bookshelf, her record collection. Six paces to the right, and her fingers slide upon the cool glass of the bay window.

She places the flowers on the end table with its beautiful view. Or so she remembers.

From the third-floor bay window, one can look upon a slice of the Inner Sunset, the cramped medley of Irish bars, tattoo parlors, and laundromats now giving way to coffee shops and tech redevelopment. On a clear day, one can see the sage-gray Pacific. Caitlyn can only feel it, the sun clawing through the afternoon fog, falling soft upon her face.

She touches the flexible fabric of the Embody chair, tracing the contours of her adjustable desk. She stretches out until she feels the safety corners, soft foam that protects her hips as much as it helps her orient herself.

Most banks prefer customers to deposit checks by photograph; few actually build software to assist the visually impaired. USAA isn't one of them. She lays Mr. Kissinger's check out on the desk, positions her smartphone above it.

"Lift camera," the app cheerfully says. "Move left. Move left. Move back. Hold steady." A click and a vibration. "Image captured. Deposit pending."

And that is that.

• • •

"THE IMPORTANT THING about hydrangeas is to keep the soil moist. They're in good light, so that's half the battle. Just don't over water."

Mrs. Bakshi is an octogenarian retiree who has lived in the next unit since her husband bought the building and subdivided it during the seventies. She is small and wide and still keeps her husband's side of the bed made despite his passing five years ago. On Wednesdays she arrives around five, bringing Caitlyn curry and rice, enough for several meals. They eat and play chess and have yet to finish a full game. They talk about books. Mrs. Bakshi complains about the tenants—their parties, their late rent, and do they appreciate how generous she is in this housing market?

Mostly, Caitlyn suspects, Mrs. Bakshi just wants the same human connection craved by all but treasured most by the old.

"What about the other flowers?" Caitlyn asks. "I think there's an orchid."

"Two, actually. We'll pot those separate. Oh, what a lovely gift you've been given."

"I'm fortunate, aren't I?"

"And too skinny. Come, I'll get you another bowl."

Mrs. Bakshi's curry fills the apartment: cumin and coriander and rich turmeric from her granddaughter's farm outside Sangli, India. Caitlyn knows not to protest. And if she did, Mrs. Bakshi would just put the Tupperware back in Caitlyn's fridge, smiling next week when she finds it empty. Rinse and repeat.

"Eat, please."

Caitlyn savors the last of the curry chicken. Envisions the colors. Golden mustard with beads of orange where the oils separate. Herself, age ten, eating at a food stall in Chennai with her friends after day school.

Then the doorbell chimes.

Caitlyn thumbs her phone, swiping to the doorbell app. Meanwhile, Mrs. Bakshi announces, "It's a young man." Caitlyn senses her peering out the bay window. "Looks cute."

Caitlyn speaks to her intercom app. "Hello?"

"Hi, it's Vincent." A familiar voice. "We met earlier. Actually, I delivered your flowers."

"Oh. Yeah, I remember your voice."

"It's the accent, right? Ozzie tongue."

"Ozzie tongue?"

"Australian," he says. "Comes out when I'm nervous."

Caitlyn smiles. "So why are you nervous, Vincent?"

"Cause of what I'm about to say. Wow, this intercom is a bit impersonal, but, um, here goes. So I've got a band. I know, everyone has a band, right? Anyway, I thought maybe if you're interested, if you aren't doing anything, you might want to come hear us play."

He says it all in one exasperated gasp. By the end his accent is so thick it sounds like *ear us pray*. Good thing the video intercom isn't two-way or he'd see Caitlyn blushing.

"That's nice, Vincent, but what if I'm not into that type of music?"

"Tycho," he says.

"What?"

"You were wearing a Tycho shirt, earlier. From the festival a few summers back."

He's right. She didn't give much thought to her shirt today, but she knows the feel of the fabric and design. A circle split into eight horizontal gradients. Tycho played at the Outside Lands Festival. She'd bought a shirt, had a panic attack. It was the last time she went to Golden Gate Park.

"Okay," Caitlyn says. "So…?"

"Oh my god, I must sound like a stalker," Vincent says. "What I meant was that my band plays post-rock electronic. You know, kind of like Tycho, only we're not as good. I mean… we're not bad. That's not what I'm saying. It's just… well, he's a legend, right?" A sigh from the other side of the intercom. "I've blown this, haven't I?"

"Well, you have crossed a few professional boundaries."

"Yeah," he says. "I'm gonna get fired."

"At least you'll have the band. So what's it called?"

"Thoughtbox. I play bass. Oh, and mandolin."

"A post-rock band with a mandolin," Caitlyn says, trying to imagine it.

"Emancipator has a violin. But he's also a lot better than we are."

"Really nailing the sales pitch here, Vincent."

"You know what? I'm sorry, really. I shouldn't have done this. This was rude and presumptive and a huge mistake. I'm just gonna—"

"So how can I listen to your music?"

She can hear him gulp on the other end of the intercom. "You want to listen to us?"

"I mean, are you on Spotify or Bandcamp or—"

"Well, we're on SoundCloud," he says. "And we're playing at Smack-Dab's this Friday and Saturday. Eight to ten. You know where that is?"

"I can find it."

"There's a poetry slam before us, if you're into that."

"No, I'm definitely not."

"I brought a flyer. But then I realized… it's not really useful."

"You'd be surprised," Caitlyn says. "Just slip it under the gate."

"Right, okay, so I'm doing that now." A faint clang from the intercom app. "Anyways, I really hope you can come."

"I just might."

"Okay."

"All right."

"Well, goodnight, Caitlyn."

"Night, Vincent."

There is a pause, then the click of the intercom disconnecting. "I'll get the flyer," Mrs. Bakshi announces. Caitlyn tells her not to worry, but it's no use. Mrs. Bakshi is already thumping down the hall, out the door, then down three flights of stairs. It must give this old woman joy, Caitlyn thinks, taking care of her young, shut-in neighbor. *Just let her have it.*

The clockwork hum of the Inner Sunset drifts through the open door. A group of patrons laughing outside the local watering hole. An evening news report from another apartment. The click and ignition of a nearby car starting up, perhaps Vincent's.

"I was right," Mrs. Bakshi says, the door creaking behind her. "He is cute."

6

SANTA ROSA
WEDNESDAY - 4:30 P.M.

SPECIAL AGENT BYUNG-SOO "BRAD" LEE OF THE CALIFORNIA Bureau of Investigation has a face so free of lines that he has been teased about his skin care routine. He does not have a routine. Nor can he grow a mustache as others in the CBI have. Even now, tired, after a three-hour interview, his smooth face offers little hint of his thirty years on this earth.

"Christ, just listen to him," he says. "He's still spinning the wheels. You think maybe it's a cultural thing?"

Carruthers isn't sure what to make of it. Her gut says that the man on the other side of the one-way mirror has nothing to hide. His story is one of immigrant hope. Hard work, sacrifice, a genuine attempt to assimilate while preserving his proud identity. He even showed up to the interview in a suit and tie. Brought his twenty-one-year-old son to interpret. Still, Carruthers agrees with this baby-faced investigator; Kembo Mlotshwa isn't making much sense.

"What I think," Carruthers says, considering her words, "is that fear cuts across cultures. Fear is universal. Makes the mind reel. Could be Mr. Mlotshwa saw whoever did this. Maybe they've got something on him. Said something."

"What, like leverage?"

"A threat, maybe. He's holding back."

Brad considers it. "Or it could be Kembo offed the professor himself."

"It's possible, but..." Carruthers hesitates.

"But...?"

She says nothing. Just studies the men on the other side of the mirror. Father and son, two steps on a genetic journey. From some angles, they could almost be brothers. And yet they are from different upbringings, different cultures. Kembo is only forty, but life has bent his body. His son sits upright, attentive. His fingers are smooth, nails not chewed but clipped. *The boy might make a good lawyer,* Carruthers thinks.

"Could be the professor caught him breaking into his office," Brad says. "Door was bashed open. Maybe he had an accomplice."

"Could be," Carruthers says.

"But...?"

"But Kembo's the night janitor. Why not just use his keys?"

"Make it look like a burglary. Maybe there was an accomplice. Maybe the professor showed up early and the job went south. An easy B&E becomes a homicide."

"Could be..." Carruthers repeats.

Brad waits for it. As an agent of the CBI, he is in charge of this case. Carruthers knows that. The image of the feds marching in, flashing badges, and taking over is a media myth. Still, she has seen the photos. If this is a homicide—and they're treating it as such—it's far beyond Brad's experience. Perhaps even hers.

"Mr. Mlotshwa's been a citizen for a decade," she says. "He brought his papers, just in case. This man's not looking to make waves." Behind soundproof glass not ten feet away, Kembo and his son are leaning together, whispering.

"Joe Rogan had this painter on with split personality," Brad says. "DID or whatever they call it. Same body with seven different personalities, all packed in. Even the paintings were different, like Picasso next to Bob Ross."

Carruthers tunes Brad out. He's talking because he's nervous. Early-career investigators often mistake silence for something to fill. *Focus on the scene beyond the glass, Denise.* Three white walls, two chairs, and a hushed conversation between father and son. The California Bureau of Investigation isn't known for a sense of decoration, but would it hurt to put a few plants in the room? Fake ones, crafted in plastic, forever perfect. Something to cut the tension, cut—

"Occam's razor," Carruthers says.

Brad nods. "Yeah, the simplest explanation is always the right one."

"That's a common misunderstanding. What William of Ockham actually said was, 'Plurality must never be posited without necessity.' You started with the crime scene. But let's have him walk us backwards from the body."

"You want to take a turn with him?"

"No. Witnesses, especially first-generation immigrants, often clam up around feds."

"Can't imagine why," Brad says. "H'okay, round four."

Kembo and his son stand as Brad enters the interview room. Respect. Yet the agent just waves it off. *Youth,* Carruthers thinks, *really is wasted on the young.*

And what does that make her? She tries to ignore her reflection off the glass. The vague, boxy shape. The suit from Macy's. Her fifties haven't been like her forties. Each year something new collapses. Her marriage and family, her figure and career. Her peers are now ASACs; one is even an assistant director. And here she is, a special agent out of Santa Rosa, field office of one. She's not here in partnership, not really. She's just a box Brad Lee had to check off.

"Just walk us through this. That's all we're asking," Brad says. "Can you do that?"

"Us?" Kembo asks, stiffening.

"Me," Brad corrects. "The collective we. The investigative arm of the—"

Kembo's eyes snap toward the mirror, toward a spot a few inches from Carruthers. "Who else is back there? It's like on TV, isn't it?"

"No, no, it's not like TV. It's—"

Kembo whispers to his son. His son shakes his head. A foreign tongue, but the tone's universal. Sudden concern.

"Wait. Am I suspect? Should I have a lawyer? I should, yes?"

Carruthers sighs. The interview is in free fall. Brad is trying to deflect and Kembo now recognizes the magnitude of the situation. She steps out into the hallway, then into the interview room.

"Take a break, Agent," Carruthers says, tapping Brad's shoulder with the case folder.

"Who are you?" Kembo asks.

Brad lingers by the door. Carruthers waits until he's gone. Then she opens the folder and begins laying out photographs like dealing cards from a deck.

A close-up of a bruised arm.

A wide shot of a broken body.

A medium shot of a neck, wrenched sideways and limp.

Doctor Charles Moore, PhD, MD, and very much DOA. Carruthers continues laying them out.

"Mr. Mlotshwa," she says. "I am Special Agent Denise Carruthers from the FBI. I'm here to listen. And I'm going to listen with an open mind. You are not in trouble. But you have something I need, and that is your story. Tell me your story, sir. Help us understand this."

More photographs. Broken fingers, bent teeth. A bone protruding from bruised skin. The images fill up the table.

For most of the laying, his son simply took it in, stunned. Now his young eyes turn to his father. "Dad, you saw this?"

Carruthers waits until Kembo shifts to a neutral posture, then mirrors his body language, his subtle wince. Bingo. "Your father's a brave man to be here. And he's fortunate to have your help."

The final photo: a faculty headshot, glossy and professional, provided by the neurobiology department. The dead professor, sitting before a blue background, smiling. Laying this picture out last humanizes the victim.

"Help us understand what happened to Professor Moore. Your fingerprints were found in his office. His blood was on your uniform. And you said someone killed him."

Kembo swallows. "Yes."

"And they were there, in Professor Moore's office?"

"Yes."

"And how big is that office? A hundred square feet?"

Kembo's son translates. His father mutters back, shrugs.

"He says, 'I don't know.'"

"Ask him how long it takes to vacuum the carpet."

Kembo doesn't need the translation. "Two minutes," he says. "Maybe less."

"And there's only one door into this office?"

"Yes."

"From the door, could you identify who you saw?"

The corners of his eyes twitch. "It is impossible."

"Dad, please..."

"Any description? Age? Height? Fair-haired or—"

"It. Is. Impossible."

"Because they were hiding? Did they have a mask or—"

"I tell you, it is impossible!" In one quick wave, Kembo clears half the photographs from the table. Silence. Then...

Kembo winces. Here it comes. Words now, spoken fast to his son. Carruthers lets them confer. She collects the photos, then mirrors the son crossing his arms, nodding. Us, yes. All in this together.

"He says, 'I've told the other man. I'm telling you. It was there, I swear. And I was scared. Very scared.'" His son squeezes Kembo's trembling hand. "He says, 'I just couldn't see it.'"

Carruthers squeezes her own. *Tilt your head. Don't blink. Furrow a brow. Now wait for it...*

Kembo wipes the corners of his eyes. Carruthers can't tell if he's crying or sweating or both. Silence. Then...

"*Chipoko…*"

The son turns to Kembo and repeats the word as if he'd misheard. Kembo nods.

"*Chipoko. Dhiabhorosi. Dhimoni,*" Kembo continues, a rhythm to his speech, each word heavy on the tongue. They come again. "*Chipoko.*" Kembo looks Carruthers in her eyes. "*Dhiabhorosi. Dhimoni.*" Then he leans back, wipes his hands as if he is done with this all.

"Dad, are you sure?"

Carruthers can feel Brad staring through the mirror. *Don't come in. Let them fill in the quiet.*

"My father, you have to understand, is not very religious. He used to say he left his gods back in Africa, so—"

"You tell this detective woman," Kembo says. "That is who do this unspeakable thing."

"Dhimoni?"

"My father says it was a ghost, a devil, a demon from Hell. That's what killed this poor man. That is why he couldn't see it."

7

SAN FRANCISCO
FRIDAY - 6:45 P.M.

THE BAND ISN'T HALF BAD, CAITLYN THINKS AS SHE APPLIES HER makeup.

Their style is distinctly electronic, stutter edits and looping chords. There is a live drummer, but they take background to samples of Carl Sagan from *Cosmos*. Traveling through dimensions, decoupling perceptions of time and space. She can relate. Vincent's mandolin adds a splash of bardic fun as it enters and exits the ethereal tunes.

The vocals, however, kill it.

The lead singer hums, mumbles, and gargles out words that make little sense. If it is a fictional language—like that sung by Jónsi of Sigur Rós—then it needs refinement. And if not, well, there are plenty of speech therapists who could take up the case. Good melodies wasted on grumbly lyrics. What a bummer.

Still, she has decided to give Thoughtbox a chance. Some bands are better live.

So here she is, ten minutes to seven, applying the last of her makeup. She navigates her face the same way she navigates her apartment: by touch and by counting. The key is routine, a good mental map, and a drawer full of Dior.

Use a blush brush, start at the apples of the cheeks, then follow the contours out toward the ears. Count the strokes. One. Two. Three.

Follow the nose to the forehead. Circular motions from forehead to temples. A smooth crescent under the eyes, from outer corner to inside. When it's done, get comfy and count down from ten.

Now step out and check in on your work.

Not bad. Her physical body is still, hands crossed on her lap. A dab of red lipstick on the end of her left index finger. Must've missed it. All things considered, a passable job.

She turns to the bay window. Outside, the city buzzes with life. A group of art students is doing the Friday night shuffle, portfolio cases swinging from their shoulders as they laugh and sip beers. A man with shoulder-length dreadlocks gives directions to a group of Chinese tourists. A car pulls up to the curb, the rideshare sign glowing in the window.

Caitlyn takes a deep breath. In the reflection, she watches her physical body mirror it. *You can do this.* Thirty-six steps to the base of the stairs. Twenty-eight blocks to Inner Haight. Two point nine miles.

Her phone vibrates. Two things happen simultaneously: Caitlyn is pulled ten feet across the room in a blink, and the world fades behind black curtains.

She stands, feels her desk. Finds the phone and wipes the lipstick from her finger.

Another deep breath. A flash of her father tying knots on their boat. That's my girl. Always stronger than she knows.

Caitlyn answers the phone, tells the driver, "I'm on my way."

SHE IS on the fifth step down from the third floor when the world tilts to the left. Her hand snatches at the railing, fingers clinging metal.

Then, with a twist, Caitlyn swings hard right.

She misses a step. Stumbles. The wall comes fast now and

brushes her shoulder. She leans back, tries to steady herself, but now her count is all off. Twelve steps per floor, but how many had she just tripped down? Two? Three?

Caitlyn clutches the railing. Feels the brick wall. Feels her heart racing. One hundred BPM. One hundred and ten. One twenty.

Downstairs, beyond the gate, the night rumbles. Somehow, life's volume has been turned up. It shouldn't be this loud.

You can do this, she tells herself. The landing is just a few steps. Then twelve more. Then the front porch, the stoop, the sidewalk, and the city itself.

Just one step at a time.

She makes her way to the landing.

Makes her way to the gate.

Finds the latch on the inside.

And opens it with a creak.

Cold fingers run through her hair, a foggy breeze. An unwanted touch of warm wind when a bus rattles past. A car stereo belts out bass drops a few blocks away.

Caitlyn feels. Is starting to feel too much.

The handle is slipping from her damp hands. Her heart drums its way up her chest. One hundred and forty BPM. One fifty-five.

You can do this, she had told herself. But where is that little voice now?

A car backfires. Or is that a gunshot?

Voices, laughing nearby. *They're laughing at you.*

Something rustles and murmurs in the bushes and she envisions gangrenous hands stretching out. The stoop is lurching forward now. The apartment building is lifting and tilting and being shaken out. She is about to fall. The earth is leaning, gravity shifting, and soon she will go sliding out into oblivion.

Then a hand brushes her shoulder. "Pardon me."

And Caitlyn screams.

Scrambles back into the stairwell.

Tugging herself now, along the railing, up the steps, three at a time.

There is an apology from down the stairs. Caitlyn doesn't hear it. Only feels her door unlocking. Only hears the deadbolts clacking shut. Inside now. Inside is quiet and warm and here the earth cannot teeter and tilt.

Six deep breaths and the apartment building settles. Caitlyn counts her pulse. Feels the vibrating phone.

"Text message," the digital assistant cheerfully says. "Caller unknown. Message: 'I'm your Lyft driver. Are you coming or what?'"

"No," Caitlyn whispers, "I don't think I am."

8

CALIFORNIA STATE UNIVERSITY, MARIN
LOFTUS HALL OF SCIENCE, 10TH FLOOR - FRIDAY -
7:00 P.M.

THREE FEET, SHE THINKS, LOOKING BACK DOWN THE HALL. THIRTY-SIX inches. A whole damn yard.

Carruthers unspools the measuring tape once more, just to make sure. Three feet from one dent in the linoleum floor to another. Five dents total, the last one ending just before Professor Moore's office.

Police tape crisscrosses the empty frame. According to the lab, the door was bent by a strong impact. That impact was Professor Moore. Enough force to buckle fire-resistant metal. Enough force to break half his ribs.

And according to the report, the force had come from inside the office.

Kembo Mlotshwa had been outside. His keys were still jammed in the knob.

Carruthers slips under the police tape. Takes in the office. Not much space for a tenured professor. Education must be feeling the squeeze.

The desk takes up a sixth of the room. An old mahogany thing with too many drawers. How had it been brought up? Probably built the facility around it.

The professor's computer is gone, turned over to forensics. All his packages have been inspected. Dead ends too. Whatever happened here wasn't a mail bomb, no chemical residue.

The CS techs left the professor's decorations. Family photos. Framed certificates and awards. An impressive bookshelf that spans the south wall.

The periodicals are dry, academic. *The Journal of Neuroscience. Frontiers in Neuroscience. Principals of Neuroscience.* The books are only marginally more interesting. Carruthers recognizes a few authors. Oliver Sachs's *The Man Who Mistook His Wife for a Hat.* Robert Sapolsky's *Stress, the Aging Brain, and the Mechanisms of Neuron Death.* The dead professor had minds on his mind.

This is going nowhere. Frustrated, Carruthers turns to the window. Ten floors up, a commanding vista of unincorporated Marin. Westward, the darkening hills, the winking highway lights and fast-food joints. At least the victim had a nice view.

Opposite the doorframe, there are scuffs where brass buckles from Kembo's uniform dug into the plaster. Another puzzle piece, clear as mud.

Doesn't make any damn sense...

She looks back at the hall, away from the elevator. Tries to imagine the world as it was that morning. What Kembo had seen. In the sterile white of institutional light, the hall frays the edge of two different worlds.

In one world, here stands a woman who has spent twenty-two years with the FBI. That woman has no answers.

And in the other world, where shadows give form to superstition, stands Kembo Mlotshwa with his explanation.

Chipoko. Dhiabhorosi. Dhimoni.

A ghost. A devil. A demon from Hell.

Carruthers doesn't doubt Kembo's recollection. The mind is a malleable thing, an organ constantly reconstructing reality. Professor Moore could have told Kembo as much. The truth hides, cloaks itself in metaphor and superstition. The truth doesn't walk right in.

But someone does.

Beneath the green glow of the exit light, a man steps out of the stairwell. He is in his mid-thirties, well-dressed in a three-piece olive suit. The glint of cufflinks, a pocket watch chain.

If he's spotted her, he gives no indication, no acknowledgment. Instead, he studies the ceiling, walking the hall in giant, awkward strides. His left hand twitches, thumb tapping against each finger, index to pinky and back. Mostly, he seems to be measuring.

The dents, Carruthers realizes. He strides toward the office now.

"S'cuse me," Carruthers says, stepping into the light. "Can I help you with something?"

"Yes," the man says, trotting over. "Hold this for a moment."

He hands her a cup of coffee. Then he turns and walks back toward the exit. A flush burns her cheeks.

"Sir, this is a closed crime scene," she says. "You need to leave."

"Yes, of course it is," the man says. "Special Agent Carruthers, is it?"

"That's right. How—"

"If you were running, and you fell, which hand would you put out first?"

Carruthers hesitates. The man stops near the exit, turns, and wobbles. A drunk? And how does he know her name?

"Left hand or right?" he asks. "Which do you think?"

"Depends what foot I was favoring, how I pushed off. Now come on, buddy. Let's clear out."

"I think I'll stay." He produces a worn leather wallet. Inside, a badge puts Carruthers command on hold. She checks the ID card beneath it, matches the face to his.

"What, is this some kind of joke?"

"What part?"

"The Foundation. That's a spook shop... no such agency."

"Are you sure about that?"

Special Agent Denise Carruthers has drawn her firearm twice

in almost two dozen years. Right now she is armed and alarmed. There's a bulge beneath the man's jacket. A police-grade Taser on his belt.

He catches her gaze, steps back. "You're a direct report to SAC Beddicker, yes? Go ahead, call him. This all checks out."

He gives her space. A little taller, but much lighter. It's been years since her last jiu-jitsu class. Still, if this goes to the floor, Carruthers gives herself strong odds she can take him.

"Keep your hands where I can see them."

Special Agent in Charge Ron Beddicker rose fast and sees the FBI not as a job but a lifestyle. Carruthers isn't surprised when the switchboard patches her to his mobile phone.

"Carruthers," he says, and she can hear classical music in the background. "Let me guess: the Howdy Doody-looking fellow found you and this is your due diligence."

"Sir, I've got his badge and credentials right here—"

"Michaels. Yeah, it's all been run up the totem pole."

"You're shitting me."

"I got personal confirmation from the deputy director's office. He checks out."

She cups the phone, whispers, "So what the hell does he want?"

"You tell me. He asked for you by name. On second thought, don't. Have a nice weekend, Denise."

The well-dressed man, Michaels, is crouching over a dent when she returns his ID. "Mind telling me why you're here?"

"For the same reason you are. Here, take a look." He lays his smartphone's light flush with the floor. Shadows stretch out. A linoleum crater and a line of scuff marks. He places his right fist against it. Not a perfect fit, but close.

Then he adjusts his squat, stretches out. His right knee touches the floor, tucking near the dent. His oxblood Doc Martens, left one flat, right one raised onto the toes.

"Curious, right?"

Like his hand, the fit isn't perfect, but it is close. The shoes obscure the dents; his knee fills in the scuff. Curious indeed.

"You ever play football?" he asks.

"What? No. I've tossed the ball around—"

"Yeah, me neither," he says. Carruthers sizes him up. He is lean, a tautness that comes from hundred-mile bike rides and triathlons. "See, I was thinking maybe it was like a runner starting off the block. But now, I'm thinking, no one starts off that hard—"

"But if they stumbled?" Carruthers asks.

"There you go."

Silence. They study the floor.

"No way," Carruthers says. "It's sealed flooring, commercial grade. You'd have to drop a hammer from six feet to make a dent like that."

Michaels's eyes flick upward. "What about sixteen?"

A sprinkler system runs along the ceiling. And an HVAC hatch, eighteen inches at its widest. "Unless there's a leprechaun with a hammer in the air vent, I'm stumped."

"As was I," he says and walks toward the stairwell door. "Until I read your report."

"My report?" Clearly, she misheard him. "I haven't filed it yet."

"No, but you've saved multiple drafts. Come."

Reluctantly, Carruthers follows, unable to shake the feeling there is something uncanny about him. For starters, he doesn't have the slow shuffle of someone on the government's time and dime. He is nimble, taking the stairs two steps at once. Then there is the suit, obviously bespoke. And his twitching left hand, open and shut, open and shut. He catches her glance, stuffs it in a pocket.

It hits her as they arrive at the next floor and he holds the door.

"You're a black kite," Carruthers says. "I get it now. You got access to a draft of my report."

"A black kite?"

"You know, fly anywhere, no strings attached. Jesus, you probably have a backdoor to every computer."

"Not every computer." Michaels pauses as they step out onto the dim eleventh floor. "Just yours."

She can't tell if that's a smirk or a grin. Something in between.

"That was a joke," he says.

"Yeah, perfect location. Dark hallway, crime scene and all. So what do I call you? Your credentials said Michaels. Is that your first name or last?"

"Both, actually."

Carruthers laughs. "Now that's funny. Like Bono or Rihanna, right?"

"In a sense." Michaels stops near a water fountain. "My parents were unconventional. Surnames, they felt, could become shadows or burdens. All my siblings were given mononyms."

"You're not joking."

"Afraid not."

"Bet the government loves that."

"Well, the DMV certainly doesn't."

Michaels raises an eyebrow. He is waiting for something. For her. Carruthers studies the hallway, the water fountain, the storage closet, and the quiet offices. Takes it all in. Then...

"Jesus, is that..."

She shines the flashlight at the floor. A familiar sight just past the water fountain. The linoleum is newer up here, the surface less worn. A fracture protrudes. Angled craters, like hammer blows against the floor.

"There's another one," she says. "What's that? Three feet between 'em?"

"Looks that way."

"Forensics didn't mention this." She runs a finger down the dent. It's less pronounced, more of a warping than an outright gash. "Probably didn't even sweep this floor."

Michaels doesn't answer, doesn't need to. Carruthers is doing the math on her own.

"These dents seem angled, not as straight on as..."

She pauses, measuring the hallway. Reorients herself. The elevator at one end. The stairwell and the green *EXIT* sign at the other. They are further away from the elevator, which means...

"Go on," Michaels says. "Run with it."

Carruthers resists the trajectory lining up in her mind. An impossible path from dented linoleum a floor below to this dark corridor. No way. Just a coincidence.

"Unless..." she says, studying the two dents. They are off-center in the hallway. The furthest one is half the size of the closer crack. A flash of a seminar, years ago. Directionality. The geometry of travel is reflected in the transfer pattern. A perfect circle means it came from straight above. But an oval, elongated...

Carruthers eyes the ceiling. *Run with it*, Michaels had said. So she does.

Her walk turns into a trot. Then she's in the stairwell, up to the twelfth floor. Down the hall to the water fountain. Orienting herself between the elevator and another *EXIT* sign. Scanning the floor.

Nothing. Just clean tiling, no scuffs or cracks.

Stupid idea, she thinks. Impossible, of course. Kembo's super-stitions have seeped into her mind, filling in the cracks with dhimonis and dubious connections.

Unless...

Squatting, imagining the trajectory. The dents aren't vertically aligned, but offset at a forty-five-degree angle, as if the floors are permeable layers on some mad trajectory. If there are dents here, that wouldn't put them in this hallway...

It would put them in an adjacent office. Room 1205.

"C'mon, no way," she says, more to herself than the spook watching her. "You've been in there?"

Michaels nods.

"And?"

A stare, nothing more. Open the door and see for yourself. So she does.

The room is a purgatory of outdated computers, cast-off cabinets, and forgotten whiteboards. A dusty place that sees few visitors.

Clearly, it has seen one this week.

"Jesus," Carruthers says, inspecting the wreckage.

"Facilities gave me the keycard," Michaels says. "They checked the logs. I swiped in last hour. Before that, it was two weeks ago. Some TA fetching a replacement projector."

"They're going to have to replace more than that."

It looks like a bull charged through the room. Whiteboards lie toppled at opposite angles. Two desks have been flipped. A third is simply crushed, reduced to splayed metal and splintered wood.

"It's like something slid into home plate," Carruthers says, following the trail.

"Or crash-landed."

"And then it ends." Carruthers stops in the middle of the room, where a single lectern has fallen. Two dents in the floor show the start of the wreckage. "What is that, twenty feet? Twenty-five?"

"Something like that," Michaels says.

His eyes trace an invisible line along the edge of the room, through the scattered equipment, and up to the ceiling again.

"You're kidding me," Carruthers says. "Higher?"

"There's only the roof above us now."

"But you've checked?"

"I have not."

"What? Why not?"

"Because I need a favor, Agent Carruthers. I trust my eyes. I trust my mind. I have a need for order and logic and lately I've had discomforting thoughts. Your report has my attention. I listened to your interview, read your notes. What interests me are the parts you wrote and deleted. Like how the only witness claimed this is the work of a demon. I wanted to see what conclusion we could uncover, together. Because the honest truth is, I'm starting to feel like Alice, teetering on the edge of some insane rabbit hole. I don't trust myself to go onto that roof with a clear mind."

"You want me to check it out," Carruthers says. "That's the favor?"

"There's a padlock on the door. I've checked. Probably to keep the students away. I'm sure we could ask facilities for a key. Or…"

"Or what?"

His pacing comes to an end at a broken desk. He gives the metal chair leg a nudge.

THE LOCK SNAPS OPEN with surprising ease. With a grunt, Carruthers retrieves the rusty halves and places them on the step next to the bent chair leg. "Kids these days, huh?"

"No respect," Michaels says.

And like that, the door is open. Carruthers surveys a flat expanse of roofing gravel beneath a canopy of low coastal clouds. "Moment of truth."

She steps out onto the roof.

"I'm sure this'll be nothing," Michaels says. "A curious anecdote, something to laugh about."

Gravel crunching underfoot, Carruthers heads off into the darkness.

Michaels feels it in his wrist, a need to open and close his hand. It's on his fingers, itching, begging. *Ignore it. Open the toothpicks, put one between your teeth. Good. Now chew and savor and pretend to be normal.*

Of course, there will be nothing on this roof. Of course, this will soon be behind him. There is no connection between a dead professor in Marin and the dead doctor in Tampa. And the others. There are no such things as chipokos or dhiabhorosi, and demons do not exist.

But people do. People with motives, means, methods. Anything else is absurd.

The gravel crunches. Louder. Faster. Carruthers reappears at the door, huffing. "Michaels, you need to see this."

Out onto the roof, where he feels like he can reach right up and touch the low clouds. Ahead, Carruthers turns a hard left past a bank of exhaust vents. Her flashlight makes wide arcs across the gravel.

They come to a stop near a protrusion of antennas. Michaels almost swallows his toothpick.

The light isn't much. With the moon behind the clouds, the shadows ooze. Still, his eyes perceive it even if his mind hesitates.

They are standing directly over the storage room now, at the edge of a dozen dents zigging and zagging eastward. There are no linoleum tiles up here, just the modified bitumen roofing with its black, granular surface, now pocked by gashes, each larger than the last.

And there, near the corner of the roof: a massive crater. Black cap sheets and roof sheathing lie torn, buckled upward and out. Five feet of impact, ringed by nothing else. No tracks or trails, not even a pigeon feather. The edge of the roof is fifty feet away. Beyond that, the next building to the east, a few hundred feet.

Michaels looks out. Up. Around. No other exits, just the same impossible conclusion. Something has come from nothing, struck the roof, and then impossibly moved through it.

"That rabbit hole you were talking about?" Carruthers says. "I think we both just fell in."

[9]
SAN FRANCISCO
FRIDAY - 8:00 P.M.

THE RITUAL IS SIMPLE, REFINED OVER A DECADE. SHE NEEDS THREE things: a quiet room, a calm mind, and darkness. The basic tenets of meditation.

The quiet comes in through custom earbuds, medical-grade silicon molded to her ears. Ten balanced armatures, twenty-six decibels of sound reduction. The same set used by Kendrick Lamar. Today's tune: white noise. A sea of static melts into a soft wall of silence. Her pulse is the only soundtrack. *Lub dub, lub dub.*

Quieting the world is easy. Quieting her mind, less so.

Some days, Caitlyn only needs to sit cross-legged and count down. Others call for a heavier touch. She has a rolling pharmacopeia: Xanax and Klonopin in the bathroom; Kentucky bourbon in a decanter; mason jars by her coffee pot, each filled with Humboldt's finest. Dark Star or Purple Candy for a soft indica buzz. Sour Diesel and Jack Herrer for the sharp lines of sativa.

Tonight, she has settled on a different herb: chamomile and a pinch of ginger, steeped for five. She sips the tea, savors the warmth spreading from her stomach.

The final ingredient is the easiest. Darkness is everywhere when you're NLP blind—no light perception. And yet, as Caitlyn settles in, the shadows expand. The darkness takes on dimensions, curtains of wet ebony.

Ten. Nine. Eight.

It starts with a flicker, a little spark. Color bleeds in; green shimmers trace the contours of her apartment.

Seven. Six. Five.

Reaching out now. Pushing a curtain aside. Here are the cool walls of her home. There is her coffee table. The bay window. This vase of flowers, dripping tarry darkness.

Four. Three. Two.

A red dot pulses in the oily sky. Sutro Tower, as seen through the window. Then the sky ripples, and the cool stars flicker. She can see Venus to the west, bright in the spring night. Sirius winks, further to the south.

One.

The flowers fall in to focus first. A backward explosion, colors collapsing, filling in petals with pinks and yellows and pale magenta, all held together by a green, leafy embrace. The vase is Tiffany crystal, the accents hand cut. Vincent was right: the arrangement is stunning.

Caitlyn stretches out, then steps out of her body. Looking back, she sees herself cross-legged and calm. The smartphone counts down, two hours. Her longest outing in years.

Caitlyn has learned that a timer is vital. When she's outside, light refracts differently and time flows in odd currents. Scuba dive too long and nitrogen builds up in the blood and skin begins to break down.

Blinking isn't that different. Caitlyn has returned to fearful confusions and week-long depressions, numb to physical sensation after too much immersion. Once, when she was eighteen and just beginning to lose sight, she had gotten lost wandering Venice at night. It took until dawn to find her hotel, to find her body in bed, bleeding from her nose and between her legs.

Now, she keeps an audio leash. One hundred seventeen minutes and counting. A respectable night out.

She looks to the coffee table. Finds the flyer Vincent left, a colorful mess of amateur graphics.

SMACK-DAB PRESENTS:
POST-ROCK PURGATORY! FRIDAY & SATURDAY 8PM - 2AM.
THOUGHTBOX. CTRL-ALT-RETREAT. MICKY'S SISTER. GREG
COHEN & BIG RED.
$30 @ DOOR!

A dozen faces on the flyer, mostly men, no band names or identification. Is this Thoughtbox, the first from the left? A handsome group. Four men, early to mid-twenties. The most prominent face of the bunch has a brooding complexion. Emo bangs and large gauge earrings. Someone perpetually auditioning for front man. Doesn't feel like Vincent.

That leaves three possibilities, all nice on the eyes. One looks like he doesn't take this band seriously. One has a kind smile. One looks like he sells corporate insurance.

Three printed maps lie before her. A map of the Tenderloin, satellite view enabled. A street view image, westward down the block. A user-submitted photo, friends posing before Smack-Dab. Whoever uploaded it had left GPS coordinates embedded in the file. Score one for assisting the blind.

It's just the triangulation Caitlyn needs.

She focuses on the images, lets them all blossom from the pages: the grid of the streets; the rise of the skyscrapers; the cheesy neon of the venue's name, Smack-Dab.

And with a blink, she is smack dab in the middle of it.

A low hum scatters a flock of pigeons. Friday night hipsters hang out on the sidewalk, hand-rolled cigarettes and half-hidden flasks. More tattoos than clean skin.

Smack-Dab is part gastropub, part club, a throwback to the rusty days of the mid-seventies, after the Summer of Love succumbed to urban decay. It looks, Caitlyn muses, like something plucked up from Amsterdam or dug out of the back alleys of Prague, south of old town. A humble place, lumpy and friendly, fast going extinct in this city.

The line stretches past the red front door, down the sidewalk. Cottage windows cast yellow on those awaiting seats. A glimpse in shows they'll be waiting a while. Smack-Dab is packed.

Caitlyn doesn't need the bouncer's permission. Doesn't even need a seat.

With a faint crack—like frost beneath soft feet—Caitlyn blinks into the bar room. The stage is set up for music, two empty mics at the ready. The poetry slam is just winding down. Perfect.

Caitlyn finds humanity fascinating. She jokes on Internet forums she hopes to rejoin it someday. But tonight, she is happy to watch it unfold.

Scene one: A string-thin Vietnamese woman, her date walking off to the bathroom. When he's gone, she reaches across the table and devours a handful of his fries.

Scene two: Two sexagenarians in near-matching zoot suits read books. A glass of red wine paired with a Paul Tremblay novel, a pint of Budweiser washing down George Saunders.

Scene three: At the corner table, where the window meets the bar, a group of guys quickly finish off their food as the floor manager stops by. "You fellas are next."

The fellas, Caitlyn realizes, are Thoughtbox, the band she's here to see. The flyer aged them upward; they're just college kids, really.

Caitlyn watches the one with the emo bangs—the lead singer —get up first and survey the bar. He tries to hide his nervousness behind an air of indifference. Struts past everyone talking, drinking, Friday night conversations few will recall.

The rest of the band follows. The insurance salesman. The portly bro who has probably spent an hour styling his hair.

The last one, the guy with the nice smile. He pauses to scan the crowds. The tables. The booths. Standing-room fans, and those dining beyond.

"C'mon, Vinnie," the bro says, rolling up his sleeve and putting a pick in his mouth. "And hey, sorry she didn't show up."

Vincent takes a last glance around the room. For a moment, those eyes settle on Caitlyn. She feels his stare. Then feels it move through her, beyond.

Nothing there, not for him to see. Just an empty patch of the pub where the air is cool and humid and the dim lights flicker.

10

SANTA ROSA
FRIDAY - 9:00 P.M.

"SORRY ABOUT THE MESS," SHE SAYS AND CLOSES THE FRONT DOOR.

After weeks of hotels with the personality of plastic, Michaels finds the touch of humanity refreshing. Twelve hundred square feet of mid-century modesty, three bedrooms, a split kitchen, and a one-car garage. Half the home's contents sit in brown boxes, packaging tape nearby.

"Moving in?"

"Moving out," Carruthers says. "Eventually. My partner and I are in transition."

"Transitioning where?"

"We're separating."

"Oh." Michaels catalogues the boxes. Decorative plates, paintings, colorful artwork. There is a theme to the packed objects, one that doesn't scream Carruthers's femininity. "Well, my condolences about the divorce—"

"Don't apologize," Carruthers says from the kitchen. "First, it's not a divorce—it's a separation. Technically, we never tied the knot. Like a breakup in slow motion. Beer?"

"Water, actually."

Caruthers hands him a bottled water. She cracks a beer for herself, bitter hops filling the air.

"And second, it's not like a car crash wiped one of us out. Separations don't happen to happy marriages."

"I see."

Carruthers raises her beer. "To clarity, and all it has brought us tonight."

Michaels raises his bottled water. "Cheers."

They take sips, water and beer. Carruthers fills a bowl with pretzels, slides it down the counter to Michaels. He sits on the stool.

"So what's your deal, Michaels? Family? Kids?"

"None that I know of."

"Dating anyone?"

"Not currently."

"Dogs, cats?"

"Someday, maybe."

Carruthers takes another sip, studies the agent. How straight his posture is. His pressed his three-piece suit. The cufflinks and tie. He might look like a mannequin at a hipster boutique if it weren't for his pores and those tired eyes. "They don't let you out of the charging stations often, do they?"

"Our batteries only last for twelve hours," Michaels says, chewing a pretzel.

"The Foundation, huh? God, I bet you've got stories."

"Not as many as you'd think." Michaels says and pulls out his tablet computer. "That reminds me, before we proceed, you need to sign some security memorandums."

"Proceed?"

"We share a mutual case. I want to bring you into the fold. I'm sorry, was I unclear?"

"Okay, first, this isn't my case. I'm advising the CBI. That's what I do. I'm the Bureau's local liaison."

"Yes, but it's not their case anymore."

Carruthers scoffs. "You can't just take it from them. That's not how this works."

"With respect, it's already been done."

"I'm sure they're pleased."

"Agent Lee is assisting. I believe the word he used was 'stoked.'"

"Yeah, well, he's a little green, if you get my drift. Forgive me, but I'm going to pass on a task force run by a spook shop. Besides, I'm on my way out."

"Your retirement isn't for another eighteen months."

"I've got a house to sell."

"Summer's a better market than spring."

"I don't fucking trust you."

"I wouldn't either," Michaels says. "I am rough around the edges when it comes to human interaction. People find me blunt. I find people confusing. You don't. You got Kembo to talk, to trust you. That's a skill I lack. And you've worked violent crimes before."

"Not this kind of violence."

"There are no violent crimes like these."

Carruthers tilts her head. "These?"

Michaels taps his tablet, swipes, then turns it to face Carruthers. It's a consulting investigator agreement, already signed by SAC Beddicker and—*Jesus*—the Office of the Deputy Director. She scrolls down, line after line, page after page.

"It's exhaustive," Michaels says. "The TL;DR version is basically that—"

"What's TL;DR?"

"'Too long; didn't read.' Like a summary. This is a temporary top-secret authorization. Compartmentalized, of course."

"Of course," Carruthers repeats, still scrolling. "Can't let the pawns see the whole chess board, can we?"

"We're more like knights. You know, sometimes I think the big secret is there is no board."

"Scary thought." This isn't the first time Carruthers has consulted cross-agency. She knows the tiers: confidential, secret, and top secret. Once, she'd contributed to a task force when a senator's daughter absconded to the Lost Coast with a militia she'd met online. Carruthers had been granted an interim public trust clearance. She has seen how fast government machines spin up with the proper motivation. In thirty-six hours the girl was found, the public never the wiser. An expired badge now hangs from the cork board at Carruthers's office, a quiet reminder that sometimes this job brings a bit of good to the world.

"So what happens if I don't sign?"

"Best case?" Michaels takes a deep breath. "The Foundation takes the wheel, puts me in the back seat, slaps national security gags on everyone. We get unpaid vacations and little red flags in our agency files that tell a few key people to keep us out of the country club. Worst case?" He shrugs.

It's hard to tell if it's the tablet's glow or the blood draining from her cheeks that gives Carruthers a grave shade. Perhaps both. She scribbles her name at the bottom of the screen. Turns the tablet back to Michaels. "I don't suppose I get a copy."

"This isn't an Apple Store." Michaels closes out the security clearance. "But I am going to borrow your printer."

"I'll give you the Wi-Fi password."

"No need," he says. "I'm already on it."

The printer starts up from the home office, the inkjet whirring and clicking. Carruthers sips her beer. "God, you guys give me the creeps."

Michaels considers it. "And you should tape over your webcams."

THIRTY MINUTES, twenty pages of paper, two beers, and a bowl of pretzels later, Michaels begins laying it out on the kitchen counter. A draft of Carruthers's report is there, key sections highlighted, including the deleted references to dhimonis. Just one piece of a puzzle. There are other pieces here, other reports, other names and agencies, local, state, and federal.

"April 21," he says and taps the first file. "Professor Karl Moore, fifty-eight, is found on the tenth floor of the Loftus science building at Cal State Marin. Autopsy concludes death due to severe blunt force trauma, external and internal. The only lacerations are from compound fractures. And the only witness is the janitor."

"Kembo," Carruthers says. "God, he was shaken."

"As he should be. Dr. Munson, the ME, said internally Moore looked like he was hit by a bus." Michaels taps the photograph of the professor. What remains of him. "That door was struck with eight thousand Newtons of force. Bone breaks around three thousand."

Michaels swipes to a second photograph. An athletic woman in a blazer. Serious eyes, a smile that is all business. Another swipe. Her broken corpse, a ruby maw where her jaw has been wrenched free.

"April 14. Doctor Deborah Anderson is found in the women's shower of the Northwest Tampa Family YMCA."

"Jesus, you think they're linked?"

"There are consistencies. Defensive wounding of the fingers, like she was fighting back. Internal trauma. Complete absence of trace evidence. Some shower room tiles were broken. Unfortunately, they were replaced by the time I arrived."

"No witnesses?"

"None," Michaels says. "Some seventeen-year-old lifeguard found Deborah, tried to initiate CPR, but..."

"Brave kid."

Brave indeed. This job has hardened Michaels, yet there are moments where humanity still impresses him. More often than not, it's at the threshold of horror where greatness begins.

Another tap on his tablet, and up comes a spreadsheet. Names run by. Dates of birth. Dates of death. He turns it to Carruthers.

"All the major medical examiners' offices are linked in case of a bio-terror attack or an outbreak. Cross-referencing suspicious deaths with ViCAP, I came up with a list of thirty similar cases over the past year. I flagged for internal wounds without external lacerations, and the algorithm narrowed it to this."

Carruthers studies the spreadsheet. Five names. Five dates of birth. Five dates of death. Locations all across the U.S. Marin, CA. Tampa, FL. Durango, CO. She tries to make sense of it, sorting by details. Height, weight, age, occupation. Entire lives laid out, just bare points of data. Then—

"Quite the educated group," Carruthers says. "Three with PhDs, one's a proper MD. One's both. All within a close age spread," she adds. "What, like ten years? I don't see anyone under fifty-seven."

"Good eye. Whatever this is, it doesn't seem to be afflicting the young."

"Tell me about him," Carruthers says, pointing to the name STRAUSS, MARK T, PhD. The bottom of the list.

"Most of what I dug up comes from Wikipedia," Michaels says. "Did an interagency search and Strauss has a clean history. Long hours at a bioengineering startup in Burlington. They build those robotic dogs. He did a TED talk."

"Wait, the thing with the head caps and mind-controlled limbs? Jesus, I saw that."

"Amazing stuff, right? They found Strauss in his engineering lab. Investigators thought he'd gotten caught up in a forklift. Closed down the facility for OSHA inspections, found nothing."

"Can't see OSHA digging this deep," Carruthers says.

"Exactly. They listed cause of death as cervical fracture due to atlanto-occipital dislocation," Michaels says. "His head was wrenched backwards."

Carruthers crunches a pretzel. The beer has made her nibbly and the photos are making her tense. Not a good combination.

"What about him?" She taps a photo of a husky man with a scruffy complexion. "Paul Donovan."

Michaels opens the file on his tablet. "Dr. Donovan spent the past decade as a DARPA contractor. He specialized in neurosensory polytrauma."

A smiling man in a lab coat. Swipe. A twisted wreck on a bathroom floor.

Crunch. Another pretzel.

"Prieta Stenvall, clinical psychologist at a rehab in Colorado."

Her website photo: friendly and attentive to a group of addicts in a circle. Swipe. A hunk of flesh mottled in contusions.

Carruthers's eyes are starting to burn. It's late, and her mind has been working overtime all week. She focuses on the web of connections. Men and women. Ages fifty-eight to sixty-eight. Professionally successful. Some politically active. Some that haven't voted since Clinton.

"The truth is, I'm not sure they're connected," Michaels says. "Or if I'm building patterns that aren't on the page. Then I hear Kembo, in your interview. Did that sound like a man who was lying?"

"No." Carruthers rubs her eyes. "But it doesn't mean he's telling the truth. I mean, I like *The X-Files*, but that's a hard pill to swallow."

"Sometimes the impossible points to the improbable," Michaels says. "In 1693 the villagers of Salem blamed their sickness on witches. Now we know it was ergot poisoning. Two centuries later men in Denton, England, went mad in staggering numbers. Turns out making felt halts with mercury causes erethism. Visit a haunted house and you're fifty times more likely to find carbon monoxide pockets or black mold in the walls. Impossible lies pointing to improbable truths."

"I'm relieved we can rule out Ouija boards and voodoo dolls."

"Not until we find who's holding the pins."

Carruthers squints. "Now here's another pattern." She sorts the spreadsheet not by date of autopsy but by estimated date of death. "Six days between Durango and Burlington. Five days to Tampa. Six to Marin. That was one week ago."

Michaels nods, his left hand begging to twitch.

"Assuming it holds," Carruthers continues, "we're about due for another one."

"Overdue, actually."

11

FOG BREAKER CAFÉ
SATURDAY - 8:40 P.M.

VINCENT POURS CREAMER INTO HIS COFFEE. WHITE AND BLACK, spinning and fusing in tawny swirls. He blows on the mug and takes a sip.

"Listen, I'm really glad you asked me to come to your gig," Caitlyn says. She fills out the booth seat across from him, the diner otherwise half empty. This is a way station for the hungry and soon to be hungover. Across from her, Vincent's plate of eggs sits half eaten. Outside, rain scours the dark streets. Turns the glass buildings into black curtains. Light smears the pavement in red and yellow to the swish of passing cars.

Caitlyn stares into those blue eyes across from her. Takes a deep breath and tries to steady her heart. Apologies, never easy. "I'm sorry I ghosted you. I mean, in a way, I did see it. I just..."

His soft fingers, trimmed nails. If she could just reach out and touch them...

"What you need to understand, Vincent, is that I'm different. And no, not in that inclusionary unique snowflake kind of way. More like, 'I haven't left my apartment in eighteen months.' What's a crazy cat lady minus cats? You're sitting across from her."

She smiles. He doesn't.

"I just... I don't interact well. With others, I mean. Actually, I don't really interact with others at all."

Vincent's eyes scour the mug. His fingers tap the silverware. A beat, a rhythm. He takes out a pen, starts jotting down words. *Cold night. Rain hums. Waiting for a call that never comes.*

"And it's not that I don't think you're nice and your music's neat. It's just... I'm not ready. Not for this."

Vincent nods, pleased. Then he looks at Caitlyn.

His pupils dilate; his gaze passes through her, beyond the empty seat. His thoughts are far off now. A sip of his coffee. Then he sets the cup down and nods at the waitress.

"Takin' any to go, hon?" the waitress says through a yawn.

"Just the check please."

She leaves the check holder at the edge of his table. Moves on to refill empty mugs. Stops to chat with a silver-haired man in the corner booth. A slow night. When it rains in the spring, the summer seems a lifetime away.

Vincent leaves a generous tip. Then he leaves the booth with his jacket.

And Caitlyn watches him go. Past the waitress. Past a quiet man in an argyle cap, eating pancakes and studying legal papers. Past a young, drunk couple, trying to quietly debate their unplanned pregnancy. On most nights, Caitlyn might stick around to listen, to hear how these new parents would solve this wrinkle. She might even wish them well. But tonight she is tired and disgusted. Is this what she's become, a cowardly ghost?

A faint rumble, followed by a low, concussive clap. Near the register, Vincent's eyes drift up to the tacky chandelier. The bulbs are flickering. By the coffee machine, an unused outlet belches twin ribbons of smoke.

At the corner booth, the waitress pauses her conversation as something outside catches her eye. The rain. It's hitting the air at an odd angle. Reflecting like crystal beneath a shower, now gone.

The drunk couple glance at a cup of ice water. The condensation is beading, freezing, falling to the counter with a faint *tinkity tink*.

The waitress cocks her head at the double doors. The rain dripping down the glass slows. Then it stops. Hangs there, beading into a shape.

A frosted blot unfolds upon the glass. Five spindly lines growing out from a seed. The shape of two hands, fingers long and crooked and cold.

Then the door shatters.

A bulge of safety glass becomes a thousand white pebbles. It all blossoms out. The shock wave hits the register, the display of pies, the day's specials. Vincent pulls the waitress away as the empty doorframe twists and crashes to the floor. The diner echoes with cries.

What comes next robs Caitlyn of all logic.

A dark form crashes into the diner, sends glass skittering, and lands on the tiled floor with a rattling thud. It rises from all fours, sinewy shoulders hyena-like and hunched. Shadows cascade down its body, oily tendrils writhing and swirling, twitching and curling. The thing doesn't move—not the way bones and muscles locomote —but bleeds, like ink in strobe-lit waters. Shifting now, from razor-sharp clarity to dendritic shadows. Its spine is a curvature of bony protrusions. Spindly fingers push into the floor, knuckles down. There is no hair upon this malformation, yet Caitlyn senses that's not skin stretched across it either. It wears the shadows like a robe, much as an octopus wears the colors and folds of coral. Yet there is a musculature, a structure beneath. A jawline traces the shape of where a mouth should be. A skull, unmistakably sapien. And its eyes, two cruel sockets dripping silver smoke.

Sockets that turn.

Scour the diner.

Scour the crowd.

"Is everyone okay?" Vincent asks, pulling the waitress up. The young couple puts their argument on hold, the boyfriend shielding his partner. "Ma'am, are you okay?" Vincent gets a nod from the pair.

"Folks, I need you to step back from the door," the waitress shouts. "Anyone see what happened?"

"Christ, probably a scooter accident," the cook says, stepping out of the kitchen.

Look at it, Caitlyn thinks. That's not a scooter. That's a nightmare and—

And nothing. No one reacts to it. No one flees this amalgam of horrors. No one even sees it.

Sees how it prowls about the front of the diner.

How each spastic movement contradicts the last.

How its hands have too many joints.

And now, how those silver eyes narrow as a cruel grin splits smoky skin.

Legs tightening, back bristling, the edge of its shadows glistening. In a barreling charge, the dhimoni leaps across the dinner and comes to a stop...

... right next to the argyle-capped man at the edge of the counter. His ham sandwich lies half eaten, his briefcase open. Sensing a change in the air, he turns, and for one terrible second Caitlyn feels it all slow down.

The raindrops outside.

The reverberating gasps.

The clatter of silverware and glass coming to a stop.

The dhimoni unfurls a hand as if caressing a flower. Runs it along the middle-aged man's stubbled face. Touches a dark finger to his rosy cheek.

Then thrusts its hand into his chest.

A dry cry echoes out. The man seizes his shirt, pries the buttons loose. The dhimoni holds on, hand sunk up to its wrist in fast-dimpling flesh. The creature twists and tugs. There is a sickening pop as the man slams against the counter. His left foot convulses, sends a brown Oxford flying.

Caitlyn, frozen. Ten years of blinking alone, of having this interstitial world to herself. Watching it all as an audience of one.

Watching now, a toe curling beneath the sock. Watching the dhimoni arch its back, plunging its hand into the man's stomach and shaking.

Screams all around, a chorus crying out.

"He's having a heart attack!"

"Call the police!"

"Somebody help him, please!"

Vincent runs over, grabs onto the man, and puts a hand on his shoulder. Then the shoulder is shattered with an audible crack. Vincent goes stumbling back.

Twisting and turning, the dhimoni lifts the man up. The cook takes a step back, makes the sign of the cross. To the patrons, this poor man is floating.

Mewling, he is flung over the counter. Coffee pots shatter. A juicer falls free. For one sad moment, that shoeless leg protrudes like an exclamation point. Then the dhimoni pounces.

Thrashing, smashing, tossing the man like a toy until it grows bored. For the space of ten seconds, the man tries to pull himself on broken fingers. Tries to cry for help with a broken jaw. Tries to rise up, off the checkerboard tiles.

Then the beast seizes him from behind, a brutal coup de grâce—

And crushes his head into the floor.

The screaming. The cries. People scrambling away. With a low thump, the cook faints.

And the dhimoni rises, calm amid this chaos. Surveys the carnage. Its back straightens to full height. The darkness sheds from its left hand. A form emerges from beneath shadows. Fingers from claws, the musculature of a man, disrobing.

Then the dhimoni's head snaps in Caitlyn's direction. A dark husk conceals all hints of humanity, spiteful eyes narrowing in—

On her.

"You... should not be here," it hisses.

It steps closer. Eyes twin cauldrons of cold silver.

"Who are you that wanders far from home?" it asks. "Answer me."

Another step. And then it's in front of her. Doesn't run, just warps right there, shadows unfolding, eyes that rip into her very mind, and now its hand stretches out, thrusting for her—

"Answer me!"

Half of the city screams past her. She is in a laundromat. In a dark office. In a bathroom at a hotel, its hot bathtub steaming. Five miles in a fragmented blast.

A bay window. A vase of vibrant flowers. And then curtains collapsing and devouring all light.

CAITLYN, exploding out from her cushion, falling sideways. Feels the floor rise up and seize her. Feels the fabric of her rug. Her heart, racing. "Warning!" her watch chirps. "Irregular heartbeat detected. Warning!"

She grasps for the coffee table. Knocks over a cup of cold tea. Fumbles for her folding cane.

Three hurried clicks and the pieces snap into place. Swinging the cane out now, sweeping left to right. The tip drags across the carpet, traces the hardwood floor. She taps the desk at her left. The couch. The end table. Each vibration confirms a familiar object, a layout she knows. Each tap fills in a line or an edge, a curve or a cushion.

This is her apartment; she feels it now. This is home, a place of safety. And yet...

"Hello?" Caitlyn calls out. "Is someone here?"

Tock.

No answer, but she senses it's there. Something, in the bathroom.

Tock.

You can do this. Follow the wall to the entrance. Follow the molding to the bathroom door. Twenty-two paces.

Tock.

She tries to quiet her mind, to steady her thoughts. *Come back to this moment, this now.* All she sees: endless shadows. And a man's head vanishing in a crimson burst. That thing in the diner.

Tock. Tock. Tock.

In ten years and hundreds of journeys, Caitlyn has never been seen. In all her travels she hardly left a trace. Yet that thing shattered glass. That thing ravaged that poor man. That thing looked back.

Tock. Tock. Tock.

Has it followed her home? Were its words true? Had she wandered too far?

Tock. Tock. Tock.

No. Caitlyn lets the bathroom door go. Hurries to the front door. Turns the bolts and rushes out into the hall.

There is only one other door atop the stairs. She finds it in four paces. Knocks on it, slow at first, then faster and faster until all she hears is the rapping of knuckles over the sound of her sobs and the patter of rain.

A SLOW SHUFFLE, slippers against the shag carpet. Mrs. Bakshi is returning.

"It was that old tree," Mrs. Bakshi says. "I've been telling the city to trim it for years. It must've given you a scare, brushing up against the window like that."

Caitlyn senses the shuffle moving into the kitchenette. A clinking of cups. A sizzle of hot water poured from a kettle. Now air redolent of white tea and lemon. And she feels a flush in her cheeks.

"Goodness, that's embarrassing," Caitlyn says.

For a moment Mrs. Bakshi just clatters and clanks. Caitlyn isn't sure the old woman has heard her words, her pathetic attempt to downplay the hysteria that had, only minutes ago, brought her to

Mrs. Bakshi's door, pounding and panicked. The only thing pounding now is her temples, a headache to come.

"Drink this," Mrs. Bakshi says and sets a cup down. "It'll help settle your nerves."

Caitlyn feels the edge of the table. Traces a line along the little cloth doilies. Follows the grooves of the old wood until she finds the cup and the saucer. Then she raises it and inhales.

"Hot cream, a spoonful of lemon, some ginger and white tea," Mrs. Bakshi says proudly. "My Dhiren called it his nightcap."

"It's delicious," Caitlyn says, savoring each sip. The cream, thickened with lemon, infuses the tea with a bittersweet kick.

"It reminds me of youthful indiscretion," Mrs. Bakshi says. "I would make it whenever Dhiren and I drank too much. Something for our belly before bed."

"You must miss him," Caitlyn says. "I sure would."

"It's the little things, mostly. His hands, and how even though he went to bed before me, they always found mine in the night. Or the newspaper laid out each morning, opened to the crossword puzzles. Sometimes he even sharpened a pencil or two."

Caitlyn can see it in her mind's eye. Decades in time lapse unfolding at this table. Black hair becoming gray. Wrinkles setting in across skin, long canyons. Thousands of meals in these very chairs. And one chair now, mostly empty.

"Caitlyn, sweetheart, how long have we known each other?"

"Four years now."

"Four years," she repeats. "I'll be eighty-six next month. When you've lived this long, you learn to spot a fib or two."

Caitlyn says nothing. Maybe if she sips her tea, Mrs. Bakshi won't press her.

"The tree isn't what scared you, is it, dear?" The chair creaks and Caitlyn senses Mrs. Bakshi leaning in. "I saw the pills in your bathroom."

Caitlyn's turn to squirm in the chair. "You... You spied on me?"

"Sweetie, they were sitting on the sink. Now, I didn't read the label—I'm no snoop—but I spent fifteen years in the city ballet. I'm old, but I'm not an old fool. Please don't try to tell me those are multivitamins."

It takes everything Caitlyn has just to say three little words. "No, they aren't."

"Of course not."

Old hands settle on Caitlyn's. Her instinct is to jerk away. Yet she stifles the fear. This is the only lifeline she has.

"You're safe here," Mrs. Bakshi says, now squeezing. "So why don't you tell me what really happened? Why you showed up to my door, your poor heart pounding right out of your chest."

Caitlyn swallows. Mrs. Bakshi knows as much about her ability as everyone else, which is absolutely nothing. It's a secret, Caitlyn's dirty secret, not because she could use it to spy, but because she *has*. Talking about blinking is admitting to all it could be used for, the good and the bad.

"I don't know where to start," Caitlyn says. "I don't think you'll believe me."

"Try me, dear." Another squeeze. "You might be surprised."

12

SAN FRANCISCO
SUNDAY - 9:00 A.M.

SHE STROKES THE GIRL'S FOREHEAD. WARM, BUT NO WARMER THAN she expects. Poor child. Best to let her keep resting.

Mrs. Bakshi leaves Caitlyn some breakfast samosas, poha, and sliced fruit with ginger. She would send her a message too, but she doesn't have a smartphone. For a while, Mrs. Bakshi had tried to keep pace as emails became text messages and taxis became Ubers. But it all moved so fast. Now, she is content with her flip phone, content to ride the bus to church on this Sunday.

There, under the stained glass of Saints Peter and Paul, she sings hymns of praise. Thinks of Caitlyn and last night's conversation, a shadow over these joyful songs.

It wasn't the poor girl's delusions but how devout she was, how certain she was of her words. How vivid the fiction her young tenant has sold herself on.

So Mrs. Bakshi kneels and prays and sends good thoughts Caitlyn's way until the service is over.

They board the bus again at a quarter past ten. Thirty seniors, bound for brunch at the YMCA. Crossing beneath the freeway, she recalls Caitlyn's story. She had mentioned a restaurant. Was it close to the Mission? Mrs. Bakshi squints at the crisscrossing power lines, the colorful graffiti. Isn't that a diner they just passed?

A compulsion overcomes her. As the bus waits for the stoplight, Mrs. Bakshi ambles down the row. "José, would you be kind and let me out here?"

"Walking home, Mrs. Bakshi?"

She has no intention of walking several miles. Nor will she fib on a Sunday. Instead, she says, "It's just such a beautiful day." Which it is. The rain has scoured the city, leaving air so pure it's like breathing mint.

The bus drops her off on the corner of Harrison and 9th. For two blocks she shuffles back, past old apartments like her own, now shadowed by corporate towers. Past a transient sleeping in the doorway of a tech startup. Her fingers tighten on her purse, not in fear of the poor but for what is coming into view.

On most days, she would have noticed her sore feet. Today, she ignores them. Her mind is rewinding to details half remembered. Images a blind girl described. The red of a countertop. A checkerboard floor. A stainless steel milkshake machine, now dented and deformed. And Mrs. Bakshi, clutching her purse, stares at the diner on the corner, its front door boarded up and taped, bright lights inside as men in hazmat suits unfurl great plastic sheets, stapling them to the windows and sealing it off.

[PART 2]

In the stone there is no pain, but in the fear of the stone is the pain. God is the pain of the fear of death. He who will conquer pain and terror will become himself a god.

— Fyodor Dostoyevsky, *Demons*

[13]
CRIME SCENE: FOG BREAKER CAFÉ
SUNDAY - NOON

A COCOON OF SPUN FIBERS, THIS ENVELOPE IN HUMAN SHAPE.
Michaels hates every inch of his Tyvek suit. High-density poly-
ethylene creates a skin-tight cling, porous enough to let water
vapor through, tight enough to seal in the sweat.

At least it's a nice diner, he thinks as he steps through the
containment curtain. Comfy booths, checkerboard tiles. Not many
greasy spoons left in San Francisco. Like stepping back to simpler
days.

Pity they've had to shut the place down.

The windows are covered in plastic. In the work lights, every
inch of the diner sheens in sharp, soap opera definition. Even the
corpse on the floor looks like a prop.

Michaels reminds himself it isn't. That is a man there. A life
and a history, hopes and dreams, the main character of his own
story, every moment as vivid as anyone's.

"Meet the late Newell Sacks," Brad says. "SFPD got the call
around midnight. We jumped on it just before dawn. We've been
fighting to keep the scene clean but the flies show up fast. No
one's moved him."

"Good work," Carruthers says.

Even behind the self-contained breathing apparatus, Brad is

beaming. "How you doing in there, chief?" Brad asks, voice muffled. "You look hot."

"I am hot," Michaels says, wishing he could wipe his forehead. "Any other insight you can offer?"

"Nope, nope," Brad says. "I'm just here to learn from the pro."

Michaels glances at Carruthers. Her eyes say, *I know. Don't ask.* She takes Brad aside. "We'll do the walkthrough. Why don't you check the security video?"

"Good thinking." Brad heads off, stepping over electric cords, around UV lights, past medicolegal investigators setting it all up. For a moment this walkthrough is quiet.

"He's interesting," Michaels says.

"He's what the Canadians call a keener," Carruthers says. "But he took the call, secured the scene, so we owe him that."

"Let's remember to send him a thank-you note when this is over."

"He'll probably frame it."

They come to a stop by the counter.

"Christ, what a mess," Carruthers says grimly.

The victim is facedown, his left arm fractured, fingers curled the wrong way. His right knee is dislocated, rising like a triangle. And the head, what is left of it, really, is a lump of black hair and bone buried in buckled tiling.

"So you're the reason I'm spending Sunday in the city," says a man kneeling beside the corpse. The ID on his Tyvek suit reads *MEDICAL EXAMINER - MUNSON.* "Michaels, is it?"

"Dr. Munson," Michaels says. "You handled the Moore autopsy up at CSU Marin."

Munson nods. Behind the plastic, his eyes are connecting dots.

"We know it's a drive," Carruthers says. "Thanks for coming."

"Government's dime. I just crank up the podcasts and hit cruise control."

"This task force prefers the same set of eyes," Michaels says. "Figure, maybe you'll see something familiar. Or something new."

"Yeah," Munson says. "A man with his head embedded in

ceramic flooring. That's new. We'll be cutting the tiles out around him. Otherwise, his face is staying. We've had a hell of a time keeping the scene cooled."

"Anything you've learned so far?"

"Well, like the Moore case, I don't see major signs of lacerations or avulsions. Skin's mostly intact, minus the head, of course. The body displays severe acute contusions." He lifts the man's shirt, exposing purple spots across a back laced with the deep red marbling of livor mortis.

A technician raises a camera and snaps a picture. *Click* goes the shutter. *Pop* go the flashbulbs. The last portrait of Newell Sacks, a mess of grim pixels.

"These extravasations of blood into tissue indicate trauma occurred antemortem. Prior to death, basically."

"What kind of weapon are we talking about?" Michaels asks.

"These injuries are nonspecific," Munson says. "If it was a bat, you'd see some abraded contusions where the skin's been scraped. If it was a hammer, some bursting as a result of the compression. Skin's elastic. Besides the fracturing of the skull, the only other cutaneous trauma I can identify is the brush burn on his arm. Road rash, from the floor."

"Could a seizure cause this?" Michaels asks. "Some sort of epileptic fit?"

"It's a thought," Munson says. "There've been cases of musculoskeletal injury during severe tonic-clonic seizures. But this magnitude? None. In a way, it's as if the trauma originated within the chest cavity and expanded outward."

"What do you mean?" Carruthers asks.

"Well, in layman's terms..." Munson glances around. The technicians are busy elsewhere. He leans in, whispers, "Think of a bag of popcorn while you microwave it." He mimes an expansion with his hands.

"You think he's been cooked?"

"No, there's no evidence to suggest that. But based on the

consistencies with Professor Moore, chances are, once he's opened up, it'll look like Walmart on Black Friday."

"Is there any way he could have done this to himself?" Michaels asks, adding, "Intentionally."

"Some of it, perhaps. But smashing his own head in?"

To Michaels, hearing the medical examiner describe it like that is like hearing his old man drop an F-bomb. "Yeah. Smashing his own head in."

"Sure, it's possible. Just not here, inside a diner."

"Why not?"

"Because he'd need three hundred feet of skyscraper to toss himself off. Now, if you'll excuse me, we've got a cadaver to excavate."

The medicolegal investigators step in, chisels and jigsaws. Motors screaming, they go to work on the tile.

A MONTH'S worth of schedules is pinned to the wall above photos of nine smiling employees. No one notices them. The investigators crowd the computer, its screen displaying the diner's security system. Old, low resolution, but at least it's in color.

"There!" Brad says. "Did you see that?"

"No," Carruthers says. "Rewind it."

They lean in, the glow dancing off their plastic masks. Michaels tries to ignore the sweat pooling in all the uncomfortable places beneath the Tyvek.

On-screen, glass is sucked backward and the doorframe unbends. "Can we get a better angle?" Carruthers asks.

"This is all we've got, boss," Brad says.

"The camera's for insurance," Michaels says. "Meant to capture sticky-fingered employees, not customers. Okay, start from there."

Brad adjusts the video feed. Half speed down to a quarter.

The perspective is high, a God's eye view of the register. To the right of frame stands the diner's double doors, the rain pounding outside. To the left, the semi-open kitchen. The counter divides the frame, from bottom to top.

A simple scene. A calm diner. Near the register, the young musician pauses, glances back at the empty booth he'd just left.

"That's Vincent James," Brad says. "I took his statement this morning."

"Anything useful?" Carruthers asks.

"Same song, different tune. Half the place is convinced they witnessed a drug-induced seizure. The other half sounds like our pal Kembo. Okay, now. Look here."

Brad raises a finger to the screen. Taps the rainy double doors to the diner. There is nothing. Just glass and the metal frames. Then, for a brief second, there is a shape. No, two shapes.

"Is that..." Carruthers squints. "That's a hand."

"Two hands," Michaels says. "Look."

The rain, hitting the door. The droplets, beading at odd angles. Two handprints, milky smudges blossoming upon glass. Then—

"Whoa!" Carruthers gasps. Silently, the glass shatters. The blast swings the frames inward. Metal folds and falls, just missing a lucky waitress.

"Back it up a second," Michaels says, his left hand begging to twitch. Wanting to be freed from the sweaty Tyvek. "Pause it... there."

Brad freezes the frame perfectly. For one quarter of a second, the glass door is no longer wet, not most of it. The raindrops are moving away from the shape of the hand. Up, down, left, right. A starburst of water.

"But there's no one there," Carruthers says. "That's not... That shouldn't be."

Again, the door shatters and glass scatters. The shot is too narrow; the carnage plays out off camera. First, in shapes rushing to help, then rushing away. Only Newell Sack's foot in frame, shoeless, as he crawls across the floor. There is a spastic kick, and the leg moves no more.

The small office hangs in utter silence. An FBI agent, a CBI agent, and a man whose agency does not exist. A thousand new questions, and no one knows where to start.

Then the phone rings. The manager's line.

"Should... Should I get that?" Brad asks.

Michaels nods. Brad raises the phone, hesitates. He is still wearing the Tyvek suit, the self-contained breathing apparatus.

He presses speaker phone. "Uh... Hello?"

A long pause, and someone breathing on the other end. Brad maxes out the volume.

"Can I help you?"

A woman's voice. "I'm calling about the murder that happened," she says. "The man in the diner, last night."

The three investigators share bewildered glances. Brad mouths, *What the actual fuck?*

"Is this the detective in charge?" she asks. "Is that how it works?"

Michaels clears his throat. Leans in. "I'm the lead investigator, yes, ma'am. With whom am I speaking?"

Another pause. Then a second voice, older, whispering in the background, "Tell them."

The young voice again, that accent hard to place. A hint of French Swiss, an undercurrent of East Africa.

"My name is Caitlyn. Caitlyn Grey."

[14]
SAN FRANCISCO
SUNDAY - 2:00 P.M.

THE MOBILE CRIME LAB IS FORTY FEET LONG, A CUSTOM RV WITH sterile surfacing and three separate sections for collection, clean up, and communication. Michaels runs a finger down an off-center tile as the mist rinses him. He towels off, dumps the Tyvek suit in the chute, and steps into the prep room, squeezing between Carruthers and Brad. Finds his suit, his cufflinks, his pocket watch.

Something about the fastidious manner in which he buttons the waistcoat, the clasps, then the cufflinks draws Carruthers's attention. It strikes her, perhaps, as a form of pageantry. To Michaels, it is a form of meditation.

"Weren't you wearing that suit the other day?" she asks.

"I wear one every day. I have twenty-two of them."

"Hold up. You have a closet with the same twenty-two suits? Did you raid Brooks Brothers?"

"One less thing to waste bandwidth on in the morning."

"Smart," Brad says. "I read that Steve Jobs did that."

Buttoning his shirt, Michaels says, "Here's the plan. Newell's ex-wife is listed as his next of kin. She's en route to the morgue to ID his body. Carruthers, how do you feel about meeting her? Having a chat?"

"Can't say I'm thrilled," she says, slipping into her shoes. "But it needs to be done."

"It does. I'm sure you'll be tactful."

"I'll do my best."

"Newell's an attorney. That's off profile for our pattern. See what she can give us. Right now, we're twelve hours closer to another one of these... episodes."

"That what we're calling these?" Brad asks. "Fucking episodes with ghost-like hands breaking windows and skulls?"

"We are not calling it anything, yet. We don't know what it is... yet. And that brings me to us, Bret... What was it?"

"Lee, sir. *Brad* Lee." He seems to deflate with each syllable.

Of course Michaels knows his name. He also knows Brad is eager to make a name for himself. A flash of Michaels, eight years ago, on an NSA task force that led to his Foundation recruitment.

This investigation, however, requires a surgical touch. There's little room for error. A wayward comment to a roommate or a cutie at a bar will compromise it all. The fastest way to rein in a fresh agent, Michaels knows, is to make them think they've yet to impress you. The best way to do that is to make them tell you their name. Again and again and again.

"Bradley, right," Michaels says. "Does the CBI have your latest polygraph and security check on file?"

"Yes, sir. And I had a psych screening last month."

"Good," Michaels says. "You're coming with me."

The junior agent's eyes widen. "Yes, sir. Want me to drive, or—"

"No," Michaels says. "You need to fill out some forms."

TWENTY MINUTES LATER, he brings the rental car to a stop curbside, blocking a hydrant. Turns on the hazard lights. The Special Vehicle Access Badge hanging from the rearview mirror is all the permission Michaels needs; it holds more legal strength than diplomatic immunity.

"All signed," Brad says, closing Michaels's tablet. "So that's it? Do I need to take an oath or swear an affidavit?"

"Raise your right hand."

Brad raises his right hand. Michaels gets out of the car, walks down the sidewalk, leaving Brad with his hand up like a cub scout.

Crisp air here, close to the ocean. An architectural shift, from downtown's metal and glass to the quintessential kitsch the city is known for. Victorian and Edwardian houses, painted ladies in tricolor palettes. Apartments, with bay windows on the second and third floors, golden sun dancing off glass.

Grinning, Brad catches up at the gate of a three-story apartment. The list displays offices on the bottom floor, four residences on two. On the third floor, to the right, the name *HAPPY TRAVELS - C. GREY*. Michaels presses the buzzer.

"You think she's serious?" Brad asks. "That she saw the assailant?"

"Maybe. Maybe not. We've locked down the witnesses with confidentiality agreements, but it won't take long for this to leak. The manager's line was unlisted, so the real question is, how'd she know we were there?"

Brad mumbles, "God, can today get any weirder?"

Then it does.

[15]

CAITLYN'S APARTMENT
SUNDAY - 2:45 P.M.

SHE DOESN'T NEED EYES TO SENSE THEIR DISTRUST. IT'S IN THEIR TONE, inflections. The subtle crinkle as their bodies shift on the couch. And the pauses, clearings of the throat masking knee-jerk reactions. Most of all, the clicking pen. That's the younger investigator; Caitlyn is sure of it. An apprentice or an intern or whatever they are called.

Still, she persists.

"Look, I know how this sounds," Caitlyn says. "I didn't call to waste your time, okay? I just want to help."

Caitlyn feels Mrs. Bakshi's hand squeezing her own. Old fingers, wrinkled yet soft and precise. She feels thankful to have someone here who believes her, even if that someone is passing eighty-five.

"It's... quite the story, Ms. Grey," the older one says. Michaels, that's his name. His voice is thick with hesitation, but not the abject doubt beneath the younger one's words. Thankfully, Agent Lee isn't in charge.

"Call me Caitlyn, please. I've never liked my last name. Too generic."

"I can relate," Michaels says. Does she sense a smile in his voice? "So, Caitlyn, to review: last night you self-induced something like an out-of-body experience—"

"Do you know what astral projection is?" she asks, perhaps too eagerly.

There is a pause, the exchanging of glances. "Uh, yes," Michaels says, adding, "I have seen *Doctor Strange*."

She clenches her toes, tries to ignore the implied mockery. She'd hoped to clarify. Instead, she's made herself sound like some mystical freak. *Tone it down.*

"Okay, so it's not like that. It's..." *Consider your words.* "When I focus on a place, slow my breathing, when I get into a meditative headspace and concentrate... Well, I can go there. Step out of my body. Watch things unfold."

"And when you do that," Michaels says, "when you step out, you're not... What I mean is, your visual impairment, it doesn't—"

"Oh no, I'm not blind," she says. "Of course I can see."

"Of course. But only when you do this thing."

"Blinking, that's what I call it. Like a form of traveling."

"Oh, I get it," Brad says. "So this travel agency, it's a play on words."

"A play on words?"

"A pun," he says. "I mean, it's not an actual travel agency, because of the name and your visual impairment and—"

"No. I run an actual agency. I'm licensed. I provide bespoke services for a very select clientele."

"Right," Michaels says. "I don't doubt it."

She senses the opposite; he doubts every word. Caitlyn reminds herself she would as well. And yet, she knows what she saw. Every place she's traveled to, every moment she's witnessed, they were all real. All those thousands of hours.

"So last night, you astral pro—you *blinked* to a diner. There, you claim to have seen..." His voice changes. He's reading, consulting the younger agent's notes. "What was it? 'A creature cloaked in shadows, but with a human form.'"

"Yes."

"And said creature 'squeezed the guts of the victim without breaking the skin'?"

"Yes," she says. "Like it was reaching into water or smoke. It just... It mauled this poor man."

"Define 'mauled.'"

"Its fingers were like... One minute they were animalistic, like claws. And then I could see human fingers beneath it."

"Beneath the creature?"

"Yes."

"The creature you saw traveling out of body?"

"Yes."

Silence again, thick and heavy. The young agent asks, "So was it like wearing gloves or a costume or something?"

Caitlyn rubs her neck. Her head throbs, her throat hurts from talking, and with each word, regret drills her temples. This whole thing feels like a mistake.

"Caitlyn," Michaels says, "what I'm having trouble parsing is, why were you at the diner? I mean, of all the places you could visit, why some overpriced throwback south of Market?"

Good question. Maybe he is starting to believe her. Or maybe he is just feeling for holes. She can't see his face, and reading his tone is like gauging the mood of a wall. Nothing to do but give the best answer, the honest answer.

"There was a guy, Vincent. I was supposed to meet him the night before."

A crinkle of turning paper. A digital pen tapping on a screen. Notes are being consulted.

"Anyways, I was there because, well, I was spying on him."

"Spying?"

"I wouldn't exactly call it stalking. More like explaining something to him."

The chair squeaks as Michaels leans forward. "Wait, so he could hear you?"

"No," she says. "No, no, I'm not... I've never actually been able to affect anything when I blink. I just..."

"You just watch?"

"Yeah."

More notes being taken. The gulp of water, the clink of a glass on her coffee table.

"So you were having a conversation with a person but he couldn't hear you."

"Right."

"And you're friends with Vincent James?"

"Sort of. We like the same kind of music. I saw his band at a pub. The thing is... well, I don't get out that often."

"But you said you saw him perform."

"I mean physically out." A deep breath, then: "I haven't left this apartment in over a year."

"Oh!" Brad says. "On account of your visual impairment?"

"More like... agoraphobia."

There. She's said it. Doesn't seem so bad now that it's out in the open. People live in cabins, in the mountains, scattered across the continent with minimal human contact. No one thinks less of Thoreau. She just happens to be doing it in a major city. So what?

"I want to leave. I've tried. It's just... I get disoriented. Dizzy. Noises amplify and I can't tell if I'm falling. Like a panic attack, I think."

Silence answers her. She holds her tongue, decides she's done enough to damage her credibility. At least she has named this affliction, this malaise that has loomed over her for the past year and a half.

"My uncle hasn't left his farm in a few years," the young agent says. "He's not agoraphobic, just a prepper with a bunker full of canned goods, so..."

Someone exhales. Michaels, she imagines. Going blind has brought a few blessings. She can't see rolling eyes, is spared the stares or glares or grimaces on the faces around her. Yet still, she can sense them. They exist, hidden in the pauses and silence, the little lip smacks, the sucking of air through teeth, the deep breath, or the slow fade of a statement that has lingered too long.

"Look, Agents. I know how this sounds. I can see where this is going. But I also know what I saw. That thing at the diner, it's real. It killed that poor man. It spoke, and it tried to attack me. And all you've got are a handful of witnesses and some crummy video. I'm telling you what I saw from my side."

"How'd you know about the video?" Michaels asks.

She has their attention now. Can sense their focus.

"The same way I got the manager's phone number," she says. "I was there in the back office, with all three of you."

16

SAN FRANCISCO
SUNDAY - 5:00 P.M.

THE OFFICE OF THE CHIEF MEDICAL EXAMINER LOOMS AT THE NORTH end of India Basin. Like the cool bodies within, the building is gray and blue, a solemn slate box between forlorn boatyards and flowered parks bringing color to this windy scratch of land. Here, the poppies bloom in Heron's Head and cargo cranes hold vigil at the bay's edge. Here, beneath storm-silver clouds and the warble of egrets, two women share a bench.

"For a while it was a good marriage," she says and pours a packet of stevia into her coffee. "Or, I suppose, it had the appearance of one. My father always liked Newell."

For someone who just identified her ex-husband from the birthmark on his chest, Eileen Sacks-Fischer is a picture of composure. *Maybe she's still in shock*, Carruthers thinks.

"And I suppose, when the divorce became an inevitability, it was my father's heart that broke first. He was a lawyer too, long retired, but in a way, Newell was his connection back into the courtroom. He would have been happy to know Newell still considered our family next of kin."

"Is your father still around?" Carruthers asks, stirring her coffee.

"No," Ms. Sacks-Fischer says. "He passed away ten months ago.

His funeral was the last time I saw Newell. After that…" She mimes a pair of scissors cutting a string. "Snip. No real connection left."

"Well, I'm sorry I couldn't be here with better news."

"Threshold moments. Marriage, divorce, receiving your ex-husband's death certificate." She pats the folder the medical examiner supplied. Dr. Munson had suggested non-facial identification. Wisely, she complied. Then the body bag was sealed, the death certificate signed. Strange, this paperwork that comes at the end of a life, forms sharing space on a park bench beside a cold turkey sandwich and a hot cup of coffee.

"It's a lot to process," Carruthers says. "How are you holding up?"

"Me? Oh, well, I'm fine. It's Sunday. I have an appointment to color my hair. I suppose I'll need to cancel." Then she looks at Carruthers. Ms. Sacks-Fischer is sixty but seems closer to eighty. Maybe it's the light. "And how are you doing, dear?"

Carruthers has seen car accident victims behave the same way. Flat answers, glazed eyes. The human mind has to chew on grief, to break horror down into digestible chunks.

"I know this is difficult, but I need to ask you if Newell had any enemies, anyone that wanted to harm him."

"Enemies? He was a lawyer, so…" She shrugs as if to say it's just part of the job.

"It could even be a debt or a bad business deal. Someone he might have professionally slighted?"

"No debts, that's for sure. Newell wasn't a gambler, and he hardly ever drank. You could set a watch by his habits. I doubt they changed after the divorce. Dinner at eight. Bed by ten. That's why it never worked out between us. He's a Virgo, you see. Virgos need structure, routine. I'm a Leo—"

"Bed by ten," Carruthers says. "He was at the diner at eleven. Does that sound normal for Newell?"

"No. No, it doesn't. And not on a Saturday night."

"Was he, you know, seeing anyone?"

"I wouldn't know. And to be honest, I wouldn't care. Our desires don't end at sixty."

"No, of course not."

"You'll be there someday. It happens so fast. Goodness, how I miss him already." Then she digs through her purse, frantic, but Carruthers already has the tissues out. Tears, salty and hot, streak the woman's cheeks as her shoulders sag and heave. Far off, the egrets take flight, calling out for each other against the bitter bay wind.

"HERE, HELP ME MOVE THIS," Michaels says and grips the dumpster. Brad squeezes to the other side, pulls on the fork pockets. With a groan, the rusty wheels turn. They roll the metal container to the edge of a chain-link fence that bisects the alleyway, then bring it to a stop against graffiti-covered brick.

"So why're we downwind of a homeless encampment?" Brad asks, sniffling. "Forensics has been all over the street."

Michaels closes the metal lid, pounds it, checking the strength. Sturdy enough. He climbs on top of the dumpster.

"We are here to get perspective." Michaels stretches out for the bottom rungs of the fire escape.

"Isn't this what Google Maps is for?" Brad asks. "Y'know, looking down and all."

Michaels releases the fire escape ladder. With a clang, the rungs slide down, stopping short of the dumpster. Where the alley meets the street, a pair of kids pause to watch this odd site: two men going up the fire escape.

"Google updates every six months," Michaels says, hoisting himself up. "We don't have six days. Forensics is at ground level, in the trench. Sometimes you need to pull back."

Twelve steps later, and they're on the next level of the fire escape. Metal clings to brickwork, dug deep into this old building. Windows offer a view of the apartments. Curtains mostly. Try this in Texas, Michaels muses, and you might get shot. Here, in San Francisco, he's more worried about used needles.

"Fog of war, that's what they call it," Michaels says. "You were in the Army. They didn't teach you that?"

"How'd you guess I was military?"

Michaels gives Brad a glance: no guesswork there.

"Right," Brad says and climbs up a level behind. "I was stationed in South Korea, Camp Humphreys. Ever been there?"

Another rattling floor, another set of rusty stairs.

Michaels says, "The less you know about me, the easier it'll make the lobotomy."

"You spooks need to get those memory-wiping lights from *Men in Black*."

"Who says we don't have them?"

"Yeah," Brad says, "but you spooks need to get those memory-wiping lights from *Men in Black*."

Michaels grins, thinking it's probably the first time he's grinned all week. Fifty rungs later, metal shepherds them out onto the roof. This is the smallest building in the neighborhood, a remnant from a bygone century. In another decade, Michaels doubts it will even exist. Solar panels will replace TV antennas; steel and glass will replace brick. But for now, the roof is sere-naded by the buzz and glow of a neon billboard advertising orange Fanta.

"Tell me what you see," Michaels says.

"I don't know..." Brad huffs. "Pigeon shit. A skanky alleyway. There's the crime scene across from that hotel."

Eight floors below, the chain-link fence bisects the alley. The dumpster they moved reveals a dry patch from last night's rain. The diner, still sealed, to the west. Michaels and Brad follow the roof to the east.

"I didn't notice them at first," Michaels says, "on account of the rain. But they're there. Follow them, down the alley."

Brad squints. "What, potholes? Welcome to the Bay Area."

"Do potholes come in patterns?" Michaels asks. "Left, right, left, right."

"Oh shit," Brad says. "Like something was running. And then... Oh shit."

"Like it passed right through that fence."

At ground level, they were almost indiscernible. From above, the indentations run west to east in a steady pace. Something heavy broke the asphalt. Then the rainwater filled it in. The indentations never let up, not on one side of the chain-link fence or the other. Not until they stop near the door of the Fog Breaker Cafe.

"Level with me," Brad says. "Have you ever seen anything like this before?"

A chirp from Michaels's phone punctures the pregnant silence. Carruthers on the ID. He waits until the connection displays *ENCRYPTED.* Then: "Michaels here."

"So I just had a chat with Newell's ex-wife," Carruthers says. A rumble in the background, the rattle of the highway. "Considering the circumstances, she's holding up. She says Newell's a straight arrow, no obvious enemies."

"Another dead end?"

"Quite the opposite, actually. I showed her a picture of Professor Moore and her eyes lit up. She remembers him. Moore and Newell were at a fundraiser. Moore got drunk, popped Newell in the chin. Happened maybe twenty years back. She remembers Moore 'cause she had to ID him to the cops."

"Moore's file never mentioned that."

"They settled it at the scene. Newell didn't press charges. He said, and I'm quoting, 'I fucked him enough to deserve that.' 'Him' being the late professor."

"What about the others? Did you—"

"Nothing. She doesn't recognize any of them."

"Maybe the lawyer's a nexus."

"He did a fair bit of pro bono. Industrial accidents, visa work. The data techs are at his office pulling files. But I've got one better:

Newell and the ex share a storage locker in Daly City. She gave me the code, one divorcee to another."

"I thought you called it a transition?"

"Whatever. I'm heading there now."

"Pick me up at the crime scene."

"I'm almost on the freeway."

Michaels swipes out of the phone app and pulls up a live map. Sixteen little dots. Red for stationary, yellow for moving, green for traveling in a vehicle. He swipes right, finds Carruthers, says, "You've got two blocks. Do a U-turn and take Potrero north."

"I'm just… Wait, how do you know that?"

"Tricks of the trade."

"Okay, you know how creepy that is? I'm not your damn Uber."

"No, of course not. See you curbside in ten." Then he hangs up.

"So what's the next move?" Brad asks.

Michaels considers it. The sun is setting, the buildings taking on the glow for which the state gets its name. Gold becoming bloodred, birthing shadows that reach across brick and glass.

His fingers twitch. It's there, an idea, the itch of connection.

Light. It travels at 186,000 miles per second. The colors now crawling across the buildings left the sun's surface eight minutes ago. They had silently screamed across a cold void, until they hit the earth's atmosphere at an angle, some scattering among dust and particles. Those that made it through now paint the world in this crimson hue.

His hand twitches as he thinks of Caitlyn in her third-floor apartment, light falling through the bay window, dark to her eyes. Humans can see roughly ten million colors, only a slice of the spectrum. But others exist. Different frequencies of oscillations, other wavelengths. UV and X and gamma rays, all around us.

Light and shadows, visible and hidden. Caitlyn, her tattooed arm and colorful hair. She must have known the back office phone number ahead of time. Okay, so how did she know about Carruthers? Lucky guess. Then what about the video?

Because she fled the diner after the attack. Then why hadn't witnesses mentioned her presence?

Because it's a ruse; she's faking it all. The blindness, the agoraphobia, the astral projection. Then to what end?

Because delusion, Michaels thinks. And the worst kind of all: self-delusion. She's smoking her own stuff. Fanning the flames of auto-psychosis. Maybe, yes, probably, she's just batshit insane.

And yet...

Kembo, and his dhimoni. Caitlyn, and her dim stare. Light and shadows, visible and hidden. It's closer now, the impossible pointing to the improbable and perhaps—

"Michaels?" Brad says. "Our next move, hello?"

Gone. It sinks back into the fog of his thoughts. Damn.

"Our next move," Michaels says, "is to get down off this building."

17

PUBLIC STORAGE
SUNDAY - 8:40 P.M.

IT TAKES THREE TRIES FOR THE METAL SHUTTERS TO BEGRUDGINGLY open. Carruthers waves away months of stale air. Michaels scours the box-lined walls with his flashlight. An armoire wrapped in plastic. Unwanted chairs stacked in a corner. Orphaned furnishings from a marriage's end.

They get to work opening old boxes, inspecting file folders. Separating personal photographs from professional letters. Sifting.

It's good practice, Carruthers tells herself. Her home will need to be reduced, simplified. Twenty years of shared living, deconstructed. Can't sell the place without stripping it down.

Too late to save her marriage. Had Newell and Eileen come to the same conclusion? Here is a photo, a picture from twenty years ago. The happy couple in a cafe, books stacked around them. Newell was handsome, strong jaw, heavy brow. Fierce eyes behind narrow glasses. The photographer had captured Eileen glancing at her husband. Adoration manifested, both love and respect. No combination more powerful.

"Makes you wonder why it didn't work out," Michaels says, glancing at the photo. He sticks it with the others, moves on to boxes of paperwork.

"The person you fall in love with isn't always the one you grow old with," Carruthers says. "Heck, our cells replace themselves every so often."

"That's a myth. Cells are different. Your trachea, for example, replaces itself every couple months. But you're stuck with your retina for life."

"You know what I mean, Rain Man. Everything's not literal."

"The Michaels-Tron does not compute metaphors," he says and moves a filing cabinet. The old rollers groan as he works the slide drawer.

"Throw in a kid, and things get tricky," Carruthers says.

"Mmm, variables."

"I'm serious. You'll see one day."

Michaels laughs. "My kids, can you imagine? They'd have cloven hooves and a penchant for turtlenecks."

"Yeah, well, at least the Michaels-Tron is self-aware. It's not for everyone, marriage or parenthood."

"Would you do it again?" he asks. "Not with me, I mean, but knowing how it turned out."

Carruthers sets a bundle of old letters aside. "And how has it turned out?"

"Hey, I can only try to read the tea leaves. You've got an ex in Florida, joint custody of your daughter, and the TSA records say it's been nine months since any of you flew. I'm just guessing here: things are a little rough on the Carruthers homestead."

"I'm good without group therapy, thank you."

"Fair enough."

She moves on to the bankers' boxes. Finds one labeled 1992–1993. Thumbs through it. Old cases, typed depositions. Hammel versus Contra Costa Power & Electric. The Estate of Davis versus Intel, Inc.

"You know what no one tells you about being a parent?" she says. "You can do everything right. I mean, you can go to all the PTA meetings and coach some sports, but when those hormones come online, it's like meeting a new person. You're juggling a marriage, a career. So you let the marriage go on standby because you think it's safe. Guess again. Now your daughter's in Florida with 'fun mom,' the one who never carried her to term, never had to worry about what it did to her body. So you bargain. Maybe agree that she'll go to college out west after two years away. Then that changes too, and now she's going to school in Virginia, but aren't you proud of her?"

Carruthers tells herself she is not going to cry. She is *not* going to cry. Not over this. And not in this fucking storage locker while her partner sorts through tax documents and... Is he even listening? Son of a bitch. No, why would he? These are the keenings of a fed on the downslope of a career. A woman without youth, soon to slip back into the shadows that come at this age.

Carruthers gives the banker's box a sharp tug. A snap as the cardboard seams crack. But this isn't a normal fold; someone has sealed two pieces together. Old tape, transparent, comes apart in clear scabs. The inside flap of the box falls free.

"Michaels," she says.

"Wow, that must be tough," he says without looking up from his binder of tax forms.

"Dammit, Michaels, take a look at this."

She empties the contents of the box, then flips it on its side. The false cardboard flap comes off, revealing a manila folder, near orange from decades between layers. Inside the folder, a single item.

A photograph. On the back, written in ballpoint pen:

9:92-CV-142578
Project Clearwater

She turns the photograph over. For a moment she thinks she is imagining it. Her eyes, tired and dry, see but don't comprehend the collected faces of the dead smiling out from the lost decades. Then she says, "Fucking hell."

. . .

Item #4B73 is tagged as evidence, listed as a photograph taken on Kodak Kodacolor VR-G, printed in 3.5-by-5-inch color format. The photograph depicts eleven subjects in the medium foreground, a picnic table, a series of trees that include ponderosa pine, white fur, quaking aspen, and western juniper. The background: snow-capped mountains, light-colored granite. Subjects are posing, most acknowledging the presence of the camera. Four known victims appear from left to right, labeled here: *MOORE, Karl; DONOVAN, Paul; ANDERSON, Deborah; STRAUSS, Mark.* Seven are unidentified.

"HOLD THE LIGHT," Michaels says as Carruthers lays the photo on a piece of white paper. She adjusts the flashlight to a wide, diffuse beam.

Michaels centers the image on his smartphone's viewfinder, holds it steady. The photo is scanned, eleven faces, most smiling, the average age under thirty.

"This has to be decades old," Carruthers says. "Moore has a full head of hair. Look at Deborah. She's got the whole punk rock scrunchy cut."

"Strauss has a Dire Straits concert shirt," Michaels adds. "We can estimate dates off that."

"So where's Newell?" Carruthers asks. "And who are the others?"

Michaels tilts his tablet so she can see. Tethered to the phone's connection, it displays the photograph, image analysis in progress. He taps a series of boxes around the faces. Then taps a list of databases to query. Facebook, Imgur, Parler, Twitter, Google, TikTok, a dozen more.

"Is that doing what I think it's doing?" Carruthers asks.

"Every hour people upload millions of photos. All those filters that age you up or fix your skin? Let social media do the work for us."

"And you've got access? I am never letting Jade use the Internet again."

"Doesn't matter. Some doorbell camera will get five hundred frames of her biking to school. Or a friend live-streaming to Snapchat. It's all out there now. You just have to know where to scrape."

The tablet flashes, confirming a series of matches. Not all, but three of the deceased. A fourth, a man slightly older, sits at the edge of the bench near the right side of the image. He is not all toothy smiles like the others, but he wears a deep confidence nonetheless. Michaels recognizes the look, the subtle poise that permeates the eyes and purses the lips of one who knows they are the smartest person around.

Carruthers squints as the name matches the face.

"Who the hell is Robert Chase?"

18

INNER SUNSET, SAN FRANCISCO
SUNDAY - 10:00 P.M.

CAITLYN'S LIGHT HAS BEEN OUT SINCE BRAD ARRIVED. SINCE HIS coffee, once hot, made its way through lukewarm to tepid and then cold. Should've brought some Red Bull.

Four hours now and the boredom has sunk its fingers into each second. No smartphone, which to his generation is like losing a limb. Occasionally, he feels phantom vibrations. What were stakeouts like before this? Just cigarettes and coffee and a pair of binoculars?

Now, the cigarettes would be a giveaway. Orange embers in a dark car. An occasional puff of smoke. Plus, this is San Francisco; combusting actual tobacco is a near felony.

Brad, in his dark clothes: gray jeans, a brown hoodie, a black cap that matches his hair and offers no tactical advantage besides helping him look the part. At his feet, three disposable thirty-two-ounce male urinal bottles.

There are games, mental exercises Brad practiced during the endless downtime between training in the Army. Brad studies objects outside the apartment. Imagines disassembling them, examining each piece, then putting it back together in reverse. He lists colors that start with the same letter. Carrot. Cardinal. Cobalt. Cerulean. Chartreuse.

He imagines himself, an agent of the Foundation, carrying out secret investigations, a modern shadow knight. Imagines Michaels, taking him to a facility deep in the Catskills, where they train with grappling hooks and a smoky-voiced woman teaches codebreaking to square-jawed recruits. In the dawn hours, instructors bang pans to rouse the agent-trainees for a surprise hike and—

A tapping on the window. Reverie shattered, Brad wipes his lip and finds himself staring at an eighty-five-year-old woman with a steaming thermos.

"She asked me to bring you something to drink," Mrs. Bakshi says. "Said you were tired. And something to eat, if you get hungry."

Brad's eyes bounce from the thermos to the Tupperware. Are those samosas and naan?

"Wow, thank you," he says, taking them, Tupperware first, then the hot thermos. The night air is crisp, redolent of the sea, and now spices, minced meats, and fried dough. "So, uh, is she... you know, is she watching me?"

Mrs. Bakshi glances up at the bay window across the street. Dark, wide, a monocle upon the timbered Queen Anne.

"It certainly makes one wonder," Mrs. Bakshi says. "Like we're kids again, and there's a bit of magic in this world. I've had a lot of tenants in my time. Even before she lost her sight, I could sense something different about Caitlyn. Don't let your dinner get cold."

And off she goes, hardly five feet tall and as strong as the tides. Mrs. Bakshi, below the amber lamps and the haze of fog, crossing the street and returning to the warmth.

"Oh, that's good," Brad says, sipping the hot chai, savoring the cardamom and clove as he watches a window where maybe, just maybe, a blind woman watches him back.

. . .

BRAD IS right about the bay window, but not about Caitlyn. For now, she sleeps and she watches, not him but herself. She watches the door as Mrs. Bakshi quietly closes it behind her. Watches her dark apartment for any shadow that crawls.

It's out there, Caitlyn thinks. That thing is out there and it's seen her face. Only a matter of time before it comes here, to this place, to the only home she's known on American soil. It is out there. And she's sitting here, just watching herself.

Just waiting to die.

"FBI, Other Agencies, Assisting in Probe of Diner Death"

By Pat Aaron and Cindy Chayefsky

RESIDENTS AND PATRONS OF THE SoMa NEIGHBORHOOD WHERE A local man died on Saturday night are still without answers as to what might have caused this gruesome death.

Late Saturday the San Francisco police received several calls that the unidentified man was in distress. Diners described an initial suspicion of choking or a possible seizure. When offered assistance, the victim reacted in a panic-stricken manner. It was only when the victim began to injure himself that the patrons intervened.

"Sometimes you don't know if it's a drug addict and he's violent or someone just having a medical condition," said Derek Harris, a witness. "It's a risk, you know? Because maybe they'll sue if you hurt them. But anyone could see this guy was in trouble."

Police have not disclosed the name of the victim, but we are told he is an attorney with decades of ties to the city.

"It's just awful," said Mei Ling, an art student who works the weekend counter. "He was very quiet and polite. Really an ideal customer."

Exactly what happened inside the Fog Breaker Cafe is still unclear. As of Monday evening, the diner remains sealed and under active investigation. Workers in hazmat suits have been seen outside. Beyond that, the police remain tight-lipped.

"Yes, we are being assisted by multiple federal and state agencies," Lin Kane, a spokeswoman for the SFPD, said. "At this time we are not prepared to give further comment."

A source who wished to remain anonymous described the Saturday night events as "bizarre and confusing" and that the victim contorted and spasmed before "bludgeoning himself to death on the floor." Residents and nearby business owners have expressed concern over the possibility of a post-COVID-19 contagion.

"It's not unheard of in cases of rabies and rabies-related lyssaviruses for a sufferer to wound themselves," said Dr. Misa Kahn, a virologist at UCSF. "It'd be wise to do thorough contract tracing."

The San Francisco FBI field office has not responded to a request for further details, other than to confirm their assistance in multiple, ongoing investigations. "The Bureau offers assistance as requested by local and state agencies on a variety of challenges," Kathleen Bell, the field office's media liaison, said.

The identity of the other agencies remains a point of mystery. Dale Brash, the owner of the Fog Breaker Cafe, declined to comment, citing a gag order.

"All deaths outside of natural causes are treated as suspicious per the medical examiner's protocol," the SFPD said. "Whether it's a homicide or a suicide or an accident, our best women and men are working to keep the community safe."

Some in the neighborhood are openly speculating. "I saw it from across the street," claimed a local source who was camped on a doorway. "That man had the devil in him. Ain't no way he done that himself."

For now, the restaurant plans to remain closed. The SFPD is requesting any information at (415) 575-4444.

(3) READER COMMENTS:

1. **Paperfan**: "Another day another sensless tragedy. My condolunces."

2. **Donald Pembridge**: "I made $73,000 last month by investing in cryptocurrency and you can too! Just visit www.43crypto-hacks.com for a free prospectus & starter kit."

3. **PatriotsOnly1776**: "Doesn't sound like a devil but the Breath of God cleaning out the wicked. So just what is the government & Lame Stream Media hiding, huh? I bet Sam Stephens has the real answers, only at The Straight Shot online."

19

LOVELACE BIOTRONIKA
TUESDAY - 10:00 A.M.

ROBERT J. CHASE, MD, PHD

  Role: Scientific Advisor, Neo-Neural Applications.

  Bio: Dr. Robert Chase brings over thirty years of clinical and research experience in public, private, and government labs to the Scientific Advisory Team at Lovelace Biotronika. Prior work includes over a decade of service as a coordinating director of the Defense and Veterans Brain Injury Center (DVBIC) as well as serving as a junior fellow and founding member of Alder Glen Analytics. He has published and lectured on a variety of topics related to traumatic brain injury (TBI), transhumanism, and the convergence of nanotechnology, biotechnology, information technology, and cognitive science (NBIC). He looks forward to helping Lovelace Biotronika reshape the face of medicine in the twenty-first century.

"WE'RE UP," Michaels says.

Carruthers closes out the doctor's CV and puts away her tablet. The lobby in front of her: a minimalist's dream. Blue slate and brushed steel and water trickling through the leafy plant wall. Everywhere: forty-five-degree angles and cool lines.

"All this venture capital and it doesn't buy taste," Carruthers says as they sign the touch screen at the guard desk. "Feels like an airport from hell."

"Your badges." The guard slides them lanyards with cards and yellow *VISITOR* labels. "Be advised there is no photography allowed. Any questions?"

Michaels has more than a few, but he's saving them for the meeting. Best not to bother the castle guards when you're crossing the moat.

"Follow the yellow line," the guard says and gestures to the right. "You're in the Mahalo room."

Sure enough, a rainbow of lights leaves the guard desk and flows along clear LED flooring, branching off in the center of the lobby into seven separate paths. They find the yellow trail, follow it to a frosted-glass door, where a TV reads, *MICHAELS & CARRUTHERS MAHALO ROOM. Please Press VISITOR Badge to Door.*

They swipe their badges. On the other side, the yellow line pulses down a long hall, a wall of glass to the left with a view of an open lab. Men and women running on treadmills, trudging on ellipticals, pedaling on bikes. Faces strain behind respirators. Skin glistens. Machines monitor each breath, count each bead of sweat. Technicians adjust sensors and offer the occasional towel.

To the right, frosted glass hints at human forms and conference tables. Squinting, Michaels can make out the pointillist shape of a man presenting to a roomful of suits. Straining, he can hear the polite applause.

The yellow line flashes, ushering them further on.

"Remind me again why we're visiting Chase here?" Michaels asks.

"We're playing to his profile," Carruthers says. "This is his habitat. He'll be at ease, maybe off guard. If he's evasive, we go in strong: badges and bad cop, press the offensive."

"All these labs remind me of college."

Carruthers smiles. "I'm having a hard time imagining you in

school. Did you sit in the front row and give the professor the creeps?"

"No. But one time I put on a blazer and taught class until the real professor showed up."

"Why would you do that?"

"Social experiment. To see if I could get away with it."

"So did you?"

"That professor got me an internship at the NSA."

The yellow line takes a hard right and ends at a frosted-glass door and the label *MAHALO ROOM*. A screen displays *HOST NOT PRESENT, PLEASE WAIT*.

"There he is," Carruthers says and points to the lab.

Through the glass, they watch a girl sitting upon an examination table, skin scarred down her left side, ear to knee. Below it, where her calves should dangle, are two stumps and a pair of hands attaching sensors. Dr. Robert Chase, a bear of a man, silver hair and soft blue eyes and lips that never rise past a horizontal line. Not when he connects the prosthetic and the scarred girl takes a few tenuous steps. Not when she giggles and turns, her young muscles fast to adapt to these mechanical legs. Not even when she says, "It feels like I don't have to think!"

"Yes, well, in a way, you don't," he says. "They have their own computer, just like your iPhone. They'll learn as you use them. Do you like the color?"

The girl runs a finger along the pink and blue detailing, where metal meets skin. "It's like D.Va in *Overwatch*."

"Yes, well, you said you liked her style. Yash here looked it up."

Yash, a young technician, smiles for the both of them. "These are your power legs now. We want you to be comfy. Bob, what firmware are these running?"

Chase's eyes rise, spotting Michaels and Carruthers. He gives them a nod. "Yash will finish up with you, dear. And be sure to ask him any questions you have, okay? Don't be shy."

He leaves the girl in the care of the technician, then stands, wobbling as he rises. With a snap, Chase extends a crutch, rests his elbow in the hinged arm cradle. He takes the other crutch, and with three practiced twists, he has it attached to his other arm. He crosses the lab fast for a man deep into his sixties.

But not as fast as the girl on her nimble new legs. No words, just two arms that wrap around Chase's waist, her smiling face pressed into his round stomach. And for a moment, he looks like he might almost smile. But he doesn't.

In the hall, Chase keys them into the Mahalo room. Inside, a jet-black table, eight Aeron chairs, and TVs at both ends. The window commands a view of the untamed peninsula, hills and hollows dotted with oak and eucalyptus and grass, emerald and dewy.

"That girl seems pretty thrilled with her new legs, Dr. Chase," Carruthers says.

"Yes, well, Rumiana had a rough life. When her father fell asleep drunk at the wheel, she barely escaped the wreck. He wasn't so lucky. New legs are little consolation for her trauma."

"Well, one step at a time," Carruthers says.

"So what's the catch?" Michaels asks. "She gets new legs, Biotronika gets the data they record? Health data too. That's the holy grail, isn't it?"

Chase lays his hands flat on the black table, studying his guests. "So how can I help the FBI?"

Carruthers coughs into her hand, glances at Michaels. There goes the plan.

"What makes you think we're FBI?" Michaels asks.

Chase studies Michaels. Waits. Then he turns his stare to Carruthers. "I have colleagues. Perks of a lifetime of service. Naturally, when you insisted on a sudden appointment, I made inquiries. Special Agent Carruthers, you're well-spoken of."

"Ah," she says, "so that was the breeze up my skirt."

Chase's stare returns to Michaels. "I'm afraid your name didn't come up at all. Which begs the question: what should I call you? Special agent? Officer?"

"Just Michaels."

"Just Michaels," Chase repeats. "From some shadowy branch that doesn't leave a print. I presume it was your plan, then, to bring out the badges if things got a bit testy?"

Michaels forces his pride back, focuses on showing nothing. *Ignore the twitch. Embrace the chaos.* "That was one angle of approach."

"Then seeing as you're not presenting me with your badges, and I am not calling my attorney, I hope this meeting can proceed in good faith."

"Yes, Doctor, that's our hope," Carruthers says, apologetic in tone. Michaels is thankful for that small mercy. He's not sure he can conjure up genuine emotion on demand.

"Sit, please." Chase motions to the chairs.

Michaels unbuttons his jacket and smooths out his pleats. A little ritual that buys him time to refocus. Chase clocked them easily. Which means he's more than a board room stiff doing the old boys club shuffle from one job to the next. Perhaps ex-military, or looped in at one time. The kind of shine that doesn't rub off. That it hadn't come up in any searches raises red flags.

"Let's get down to brass tacks," Carruthers says and places a picture on the table. A copy of the photograph from Newell's file. An estimated date between 1988 and 1991. Eleven young faces, Robert Chase at the edge. "Do you recognize this photo?"

"Of course I do," Chase says. "What an extraordinary group of minds. We were under orders not to take any photos. Clearly, not all rules were followed."

He places the photo back on the table with a reverent tenderness.

"Why don't you tell us about Clearwater," Michaels says and turns the photo over.

"Clearwater?"

"Clearwater," Michaels repeats. "That's a docket number scribbled on the back. We found a reference to it in the federal courts, a civil suit. You're named a defendant. So is Clearwater. But the case text is curiously absent."

"Not so curious, I'm afraid," Chase says. "However, seeing as this meeting is not about my employer's business, I have nothing more to add." Chase stands up and reaches for his crutches. "Good afternoon."

Carruthers stands up at the head of the table, blocking the way. Chase is a big man, but she's a sturdy woman. How far could he get without those metal poles? Hesitation, then: "Dr. Chase, let's try a reset," she says cheerfully. "My colleague has some additional photos we'd like you to consider."

She doesn't say which photos, but Michaels is already swiping his tablet, scrolling fast. "Three days ago," he says.

When he turns the screen to Chase, the man isn't quite sure what he's seeing. Pixels of pink and red, rivulets of crimson and shattered gray. Human minds are wired to seek patterns—and faces—but it's difficult to identify a face when it's been crushed into the floor.

"Good God," Chase sputters.

"Nothing? How about now?" Michaels swipes to a picture of the same man, Newell Sacks, smiling from his social media profile.

"Ten days ago." Swipe. Professor Moore, lying on the slab, one eye open, the other a concave of bone. "Oh, and here's a refresher."

Swipe. Professor Moore, smiling from his faculty bio beneath the title *Distinguished Educator Award*.

"A week before that."

Swipe. Deborah Anderson, her mandible a raw hollow. Swipe. Her laughing face as she poses with her family for a Christmas card.

"Stop, please—"

"What is Clearwater?" Carruthers asks.

Swipe. Mark Strauss. Head wrenched so far back his throat has burst open. Then the company's executive team, a photo all confident smiles and pearly whites and endless potential.

"Enough!" Hands trembling, Chase removes his glasses.

Swipe. Paul Donovan. Swipe. Prieta Stenvall. Michaels takes the copy of the old photo, grabs a board marker, and draws an X through five of the faces. Six left, including the man across from him now.

"Here's what I think," Michaels says. "That smug mug you're wearing in this photo? You didn't quite belong to this group. You weren't their peer. You were, what, twenty-nine, thirty?"

"Thirty-two," Chase whispers.

"Those are post-doc years, Dr. Chase. You've accomplished a lot. But when I look at your CV, I can't find anything prior to '92. Same with everyone else in this photo."

"It's like you all took gap years," Carruthers says. "Right around the time a federal case goes to court."

"Which tells me," Michaels continues, "that you all got wrapped up in it. They did something to you, Dr. Chase. Something you can't talk about. Someone you can't name."

"You've got this all wrong—"

"Do I? 'Cause the pattern I see continues like this…"

Michaels marks an X through another face. Then another X. And at last a fat, black line right through the young face of Robert Chase.

"Now I don't know if you're next or last, but I can promise you this: if you withhold any useful information, that's obstruction of justice."

Chase lowers his head, whispers, "Were there fingerprints found?"

"There were not," Carruthers says.

"But were there finger-like prints? Burned tissue? Subcutaneous, perhaps, or internal—"

"Multiple organs showed severe bruising," Michaels says.

"Beta burns from hot particles," Chase says. "Instruct your pathologists to wear lead aprons."

"Dr. Chase, help us help you," Carruthers says. "We need to know what they did to you."

"I told you," Chase says. "You've got it wrong. They didn't do this to us. If this came from Clearwater, we made this."

It sits in the corner of corporate storage, beyond a chain-link fence Chase unlocks with an old key. They squeeze past shadowed chairs and dusty TVs. Michaels watches Chase navigate the basement by memory, crutches touching boxes. It reminds him of Caitlyn, how she moved through her apartment.

"Project Clearwater," Chase says in a reverent whisper. "We were a paper company. You've heard that term?"

"Off the networks, off the grids," Michaels says. "I'm familiar with it."

The expression is dated, a relic from the days of Eisenhower to Reagan. When Afghan rebels needed Stinger missiles to take down Soviet planes, paper companies helped make it possible. The mandate was simple: maximum effectiveness with zero records. They didn't exist, except in a few paper ledgers.

"Then you know the protocol," Chase says, "the burndown that comes at the end. Clearwater was my creation. The first fifteen years of my adult life, from a soldier to a doctoral researcher, were focused on it without distraction. And then it was taken from me. The moment you showed me that photo, all the years and all I've accomplished fell away. I've done what they wanted, kept quiet. For thirty years I knew this ax would fall. I just didn't know when. Or who would swing it."

Chase activates his phone's flashlight, illuminates a rolling multimedia cabinet and opens the door. There is a knob, and another door, thicker still. A safe, sitting here in the basement of the company Chase helped build.

"I must warn you," he says, "if you're here to put a bullet in my head, this is not the only copy. Instructions exist, a fail-safe. Certain publications will receive a copy in the event of my death."

"Yeah, plugging our only solid lead," Carruthers says. "We'd have to be the world's worst assassins."

"Death doesn't frighten me," Chase says, turning the dial. "Not at this age. No, what keeps me awake is how close we came to changing the world. The work we do here at Biotronika has been my fallback."

"Hell of a second act," Michaels says.

"Yes, well, the heart yearns for a third." A stop of the dial, a turn of the lever. The safe moans. Four feet of darkness and dusty metal and the only thing that sits on the shelf is a single Betamax cassette.

"Michaels," Chase says, pointing with a crutch. "Do us a favor and drag that old thing over."

The old thing is the TV cart in the corner. Michaels wheels it over. Carruthers finds a dusty power strip and connects cables. RCA to a coaxial convertor. She tunes the dial to channel 3. The tape goes in with a click and a whir.

First comes the darkness, then the static. Michaels adjusts the tracking. There is sound, but no image yet.

"In the fifties, the CIA began a test program known as MK Ultra," Chase says. "No doubt you've heard of it."

"Government dosing citizens with LSD," Michaels says. "It's conspiracy theory canon."

"As it should be," Chase says. "Conspiracies, though often absurd, occasionally reflect a deeper truth, like light passing through water gives hint of some scaly form. I was born during MK Ultra's beginnings. I remember America's fear. The Russians achieved thermonuclear advantage. The Chinese pushed us to a truce in Korea. Sputnik was circling the globe. One of the goals of MK Ultra was to fortify the last castle we had: the American mind. Guard it from outside influence, or seize the keys when needed."

"Yeah, except it didn't work out," Michaels says. "I've read the findings. Even the files the CIA claims were destroyed. All MK Ultra proved is that if you give someone enough LSD and abuse, their synapses rewire. The mind and reality file for divorce."

"Indeed, you are correct," Chase says. "At its best, MK Ultra gave us Ken Kesey and the flower children. At its worst, it gave us the Unabomber. But it also gave us data. Eighty-three institutions, from prisons to universities, all taught us what failed. I spent my graduate years parsing that data. Edison said it took ten thousand tries to build the lightbulb. For us, it took only twelve."

Michaels smirks. Most people who compare themselves to Edison are a pale shade of light.

Then the video begins and he thinks, *How very wrong*.

[20]
REDACTED

"AND WE'RE RECORDING," HE SAID AND GAVE THE PROJECT LEADER A thumbs-up. "Bob, say something for the camera."

"Something for the camera," Robert Chase said and returned a curt nod.

Dr. Ibrihim panned the shoulder camera around the lab. "You know, when Oppenheimer saw the bomb, he quoted the Bhagavad Gita. Any words of wisdom?"

Chase tapped his cane. "How about, 'Let's make distance a thing of the past'?"

Not the young doctor's finest words, but good enough. Especially with a two-star major general standing beside him. Robert Chase, age thirty-three, which is also how many millions of dollars this moment has cost.

"Dr. Locke, please bring out the subject."

The major general moved to the window and peered down into the test chamber. Forty feet of terraced concrete, enough tape drives to store a whole gigabyte of data.

"So those are the deprivation units?" the major general asked as Dr. Beane and his technicians tightened the final valves. "They don't look like much."

"Pods, sir," Chase said. "They heat the air and water to match the subject's core temp. It requires precise calculations."

A grunt from the major general. "What's with the salt water?"

"For buoyancy, sir," Dr. Chow said from the station right of the observation window. "The brain requires the absence of stimulation to induce decoherence. Floating helps."

"Isn't that what the damn drugs are for? I've had to lock horns with the DEA."

"William McNare is our chemist," Chase said. "He'll fill you in."

McNare swiveled his chair to face a chest of medals and stripes. McNare, the only one in the lab without a lab coat. Without a PhD or an MD. McNare did, however, have a criminal record, one that he cops to with pride. He was a graduate student when the DEA raided his chemistry lab. After that, the nation's MDMA supply dropped by sixty percent.

"Well, Mr. General Man," McNare said in a slow drawl like nails on a chalkboard to the major general. "It's like the ad goes: this is your brain..." He tapped the computer keyboard, bringing up a green pixel map of folds and ridges. "And this is your brain on the Dee Zee train." Another tap. The green pixel brain, pockmarked now, dark spots scattered about. Like snowflakes or shadows. "And this is your brain decoherent." A third tap, and the green image showed a brain almost identical to the first.

The major general grumbled, "Someone translate what Shaggy just said."

Swiveling and grinning, McNare pulled a leg up onto his chair.

"What Willy means," Dr. Moore said, giving the unkempt chemist a nudge, "is that DZ3 jumpstarts a mental refraction that allows consciousness to separate from the physical self. Like laying train tracks. Once the mind is primed, it redistributes its mass to facilitate *mens corpus*—the mental body—so to speak."

"I thought DZ3 was just ketamine and acid. Hippy shit."

"Yeah, and a diamond is just carbon, Señor," McNare said, "but try putting coal on your wife's finger. See what that gets ya."

At his computer, Dr. Linamore covered a smirk. The major general nodded, but his eyes said otherwise. "So you've spent Pentagon money to fry twelve brains. I could have done that for the cost of some moonshine."

"That's some gnarly mash liquor," McNare said.

The major general eyed him with contempt, turned to Chase. "This could be staged in a warehouse."

"And the measurements would be meaningless," Chase said. "We're competing against radio waves and cosmic rays to isolate the exact moment the body and consciousness split. This facility serves as an amplifier. Without it, we'd be searching for a spark in a sandstorm."

"The subject is ready," Dr. Locke said.

Camera still on his shoulder, Dr. Ibrihim followed the major general back to the observation window. Below, Dr. Beane and his technicians had pushed carts beside each pod. Respirators, blacked-out gas masks, bundles of adhesive electrodes.

And a young man with red hair, dressed only in scrubs.

Button by button, they removed the scrubs until he stood naked, lit by the bright lights above. Then came the electrodes, and he flinched as the tape stuck to skin. Chest, arms, legs, the base of his spine. Next, the lubricant and the latex suit, a sucking pop as he slipped in, feet first, pulling it up until the zipper climbed his back and fastened to the clasp at the nape of his neck. Last was the mask, placed on his head with ceremonial reverence, sealing him off. A hose connected to an oxygen tank.

Through the prep, the major general hardly blinked, yet his hand bunched up against his slacks into a tight fist. This was all too weird for him.

"So that one of your psychic spies in training?" the major general almost spat.

"Dr. Strauss prefers the term 'decoherent,'" Chase said. Another grunt from the major general. Chase waited for more questions, but none came. He knew better than to keep talking to a man looking for any reason to shut this all down.

Tenderly, Dr. Beane led the young man to the open pod. Inside, glistening dark waters. They helped the subject step in, feet first, now floating. Then they closed the pod.

Chase had to admit, it was a remarkable design. So elegantly crafted the seams faded like the lines of an Italian sports car. A hiss filled the room, mic feedback, then...

"Teddy, can you hear me?" The voice of Dr. Tannen, from her station beside the observation window. Her desk could barely contain a rack of Sony TVs, video feeds running and peppered with static. Wide shots of the chamber, close-ups of the pods. An infrared feed from inside.

"Hi there, Sian," Teddy said, voice warbling over the intercom. "How ya doing today?"

"We're doing well, Teddy. Thanks for asking. Yourself?"

"Not too shabby, thanks. But I've been having those dreams again."

The major general turned to Chase, asked, "What dreams?"

"As the brain redistributes, we've noticed an increase in lucid dreaming," Dr. Tannen said, switching the mic off. "Karl here has a theory that it's the brain's autobiographical self redefining its perimeter."

"Yes, a mental dysmorphic disorder," Dr. Karl Moore said. "Like your reflection after you shave, or a picture after a big diet. Our mens corpus struggles to cohere with our real image."

"So what?" the major general said. "My wife sometimes dreams she's Doris Day."

"With respect, sir," Dr. Moore said. "Your wife doesn't step out of her body. It can be problematic to find yourself if your sense of self is no longer defined by your self."

The major general clenched his jaw. "So far I've heard a lot of wobbly words that cost millions." He eyed Chase. "Robert, you're nearing the end of the runway."

Chase squeezed his walking cane. It took every ounce of

willpower not to call the major general what he was: just another myopic meat shield with no vision beyond his nose. Chase knew the military. It bred camaraderie, yes, but also complacency. Outside rare acts of battlefield bravery, it's an institution that punished the bold, the independent, the thinkers. He'd have to rub the major general's nose in the future just to show him it's there.

"Dr. Tannen, would you give Teddy his countdown? Let's show our guest how high our subjects can fly."

THE FIRST SIGN he noticed was when the countdown hit twenty. A flicker in the test chamber below. The major general's eyes left the pod, shooting up to the klieg light dimming along the catwalk.

At fifteen seconds, there was a flash of static upon the video feed from inside the tank. Teddy's masked face, all darkness and glistening plastic, vanished behind blooming noise.

At eight seconds, the printers began buzzing, needles tracing mountains and valleys.

At three seconds, there was a smell, like the pavement after a thunderstorm. The major general sniffled. Then it was promptly wiped from his mind.

The concussive wave hit him in his gut, in his bones, in his bladder. A low, subsonic rumble that signaled a displacement of air. Instinctively, he went for cover. Stopped when no one else moved.

"And we've got decoherence," Dr. Tannen said. Then, into the mic, "Teddy, how are you doing now?"

"Just swell, Sian—"

"Christ." The word burst from the major general, who turned, spun, searching over his shoulders. "That was right beside me."

"Technically, it was above you, my man," McNare said. "As in, the higher dimension."

"It's a quantum echo," Dr. Moore added. "That's why it sounds like it's all around you."

"Can he hear us now?" the major general asked. "Can he listen in?"

"If he projected himself in here, yes," Dr. Locke said. "But for now he's getting audio in the pod. The mens corpus has trouble passing through glass, water, really anything that refracts."

"I want to see the subject in action."

"Look at the test chamber," Chase said. "There."

"Where?"

"Teddy, I would like you to move to your first target," Dr. Tannen said. "Audio description incoming shortly." She switched the audio feed to the floor of the test chamber. "Dr. Beane, set up primary calibration."

A flurry of activity on the concrete floor forty feet below. The squeaking of a medical cart holding several objects: a marble, a baseball, a basketball. Hands unrolled a white mat, upon which was stenciled $7z41o+$.

"Teddy, your blind site for today is as follows. Seven, zeta, four, one, omicron, plus." Dr. Tannen repeated it, the machines clicking and whirring, needles scribbling ever higher mountains, ever-deepening valleys. Then a low pulse. And something else...

"Is that..." The major general squinted, leaned toward the window.

"Turn your noggin, boss," McNare said.

"What?"

"Your head." He tapped his temple and raised his index finger, slowly turning until he was looking sidelong at his finger.

The major general gave it a dismissive try. A religious man, he had now taken his lord's name in vain for a second time that afternoon. There would be others.

"Told ya," McNare said with a grin.

"That's... There's something down there. A shimmer. That can't be."

"Our subjects have been able to form basic mens corpora for six weeks," Dr. Locke said proudly. "And their progression has been exponential, to say the least."

The major general looked down at the chamber, straight on. Nothing. Then, turning his head, sidelong. There it was, a shimmer, and...

Were those legs?

"Dr. Locke," Chase said. "Let's show the major general some kinetic demonstrations."

The show hadn't even begun and the guest was eating out of their hands.

HE NODDED when the marble lifted off the metal cart. He almost smiled when the baseball hovered in midair. When the basketball rose and slowly started spinning, that was when a grin split the major general's stony face.

"Good job, Teddy," Dr. Tannen said into the mic. "Go ahead and take a breather."

The major general furrowed his brow. "He's out of breath?"

"It's a figure of speech, sir," Dr. Tannen said. "A mens corpus doesn't require oxygen."

"What are the IVs for? More of that DZ3 crap?"

"Nutrition," Dr. Locke said. "The subjects burn thousands of calories an hour. More, the heavier they lift, the farther they travel."

"How far have they gone?"

"That we've confirmed double blind?" Dr. Locke asked. "Just outside Syracuse."

"New York. Hmm."

"Sorry, sir. Syracuse, Italy."

The major general scoffed, turned to Chase, who gave him a nod. It's true.

"Tell me, Robert. Can you move something living?"

THE PARAKEET SQUAWKED as the cage was placed on the metal cart. Blue and white plumage, wings fluttering and flapping and banging against the wires. The technician stepped back, hurried from the test chamber.

In the observation room, Dr. Linamore turned to Chase, said, "Bob, I'm not comfortable with this."

"Noted, Francis. Thank you."

Dr. Linamore's lips tightened, and his nostrils flared. He returned to his station.

Clearing her throat, Dr. Tannen clicked on the microphone . "Uh, Teddy, we'd like to try something different. Kind of a new activity for us, okay? There's a bird in a cage. We've—"

"You want me to hurt it?" asked the voice from everywhere. An echo, hollow and cold. "Is that it?"

"Yes, Teddy, you need to show us you can do this. There's no shame. If you grip it by the neck, it will be quick. This'll be the final activity for the day."

"Then I can leave?"

A grim look passed between Dr. Tannen and Chase. A small nod from the project leader.

"Uh, I'm sure any day now," Dr. Tannen said and glared at Chase.

"Focus on the task, Theodore," Chase said, leaning into the mic. "Remember your training. Relax. And know that when history speaks your name it will be among those great pioneers who crossed continents, those brave souls who touched the stars."

Silence in the observation room. Silence in the test chamber. Then a spike in the printouts. Needles scribbling, rising. The major general leaned against the window.

A click from below. The creak of metal. The cage door fell open and the parakeet hopped through and took flight in a smooth bloom of feathers. Blue and white wings spread and flapped and fluttered as the free bird soared and circled the wide-open chamber, higher and higher.

"Then I can leave?" the parakeet mocked. "Then I can leave?"

The parakeet tilted and banked, gliding close, closer, coming alongside the window and the major general and the observers, full of elegance and mastery of the winds.

"Then I can—"

A burst of blue feathers. A wisp of red mist. The dead bird thumped, hitting the catwalk, rolling off, and falling down, down, to the cold concrete below.

[21]
SAN FRANCISCO
TUESDAY - 5:30 P.M.

EYES ITCHY WITH PIXELS AND STATIC, MIND HUMMING WITH THE PAST, Michaels switches off the video, the fourth time he's watched it. Carruthers parks at the edge of Chinatown, turns on the hazards. For a moment, they soak in the city.

"I feel like reality just got thrown in the blender," Carruthers says. "Mind telling me what we're doing here?"

"We all work for somebody," he says and opens the door. "Go home, Denise. Get some rest."

For two blocks Michaels walks, absorbing the evening. The banter of Mandarin and Cantonese, the clatter and clank of restaurants packed with tourists and locals. He takes his time, trying to turn chaotic thoughts into precise words.

Downwind of the Golden Gate Cookie Factory, the Red Lotus Hotel caters to frugal business travelers from the Far East. The building is bland, five floors of dusty windows rimmed in chipped gold. More smoking rooms than nonsmoking.

NO VACANCY, reads the counter sign. To Michaels, this doesn't apply. Room 320 is held in perpetuity for employees of Northwestern Gravel & Tract, LLC. Different names have checked in over the years. Tonight, he is Tom Spalding, who is visiting his daughter in Alder Glen.

Not that the attendants care. Here is a high school student studying AP biology, his notecards a mix of Mandarin and Latin. Michaels hands him Spalding's ID, and the kid returns a room key, then returns to his homework.

Three floors later, and Michaels inserts the old key. There is a second lock, one embedded in the door's peephole, a biometric sensor no different than those on most smartphones. It scans his face, matches it with a database of Foundation agents, and tells the knob to unlock. Sometimes it takes a few tries.

A simple room, this corner suite with blackout curtains, mesh wiring covering the window, the musty bed. A TV sits in the corner with a camera atop it.

Often, people assume the government has access to technology twenty years ahead. Quantum computers, nano tech, devices that can read minds. The truth is more subtle. Sure, the Foundation redirects some pre-release shipments from major manufacturers, but they have a contract. The rest of the tech can be found on Amazon. This TV is ten years outdated. The camera houses old optics. Even the closed-circuit network and encrypted connections are slower than the Wi-Fi at Starbucks.

But this sanctorum is robust and reliable. Most of all, it is secure. This room is one big Faraday cage, the walls lined with aluminum and steel, EMI and RFI shielding. There isn't a place in the city that kills more cell phone signals. Michaels pities those who check in one floor below.

He turns on the TV. *CHANNEL 99 - No Signal.* He checks his pocket watch. Two minutes to six.

There are four bottles of water in the mini fridge. He takes one and paces. The room comes with a desk, and there upon it sits an ashtray with a pack of toothpicks and a note: *Nice work in Tampa.*

The best way to keep its agents in line is to keep them on their toes. This the Foundation knows. There is no conspiracy of lizard people, no sentient crystals running the UN. There are field agents like Michaels, sometimes tasked with investigating each other. The North Korean regime keeps order with social self-policing.

The Russians use *sistema*. This gift of flavored wood's meaning is clear: *We're watching*.

"Assholes," Michaels mutters, dumps the toothpicks in the bin. He lets his left hand tap simple primes to the count of ten. Sips his water. Waits.

At two past six, the TV flickers. The connection still reads: *CHANNEL 99 - No Signal*, but as the sign at retailers says, this is for display purposes only. The wide-angle lens is always on.

"You've lost some weight," says a voice before the video syncs up.

The man on the other end of the connection takes up half the screen. Coordinator Nox is tall, thin, his face a flat mask. He looks like he might just read off the weather. His eyes say otherwise. Latent darkness swims within those green eyes, the hint of grim tasks done in veiled service. Since joining the Foundation eight years ago, Michaels has met Nox in person three times. He can remember every detail, down to the color of the man's tie.

Most concerning of all, there simply are no rumors. Every one of Michaels's superiors at the NSA had an institutional reputation. Nox simply appeared with the Foundation, like a shark in the sea, quiet and comfortable in his own powerful currents.

"You still on that diet?" Nox asks. "The starvation one."

"Fasting," Michaels says. "And yes, week twenty-one."

He doesn't like calling it a diet, but he supposes that's what it looks like from afar. It's a lifestyle; it brings needed clarity to his thoughts, keeps his blood sugar from becoming a bad roller coaster.

"Well, good for you. Michaels the machine." Nox clicks his tongue. "Not big on the small talk tonight?"

"We both know I'm not good at it, sir."

"No, no you are not." Nox leans in, face filling half the screen. Michaels shifts as the coordinator's green eyes peer through a thousand miles of fiber-optic lines. But Nox's attention is elsewhere. A keyboard clicks and the left half of the screen fills with images and text. Michaels knows every word and line.

"How much of my report have you read?"

"Enough to be piqued," Nox says and zooms in on an image. Carruthers, an agency photo, perhaps five years ago. "These friends you're making, their involvement seems broad, given the mandate of your task."

"Which is to investigate the cause of death in five anomalies and counting."

"Investigate, contain, control," Nox says. "That fiasco at the diner made the news."

"With respect, sir, we can't control what we don't understand. This task force is held together with goodwill. Best to keep things friendly. Otherwise, they clam up on us, lock us out—"

"They can try," Nox says. "But your point is taken. Tell me about Denise Carruthers."

"She's solid," Michaels says, glad this isn't a lie. The Foundation is known to use audio-visual polygraphic analysis. He wouldn't be surprised if Nox is running it now. "We'd be a lot further behind without her."

"Same with this greenhorn, Brad Lee?"

"He's eager, means well. I gave him the speech. He signed the forms so he knows what's at stake."

"Good. Some idiots online are calling it the God's Breath Killer."

"That's not from our end, sir. Everything's airtight."

"Our intel agrees. Now keep it that way. We both know a full clean isn't pretty."

"It won't come to that, sir," Michaels says.

A nod, but the coordinator holds his stare. Perhaps the software is picking up doubt in Michaels's voice. An honest fear. He's seen what happens when the cleaning crews get called. Jobs are lost, and houses are sold. Bank accounts closed and identities changed. A dozen gag orders without expiration.

At best, it means lifetime surveillance for all involved. Every email and phone call, every Instagram pic and Snapchat, all interactions algorithmically catalogued and scrutinized.

At worst, a permanent vacation. A news story about a gambling debt, child pornography found on a work computer. A suicide note in a jail cell, a one-way ticket to Thailand, misdirections hiding extractions to places scrubbed from Google Maps. Islands marked as bird sanctuaries, surrounded by a thousand miles of nautical nothing.

"Well done," Nox says, nearing the end of the report. "I'm confident you'll keep things under control." He swipes the screen from his end. The picture shifts, images of Caitlyn. A passport photo, her California ID, and bank records now. She's worth more than Michaels had assumed. Much more.

"This woman, Caitlyn," Nox says, "you think she's connected?"

"She believes she witnessed something, yes."

"Witnessed? A curious term, considering her condition."

"It's challenging to wrap my mind around it," Michaels says. "But it maps with what I've learned this afternoon."

Nox pauses, stares directly into the lens. "This report was filed last night. What's changed?"

Michaels takes a sip of water. Not because he is thirsty but because he desperately needs a moment to parse his thoughts, to wrangle these wayward ideas, sort them into a believable order, and to tell the impossible to the most dangerous man he knows.

"Sir, have you heard of Project Clearwater?"

AND THAT'S THE THING, FOLKS. THAT'S THE THING ABOUT THE
liberal mainstream media. They will not tell you the truth, the
uncomfortable truth, for fear it may trigger you or shatter your
safe space. But you listen to me because you want the truth, the
whole truth and nothing... See, I have a commitment to freedom,
and freedom discomforts you, let me tell ya.

But first, I have some breaking news. You heard it first here,
folks. This one in from our Patriot Chat forum, a hot tip that the
FBI are investigating a series of killings—brutal attacks, from
what our source tells us—spanning several states, and I have
exclusive word that it has been dubbed the God's Breath Killer—
yes, you heard that—the God's Breath Killer, because, and again
this is an exclusive here at *The Straight Shot*, word out of San Francisco—you know, our favorite failed socialist sanctuary state—
and folks, from what I'm told, witnesses were helpless to stop a
vicious attack that fits the pattern of four killings in as many
weeks. Four American lives taken—stolen!—that's right.

And if I'm being honest here, it makes me wonder what our
government is doing to protect its citizens. Or if it isn't—as I've
said right here on the show—if it isn't perhaps complicit? Lot of
skeletons in the deep state's closet after all, but hey, people want

to cancel this show 'cause I use a few naughty words, 'cause I ain't woke. Well, that should tell you something, friends. More details coming soon in these strange and troubling times.

And speaking of safety, I want to tell you, dear listeners, about a special offer from our new sponsor: Castle Doctrine Safety Shelters. Yes, that's right—

22

FBI FIELD OFFICE, SAN FRANCISCO
THURSDAY - 8:00 A.M.

HE HAD TRAINED AS A FIELD AGENT—NOT A COORDINATOR—TO avoid leading a team. Yet here he is, walking into the conference room, trying to ignore his rumbling stomach. He tries to ignore the murmurs of the special agents, the squeak of the cable as he connects his tablet to the lectern. Sixteen pairs of eyes upon him. Stony faces wondering why he has summoned them here.

Michaels takes a deep breath. Notices a female agent in the back. She's tapping away on her smartphone. He spots someone checking the stock market. Feels the carpet beneath him, a solid anchor.

"Good morning," he says. "Some of you took red-eyes to get here. You have my thanks. Before we start, Special Agent Carruthers will collect all electronic devices."

Confusion crosses her face, fast erased. She tells the room, "Power 'em down. You heard him."

Grumbling around the conference table, then clattering. The agents place their phones on the table, facedown. A few power them off.

Michaels continues. "Surrendering your devices constitutes a fully enforceable acceptance of the forthcoming joint task force assignment, classified beyond top secret. Any disclosures henceforth are a violation of US code 18, section 798. Folks, there is a door behind you. Consider it now."

He waits for Carruthers to collect the devices, placing them in a container and zip-tying the lock. He sips his water and counts down from ten. No one goes for the door.

"I'm Field Agent Michaels. As of this morning, all of your active cases have been reassigned. This comes from the deputy director herself. Your SACs and ASACs are aware of the uniqueness of this assignment. As the investigator in charge, I am your direct and only supervisor."

A low hiss, a dozen pairs of lungs sucking in air. Michaels scans the eyes. An older agent, Maddox from the San Diego office, seems to be squinting. Anand, an auburn-haired agent near the window, is sizing him up. Michaels forces himself to make eye contact with every set at the table. His palms are moist by the time he's done.

The chair squeaks as Anand leans against the table. "Why are we really here, sir?"

"To meet someone," Michaels says and presses the tablet. "This is the late Newell Sacks." Sixteen feet of screen turns crimson and gray. A video, close up. Like bubblegum coming off a shoe, Newell's face clings to the cratered floor. Gloved hands do their best to separate tiling and tissue.

An agent stifles a gulp. Another wrinkles her nose. Hard stomachs all around, some turning sour.

"Four nights ago Mr. Sacks was murdered at a diner in clear view of a dozen hungry customers," Michaels says. "His skull was crushed with the force of a jackhammer. Yet no one was able to identify the assailant."

A click. Another clip. The security footage of the diner door shattering inward. Hints of carnage at the scene's edge. Befuddled agents lean forward. One removes her glasses. A low murmur passes through the group.

"Eleven days prior, this man, Professor Karl Moore, was assaulted in his office."

Familiar pictures now: a shattered door; indentations on the floor; and the body, Professor Moore, splayed across the office, a sculpture of pain.

"The victim shows defensive wounds typical in strangulation. His hyoid bone was fractured." Michaels traces a line across his Adam's apple. "Laryngoscopy reveals lacerations to the pharynx, spinal fracture. The base of his skull was shattered, suggesting an assailant of tremendous strength. Atypical, however, was everything inside. His liver was ruptured, his heart crushed. Organ tissue showed concentrated radiation burns in the shape of fingers, roughly eight inches in length. A janitor witnessed the assault. And the only description we got was this: 'chipoko, dhiaborosi, dhimoni.'"

"Dhimoni," says a freckled woman in the first row. Freya, Michaels thinks. No, Faye. "That's like a voodoo spirit, isn't it?"

"Demon," Carruthers says and begins passing out a tablet to each agent. They power on the devices and study the files. Michaels cycles through the photos, faster now. Just the highlights.

"Nineteen days ago Deborah Anderson was found in the shower of a Tampa YMCA. Similar wounds, similar MO. Here's Mark Strauss, twenty-six days ago in Burlington, Vermont, and so on, leading us back to last year, where one William McNare, aka Kermit the Hermit, a self-taught chemist, was found dead at his ranch lab outside Bozeman, Montana. In the eighties McNare got caught synthesizing top shelf molly and talked his way into lifetime immunity. Recently, the Esalen Institute sourced LSD from him for Psychedelic Integration Week. When McNare didn't show with the doses, they sent somebody to check. He was decomposed, mostly. What the flies left showed incisions to the bone, torture. Forensic anthropologists estimate his TOD around Thanksgiving."

"So, what, our unsub is a demon?" a blond agent asks. Kruger, Michaels thinks. He shaved his beard since his last agency photo. "Are we being issued holy water?"

Awkward sniggering. Michaels tries to read the room. Is this nervous humor? A challenge to his authority? Social cues vex him, and standing here reminds him why he prefers to fly solo.

"Holy water won't help us," he says. "But neither will bullets. These crimes were committed by a human, but the hands were something else."

He taps the tablet, cues up the video. Hesitates.

"This is what we're up against."

Then he presses play.

"THAT'S NOT FUCKING POSSIBLE," Kruger stammers. For a Mormon, he swears like a sailor. "God in heaven, that can't be fucking true."

It's in all their eyes now, rational thought and doubt fighting it out, evaluating each frame. That's why he plays the video back twice.

In the end, it's Faye who maintains poise. "So let me get this straight. While the government was funding a war on drugs, the military was frying minds to create... what? Psychic assassins?"

"Telekinetic," Carruthers says. "Technically, that's what they are."

"Yeah, but that's not possible," Kruger says. "Is it?"

"Eighteen hours ago I said the same thing," Michaels says and spots the shadow entering from the back of the room. "But it is true."

"The Manhattan Project gave us the bomb," says a syrupy voice. "Project Clearwater was my contribution, I'm afraid." Dr. Chase circles the table, crutches on the thin carpet. *Fump, fump, fump.* "Recently, scientists attained a rudimentary form of quantum communication. Two photons, entangled, like genetic twins. One here on earth, another five hundred kilometers above, on a satellite. Any changes to the earth-based photon result in instantaneous change to the entangled mate, up there."

Chase snaps his fingers. "They've learned what we accidentally discovered: distance is irrelevant. Project Clearwater was to be our masterpiece, a chance to free the mind from the failings of the body. But we lost control. So we buried it, denied it, and for thirty years now, we've been living on borrowed time."

"Half of Dr. Chase's original team is dead," Michaels says. "That's the connection. They're being hunted and killed. One by one by one."

"Okay, so if that's the case," Faye says, "what's the MO for the lawyer?"

"Newell Sacks brought about a class-action lawsuit on behalf of the test subjects," Carruthers says. "Or that's what they thought, right, Dr. Chase?"

"It would be fair to say Mr. Sacks played for both teams. Certainly harder for one."

"God's Breath Killer," Anand says. "Now it makes sense."

"Don't," Michaels says. "Don't use that name. It's a person."

"Yeah, a person who can go anywhere," Kruger says. "I mean, where do you even begin?"

"In this room," Michaels says. "We start here, with this list of test subjects. We locate them. They're not ghosts out in the ether. They're not demons. They have a body. A home. They eat, they crap, they sleep. That last one probably more than usual. This skill, from what I understand, comes at a cost."

"Correct," Chase says. "All subjects displayed post-projection neurological trauma. Headaches, confusion, inability to concentrate. Decoherence requires a tremendous amount of energy."

"So we hit the perp while they're recharging," Michaels says.

"Yeah, but they could be anywhere," Maddox says.

"Without basic orientation, they can't project," Chase says. "They need reference points, a way to mentally construct a destination. Photographs, a video, a strong memory of a location. The more senses, the better."

"There were eleven test subjects," Michaels says. "Two are deceased. That's Tae Hwan Kim and Cynthia Nesbit. One's living abroad. That's Zara Eisler. The other eight are scattered across the

U.S. Carruthers and I are starting with Theodore Jensen. Your targets are on your tablets."

Faces fill the tablet screens. Men and women at the far edge of middle age, most gone silver. The photos run the spectrum of quality, from crystal clear employee pictures to fuzzy DMV photos from a decade past. Five men, three women. Smiles, frowns, faces no different than those seen on the street.

"I want full surveillance starting this afternoon," Michaels says. "Coordinate with your field offices. Look for anything odd: travel patterns, high water bills, a hyperbaric chamber in their basement. Keep your distance but use discretion. Be ready for coordinated takedowns. We're in dark territory, past the edge of the map, and time is ticking."

He holds up his pocket watch. Silence.

"That means go," Caruthers says, and the room explodes in a flurry of activity.

OPERATION CLEARWATER RETRIEVAL
For Authorized Eyes Only - Penalty 18 U.S. Code § 798

S1. EISLER, Zara
Status: Missing
Location: Unknown
Assigned to: Maddox & Anand

S2. JENSEN, Theodore
Status: Alive
Location: Central City, Iowa
Assigned to: Carruthers & Michaels

S3. KIM, Tae Hwan
Status: Deceased
Location: Gyeongju, South Korea
Assigned to: N/A

S4. MAYER, Felix
Status: Alive
Location: Seattle, Washington
Assigned to: Pendergast & Kang

S5. MUNDAY, Jamal
Status: Alive
Location: Eugene, Oregon
Assigned to: Lowe & Romero

S6. NESBIT, Cynthia

Status: Deceased
Location: Twin Falls, Idaho
Assigned to: N/A

S7. NUEHOUSE, Margret
    Status: Alive
    Location: Keene, New Hampshire
    Assigned to: Alvarado & Fong

S8. OATES-DEANNA, Lucille
    Status: Alive
    Location: Savannah, Georgia
    Assigned to: Flick & Dunning

S9. PECK, Martin
    Status: Alive
    Location: Boulder, Colorado
    Assigned to: Crouch & Konrath

S10. STEPHENS, Sam
    Status: Alive
    Location: Scottsdale, Arizona
    Assigned to: Kensington & Faye

S11. WHITEHEAD, Patricia
    Status: Alive
    Location: Weatherford, Oklahoma
    Assigned to: Berrong & Kruger

23

FBI FIELD OFFICE, SAN FRANCISCO
THURSDAY - 9:00 A.M.

ADRENALINE HAS A HALF-LIFE OF TWO TO THREE MINUTES. YET AN
hour after the meeting, Michaels still tastes metal. The dull carpet
floats five miles beneath him. He balls his fists just to feel something solid.

"I've spoken to my board," Dr. Chase says, joining the field
agents at the elevators. "They've offered to lend you the jet. It's
being fueled now."

"Thank you," Carruthers says.

The elevator car arrives. Eighteen men and women file in. The
largest team Michaels has managed, a fact he keeps to himself on
the ride down.

"If I may," Chase says, "there's an alternative. With the right
lab, the right team, I could generate a list of likely assailants. All
I'd need is time with the suspects—"

"No," Michaels says. "We're on murky turf, legally speaking.
This is a prosecutorial nightmare. That's why we need the element
of surprise, catch them in the planning."

"You'll be safe, Doc," Carruthers says. "We've arranged
protection. They'll have the details downstairs."

"When we shuttered Clearwater," Chase says, "when the

lawsuit drained our funds and the facility was mothballed, there were rumors of witness protection. We thought it foolish. Perhaps we weren't thinking on a long enough timeline. Our folly as a species."

Michaels says, "The important thing is that we keep this quiet. They can't know—"

The doors open, and the thought vanishes.

"What the hell is she doing here?"

At the far end of the lobby, one hand clutching the security desk, the other holding her folded cane, stands Caitlyn. Sunglasses mask an empty gaze, yet she faces the elevators expectantly. The desk attendant whispers something, leaving Caitlyn smiling as he intercepts Michaels on the secure side of the metal detectors.

"Sir? She asked for you specifically. And I told her you didn't work at the Bureau, but here you are, like she promised."

"So much for security," Carruthers says. "Imagine a whole team like that?"

Chase doesn't have to imagine. He is already there, introducing himself.

"Ah, here they come now," Chase says. "I do hope we'll talk in greater depth soon. Your talent deserves special attention."

"Thank you, Doctor, but I just want to help."

Carruthers identifies herself, gives Caitlyn her elbow, and leads her to a section of chairs with a view of the fountain. Sensing the sun, Caitlyn turns her face to let the warmth caress her cheek. She can hear Michaels grinding his teeth on a toothpick.

"First, let me just say that I tried to reach out. You ignored my calls."

"We got over two hundred yesterday," Michaels says. "I spent twenty minutes on the phone with a man claiming to be the Zodiac Killer reincarnated. He said he had proof. Just drive down to Morro Bay with a film crew. He'll spill the beans."

"Well, did you?" Caitlyn asks.

"We sent someone," he says. Brad Lee, to be specific. Still fuming about being left out of the manhunt. "My point is, we're handling it."

"Can you?" Caitlyn asks. "What was it you said upstairs? 'You're past the edge of the map.' I can help."

Carruthers tries not to smirk. Michaels tries to ignore the sheen forming on his palms. Since this case started, a persistent whispering: all logic is falling away. When he tries to visualize perfect prime numbers, he sees only noise.

"No, not happening," he says. "We don't have room for travel consultants."

"I'm not a consultant. And I'm not charging a fee. What I am is the only witness you have."

"You're blind—"

"But not stupid. Let's be honest, Agent Michaels, you don't like me."

"You make me uncomfortable," he says. "If we're being honest. You're an aberration. I can't classify that."

"Doesn't quite fit in a box, does it?"

"Not quite."

"Good. Honesty. You know what I hate about being blind? Everyone finds an excuse to say you're brave or noble or whatever. Somedays, like today? I'm just a stubborn cunt."

Carruthers's guffaw echoes across the lobby. Two agents turn their heads.

"I don't care if you like me," Caitlyn continues. "I don't care if you can't understand me or classify me. Neither can I. It took a lot of Xanax to get me here and I'm not going home to wait to die. The only thing I care about is stopping whoever—or whatever—Dr. Chase created. That puts us on the same team. Now, I've seen what you're hunting, what it's capable of. If your suspect walks through a wall, I can track where they go. Face it, Agent, without me, you're going in blind."

When Michaels opens his mouth, he finds there are no words that follow. His lips settle tight, a crack splitting his face. Then he turns to Carruthers. "Can you believe this?"

"Yeah. And I agree with her too."

"So," Caitlyn says, "is the first stop still Iowa?"

24

LEARJET 70 N753LL
THURSDAY - 9:45 A.M.

BENEATH SAPPHIRE SKIES, THREE JETS TAXI DOWN THE RUNWAY AT Moffett Field. The flight plans are filed for El Paso, Seattle, and Iowa. Dr. Chase's name has procured the use of a Learjet 70 from Lovelace Biotronika. The other two are on loan from the Justice Department, former sex-trafficking planes repurposed into government service.

Five days after the worst night of her life, Caitlyn Grey, age twenty-six, grips the armrests, feels the tarmac's vibrations, hears the roar of twin jet engines, and senses the earth falling away as the skies open up.

DESPITE THE PORTRAYAL on TV of kicking in doors, despite the plots of airport novels, the Bureau is still a bureaucracy, one cut from the same cloth as the DMV. It moves slow, until it doesn't. For most of the flight to Iowa, Caitlyn listens as Carruthers calls field offices, fires off emails, and follows up on surveillance authorizations. Tedious work. First, securing memorandums of understanding with state and local law to form a joint task force. Next come the cross-deputizations. Finally, there's coordination, getting everyone together, on the same line, at the same time, and with the same goal in mind.

"Listen carefully now," Carruthers says, raising her voice over the hum of the engine. "We'll touch down in an hour. Until then, your team needs total concealment, understand? This is a surveillance operation. Zero contact until we're on scene."

Beneath Carruthers's words is a deeper implication: how do you surprise that which can leave its own body? The plan, for now, is to blend in and wait.

So Caitlyn waits, unable to get comfortable, unable to sleep, unable to ignore the hum of the engine.

She tries to visualize her surroundings. By touch, she knows that the chair is leather. Perhaps brown. There are USB ports and a pair of noise-canceling headphones that retract into the headrest. There is a call button with braille lettering. There is in-flight Wi-Fi through which Caitlyn sends a text to Mrs. Bakshi, asking her to see to the flowers while she is gone.

But what landscape passes below? Caitlyn has only movies set in the American Midwest to draw upon. Are the plains as golden as the fields of east India? Caitlyn, who has walked along the Great Pyramid in the moonlight, who has dived with pink dolphins in Laos as a child. This is her homeland, her country, yet a place as foreign as the far side of the moon. And now, moving over the heart of these lands, she thinks it's a shame it took horror to push her past the front door.

25

OPERATION CLEARWATER RETRIEVAL

NOON, SEATTLE TIME, THE SAME TIME CAITLYN'S MORNING XANAX IS fading, three featureless SUVs leave the Seattle FBI field office in a convoy. Their destination: the port of Seattle. Their target: Felix Mayer, fifty-five, a load operator on second shift.

By all public accounts, Felix is an upstanding citizen. He has no bankruptcies, no arrests. Eighteen years as a longshoreman brings in a union salary of eighty-six thousand dollars. He fully owns a bungalow on South Orcas in the gentrifying Georgetown neighborhood. He has a Labradoodle named Sasha. He is learning Spanish. At nights, Felix likes to visit the university and listen to lectures on art.

Occasionally, he takes a week off and travels. Sometimes to Las Vegas, sometimes to Atlantic City, and sometimes to an upscale Indian casino, Two Rivers or Red Wind or Muckleshoot. It is an unremarkable pattern, one undertaken by millions of Americans whose gambling feeds the economy.

Except when Felix visits.

His tax returns show consistent winnings, an unbroken streak of good luck. Added to his longshoreman salary, Felix sits in the middle of the second-highest tax bracket. His 1040s are honest and thorough, consistent with the records of the state gaming agencies. On paper, Felix is a semiprofessional gambler, one of the few who have found the blade's edge between calculation and chaos.

Felix, however, does not play cards. He bets on those who do. His wagers are locked in at the last possible chance. It's as if he knows which cards are worth holding, which hands are hot, and where the roulette ball might rattle and bounce.

Felix Meyer, perpetually single, otherwise unremarkable, but for one fact: a twenty-seven-month stint at a facility in the high Sierras, a place that lies in the maw of a mountain, by a river and a canyon named, in the tongue of the Miwok people, Clearwater.

IN BOULDER, Colorado, on the soft grass of Norlin quad, near Hellem's building, Martin Peck, fifty-seven, an adjunct instructor and author of four rejected manuscripts, meanders back to his office, clutching his fifth novel, the one that will surely get noticed, get published, get him back on the track to tenure and fame. Martin Peck does not notice the two men playing frisbee across from his office. Men much older than undergrads, too care-free to be graduate students. Men that notice him and speak in a low whisper as he passes.

AT THE BUNS Away Bakery in Savannah, Georgia, Lucy Oates-Deanna steps out back to take a delivery. The mixings are a day early. The driver, a substitute, fumbles the order forms, twice retrieving the wrong boxes from his truck. Despite her headache —which comes often these days—Lucy smiles. This is the post-lunch lull, a time of few customers. She signs the delivery receipt, leaves the mixings in the walk-in fridge, and returns to the register to see two customers leaving.

"Sorry, fu-fu-folks, I was out back," Lucy says, breathing deep to tamp down her stutter. "Hope I didn't keep you..." She trails off. The men are taking their business elsewhere. Lucy notices the bag one carries; she does not notice the black clock within it. It is the same type of clock that hangs above her register. A clock with a good view of her store.

AT THE NORTHERN edge of Scottsdale, Arizona, where the Saguaro and Palo Verde trees grow on the bronze slopes of the McDowell Range, Sam Stephens, known to his millions of viewers as "the Straight Shooter," takes a break from his midafternoon blogging and steps out of his home office. The veranda provides a view of the neighborhood, a development still in its infancy. Here, he can watch electricians from APS Electric and SRP Electric arguing beneath a power line, two vehicles angled like cats in a fight. Sam smirks. Just another example of big bureaucracy stumbling over itself. Then his smirk fades, subsumed by a prickle of fear. Why does one electrician have a truck while the other drives a van? Where is the uniform on that shorter man? Is the pickup missing its license plate?

Sam knows the government's tricks, its deep state operatives dug in like weeds. That power line also brings cable and phone. Is his home studio compromised now? He makes a note to switch VPNs, to disable location services on his phone. A new idea for his next show: how to live off the grid.

What Sam doesn't see is the glint off a lens, just inside his neighbor's house. A house that had been on Airbnb until two hours ago.

IN WEATHERFORD, Oklahoma, Patricia Whitehead, fifty-six, resident of the Brookdale Assisted Living Facility, smiles as the deliverymen from Home Depot replace her refrigerator with a fancy new one. She spends the afternoon customizing the touchscreen and marveling at the clarity of its camera.

. . .

In KEENE, New Hampshire, while admiring the spring bloom of her garden, Maggie Neuhaus, fifty-five, scolds her half-chow Muffin for barking at the Spectrum man who is fixing the neighborhood cable.

In EUGENE, Oregon, Jamal Munday leaves the tent encampment and pushes his belongings in a cart painted neon and named Further. His destination: Whole Foods. His plan: play a few new tunes on the ukulele and busk for some change. And to fend off the daylight hallucinations that have plagued him for years. He will ignore them, yes. Ignore the shadow people with no eyes. The hobgoblins skittering within bushes. The men in black who follow him, thinking, perhaps, they haven't been noticed.

By MIDDAY, systems are online. Microphones, cameras, and GPS sensors stream terabytes of data, first to antennas, then satellites hidden from registries, and back down now, beamed directly into the tablet, lives transmitted here as photons for Michaels's eyes.

26

CEDAR RAPIDS, IOWA
THURSDAY - 3 P.M., CST

A SQUEAL, THE WHINE OF BRAKES. THEN THE LOW HUM OF decelerating jet engines. A moment later there is a whirring motor and the clang of the stairs. Caitlyn, led down the aisle, down the steps, and out onto the tarmac, now takes in a lungful of Iowa. Spring, a time of tall clouds. Showers that come without warning and flee just as fast. Sweet heat off the asphalt, rubber and gas and steamed puddles that follow the storm.

They are shuttled from tarmac to freeway. Damp manure as the SUV speeds east on Highway 30, sirens screaming.

The Elks Lodge is thick with the scent of Costco muffins and coffee poured fast into Styrofoam cups. They eat sandwiches and sliced apples brought by the Iowa state troopers. Caitlyn focuses on the accents—all men—and after fifteen minutes of chatter, she has an ear for the locals and who moved here in later years, when diction stiffened behind less flexible tongues.

And she senses the troopers' eyes on her. They're wondering, but never asking, why is this blind woman with these federal agents? She speaks little. Of her own accent, she is self-conscious. No effort can hide the twang imbued from schooling abroad. The crackling South African that creeps when she speaks fast. Or the way she rolls her R's, learned from a tutor in Manila.

She rubs her socked feet against the carpet. There is a sadness to this lodge. All the parties and weddings, all the morning meetings and nighttime pledges of sobriety tamped into the fibers. She can almost hear the lonely hum of the vacuum cleaner, this room's only regular guest after the law enforcement officers unplug their computers, pack up the SWAT gear, and roll out.

"We've had full surveillance of the Jensen farm from three positions for an hour now," says a voice identified as Special Agent Kelly from the Omaha field office. "Linn County SWAT knows the area so they're taking lead. They have a utility vehicle out on Sawyer Road now, pretending to upgrade the Balisors. You know, those lights keeping planes from hitting the power lines. Good news: the boom lift is about seventy feet up with a perfect view of the farm."

"Can you get sniper coverage?" Michaels asks.

"Already done. The spotter's dressed in civvies. The sniper's reclining in the basket."

"What about the other two positions?" Carruthers asks.

"Less tactical, but good in a pinch. We've got the county inspector at the neighboring farm, supervising a cellular antenna inspection. Another spotter's up top. To the west, we've positioned SWAT in ghillie suits past the hoop houses. There's a mess of horses, so that's affecting line of sight."

"The farm's a misnomer," Michaels says. "Technically, it's a horse sanctuary."

"Aw, that's sweet," someone says. Laughter. The kind laced with testosterone and a tilt toward conflict.

"This is Undersheriff Acosta," Special Agent Kelly says, "our local liaison. We've worked JTFs before. Cross-border meth runners, oh, and a pair of dumdums trying to storm the inauguration."

"We've got mutual investment in keeping the peace," Acosta says. Caitlyn picks up on the subtle way he flattens secondary vowels. Mutual. *Mu-tul.* "Usually Agent Kelly just gives me a holler and we coordinate long distance-like. When we got word this convention's coming together, I thought, 'This is big.' So y'all mind telling us what hornet nest we're poking?"

Michaels says, "This is Theodore Jensen." A shuffle of papers, hands passing them down. Someone taps Caitlyn, holds out a paper, then murmurs an apology. Still, she takes the handout to give her collapsible cane a rest.

When the curtains fell, Caitlyn mourned the loss of her vision. More so, she mourns the image that followed: a blind woman, hands clutching her cane in quiet supplication. An invisible sign: *Pity me.*

"Theodore Jensen is forty-eight years old," Michaels continues. "Left is his last known photo, courtesy of the DMV three presidents back. On the right is computer-aged. Theodore is a unicorn in our digital age. He has no social media, no online footprint. Other than a government stipend, he has no income. Theodore is unmarried, a live-at-home with his mother Susan Jensen, just shy of sixty-eight. That's her on the bottom. She's a licensed veterinarian and runs the horse sanctuary."

Caitlyn can hear Michaels pacing now, his shoes scraping the rug. He cycles through slides. *Tap. Tap. Tap.*

"Theodore has a short history of psychiatric internment, twenty years back. As well as an assault charge when he was a freshman at Missouri Baptist. His roommate mouthed off about his mom, and Theodore about lost it. He beat the kid with a leather-bound bible. Then he turned the other cheek, drove the kid to the hospital, told the cops everything. The DA got community service out of it. And this, folks, is where our records of Mr. Theodore Jensen come to an end."

Not entirely true. Locked away in Dr. Chase's mind is a second file, one he'd relayed to Michaels after the FBI meeting. Caitlyn had watched them in that windowless room.

Fifteen minutes later, and the convoy of trucks ferrying SWAT and FBI roars down the highway, out of Cedar Rapids and into unincorporated Linn County. Carruthers drives while Caitlyn sits in the back. It's Michaels's turn now, to channel Dr. Chase from six hours ago.

"Chase called him Teddy and warned us to be careful," Michaels says. "Apparently he's the most powerful of the group."

"That would have been useful fifteen minutes ago," Carruthers says, "while we were making tactical plans."

"Higher-ups want to limit informational leak," Michaels says. "Linn County just needs to keep the crosshairs on Teddy."

"So this is the cool kid's car," Carruthers says. "Okay, what's the scoop?"

"He was seventeen when he joined Clearwater, the youngest by four years."

"How'd a minor consent?" Caitlyn asks.

"Military volunteered him. He was homeschooled, got his GED at sixteen. His mother authorized his Army enlistment, ergo Clearwater. Chase was scanning enlistees for certain traits and Teddy came up."

"Nothing like a young mind," Carruthers says.

"And deeply religious," Michaels adds. "There's a decrease in neural activity in the parietal lobe. Basically, it softens the edge between the self and the outside. Atheists and agnostics test less susceptible, so—"

"So you're not on the shortlist for round two."

"None of us are," Michaels says.

"Speak for yourself," Carruthers says. "I meditate. I go to Christmas mass. I fasted for Ramadan... once. I've got my bases covered."

"And so do the snipers," Michaels says. Ahead, the SUVs turn left off Country Home Road and onto Highway 13. Michaels continues. "Now hear me out: driving up with FBI and SWAT is one tactic, but it won't roll out the welcome mat. We need a more subtle approach."

"You want a sit-down?"

"I want to avoid provocation. I'm looking at the Jensen electric bill for the past year. It averages almost two grand a month."

"That's some bill," Carruthers says. "Maybe they're powering a sensory pod in the basement?"

"They're powering something."

The SUVs turn right, merging onto West Maple Street, which then becomes Main. Central City, Iowa, population 1300, blows past them in a blink. A kayak rental store, a pharmacy, Foxy's Chill & Grill. Under the train tracks and out onto Sawyer Road. A sign thanks them for coming. Then the sign at the Baptist church warns of coming damnation.

Michaels radios the lead vehicle and they pull off at a driveway. Carruthers guides the SUV past the utility truck at mile marker seventeen. The radio squawks, "We've got eyes on you, envoy. Driveway's clear. Follow it past the pond. The farmhouse is a quarter mile up the hill. No movement all afternoon. Over."

"Copy that," Michaels says. "Turning into the Jensen driveway now. Over."

Asphalt becomes gravel and dirt loosened by rain. Caitlyn tastes clay. To the right: a pond, verdant and teeming with ducks rooting among cattails.

What beautiful land, Carruthers thinks. Could she ever learn to tame such a place? Or maybe she could accept it for what it is: wild and overgrown and home to those who take life a little slower. Maybe she could even find such a patch east, near her daughter, close but not encroaching.

"Movement, to your right," the radio squawks. Michaels spots it emerging from the thicket. A three-legged dog follows the SUV, barking and limping and wagging its tail.

"So much for the element of surprise," Caitlyn says from the back seat. She feels the SUV rise as it crests a hill.

"Envoy, this is cell tower. We have visual on you. There's a clear path to the farmhouse and… Wait, there's movement. Someone's stepping out of the barn. They're… It looks like they're holding something. Is that a firearm? Envoy, be advised there is a female, possibly armed. Wait… she's putting it down."

"Envoy to cell tower," Michaels says. "Visual confirmed. Be

advised she appears to have placed a captive bolt pistol on the bench outside the barn. I don't believe her to be a threat. Over."

"Copy that. She's making her way to you. Over."

"Go ahead and park ass in," Michaels tells Carruthers. Gravel clatters in the undercarriage as Carruthers executes a three-point turn. "Watch the house while I parley with the matron."

The groan of the emergency brake, the click of the seatbelt, then the crunch of pea stones underfoot.

"What's a captive gun?" Caitlyn asks.

"It's what they use to euthanize animals," Carruthers says.

A *thump* on the passenger side of the rear door. Then the eager snout of the three-legged dog, nostrils fogging up glass.

"And what's that?" Caitlyn asks.

"That would be the dog. Wait—"

Caitlyn rolls down the window. In a gust of dusty fur and hot breath, the dog jumps onto the running board, tail wagging against the door. It does a three-legged jig and presses its face to the gap. First comes the cold nose, then the warm tongue.

"What a good fella," Caitlyn says as the snout alternates between snorts and licks.

"Real professional," Carruthers says. "Rolling up under sniper cover and petting the pooch."

"Probably against everything in the handbook."

"Well, if it's not, it will be."

Carruthers keeps her eyes on Michaels as he hands something to Mrs. Jensen. A glint of metal, a fold of leather. She studies the badge a few beats. Out comes the warrant. Mrs. Jensen looks older than her sixty-eight years, but stronger as well. Country miles and country muscles. Carruthers respects that. She grew up in rural, religious Kentucky, spent her whole career running away. Retirement on the horizon, and now she's coming full circle. Looking upon the wrinkles of hard labor—so familiar from her youth— and now filling them in with nostalgia.

Mrs. Jensen returns the badge to Michaels. He motions for Carruthers to join them. "Stay here," she tells Caitlyn.

"Wait. I need to know where we are."

"What?" It takes Carruthers a second to catch on. "Wait, why?"

"If you run into trouble," Caitlyn says. "You've got eyes up there. You need eyes down here."

Carruthers hesitates. A few hundred yards isn't a problem for snipers. But the walls are. If there's trouble inside, they have a code word and firearms. And still... The dhimoni had killed quickly. Only a second to turn the lawyer's head into paste.

"Okay, so there's a grain silo," Carruthers says, starting from the northwest. "The silo's old, maybe fifty or sixty years, paint gone to a rusty tone. There's a barn, also rust. A dozen horses out running in the pasture. Hoop houses—like greenhouses with plastic. There's a tree close to the house, huge, black walnut with a scar down it, probably from lightning. The farmhouse is mid-century, two floors, robin egg blue vinyl siding and asphalt shingles. Is that enough?"

"We'll see," Caitlyn says and gives the dog a scratch behind its floppy ears.

THE LATE AFTERNOON SUN, golden and warm, reaches inside the farmhouse and gives the shadows sharp angles. Susan Jensen knows this living room by heart, has to remind herself to turn the light on for her guests.

"Long day," she says and stops at the edge of the kitchen. "Had to put a horse down. Not much you can do when they go lame. I'd offer y'all a seat, but you don't strike me as the sitting type. So what have I done to earn the ire of old Uncle Sam?"

"We have no reason to believe you have, ma'am," Michaels says. "Actually, we're here to speak with your son, Theodore. Is he around?"

She considers them. These two strangers. Belt badges. Lumps under their blazers, about the size of a Glock.

"Teddy's here," she says. "Odd to see the feds showing interest, considering our history. Can I fetch you something to drink?"

"I'll take a pop, if you've got one," Carruthers says.

"A pop it is," Mrs. Jensen says and seems pleased to be moving from the living room into the kitchen.

A pop? Michaels mouths. Carruthers shrugs.

Mrs. Jensen fishes a bottle of Coke from a fridge nearly as old as she is. She pops the cap against the counter and passes the bottle, beaded and cool, to Carruthers. Michaels glances at the dining room, the antique gun cabinet, the shotguns and pistols. Three empty spaces.

Mrs. Jensen turns her gray eyes on him, from shoes to sunglasses. "I'm afraid we're fresh out of Perrier."

"I'm fine," Michaels says.

"I'm sure you are. Now, you'll have..." She drifts off, eyes lingering on something just beyond Michaels's shoulder. There is a faint groan, old wood in the shadows. Motes of dust in a sunbeam, now dispersing. Just an empty doorframe.

"Ma'am, if we could talk with Theodore—"

"Teddy can't talk to you," she says, and her eyes take in Carruthers now. "You didn't say which agency this one's with."

"Special Agent Carruthers is with the FBI," Michaels says.

"The F-B-I," she repeats. "Tell me, should I have my attorney present?"

"You can," Carruthers says. "That's your right, absolutely."

"Of course, I can't imagine your attorney's close by," Michaels says. "That was a slow drive here. In the meantime, we'd have to execute the search warrant. A full toss, that's a lot of work. It'd turn this friendly visit into a formality."

"That's never as pleasant," Carruthers says and sips the Coke.

Mrs. Jensen scoffs, taps her finger on the counter. "It takes the county a week just to de-ice the roads. Funny how fast gov'ment moves when it wants something."

"Big ships take time to turn," Michaels says.

"Ma'am, if we could speak with Theodore, that'd be best," Carruthers says. "You said he's here."

"He is. But he's not on speaking terms with anyone. Now what the dickens do you want to see Teddy for?"

"That's classified," Michaels says.

Mrs. Jensen flicks her hand like she's waving off a bad smell. "That's supposed to make me open my son's bedroom? Last time folks like you came around, I had a family. Now all I've got are remnants."

"What do you mean 'you folks'?" Carruthers asks.

"That program, Clearwater. I know that's why you're here. First you ruin his life. Then you threaten us into silence. Now you're here to talk and I'm supposed to just give up my son? Some fed and a G-man, both packing heat?"

There is a clack of wood, the creak of a spring. The three-legged dog limps in, wagging his tail. Caitlyn at the door now, cane tracing the edge of the rug.

"He's in there," she says and points to the dark hallway that ends in a sky-blue door.

"No!" Mrs. Jensen is spry for the cusp of seventy. She clears half the living room by the time Carruthers catches her in a tight embrace.

Michaels brushes back his jacket to clear his holster. Brandishing, he clears the living room corners, then hits the hall hard, fast. Checks the bathroom: good. Mrs. Jensen's bedroom: empty. Hits the sky-blue door while she shouts: "No! Don't hurt my boy!"

The dog is barking now, limping around the living room, its tail swinging wild. Caitlyn feels it hobble past, feels the whole house teetering toward violence, and now she is shouting, "He isn't armed. Teddy will never raise a weapon!"

Her words die behind the cries of Mrs. Jensen and the squawking of the radio, intrusive static cut by voices demanding to know, "What the hell's going on? Status report. Over!"

Michaels throws open the bedroom door, clears the darkness, and lowers his gun, muttering, "Shit."

• • •

THE MACHINES that keep him alive take up a quarter of the bedroom. Machines that breathe in measured clicks. Machines that push liquid food through tubes to a hole beneath his ribs. Machines that rumble and turn, sucking dark blood out and pumping bright, clean blood back in. Machines and screens, so many numbers and lines that Carruthers feels like she's looking at the cockpit of a plane.

And here sleeps Teddy Jensen, so sallow and gaunt he looks not like a man in his late forties but some stillborn thing, more tubes and tape than soggy matter and patchy red hair. A monitor lists a bed weight of seventy-five pounds; that includes the quilt and electric blankets. When Carruthers presses her hand to the corner, the weight jumps to ninety.

"Here," Michaels says and brings Mrs. Jensen a glass of water. She sits in a well-worn rocking chair, bedside. They give her time to compose herself.

"You'll have to forgive me," she says, throat dry. She places the water on the nightstand by a stack of books and a bible. Adjusts a blanket. "I've had trouble trusting the gov'ment after what my family has seen."

"That's understandable," Caitlyn says. A curious thing: she reaches out, finds the old woman's hand, and gives it a squeeze.

"How long?" Carruthers asks. "You know, how long has he been…"

"A few years since he stopped responding entirely. Before that, there were symptoms. Signs ignored at the time, so obvious in hindsight. Mood swings. A seizure at church. He'd say he was spending his day with the angels. Or he could see the whole world at once. Then he'd go quiet-like. Or that he was young again, back in Clearwater. And he slept. Sometimes days at a time. I thought it was melancholy and prayed he'd get better, but the truth was, my boy, his mind was shutting down. All the parts were dying while he was awake."

"Do they know what caused it?" Michaels asks.

"Course they know. They just can't admit it. Idiopathic non-fetal cerebral redistribution. It's all right here." She passes him a yellowed folder.

The words are the usual hyphenated prose that masks medical speculation. Sequenced PET scans show a decade-long story: a brain transforming. As the parietal lobe in the rear swelled and crowded the skull, the frontal and left temporal lobes collapsed in on themselves.

"First they thought it was mad cow," Mrs. Jensen says. "You can imagine how well that went over, here in the farmlands. Had the FDA and CDC camping out for a month. Then they thought maybe it was ALS or Parkinson's or Alzheimer's."

"Alzheimer's would show reduction of mass," Michaels says. "Not redistribution."

"You've some experience with it?"

Michaels nods. "More than I wish."

"My son's experience doesn't have a name. Least not one insurance will cover. Teddy, he's had to fight this battle alone."

Michaels turns the charts. Scans show a darkened patch in the mid-brain. The pons, the basilar artery, part of the thalamus: all gone. He closes the chart, hands it back.

"We have to ask," Carruthers says. "Have you reached out to any of the members of Clearwater?"

"Victims," she corrects. "And no, who would I contact?"

"When the settlement was arranged, there was a lawyer who handled the class action suit. An intermediary—"

"Sacks," she says. "Weasely fellow. Kept how much? Seventy percent? I hope his Cadillac can carry his conscience."

"It's probably a struggle now," Michaels says, exchanging a look with Carruthers. "So after the settlement, you didn't have contact with any of Teddy's cohort?"

"No, no, that's not quite right," she says. "There was someone, but he wasn't a victim or a scientist or whatever you call it."

Carruthers leans forward. "So who was he?"

"More of an employee or an orderly, I think. It was... what, nine or ten months ago? He came looking for Teddy and I told him what I told you: Teddy was infirm. He didn't take the news well. I figured maybe they'd been friends. He said, and I remember it well, he said he was going to make things right."

"Do you remember his name?" Michaels asks, already on his tablet, pulling up a list of everyone who drew a paycheck from the Clearwater fund. "Any distinguishing marks? Hair color?"

"Robert or Randall," she says. "He had a scar, this ways, across a cheek and ear."

"Was this him?" Michaels turns the tablet to Mrs. Jensen.

"Roger," she says, reading his name. "I'm not sure. That's an old photo..."

Michaels swipes away the employee photo. With a couple taps and pinches, he has the most recent public photo, courtesy of the Texas Department of Veterans Affairs. There is no beard, and the lighting is washed out, institutional. But there it is; his cheek bears dimpling that could be mistaken for acne scars if they'd been on both sides. His left ear, cut and cauliflowered, part of it missing.

"That's him," Mrs. Jensen says. "Deuteronomy: 32:35: 'Their calamity is at hand.'"

"He said that?" Carruthers asks.

"Didn't have to. He had it tattooed on his arm."

Carruthers whispers to Michaels, "I'm going to get a BOLO for this guy, see if we can't squeeze fast."

"Do it."

Caitlyn feels the floor groan as Carruthers hurries out.

"Your son, Teddy," Michaels says, "before the coma, would he have known of anyone with intent to harm those involved in the program?"

"Take your pick. Everyone involved's got plenty of reason. And you still don't get it, Agent. My son, he's not in a coma. Never said he was. He's here, now, locked in. Teddy was born in this room. One day he'll die in it."

Caitlyn traces the edge of the medical bed with her fingers.

The electric blankets, the quilt, the faded stuffed animals of Teddy's childhood. She follows a cord and comes to a blood-oxygen monitor taped to a skeletal finger. Then she gives his shrunken hand a gentle squeeze.

"I'm so sorry for your suffering," she says. "Both of yours."

"Thank you, dear," the old woman says. "It's been an age since we've heard that."

DECADES OF FARM work have calloused the old woman's hands, but to Caitlyn, they are suffused with a mother's touch. Mrs. Jensen guides her out onto the porch. Caitlyn can almost sense the gloaming, an orange tint behind the black curtains. Murmuring birdsong and the cry of a migratory loon carrying up from the pond.

"Your son is lucky, Mrs. Jensen. This is a beautiful home."

"I was hoping maybe he'd take over one day. I was a nurse before I became a vet. Funny how it worked out. Teddy'll be my last patient. After that, it's horses 'til the good lord takes me. I prefer them to people. The beasts don't pretend to be civilized." She shifts against Caitlyn, lips at her ear now, whispering, "Stay far away from these folk. They're hunters. They'll use you to find a scent, but what then?"

And as sweetly as before, she takes Caitlyn by the arm, places a hand on the small of her back, and guides her into the SUV. There is the click of the lock. Pleasantries and the offer of follow-up calls. Caitlyn tunes out the chatter as a thump hits the window.

"Hey, you." She stretches her hand out and gets a hot snout in return. "Take care of the farm."

A whistle and the dog is gone. Soon, Caitlyn feels the hilltop receding, then the gravel. Next comes the highway, smooth asphalt lulling her to sleep.

27

SAN FRANCISCO BAY AREA
THURSDAY - 4:30 P.M., PST

THE PHOTOS FROM THE CS TECHS COME IN AS HE'S CROSSING THE BAY Bridge. An old motor home, Fleetwood Jamboree, 1989, with Texas plates. A botched burn job. When Brad sees the interior, he pushes the accelerator to ninety, hits the red-and-blues and cuts through traffic. In less than twenty minutes, San Francisco is behind him, the Oakland impound yard ahead. Another ten, and he's walking the lot.

"Fire crews found her this afternoon in the airport's long-term parking," the impound officer says. "Normally, they give RVs a few days, but we've been having a problem with van dwellers. It gets to be a sanitation issue."

"What's it cost to park per day? Twenty bucks?"

"Thirty-five."

"Can't say I blame 'em. A thousand a month, plus your own toilet. I pay three grand for two roommates and one bathroom."

"That's the Bay Area for ya."

The officer unlocks a chain-link gate and leads Brad into the heart of the lot. An abattoir of metal, a cemetery for the American dream. Moldering jalopies share space with low riders and Teslas. Trump-stickered pickups rust beside Priuses decorated with

Bernie for President. In this way, the impound is more egalitarian than the community it serves.

"So that's it," Brad says as they round the corner. The CS techs are mostly packing up. A few linger, chatting with the responding officer. He waves Brad over and they start their walk-around.

"Most of the smoke damage is cosmetic," the officer says. "The doors were locked, so the fire crew broke the passenger window. Thankfully, the RV was empty."

Brad scans the license plate with his phone, sends it to Michaels. They continue around the RV, Brad snapping pictures along the way.

"Fire crew thought it might be meth chefs burning a cook truck so they called the bomb squad. Your BOLO came in about the time it got the all-clear."

"Good thinking on the bomb squad. I tossed a tweaker's car in Antioch once. He'd rigged the airbags with ball bearings, like a claymore mine. Turn the ignition without activating the safety— boom—there goes everything above your shoulders."

"Jesus. How the hell'd you find that?"

"We didn't," Brad says. "The guy got drunk and forgot to disable it. Saved us the trouble."

"That must've been a mess for the scene cleaners."

"I heard they just compacted the car." Brad puts on a fresh pair of nitrile gloves, nods to the officer. "Mind holding the door?"

"Go in. Have a peek."

A slurry of water and yellow monoammonium phosphate drips down the steps. In the RV's sooty kitchen lies a spent fire extinguisher. A hand over his nose makes no difference; Brad tastes chalk and ash. The responding officer waits outside.

"The big thing's in the back, by the mattress," he calls out. "Figure that's why you're here."

The BOLO hit had put the RV on Brad's radar. But it was the photo of the metal object that put Brad's accelerator to the floor. Here, in the back, in the still smoky air, sits a coffin-sized object. Hastily made of metal and plastic. Like a homemade bath, what his uncle calls a hillbilly hot tub. A round end stock tank, galvanized metal, seven feet long, three feet wide and equally deep. The lid is open, askew. Inside, Brad finds a tarp and sound-insulating foam and darkness, wet and glistening.

"What's this?"

"Salt water," the CS tech says. "Maybe they had sore feet."

"Okay then, why the mask and tank?"

The GP-5 gas mask is popular with cosplayers and fetishists and those who want to look like a Soviet nightmare. It is rubber, enclosing a wearer from nape to neckline, tight enough to block out a biological attack. The eyes, two ant-like glass circles, have been painted black. A hose runs from the respirator to a metal tank where the indicator gauge reads empty.

"Nitrous wouldn't surprise me," the CS tech says. "We'll have the lab swab it, but we wanted you to see it *in situ*."

Brad steps back, panning the camera for a wide shot looking frontward from the rear. "The fire started in the kitchenette?"

"Yep, gas stove, over here." She points to the darkened streaks, the spatter of oil. "They filled this pot with rags, poured in the oil, turned the flames on, and went for a walk."

"I did something similar in college," Brad says. "Fell asleep cooking ramen. Doesn't this strike you as a lousy way to torch an RV?"

"Well, considering whoever did this was huffing fumes in a home-built water coffin, I can't say it's surprising."

Brad shines his flashlight beneath the front seats. Passenger first, then driver's side. A loose gospel CD. Crumbs, hair, pennies.

"They left plenty of DNA," Brad says.

"We got toenail clippings too, in the bathroom. And dirt. Lots of dirt."

Brad squints, shining his light into the driver's side seat belt. "Did you get this receipt?"

"What receipt?"

"Hold the torch please."

The CS tech aims the flashlight down at a wad of paper, checkered red and white. Just a corner caught in the webbing of the seatbelt. "I'm guessing the techs probably thought it was the warning label," Brad says. He pulls out tweezers and an evidence bag. Sure enough, retracted, it looks like any other safety label. He gives the paper a tug, and out it comes.

"That's a funny receipt," the CS tech says.

"Zippy Burger," Brad says, carefully opening it. Three photos: wide, medium, close-up. "They do these old-timey checkered receipts. More of a Midwest thing, but you're missing out if you haven't had the okra fries. Huh…"

His stomach knots. The paper is greasy, ink faded in spots. The order: an Atomic Burger, a side of Cheesy Shock Fries, and an extra-large Mountain Dew. There, in the upper corner, is the store location: PTLMA. And the date: nearly two weeks ago.

Closing his eyes, Brad can see the line of cars at the drive-through. The only Atomic Burger west of Sacramento sits at the edge of the freeway, south of Petaluma, within spitting distance of Cal State Marin. This burger, Brad realizes, was ordered while the professor's blood was just starting to dry.

[28]

LEARJET 70 N753LL
THURSDAY – 6:45 P.M., CST

FROM FORTY-ONE THOUSAND FEET THE SOUTHERN TERMINUS OF THE
Appalachian Trail is a twilight scar, purple where Tennessee meets
Georgia. From the in-flight map, it is just a passing shadow. The
USA is vast, a fact most Americans forget: a continent pretending
to be one country.

Cell phone signals can't reach this altitude and the airplane's
body blocks satellite phones. So when Michaels's seatback phone
rings, he knows it is urgent.

"Talk to me, Brad."

Five minutes later, he is in the cockpit, the phone to his ear and
a new flight plan on-screen. The captain inputs the destination;
autopilot confirms it. Carruthers doesn't notice, but Caitlyn does;
her senses are attuned. A change in routine, a tilt to the plane,
acceleration. She waits until Michaels returns to his seat, then she
asks, "We're not going to Savannah, are we?"

"THIRTY MINUTES AGO, agents from the Dallas field office and the
Texas Rangers hit the house of Roger J. Fenton," Michaels says
and lays his tablet out on the tray table. "Roger was not home.

And judging from the state of the place, he hasn't been there in months."

Carruthers swipes through the files. The rap sheet reads like two different men. Prior to 1990, Roger was a low-grade defense contractor with security clearance. Before that, a stint in the navy food services, aboard the submarine USS *Batfish*. Roger spent most of '88 in the Persian Gulf, chasing Iranian boats and guarding the USS *Theodore Roosevelt*.

After 1991 it's a shopping list of misdemeanors and the occasional felony. DUIs, warrants for child support, assaulting an officer. Roger did six months for stealing copper in Pensacola. Carruthers struggles to connect the stoic face of the navy crewman in '87 to the scarred mug shot a decade later.

"Roger's been busy touring the land," Michaels continues. "Before the Bay Area, a license plate reader caught his RV in Tampa, four weeks ago. Before that, Burlington, where he racked a ticket for dumping gray water. Then in Durango and a dozen points between."

"He's been near at least four murders," Carruthers says. "Same time."

"But Roger wasn't in the program," Caitlyn says.

"He was a guard," Michaels says. "There was an escape attempt. Gas was deployed to incapacitate the subjects. I got off the phone with Chase, and it turns out Roger was pulled into the mess. He was collateral damage."

"How collaterally damaged?" Carruthers asks.

"Enough to be angry. His VA records show ongoing neurological issues. They coded it as some variant of Gulf War syndrome. Like Teddy, health insurance didn't play nice. And when the test subjects sued, who do you think was left off the plaintiff list?"

"They hung him out to dry," Carruthers says, swiping back to the empty space from 1988–1991. "Christ, that's motive. So what about means? How could he... decohere?"

"Chase said it started with the molecule, right? DZ3 lays the tracks. Chronologically, the first victim was McNare. He synthesized the entheogen."

"This feels like a stretch," Carruthers says. "This file, this guy Roger, he's scattered."

"Not too scattered. Oakland found a homemade sensory deprivation rig in his RV, gas mask and tank. They swabbed the hose. Guess what came up? Aerosolized DZ3. He's been homebrewing this stuff."

"So where's he now?" Caitlyn asks. "He's not in his RV, and we're not heading to Georgia."

"Roger dumped the RV on Sunday, right after the lawyer. Tried to torch it too, but he botched the job. Maybe being seen spooked him. I don't know. He bought a ticket to Boston, been there since."

Carruthers swipes over to the list of scientists out in the wild. Seven potential targets, seven locations, including Dr. Chase. Only he knows what is out there. The rest are under silent surveillance. "I'm not seeing anyone local to Boston or New England."

"Because there aren't," Michaels says. "But this weekend, the Society of Clinical Neuropsychology is having its yearly meeting. The keynote speaker is Francis Linamore."

"You have to tell him," Caitlyn says.

"Agents are following him."

"Agents are useless," Caitlyn says, indignant. "He'll tear right through your protection."

"We can't just gun him down like John Dillinger, okay?" Michaels snaps. "This has to be surgical. We have to catch Roger with intent. There's prosecutors and grand juries and a whole chain of evidence. This needs to play out to a conviction."

"You think this'll see a jury?" Carruthers asks. "Please. The Foundation'll ship him off to a black site, spend the next thirty years taking him apart. You know that."

"No one knows that," Michaels says. It isn't the first time he's lied to them, but it's the first time he feels guilty about it.

"So, what, Francis is just bait?" Caitlyn asks.

"Yes," Michaels says and rubs his temple. "He's a worm on a hook. And we're trying to catch a fish that cost forty million dollars and can kill with its mind. That's my mandate."

The plane banks again, turning north-northeast, the turbofan engines humming loud in the darkness. Behind them, the dark scar of the Appalachian Trail. Ahead, the Eastern Seaboard, one hundred million people getting ready for bed. And down there, somewhere, one stalking his prey.

BOSTON
THURSDAY - 8:15 P.M., EST

SPRING IN BOSTON. WARM ENOUGH FOR SKIN DURING DAYLIGHT. Cold enough for pea coats and scarves after dark.

The edge of Beacon Hill. Brick row houses lit by antique gas lanterns, some nearly two centuries old. In this amber darkness, a few miles from where Paul Revere began his ride, now walks a man on his own nocturnal journey.

Roger Fenton is a friend of the shadows. Where once great shapes in gas masks cackled from a gray waste of fog, now here he stands, vivified by night. He clutches a fountain pen and a leather-bound journal. The binding is hand-stitched, the paper no mere scratch pad for students but Japanese vellum.

These are his tools: his eyes and his mind. He sucks in the world in spastic strokes of his pen.

This is his mantra when it comes to his writing: size, shape, distinguishing characteristics. Size: three hundred feet of old cobbled road. Shape: lumpy stones and ivy-draped brick. Distinguishing characteristics: these warm honey lamps.

He was a serviceman once, and he served in the belly of a great metal beast. Now, he is more. Scribbling, his fingers tremble as the alley transforms. A concrete hall, klaxons, flashing red lights. Chemical fog, rolling, roiling, coming toward him. Roger closes his eyes, braces for—

No. A different life. A time without purpose. He has slept with his light on for decades. He has dreamed away too many days. No longer.

Opening his eyes, Roger watches the subterranean corridor fade as the cobbled stone of Acorn Street gives way to the brick houses of Willow and Chestnut. He caps his pen, gives the ink three breaths to dry. Then he moves on.

Do not envy those who dwell here, he tells himself. These quiet structures, steeped in history and warmth. He, too, once saw such a future. Of laughter, and early suppers on Thursday. Of open windows, and curtains spread in supplication to the wind. Of mirth and meals made for visiting friends.

As Roger pauses beneath one such open window, his mind drifts. A fortuitous assignment, and how pressed his uniform was that first day at work. Good things come to those who wait. And so he waits in this subterranean corridor, yes. Waits for his wife's letters. Waits to tell her that with this job he will become the first Fenton to go to college. He is studying to get his associate's degree. Then beyond that: the walls of higher education. He will—

Shit. Roger pinches the bridge of his nose. He's caught in yesterday again. Lost track of the tense and fell into a loop. Not caught, *robbed.* Yes, that's what they did.

Roger takes out his pill bottle and plucks out three Imitrex. He crushes them between his teeth; the bitter tastes sweet. He can crush other things too. He leans against the wall, waiting for equilibrium to return. Why is he here?

He studies the written wisdom on his wrist, tattooed. Deuteronomy: 32:35. The words come to his heart:

Vengeance is mine, and recompense; their foot shall slide in due time; for the day of their calamity is at hand and retribution shall make—

"Haste," Roger says.

Purpose returns. A warm surge bringing definition to his vision and guidance to his feet. He steadies himself against the brick wall. Above, a family eating dinner laughs, their voices drifting down from the dining room and into this alley. Roger laughs with them. Aloud and with tears in his eyes.

He has direction. He finds the path, past the gold-domed state-house and down to where the buildings rise high and the streets screech with Thursday-night traffic and a homeless man begs for change and Roger obliges and tithes generously. Now, Roger comes to his great destination, gives the bellman a nod, and steps into the hotel's opulent lobby, this palace of finery.

DR. FRANCIS LINAMORE, clinical researcher at King's College, London, senior fellow at the Spatial Mind Foundation, father of two, collector of medieval manuscripts, and recovering alcoholic three weeks shy of his ten-year coin. He stands at the lectern, staring into the stage light. The screen behind him: a highlight reel of his work in Bali. Sun-kissed children smiling back, wide-eyed and beaming and now free of brain tumors.

"Right, I'm not hearing any sound," Francis says, pressing the clicker. "This slide should have audio."

The stage tech taps buttons at the console. The PowerPoint flickers and vanishes. Typical. This is why he generally avoids regional conferences. At his place in the game, these small-scale frustrations should be gone. If his PowerPoint is going to crash, at least let it happen in Zurich or Vienna or Tokyo.

The stage tech asks, "Did you convert the audio to a compatible format?"

Francis studies the presenter slide, the curious X where the audio should be. "Let's mark slide five for revision."

The stage tech makes a note. Boomers. Tomorrow, this room will be filled with a few hundred doctors. Hopefully they handle their patients more carefully than this keynote speaker handles basic tech.

"H'okay, let's try it from the beginning," the stage tech says. "Opening slide. Cut lights. Cue video. You enter stage left..."

Francis walks out, waves to the empty auditorium. Then—

"Cue your presentation. Slide one: opening remarks. Slide two: state of neuropsychology..."

He drones on. There is light in the far darkness, a line that spreads into a rectangle. Francis raises a hand to shield his eyes. The ballroom door is ajar, a shadow at the threshold.

The stage tech says, "If you're setting up chairs, can you hold for fifteen?"

The shadow simply stands there, backlit by the warmth of the adjacent lobby. Chattering drifts in, evening conversations, the clatter of silverware as a food cart rumbles past.

"Sir, do you need something?"

"Oy, dummy," Francis says. "Close the bloody door."

When the shadow's hand dips into a pocket, Francis scans for a close exit. This is America, after all. Quick tempers, ample triggers. A flash of light, a click.

The shadow lowers the camera. "Jolly good show, Francis," says a guttural voice that comes from a dream.

And then the rectangle becomes a sliver of light and the door closes.

FOR THE FIRST time in years, Francis finds himself walking into a bar. Thursday night, thirsty Thursday in Boston, seats mostly filled. He finds an empty stool at the bar, down from three college girls out on the town. The bartender pours mixed shots—Bailey's, Kahlua, and Grand Marnier—and the girls knock them back, giggling and taking selfies.

The bartender turns to Francis. "What can I getchya?"

"Laphroaig, three fingers, couple drops of water. And the Angus burger."

"Rare?"

"Yes. And you know what? Fetch me a ginger ale instead."

"No Laphroaig?"

Francis shakes his head. When the ginger ale arrives, he grips the sweating glass and takes stock of his thoughts as they'd taught him in AA. One day at a time.

Why, then, had tonight brought him so close to relapse? The rehearsal was stressful, yet no more than others. The Boston climate is nice. Objectively, he is at the apex of his career; he knows this. He has a family, twin daughters in college. And sure, they are probably doing shots at a pub in Leeds, but they are wise enough not to share it on social media. Yes, Francis is grateful for many things, especially coming of age before digital records.

He is halfway through the Angus burger and onto his second ginger ale when it happens. The girl to his left—the one with the bubblegum hair and squeak-toy voice—teeters and falls, taking her pint glass with her.

She bounces and laughs. The pint shatters. A distinct crackling as glass comes apart. And for a moment, Francis recalls a noise from when a man had smashed his way through a one-way mirror. They had donned gas masks that day, but the glass still crackled and crunched. And the security guard tottered through. His name, his name, what was that poor idiot's name?

The girls are laughing and giggling now. The bartender is helping them pack up. And Francis, six weeks shy of his sixtieth birthday, lets the fog of late middle age swallow his reverie. He bites into his burger, thinks of tomorrow, and gives no further reflection to the man from his past who is standing outside, glaring in through the window.

FIVE SEATS down from Dr. Linamore sit Parker and Quon, agents from the Boston field office of the FBI. They arrived after he did and ordered only appetizers, prepaid in case they need to leave fast. They take turns, Parker watching the doctor, Quon pretending to watch CNN. Some blowhard speculating the God's Breath Killer began as an Internet meme. An online mind virus refracting social psychosis.

When the doctor pays and leaves, they follow. Parker fakes a phone call in the lobby. Quon tarries by the elevator. The doctor is slow, seemingly lost in thought, and Quon wonders if he can hold his position without blowing the tail. He is about to give Parker the switch signal when the doctor ambles over, newspaper tucked under his arm.

"What floor?" Quon asks as the elevator doors close them in.

THREE HUNDRED AND seven miles from Boston's Logan Airport, Carruthers hangs up the phone. She sets her watch to Eastern time, 9:00 p.m. When Michaels returns from the cockpit, she gives him a thumbs-up.

"The doctor's in bed," she says. "Room 1511, by himself. One agent's stationed in the hall. The other's checked in next door."

"How'd you manage that?"

"I bunked with the ASAC during management training and she's tight with Boston PD. The hotel thinks we're running a counterterrorism drill. Now all we need is the warrant on Roger."

"I'm working on that."

"Why can't you just grab him?" Caitlyn asks.

"Because of due process," Michaels says. "If we did, it would taint the evidence."

"The sugar bowl maxim," Carruthers adds. "If you have a search warrant for a stolen TV, you can't go looking in the suspect's sugar bowl. It's unreasonable, and anything you find would be invalid. But if the warrant was for, say, a stolen diamond, well, go look in the sugar bowl."

There are ways around it; this they both know. Parallel construction—a form of evidence laundering—creates a dummy case to skirt Fourth Amendment issues. Michaels could pass a tip to the FBI via Carruthers. The agents—acting in good faith—

would take Roger in. A false beginning, until the real investigation catches up. But that introduces variables, witnesses, more loops to be closed.

"It's important to follow rules," Carruthers says.

"The killer doesn't," Caitlyn says.

"And that's the difference between us."

Caitlyn senses a phone vibrating on the tray table. Michaels's call lasts thirty seconds and he paces the whole time. Then he hangs up.

"That was Brad, in California," he says. "Check your messages."

Carruthers taps her keyboard. Most keys sound similar, but to a trained ear, a few stand out. The thumb hits the spacebar harder, and it bounces back with a little more heft. "No way," Carruthers says. "I'll have Boston FBI prep the takedown with SWAT. You getting that warrant?"

"Any minute now," Michaels says.

Caitlyn feels the woman's heavy footsteps; she's hurrying to the quiet end of the plane.

"What's happening?"

"Brad's an MVP, that's what," Michaels says, cupping the phone. "He ran Roger's ID past some motels in San Francisco. A night receptionist recognized him. Said he paid in cash, demanded a room with a view right across from the diner. He made one phone call, from the motel to the lawyer's office. The secretary said it was about Clearwater."

"So Roger baited him out," Caitlyn says. "Now can you arrest him?"

"With that? Maybe. But we can put him away with this: toenail clippings in the RV are a DNA match for tissue scraped from William McNare's teeth. Roger was the last thing the hippy chemist ever bit. We'll have Boston SWAT kicking down his door in thirty minutes or less."

Caitlyn feels the shift as the tablet leaves the tray table and an inflight phone is lifted from its receiver. The airplane buzzes with

voices, motion, excitement. Beyond the black curtain that has
come to separate her from colors and shapes, only a few hundred
miles away and closing, there is a monster. And beyond the
curtain there is also a promise. Justice, moving swiftly, turning her
sword and blind eyes upon Boston, where a man of shadows plies
the night.

[30]
BOSTON
THURSDAY - 9:00 P.M., EST

Ever since a Monday in mid-April when two brothers turned the Boston Marathon into a field of torn flesh, the FBI and the Boston police have maintained close ties; agents and officers keep desks in each other's departments. Better a colleague down the hall than a stranger on the far end of the phone. Special Agent Renee Coates and Detective Bud McShane are paired when the call comes in.

At 9:17 p.m., their van leaves the FBI field office in Chelsea, north of Boston. Lights flashing, it speeds down Highway 1, crossing the Tobin Bridge, where fishing boats sputter in the Mystic River below. Detective McShane drives too fast for Special Agent Coates. Normally, she would insist they give the sirens a few squawks before rolling an intersection. Tonight, there isn't enough time.

The Special Operations Unit within the Boston PD maintains the roster of Tactical Operations, officers cross-trained in SWAT and ready for call-out. Six are suiting up when the FBI van arrives. Another six are on the way. McShane and Coates park in the garage just in time to see it: a black and blue juggernaut, Lenco BearCat, more tank than truck. The SWAT team is on weapons check. The rear doors of the armored truck are open, ready to swallow the Kevlar-clad warriors. McShane and Coates are the first in, then the SWAT team. With a gut-rumbling purr of V8 turbo diesel, the dark beast is off, charging onto the foggy streets.

Inside, buckles are clipped and belts are cinched. McShane verifies the cams and monitors are synced to Mobile Command. Coates connects her tablet to the tactical display. The destination is five minutes away. No time for a long briefing; an info dump will have to do.

"Okay, folks, listen up," Coates says. "Commander Harrison will brief tactics in a moment. But first—"

"Harrington, ma'am," the team leader says.

"Harrington, right," she says and turns to the screen. "Now, this is the face of Roger Fenton, age fifty-five, currently a suspect in multiple homicides. He arrived in our fair city three nights ago, and it's the belief of federal law enforcement he's here to continue his work. Let's show Roger a proper Boston welcome."

A few nods and a chuckle. For some, these moments before a takedown exist in liquid. Time thickened and heavy yet passing too fast. For Operator Chaco, it's what he signed up for. Just like the Army, even some of the same toys. The heavy metal over his earbuds helps with his heart rate. Helps keep his mind off his trembling feet.

"An hour ago, Roger's credit card hit the processing systems at the Hotel InterGlobal, on Atlantic," Coates continues. "He's checked in to Room 1620. That's four from the top. FBI have plain-clothes on-site, and all quiet. If we're lucky, he dozed off and is dreaming sick little thoughts—"

The BearCat takes a sharp turn, pushing the SWAT operators shoulder to shoulder.

"—but even so, go in fast, make a clean arrest."

Team Leader Harrington, on comm with surveillance, briefs the team on approach. The hotel hallway, the stack, the fallback if Roger barricades himself in the room. With no cover and conceal-ment, there's no room for error. "You hit your AOR fast and smooth, no cowboy shit, clear?"

O'Neill elbows Chaco, tugs out an earbud. "Focus up."

The Cordura handholds sway from the ceiling. Narrow streets now; they're close. "All right, last turn," Harrington says.

"Last turn," the team repeats, eyes dancing off each other. Deep breaths now.

"And one more thing," Detective McShane says. "Do not let this guy close his eyes for more than a blink."

Laughter, bemused and nervous.

"That's not a joke. Apparently he's got some medical condition."

"Yeah," Chaco says, "it's called an impending ass-kicking."

THE INTERGLOBAL'S chief of security opens the kitchen loading dock to receive tonight's delivery: six of Boston's finest, followed by the detective and the FBI's task force liaison. There are others watching but not present. The head cams and chest cams stream wide-angle views in crystal clear 4K at sixty frames per second. One such audience sits in a Learjet, watching in 1300-millisecond latency. Not quite real time, but close enough.

Inside now, combat glide, smooth and fast where the kitchen staff clears a path. Kevlar and carbines rattling past boiling pots. Cuban hip-hop from a wireless speaker. For a few curious seconds, the beat matches the pounding boots.

A hundred and twenty yards across Purchase Street, the High Street Tower offers the only direct view into Roger's hotel room. A postmodern high-rise, the tower is also home to Fire Engine Company 10, who are happy to assist BPD SWAT. Sniper Gayne takes the service elevator to the seventeenth floor, takes position at the end of a hall with a view across the Kennedy Greenway. In seconds he has the digital scope glassing Room 1620. There is Roger, motionless in bed, dim light playing across the sheets. Gayne tethers the video and streams it back to Mobile Command.

"Confirm, suspect fell asleep watching TV."

When the InterGlobal service elevator opens with a ding, the

SWAT team fans out, down the beige hall of the sixteenth floor. McShane and Coates hang behind, waving two civilians back into their room. O'Neill's on point, Chaco covering on approach. To the left is Harrington with eyes on entry. "That's the door," he whispers and verifies his team sees where he's pointing.

Like all rooms, 1620 has a fire-rated inward-opening door. O'Neill and Chaco squeeze to opposite sides of the frame. A clang as a plate carrier smacks against a firehose container, and all eyes snap to Chaco. Fuck. Everyone holds their breath.

Harrington checks the video from Gayne. "Mobile Command, confirm target is still asleep?"

"Confirmed."

Harrington gives the go-ahead. Anipen, on breach one, hoists the keycard. Barton, all shoulders and chest, takes up second breach and readies the ram. Inhale, exhale. They're in the fatal funnel now, and hotel doors are the worst. If the keycard fails or the swing bar inside is latched, it's going to be a dynamic entry, loud and costly but always exciting.

The keycard doesn't fail.

With a green blink and a double beep, the door opens. A sigh of relief and then a quick push. Chaco and O'Neill buttonhook into the room, take positions in the corners to clear space for the team. Guns and lights painting the room, the rest of the stack pour in, shouting, "Police, down! Show your hands!"

SEVENTY-TWO MILES AWAY, as the Learjet begins a rapid descent toward Logan Airport, Michaels and Carruthers watch the illuminated darkness in high definition. From the chest cams and head cams they get multiple views. A textbook takedown in sixty frames per second and only the hint of a stuttering connection.

Over the headphones: "Police! Hands behind your back now. Cross your legs."

The drumming of boots, loud even on carpet. A cry of protest:

"The hell is happening, man?" Hands, pinning the man in boxers and flex-cuffing his wrists.

"What was... shit," Carruthers says, fumbling with her headset. "Special Agent Coates, please verify ID. Over."

"Copy that." Coates's chest cam pushes into the flickering room, bobbing and scanning. Arms reach out. "Turn him over."

Four sets of hands follow the command. Gloved fingers probe skin. Michaels props his tablet next to Carruthers's laptop. Brings up a picture of Roger. Compares it to Coates's chest cam.

"This is Michaels. I need light on his face and a steady view. Over."

"What's he saying?" Caitlyn asks.

"Shh," Carruthers says.

Through the commotion, the suspect's voice comes in. "... paid me... not... room." There is a hiss of static. The video downgrades to HD.

"Everyone shut up!" Michaels says. "His face. Show me his face."

The flashlights are washing him out, too much grain against the shadows. Someone turns on the bedside lamp and the face that fills the screen is not Roger Fenton's.

"—fucking told you already," the man says. "He paid me to take the room. A clean bed, a warm shower. That's what he said!"

"Who said that?" Coates asks.

Michaels clenches his teeth. At some point, he leaned forward and now there is no more room on his seat.

"He knew we were coming," Carruthers says. "Jesus, he faked us—"

There is a low-frequency pulse, a bass drop over audio. And it drops and it drops. Video stutters, downgrading to 480p. Across the street, Gayne's digital scope blooms white. Static crawls, skips, stretches across the room.

"Whoa, I've lost visual."

Then there is a shout. Sudden, spastic, to the right of O'Neill's body cam. Nine pairs of eyes and no one understands what they are seeing.

Operator Chaco, in full tactical gear, is crawling up the wall. He turns, twists, pirouettes. His boots dangle eighteen inches off the ground.

Then he is flung across the room and into a lamp.

Shadows dance and stretch. Next come the cries.

"The hell is that?"

"Lights! Get lights on the window!"

"There's someone moving by the—"

Another low hum. The feed stutters, takes on a pixelated mosaic. A few frames a second, flashes really. Behind it, shouting voices in screeching burps.

"Oh my god, did you see—"

"That's impossible—"

"Get it off me! *Get it*—"

A flash. One of the SWAT operators, suspended in the middle of the room. Feet kicking, arms flailing, like a dancer on wires with no wires to be seen.

Next comes the gunfire. A drumroll blast, muzzle flashes, and the screens go sideways as the SWAT team dives for cover. A smoking M4 carbine falls from the operator's arm. Then the arm breaks with a crack.

"What's happening?" Caitlyn asks. "Is he there? Is Roger there?"

"I... I don't know," Michaels says. "Something's there."

Caitlyn inhales. A buzz over the intercom: the captain telling them to buckle up for the landing. The hum of motors on the wing, flaps extending. *Steady yourself.*

"I can go there, now," Caitlyn says. "Maybe I can stall him."

On-screen: a room full of confusion, chaos, the impossible. Two SWAT operators are retreating into the hall. A third is dragging his colleague into a stairwell as a guest runs past. Everything is falling apart.

"Michaels, we can't handle this," Carruthers says.

"Hold fast," Michaels says over the line. Then, to Caitlyn, "How do we do this?"

"I need quiet. Use the noise-canceling headphones and give me directions."

"Carruthers, handle the backup SWAT," Michaels says. He plugs the headphones into his tablet, switches them to noise-canceling and sets his mic to input. "Can you hear me?"

Caitlyn cups her ears, nods. Michaels pulls up a map of Boston while she brings her knees into an improvised lotus position. A deep breath. She holds it for five. Feels her face relax. The airplane is a vibration, distant. Another deep breath. *Now hold it for ten. Release.*

Caitlyn, in the darkness. *Feel the curtains. Feel the texture.* There, where it's parting. *Reach out now.* Her thumb grazes black velvet. *Count down from ten... nine... eight.*

And she tells Michaels, "Go!"

"It's a large building," he says. "Twenty-one floors of glass and metal. Uh... it has a glass facade..."

Push the curtain aside. See the glimmer of light. Glass, glass, endless and shimmering. Metal towers scraping an oily sky. Ten thousand similar buildings, too many. Static now, overwhelming.

"That's too vague," she says. "Pictures. Do an image search. Get me into this plane and I'll work over your shoulder."

"Yeah, sure, this is totally normal," Michaels says and pulls up a picture of downtown Boston. "Okay, this plane. It's a Learjet 70. Uh, there are six seats plus a table—"

"C'mon, use your vocab! What makes this plane special? Start with your chair, then work your way out."

Michaels studies his chair. "It's leather. Marbled resin armrests. There's... There's a stitch that was replaced. It should be black, like the rest, but it's not. Maybe whoever restitched it must've been colorblind. Or just lazy. The chair is black and gray. But the stitching, it's an olive color. What else? The armrests are like when you put too much cream in your coffee and it hasn't quite mixed. There's a line of excess plastic on the in-flight tray, maybe when it was molded. Okay, the carpet…"

The curtains part. Beyond it: a chair, luminous and infused with tendrils of color. A leather throne nested in shadows. There are buildings beyond, below, rushing past in a blast of yellow and red. Caitlyn is soaring through a petrol sky. The floor fills in, wires and pipes and layers of luggage. A field of fibers sprout, weaving the carpet as he talks. Then comes Michaels, first a shade in a chair, then clothes, then flesh. His lips move. He is talking, and from a distant place she knows his words are piped straight into her mind. But here, his lips move slow. Each syllable like syrup. "Not… sure… she… can… hear… me…"

Caitlyn wants to tell him she can, but talking risks ending the blink. This link is weak, shaky, tilting with the pitch of the plane. Damn hard without chemical assistance.

A deep breath. She focuses on Michaels, whose face is lit up by…

Two rectangles of light. There they are, the sources of the reflections in his glasses. Carruthers's laptop and his tablet.

Caitlyn takes in the pictures. Stuttering glimpses from a video feed. A man in body armor being slammed against a wall. Someone cowering behind a bed. A long, low angle, fingers digging into the hallway carpet, crawling. A glance upward at a door: 1620 in cursive gold script.

She sees the door now, just beyond the chair and the cockpit. A clear frame…

Then the curtain falls, concealing it. More. She needs more to fill in the dead space. Images on Michaels's laptop: a modern lobby with a glass atrium, a long check-in desk. She can see that to her left, beyond the wings dipping into the night sky.

She feels a small pop, right behind her eyes. Then the floor falls apart.

"You should see Fenway Park in the spring," says a voice she hasn't heard in a decade. "There's something about the high ones, the nosebleeds behind home plate."

He sits one row in front of her, the baseball stadium otherwise empty. He pulls on a wet rope that dangles over the balcony and into the section below.

"Daddy?" Caitlyn asks.

Another tug on the rope. "It's a curious thing. How the light seems to sweep across the seats. And the crack of the bat, it travels, like thunder on the open sea. Makes you feel part of something bigger."

A final tug of the rope. Seaweed and barnacles and something metal clattering down in the chairs. Her father's hair is just as she remembers, the first signs of gray in thick, shaggy black. Hands imbued with a tropical tan. He wipes his brow, and if he turned, she could just see his face. *Please turn, Dad. Please turn around.*

"Sure hope your mother and I can take you there some day, kiddo." And he drops an anchor onto the chair. "Maybe one day soon." He does not turn.

A crackling release, depressurizing deep behind her eyes. Her father is gone. So is Fenway Park. A flood of images swallow the stadium: Paul Revere's house from an old textbook; the Boston commons on the wall of a travel agency in Berlin; the Mystic River, and the movie of the same name; a parade, down streets, past colonial houses and then—

Caitlyn is in the hotel lobby. Distant alarms cry out as staff direct guests away from the elevators. Outside, through the windows, cop cars brake hard, one jumping the curb. Behind them: a fire truck and a second SWAT van unloading.

There is a crash high above. Glass salts the asphalt, and heads crane skyward. Caitlyn doesn't need to walk or run; she simply looks out at the sidewalk and then she is there.

Up. Is that a chair falling through the air? She ignores the screams. Focuses on the broken window, the curtains dancing through like ribbons in the rain. Sees the flickering lights inside.

Sixteen floors, sixteen miles. It makes no difference. Caitlyn visualizes the window, the room beyond, and now she is in it.

The walls are pockmarked. Bullet holes, impact craters

where Kevlar and flesh met drywall. A smear of blood. Furniture toppled and tossed aside, chairs splayed and snapped. The only SWAT operator who isn't unconscious or crawling is being dragged by his foot to the wide-open window.

Dragged by a windswept man visible only to her.

Roger, his skin liminal and smoking, pulls the SWAT operator like he's hauling out the trash.

"Hey!" Caitlyn shouts and blinks herself across the room. Thirty feet in a thought, faster than her voice. Her hands strike Roger in his back. The momentum sends him stumbling, out through the window, down, down.

Something remains. A static transference between two mental bodies. Then a flash before Caitlyn's eyes: wet skin in dark, steaming waters. A bathtub.

A second flash: long desert roads, and Roger driving the highway in his RV. He senses something behind him, turns to see—

Caitlyn, in the hotel room, raising her shimmering hands. Was that Roger's memory?

Free, the SWAT operator stumbles out of the room. At the fluttering curtain, Caitlyn looks down. Had Roger fallen the whole way?

Then she feels that subsonic pop. Roger appears in the room, body swaddled in mist. He is not like his mugshot; his face is unscarred. A hazy specter, vibrating in and out of focus.

"You..." he hisses, eyes narrowing to dim slits. "How can you see me?"

"I can see you," she says. "And I can stop you."

"You're not part of God's plan."

"I'm a wrinkle. Now give yourself up, Roger. The police have you surrounded."

"You... know my name." It isn't a question but some frightful epiphany. Fear widens his eyes.

Then he turns and runs through the wall.

Caitlyn doesn't think. Doesn't question. Doesn't wonder what's on the other side. She just follows him.

The adjacent room is empty. The one after that is being evacuated. In the third room, she catches a glimpse of Roger, blurry body diving into the floor.

She dives after him. Past pipes and ducts and nests of electrical cables. Comes to a stop in a dark bathroom.

Dammit, she's lost him. Somehow, he had—

A body bursts from a bathtub, wet and steaming and wearing a gas mask. Roger yanks the rubber free from his face—his real face—and crawls onto the tiles.

"No, no no no. Too soon. Not like this."

He grabs a pile of clothes by the toilet. Sweatpants and a gray hoodie cling to heaving, wet skin. Trembling, it takes him ten seconds to pull them on.

"You can't run, Roger," Caitlyn says, her voice a breeze in the darkness. "I'll follow you and—"

There is a shuddering. The world tilts to the left. Caitlyn, falling through the wall, through the ceiling now, up, up, where the spinning sky swallows her and the black curtains drop.

"What was that?" she gasps, feeling the shapes around her. Plastic, an arm rest, somebody's hand.

"A bumpy landing," Michaels says. "Jesus, you really were there. It all just stopped."

"He's three rooms down, one floor below. He's in sweatpants and a gray hoodie."

The jet engines whine. The runway rattles. Michaels relays the description into the mic.

"I can follow him," she says. "I just need to get my balance—"

"Caitlyn, we've got it now. Take a deep breath."

She feels the tears on her cheek. How fast they'd come. *Dammit, not now, no time to cry.*

"You did great," Carruthers says. "Let the police handle it."

"I *need* to stop him."

"And that's what you did," Michaels says. "Here, take this. Wipe your cheeks."

She blots her eyes with the cool napkin, catches the scent of copper.

"I didn't mean to cry. I just got worked up."

"Caitlyn, you're not crying," Michaels says. "You're bleeding."

[31]

THE INTERGLOBAL HAS SIX STAIRWELLS AND EIGHT ELEVATORS, AND within minutes most are swarming with officers. Boots clap off concrete, shouts of "clear!" as armored bodies push up, floor by floor.

On the eighth, a glimpse of a man in wet sweatpants doubling back into an elevator.

On ten, a hooded shape darts into a stairwell.

Between floors twelve and fourteen, the police and the backup SWAT team convene as Roger disappears behind an unlabeled door.

"He's on thirteen," an officer says into the radio as the two groups merge. "Looks like HVAC, no guest rooms here."

Every building of a certain height hides floors dedicated to ventilation and plumbing. Some are called Mechanical Floors or Service Floors and some are unlabeled. Here, no guests are booked for the thirteenth floor, and without a keycard, the elevator zooms past. But tonight, Roger is taking the stairs.

WHILE A DESPERATE MAN crashes into a folded ladder and stumbles past humming fans, two miles away a black Ford Explorer enters

Sumner Tunnel. Sirens and lights as the escort motorcycles clear traffic. The deputy on the lead bike listens to the radio, trying to make sense of it all. The chaos downtown, the pickup at Logan. He'd never been to the private terminal before. Never escorted feds from a Learjet to an active crime scene.

Feds, and a blind woman.

Exiting the tunnel, the deputy can't shake the feeling that there is a storm coming. A charge in the air. And improbable as it is, the SUV trailing him is the source.

Silly thought. *Focus on the road.*

In the Explorer, Caitlyn's head thumps against glass. Like a rubber band, her mens corpus snaps back, and now comes the darkness.

"I can't focus. The motion, the bumps, it bleeds over."

"Don't worry about it," Carruthers says. "You've done enough."

"They've got him pinned on the mechanical floor," Michaels says. "There's no way out." He fingers his earpiece, listens. "They're deploying flashbangs to flush him out. Look."

Sure enough, from five blocks away, the hotel looms into view. The facade, a teal grillwork of glass. Then a bar of windows brightens in pulses. Shadows, rifles in hand, frozen in mid-motion like a flickering zoetrope.

"Game over," Carruthers says. "They'll have—"

A distant pop, nearly noiseless, and if Carruthers hadn't been fixated on the building, she never would have seen it. One window is dark. Then it is not. A flower of shards opens up.

"Oh shit," the driver says. "Oh shit, oh shit, you see that? Something just fell from the hotel. Oh, Christ, what was that?"

Silence for the space of a few heartbeats. In that emptiness, Michaels keeps his finger to his earpiece and closes his eyes.

"That was our suspect," he says and lets out a deep sigh.

· · ·

WITH THE FIRE DEPARTMENT ASSISTING, two EMTs push the stretcher to the path that ended Roger's descent. No need to hurry, but they always do. News vans circle, vultures eager for a glimpse of the meat.

In a bed of snapped branches, where the grass meets the sidewalk, the EMTs find Roger. One look tells them this is a recovery operation. The body is broken, the gutters steaming crimson in the fog. Roger isn't the first jumper the EMTs have seen, not even the first this year. Still, there is something sad about this twisted man, one shoe on, the other knocked off from the impact, lying sideways in the storm drain, fast filling with blood.

32

HOTEL INTERGLOBAL, BOSTON
THURSDAY - 10:00 P.M.

LONG BEFORE THE EVENTS AT THE HOTEL INTERGLOBAL BECOME THE subject of classified hearings. Before the name Roger Fenton becomes synonymous with the God's Breath Killer. Before cleaning crews are dispatched from an unknown yet surgically effective agency. Before all of this happens, Michaels stands in the parking lot, thinking, *How do we tame this runaway narrative?*

Unlike San Francisco five days ago, and Santa Rosa two weeks back, there are dozens of witnesses here from local, state, and federal agencies. There will be no debriefing en masse. No way to gather the wounded, some who are already on the way to the hospital. While doctors set bones, there will be questions. Calls to worried wives. Radio chatter.

The odds of a conspiracy collapsing can be mathematically calculated. As the quantity of conspirators increases, failure trends toward inevitability. Cover-ups complicate matters. Technically, a cover-up is an additional conspiracy with an ongoing cost of maintenance. The more people involved, the more conspiracies crammed under a grand tent, the sooner it all comes down.

It took six years before Edward Snowden exposed PRISM from the heart of the NSA. At the time of the moon landing, NASA employed 400,000 people. Had the landing been faked, its exposure would be certain in under four years. If faking climate change or lacing vaccines with microchips were schemes of the global scientific community, they would have only lasted for three.

These are the calculations racing through Michaels's mind. When he factors in outsiders, tonight will be tight. The days that follow will be critical. So, time to work.

Within half an hour, he has a list of Roger's primary contacts. Carruthers compiles the secondaries: radio operators, hotel personnel, armory sergeants that helped Boston SWAT gear up. Then it's on to debriefing, sealing affidavits, cataloguing and classifying. Not thrilling but methodically exhaustive by design. Movies always skip the paperwork. Too bad. Michaels finds it as complicated as the chase.

At 10:30 he puts in a brief call with his coordinator. Unsurprisingly, Nox is up to speed. Perhaps he watched Roger's final moments playing out in crisp colors. Streamed it through fiber lines reserved for the president, the Pentagon, and those with a skeleton key.

At 10:42 Michaels tours the mechanical floor. Police tape covers the shattered glass, Roger's final dive. Michaels visualizes the trajectory. A long jump, out and down, onto the Rose Kennedy Greenway. The broken limbs of a magnolia trace Roger's final descent. Below, CTS decon is power washing the concrete.

At 10:51 Carruthers finds Michaels in the elevator and gives him the news. Roger was pronounced dead on arrival. *Good*, Michaels almost says, but he holds his tongue.

At 11:07 they sign forms taking collection of Roger's belongings, which include 1× gas mask, 1× gas tank, 1× key to a self-storage locker, 1× digital camera, 2× notebooks, including handwritten descriptions of nearly a dozen locations across the country, half of which are crime scenes. Missing pages, misspelled words, entire paragraphs crossed out. The final entry is two pages. A description of the Marriot conference rooms. And a conference pamphlet featuring Dr. Francis Linamore, brown ink beneath it: *ROOM 1511*.

"Makes your head spin, doesn't it?" Carruthers asks, bagging the journal. "We're here, going through this kill list—probably going to be sorting for a month—and Francis is a mile away, sleeping without a care in the world."

"That's what we do," Michaels says, rotating the fountain pen. The finial has been chewed down, more potential DNA. "A good foundation keeps everything stable."

Carruthers's phone chirps. "Damn, Caitlyn's downstairs. I thought you got her a hotel?"

"I thought you did."

They share a grin. Somewhere, somehow, in the past ten days, they've grown a little closer.

"You okay with the final walkthrough?" Michaels asks.

"I'm sure we'll manage without you," Carruthers says. "Go. Get her a hotel room. And one for me too. And whatever docking station you plug into. But not here. I need distance from this glorious mess."

Michaels stops by the elevator, watches Carruthers heading back into Roger's room. He calls out from his island of quiet. "Denise, you did good."

"Well," she corrects. "We all did well."

[PART 3]

They are not long, the weeping and the laughter,
    Love and desire and hate:
    I think they have no portion in us after
    We pass the gate.

They are not long, the days of wine and roses:
    Out of a misty dream
    Our path emerges for a while, then closes
    Within a dream.

— Ernest Dowson
Vitae summa brevis spem nos vetat incohare longam

33

The Hyatt Regency is a fifteen-minute drive from the crime scene, along the narrow streets of Boston's downtown crossing. Michaels and Caitlyn hitch a ride with a rookie officer who chatters the whole way. Caitlyn is quiet, and he has come to assume that silence means she is either thinking or sleeping. The third possibility—her trick that led them to Roger—comes from a different quiescence, more monk-like than solemn. After they check in to the hotel and Michaels hands her a keycard, she finally speaks.

"They said he broke the window and leapt. I heard someone saying they tried to stop him."

"Yeah, that's what I've been told."

"Did you see him?"

"Did I see Roger's body?"

"Yes."

"Yeah, when they were loading him into the ambulance."

"And? How'd he look?"

"Like he won't be bothering anyone anymore."

Caitlyn nods. "Good."

They stand by the elevators, waiting. The clink of glasses and the clamor of the nearby cocktail bar drifts out. Someone laughs.

"That's the hotel bar, isn't it?" she asks.

"It is."

She wipes a lock of hair from her cheek. "Have a pint with me, agent. We're in Boston, after all."

WITH TACT, timing, and a few curse words muttered her way, Carruthers intercepts the body cam footage as it makes its way from SWAT Mobile Command to the police station. She downloads .MP4 files from all six cameras of the primary team and five from the backup team. One is unrecorded, operator error.

Sitting here, in the back of Mobile Command, she cues up video after video. There are glimpses, flashlight images. The man in the bed, now identified as a transient, flex-cuffed and fleeing the room as an invisible assault rages on. Bones snapping. A SWAT operator tossed like a doll. Nauseating, all of it. Like the room became sentient and tore itself apart.

The second wave of SWAT came directly from the station. Carruthers watches as the teams catch up to Roger in the stairwell. Glimpses of a man running past industrial cooling units, lockers, Internet switches. Shouts of "Clear! Come out! To the right! There!" The adrenaline chatter people never remember. A distant vibration, and the cameras pan hard left. The window is pebbles. A scream comes quick and ends; jumpers are rarely silent. Then the cameras rush past storage bins and HVAC piping and the hole comes into view.

Tempered glass doesn't break like its annealed counterpart. The entire pane is gone. Only a few holding bolts remain, the rubber seals drooping in the darkness. Two of the cameras step close enough to look out and down. Thirteen floors below, Roger is just a gray shape, breaking branches and then coming to a hard stop.

Carruthers logs the time and bags the cams. There's an odd weight here, holding a human's final seconds. And as she steps out of Mobile Command, she looks up to the open window, which is now crisscrossed with police tape and safety board. The last of Roger has been hosed off the concrete. Tomorrow the window will be repaired. In twenty-four hours, it will be business as usual.

She taps her phone, starts composing a text to her daughter. It has occurred to Carruthers they are on the same time zone. There will be paperwork and depositions to handle, but maybe, when she's done, she could fly down to Florida.

Hey sweetie, it's Other Mom. I'm on your coast and wondering…

She pauses, thumb over the *send* button. Who is she kidding? They haven't texted in two weeks. Haven't talked on the phone since she found out about Berkeley. It kills Carruthers how that all turned out. Two stubborn women, a generation apart, each communicating with silence. And now, filled with the thrill of stopping evil—real evil—Carruthers can't work up the courage to share it with the most important person in her life.

Coward, she thinks and puts her phone away.

BEYOND THE CURTAIN OF SHADOWS, there is warmth and laughter and the clink of glass. She steadies herself against the table with one hand. With the other, she finds her beer bottle. A sip confirms the worst: it's almost empty.

"Can I ask you something?" Michaels asks.

Caitlyn senses the buzz in his voice. Men sometimes gain an effervescent inflection when they drink. "That's the phrase people use when they really mean, 'Can I ask about your blindness?'" A creak as he shifts in his chair. "But go ahead. Only if I get to ask one as well."

"Well, that depends on the question."

"Relax, Hoover, I'm not going to grill you on chemtrails. We're just having fun."

"Be advised, I'm under strict orders to avoid fun," Michaels says. "I believe it's a fireable offense."

Caitlyn smirks. Her mesmerizing gaze alternates between focused and far-off. And yet he knows he shouldn't read into it any more than someone should analyze him by his preference in bourbon. Such things do not define people, only give them texture. He likes that he can sit across from her and not worry about eye contact. Social interaction is exhausting, an ever-changing simulation of expectations and outcomes. With her, it's different, relaxed, in part due to her blindness, but mostly due to her kindness.

Another sip of bourbon. "You were right. It's a question about your vision."

"Well, shoot, Agent. Now I think less of ya." She drains the last of her beer and raises a hand, signaling in the general direction of the bartender. He shouts a confirmation, and Caitlyn returns a thumbs-up.

"So what does this feel like?" Michaels asks. "I mean, drinking a beer or getting a buzz on or—"

"Smoking a joint?"

"Yeah, I guess. Sensory perception interests me, especially—"

"If you're sensory impaired? Okay, try something for me. Close your eyes."

"If you're planning on ditching me, there are better ways."

"Not yet, but I might spit in your drink. Now go on, close them."

He shuts his eyes. Darkness, then movement, a shift of the table. Her elbows perhaps, lifting off the edge. Warmth passing by on his right.

"Listen to the room. You hear that couple to your, maybe... nine o'clock? They're fighting. Something about money. They're trying to do it quietly, but that just makes it louder. No one whispers in public when it's good. Hear them?"

Michaels strains to isolate their voices from the last-call chatter. Nothing. Just a dozen conversations. And then it emerges: a man's nasally intonations and a woman's cutting response.

They're past the opening arguments and deep in the cross-examination of their marriage.

"Your eyes still closed?"

"Yes."

"So how do your toes feel, going into your third bourbon?"

"Warm. Like a nice pair of socks."

"And my voice, what am I doing now, while I speak?"

"I dunno. Tilting your head?"

"And you, Agent Michaels," she says. The table shifts again, and her hands are on his wrists now, following his forearm, up his elbow to his shoulder, his neck, his cheeks. She takes his face in her palms. He beholds their softness, the velvet touch as her fingers rise from his jaw, finding the hollows of his cheeks. "When you smile, you exhale through your nostrils, just a little. Like your nose is making way for the corners of your lips to rise, but you fight it. Ah, you're doing it now. I've embarrassed you." She lets go.

"You've surprised me. Lot of that going around."

"So what's it like? It's like touching the darkness and letting it touch you back. It's submission and serenity and a whole lot of fucking trust. You can open your eyes."

The dim lounge is momentarily bright. He watches her follow the edge of the table back and settle into her seat. A new beer sits to her right and the pretzels have been refilled. She pops a few into her mouth.

"Does that answer your question?"

"Not in the slightest." He laughs. And damn, she is right: he does exhale to stifle his smile. "I meant, like, do you get the spins if you can't see?"

"Ask silly questions, win silly prizes." She takes a sip from her beer. "My turn."

"Fire away."

"Where's home for you? Carruthers pegs you for Seattle. I'm getting a Brooklyn vibe."

"Home? I have a condo in St. Louis I haven't seen in months. My houseplants are probably dead. Does that count?"

"Succulents," she says. "Perfect for absentee homeowners. One ice cube once a month and you're golden."

"I'd find a way to kill them. What's the opposite of green thumb? Black thumb?"

"Murder feet."

"Murder feet?"

Alcohol-flushed, she nods. "That's the technical term."

"Right, well, when it comes to plants, that's me: Agent Murder Foot."

"What's the strangest case you've ever worked?"

"Isn't it my turn?"

"You asked a question: what's the opposite of green thumb?"

"That's... well, technically, I guess. Okay, strangest case: this one, by a long shot."

"Excluding this. Carruthers called you a Sasquatch catcher. I saw the way the FBI looked at you in the meeting this morning."

"That really was this morning, huh?"

"So, weirdest case. Or let's say in the top five. And don't stall by taking a sip of whiskey."

Wow, she is perceptive. The glass is almost at his lips.

"The Frankengoat of Wyoming."

She leans in. "Oh, this night just got interesting."

"I was new, just poached from the NSA. We caught some chatter about this phenomena in the backcountry of Wyoming. Hunters, ranchers, good old boys out on BLM land. Most described the entity as goat-like, but patchy, its parts a bit wrong. Someone swore they saw it walking on two legs."

"So was it Internet weirdos? Like Slenderman?"

"We thought so, at first. But then some photos came in. A drone video, only noticed when the operator checked it later. Some trail cams. And a hunter, way off-season. Image analysis proved they were undoctored. So there it was, three sets of visual evidence, another half dozen accounts, all swearing they'd seen the Frankengoat of Wyoming. I drew the short straw and hiked a week into the Beartooth Mountains, near the Montana border. I am not a camper. And after a week without conversation, the mind tends to... wander. That's when I saw it."

"The Frankengoat?"

Michaels nods, then realizes the gesture was more for his own telling than his audience. "Predawn, I was coming into this canyon knee-high with fog. A few hundred wild goats grazing. And there it was, this... freak. I mean, I was a thousand feet away, and even then, I could tell it was all wrong. The horns were huge, almost branches. The fur was a bad quilt. And it didn't walk but sort of staggered, sick-like. All the goats kept at a distance. I shadowed it for about two hours as it trailed the herd. Its eyes caught the dawn and lit up like embers. I had a rifle and a scope so I glassed it. Kept my crosshairs on it as it hobbled around and twitched. Then it stood up."

"It stood up? What, on its rear legs?"

"On its rear legs."

"Like a bear?"

"Like a very tired person in a goat suit," Michaels says. "It unzipped itself and I watched as a guy in his twenties stumbled out, found a bush to squat, and did his business."

"So was he like a furry or something?"

"A grad student. Some German studying the migratory patterns of mountain goats. It was mid-May and he'd been at it since late February. He was getting monthly care packages in a bear box at the trailhead. God, I couldn't get within ten feet of that goat suit. It was ripe."

"So the great Frankengoat of Wyoming was a student. Did he know how close he almost came to getting shot?"

"I told him but it didn't seem to click. He had this glazed look, feral. Like those photos of people in the old west when they first saw a camera."

The bartender stops at the table. "Last call, folks."

"Aww, you think that applies to us?" Caitlyn whispers, "We're heroes."

Michaels considers the dim bar, the patrons now clearing out. The bourbon like warm coals that could use some rekindling. "Give me a moment."

Caitlyn senses the table shift as he stands up. His shoes shuffling against the rug. She likes to think she is doing well, or well enough. Still, sharp fear occasionally cuts her buzz and renders her keenly aware that she is not only socially interacting but also three thousand miles from home. In reality, and not in her head.

A breeze of body heat passing to her right. The clink of something heavy placed on the table. "He said we can stay as long as we lock up."

"No shit?"

"No shit," Michaels says. "He locked up the cabinet but I procured us a bottle of Cragganmore."

"That badge sure opens a few doors."

"Yeah, it can," Michaels says. He leaves out how five hundred dollars also bought the bartender's trust.

"To opened doors then," Caitlyn says and raises her beer.

"Here here."

In the dwindling hum of the hotel's bar, under the dim buzz of unpronounceable alt-rock bands, they toast to each other.

CARRUTHERS, waiting for the elevator as the guests filter out of the cocktail lounge. She smiles to a young couple, their mood dour, the martinis seeping from their pores. They don't smile back.

Beyond them, in a far dark corner, she catches a glimpse of colorful hair. Caitlyn, having a drink, and Carruthers thinks she might just go join her.

She stops at the entrance. The sign says CLOSED and the bartender's wiping the glasses. There's someone else sharing Caitlyn's table, posture intimate.

Good for them. Carruthers heads back to the elevator, to her room, to her bed, alone, and within seconds, exhaustion embraces her.

THREE FINGERS further into the bottle of scotch, Michaels asks, "So what's your story?"

"You don't have dossiers on me?" Caitlyn asks.

"Nothing a quick Google search wouldn't show."

"My story, huh?"

Michaels observes her right hand reaching out, tracing the edge of the table, cutting inward, and finding its way to the bottle. She brings it in close. With her left hand she does the same, follows the edge, sweeps inside, finds the glass. Satisfied with the placement, she uncorks the bottle, raises the glass, and tips them together. A one-two pour, near perfect. "My story isn't very interesting."

"As someone who profiles and obsesses over deviancy, I respectfully fucking disagree."

The corners of her mouth rise and her gaze falls toward the far corner of the bar. She is a book of infinite secrets. Her smile coyly acknowledges this.

"Let's start with your accent. I detect Eastern European, East African, and maybe some French. You grew up abroad, moved. Military family, I'm guessing."

"Professional hippies. I went to international schools until fourteen. Then I was homeschooled, different country each year. I didn't really consider myself American. I mean, that was just the passport I had."

"It's a good passport to have."

"Sometimes. But it also made us targets. My parents weren't rich, but people acted like we were. 'You're American. If you get in trouble, just call the embassy.' Like we were on a first-name basis with the chief of consular services."

In the NSA, Michaels had met expats that assumed Uncle Sam was there to assist every citizen who got robbed or locked up abroad. The truth is the opposite. Uncle Sam might airvac a high-value citizen, but the days of helicopter rides off embassy rooftops died with the fall of Saigon. There are nine million in the American diaspora. Burst your appendix in Bhutan, you're finding your own doctor.

"Your file mentioned Argentina."

"We were there for a time." She counts her fingers. "Brazil. Colombia. New Zealand. Indonesia. India. Kenya. One year in a place, and then we'd move on. My mom was an NGO consultant. My dad helped expats with financial planning."

"Must have been nice growing up all over."

She strokes the Polynesian tattoo on her wrist. "Sometimes it feels like a different life. Americans have all these assumptions, like this is how the whole world is, here in Boston or San Francisco or wherever. That they've got it better than the rest. Land of the free, but oh, you better have a car."

"But you're an American."

"See, that's my point. Abroad, I considered myself human. American is just part of my identity, a slice, like life before the curtain came down."

"The curtain?" Is she tapping her left temple? No, she is gesturing to her eye. "Ah, that must've been hard. Seeing the world, then, you know... not."

"It came in waves. Little floaters here and there. Things in the corner, out of focus, like breezy curtains."

"What's the last thing you remember seeing?"

"My parents..." she says. "Drowning."

Michaels swallows. What to say? *I'm sorry?* A default response, but Caitlyn seems to hate shallow formality. Instead, he says, "If you want to talk about it, I'll listen. If not..."

She finds the glass and pours a sip. Beyond the curtains that hang in her mind, she can still picture the golden flecks of the sun on the East African coast. "We were sailing south, off Mombasa," Caitlyn says, "following the Mozambique Current. We'd had the boat for a few years. A Cal 40, nothing special, but it was home. I don't remember what we hit. A container or a shoal, at least. That's what they told me, later, when I woke up from my coma. Our maps were outdated. Three of us went in the drink. A week later, only I came out."

She stops there. No need to mention the details in polite company. Flashes of the hull splitting like twigs. How the kitchen collapsed. The fiberglass and wood formed a lattice, and the waters mixed with oil and gasoline and coated her throat.

"You were at sea for a week?"

"A life raft," Caitlyn says. "I don't remember how I got there. But I do remember watching myself sleep. I remember the nights. I'd go for these walks across water like black glass. I'd look back and see that dinghy, the little light blinking, stars above mirrored below. And everything seemed... okay. I'd watch these great fish circling in the deep: iridescent eels, Moorish idols with their ebony and yellow stripes, and bell jellyfish towing tendrils of silk. I fell in love with it all. I couldn't be angry that my parents were gone, because they weren't. They were the sea and the fish now. They would make their way to all corners of the planet just as they'd wanted. I could not be angry. I just missed them. And I sensed that if I walked too far, I might never come back. That's when the fishing boat found me. They were Bengali, and I think they were disappointed they didn't get a reward. An American girl, at sea, right? Like finding a mermaid. The rest of that year was flashes. Physical therapy. First in Nairobi, then in Cape Town, then London. There was a doctor here at UCSF doing new things with retinal stem cell injections. A needle in the eye seemed like a fair trade, and it worked too, at least in fifteen of the sixteen subjects."

"Those are bum odds, Caitlyn. I'm sorry."

"Yeah, well, at least I got to watch the curtain drop here, in my home country."

"Your parents would be proud," Michaels says. "I mean that. Roger had a kill list with seven more names on it. We cut him off at the midpoint. Seven lives are sleeping safe. Because of you."

"You would've found him."

"Maybe. Maybe not. We got lucky and you sure helped."

When she smiles, he thinks it might be the most beautiful smile he's ever seen. The corners of her eyes make tiny creases, two crescents just for him.

Beautiful because of the sincerity.

Because of her strength that led to this moment.

"Walk me back to my room, Agent Michaels."

THE ELEVATOR DOORS are hardly closed when she takes the hand that is holding her elbow and guides it to her waist. Whether he pulls her into his embrace first, or she pulls his face to hers, it is impossible to say. In the ride up nine floors, they feel only each other. Sticky lips, beating hearts, desperate hands against fabric and skin, fueled by adrenaline and good scotch and the shared vulnerability that they are strangers here, in this new town, and that maybe they can be new people too.

Giggling, stumbling, walking down the hallway. They pause by her door as she finds the lock and slips in the keycard. She feels the light switch and turns it on as a courtesy. Caitlyn doesn't need to cloak herself in darkness to be comfortable with her body; she knows others find it pleasing to behold.

Yet Michaels lingers at the door. His fingers slip from her hand.

"Caitlyn, I want to... Trust me," he says. "But I shouldn't, really."

He drinks her in, backlit by the lights, perfect and mysterious, her confident grin giving way to something harder. "I'm not drunk," she says. "I'm not some pity case being taken advantage of."

"No, no, I didn't mean that. It's just that..." Her gaze becomes a squint. His skin tightens, body awkward and clumsy. She just took a leap of faith and he stepped back from catching her. "It's just that technically we're still working together. This could taint the investigation."

"Taint, huh?"

"Poor choice of words."

A smirk, polite, all the spontaneity from the elevator now gone. This is it, a receding glimpse of what could have been. One future fading.

"Well, Agent Michaels, I respect your professionalism." She leans forward, hands finding his chin. She places a soft kiss on his cheek. "Goodnight. And thank you for a memorable day."

He pauses at the door. "You know, after this is over, I mean, once we wrap up the paperwork. Who knows, right?"

"Yeah, who knows?" Her fingers find the light switch, bathing the room in darkness.

"Who knows?" Michaels cringes as he takes the elevator down. "Just ask her for a rain check, you idiot. Who knows?" It isn't the worst line he's ever muttered. But it's in the top three.

BOSTON
FRIDAY - 7:45 A.M., EST

"CHRIST, YOU LOOK WORSE THAN ROGER," CARRUTHERS SAYS, SITTING down at the table.

Morning, and the hotel's breakfast is in full swing. Silverware scrapes plate as guests load up on omelets and dry bacon. Business calls compete with CNN. Despite promising to sleep until Tuesday, Carruthers is in fine form. To Michaels, every light is too bright.

"You look like my phone when I leave the cable at home and try to make twenty percent last all weekend," she adds.

"I didn't sleep very well," Michaels says between bites of a Denver omelet.

"And you smell like a gas station. You didn't mix, did you?"

"Mix?"

"Beer plus liquor, never been sicker."

"No. I stuck with whiskey."

Carruthers opens her laptop and digs into her eggs Benedict. "The swabs off Roger's party toys came in," she says. "Have you read them?"

Michaels shakes his head. The room wobbles with it.

She turns her laptop around. "The tank in Roger's hotel room is a match for the tank in Oakland. DZ3, mostly LSD mixed with something called Vetalar."

"That's a horse tranquilizer, brand-name ketamine."

"Together it's some potent party vapor. Really spooked the lab techs. I had to assure them it wasn't something new on the street. Good news is it's short-acting. Bad news is it's seriously caustic to the brain. It corrodes the insular cortex. You know what that's responsible for?"

"No."

"Hold up. I'm going to savor this Folger's moment." She sips her coffee.

"You through?"

"This cocktail obliterates the ego. Total separation. That'd explain why Roger's mens corpus didn't match his physical self. Hell, take enough and he'd project an eggplant."

"That's unsettling." Michaels turns around, waves. "S'cuse me! Do you mind turning the TV down?"

The hostess obliges, silencing Anderson Cooper. A few surly travelers give Michaels the stink eye. He doesn't care.

"You're cute when you're hung over," Carruthers says. "Anyways, let's review: we've got a dead man driving coast to coast with a kill list and enough chemicals to fuel a rave."

Michaels closes his eyes, rubs his temples. Imagines Roger, behind the wheel of the RV, rumbling down the interstates. Snapping photos and crossing off names with his stupid fountain pen. Roger, talking to himself as his mind starts to melt.

"So the timeline is Roger kills the chemist, McNare," Michaels says, "Does it the old-fashioned way, face to face."

Michaels pictures it: deep cuts, then the promise they would stop. If only McNare would just give up the formula, teach Roger how to cook it. Desperate lips spilling secrets as the pen moves across paper.

"Something feels off," Michaels says. "So Roger spooks in SF, ditches in Oakland, and this was plan B?"

"Or plan J, K, and L," Carruthers says. "He had a locker here in Boston with more cocktail, ready to roll."

"Then why torch his RV? Why not just let it sit until it gets towed instead of drawing attention?"

"I don't know. Maybe huffing industrial quantities of psychotropics stunts the judgment? Just a thought."

"This feels like we got too lucky."

"We did. We have Caitlyn. Roger wasn't anticipating that. Speaking of getting lucky, how's she feeling this morning?"

"I don't know, why?"

Carruthers tilts her head.

"What?"

"Nothing. I mean, I saw you two closing out the bar. Judging by the body language, I guess I got the trajectory wrong. What's our move from here?"

Michaels checks the updates on his tablet. "I'm briefing my supervisor. Then we'll pull surveillance by the end of the day. We're waiting on the Koreans to get us Tae Hwan Kim's death certificate. Zara Eisler's still a ghost. Interpol's got nothing."

"Think we'll ever get the big picture?" Carruthers asks. "The chessboard past endgame?"

"Someone will. That's past my pay grade. Best we can hope for is a glimpse. A few key moves that turned out all right."

The waitress takes their plates. Michaels hands over his credit card. When she is out of earshot, he leans in.

"You know what I keep coming back to? This feels like more than revenge. Like a need for closure. Maybe this wouldn't have happened if Chase and the government had taken responsibility. Roger—hell, everyone in Clearwater—they got a raw deal."

"This country's built on raw deals," Carruthers says. "Roger got boned by bureaucracy. Teddy's in a coma. You've seen the cohort's prognosis. They've got more medical problems than the first responders on 9/11. Most are nearing sixty and Chase thinks few will make it to seventy. But just 'cause Uncle Sam stiffed you doesn't mean you can go on a rampage."

"No, of course not," Michaels says. "But there should be some sort of accountability."

"Boldly spoken for a government spook."

"A spook with a migraine."

The waitress returns with the receipt. Michaels signs it, leaving a generous tip.

"And Michaels," Carruthers says as they walk through the lobby, "don't start growing a heart. It'll take blood away from that beautiful mind."

HE PICKS up the braille embossing from the hotel's business center. He inspects each page, the print on the front, the raised dots on the rear. For good measure, he attaches *SIGN HERE* stickers to the signature line. Maybe it'll help.

Upstairs, he knocks on the door. Nine hours ago he'd stood here, invited in, and he'd refused. What an asshole. And now here he is, delivering a folder full of NDAs, contracts promising federal penalties for disclosing any aspect of the case. *Good luck getting Caitlyn in the mood after this.*

Another knock, another thirty-second wait. It is a quarter to nine, and he imagines her curled up beneath the sheets, one foot poking out, a different tint of polish on each toe.

He slides the folder under the door. Takes out his phone. Writes her the following text:

> Caitlyn, thank you for your assistance. I slid some forms under the door for you to sign. I'll be by later.
>   -Michaels.

WHILE THE CONNECTION ENCRYPTS, Michaels studies his video reflection: puffy eyes, dry lips, his cheeks pallid like the walls of a truck stop bathroom. Then his supervisor fills the screen, backlit, blown out by white. Nox is traveling.

"News says you've been busy out there," Nox says.

"It's under control, sir. Or rather, it will be soon. I've got some containment ideas—"

The supervisor waves his hand. "We're already on it."

"You're handling it?"

"We're flooding social media with deepfakes. Everything from a training exercise gone wrong to Harvard kids with club drugs."

"You're diluting it," Michaels says. It was half question, half statement. Tactically, introducing misinformation has risks. It can draw attention back to an originating event. Often, there's gravity there. It keeps the public talking, unless—

"Word's out on the God's Breath Killer," Nox says. "Branding has stuck, whether we like it or not. We'll leak an update, buy you some time. Now tell me about Roger. You're sure he's on the slab?"

"Absolutely. Facial and fingerprints are a match. Rapid DNA linked him to several hits in CODIS. We'll be closing a few cases for the FBI. And we're flying Dr. Munson in for the autopsy. I don't expect any curveballs."

"We'll send a friendly to assist. What else?"

"A cadaver dog in Texas dug up a corpse behind Roger's shed. His dog. Looks like he tested DZ3 on it around Christmas, probably trying to get the dose right."

"Yes, I just read about that."

So what else have you read? That detail hadn't come from Michaels's report. Someone else is feeding the coordinator information.

"Let's talk containment," Nox says.

"A challenge. We have twenty-two primary contacts with Roger in the past two days, from the concierge to SWAT to the transient he paid to throw us off. Secondary contacts are pushing two hundred. That's just an estimate."

"Focus on the primary, locals only. Get signatures. We'll dampen secondaries, plus the feds. What about Ms. Grey?"

Michaels's finger twitches. "What about her?"

"Thirty-six hours ago your report listed her as a dead end. Now she's a tactical ally, on-site. What changed?"

"My mind, sir. Frankly, I saw it fit to bring her in. As a specialist, given her ability—"

"And after she eavesdropped on a classified briefing."

"Yes, sir." Michaels's posture straightens. "The thing is, if Caitlyn hadn't gotten involved, we'd still be sweeping the Inter-Global for Roger. Maybe she's the reason he fled to Boston, maybe not. But she's definitely the reason we found him."

"How fortunate for us that she chose to get involved."

Silence. A hard stare near impossible to break. Michaels wipes a clammy palm on his knee. "Sir, is there something you want to say?"

"Keep up the good work, Agent," Nox says. "Keep Caitlyn close. She could prove useful. Oh, and some advice, man to man: never turn down a good thing."

The last thing Michaels sees before the connection ends is a knowing smirk on Nox's thin lips.

THE CLASS-ACTION LAWSUIT AGAINST CLEARWATER AND THE UNITED States government listed eleven plaintiffs. Two are deceased. One is in a coma and well on his way. One is MIA, last seen boarding a bus to Mexico. The seven who remain stateside may feel alone, but they are not. For the past thirty-six hours, they have been tailed by rotating teams, mostly ignorant they were persons of interest in a nationwide manhunt. They can go about their lives being silently extraordinary.

At 10:00 a.m. EST, the orders go out to six states and fourteen agents. Operation: Clearwater Retrieval is on pause.

AT THE BUNS Away Bakery in Savannah, Georgia, Lucy Oates-Deanna sips her coffee and watches the news. After another suspension, the ex-president is back on social media, bemoaning stolen elections and big tech. Lucy's hemorrhoids are flaring. Though they are physiologically unrelated, she equates the two.

Beneath the headline, a crawl reads, *FBI tightlipped; sources say the God's Breath Killer dead in Newark car crash.*

. . .

IN BOULDER, Colorado, adjunct Martin Peck teaches his Friday seminar on existentialist lit. While the students form groups for a close read of Cormac McCarthy, Peck glances out the window to the emerald grass of Norlin Quad. Another gorgeous Colorado day, with summer around the bend. He thinks of his abandoned novels, four shameful stacks yellowing on a shelf in his duplex. He thinks about the pleasing shorts on the women's jogging team. He does not think of the two men playing frisbee in the shade for a second day in a row.

IN SEATTLE, longshoreman Felix Mayer feels an odd click, like a light, long dormant and dusty, now buzzing bright orange in the basement of his mind. Ever aware of such sensations, Felix decides he is clocking out early. He hits the road, driving past his house, straight east, into the rising sun, the Great Cloud Casino on his GPS. Two cars back, a tan Ford Taurus follows.

OUTSIDE SCOTTSDALE, ARIZONA, "THE STRAIGHT SHOOTER" Sam Shepard is sweating up a morning storm in his garage studio for an online audience of three million. His desk, a polished crescent, aluminum and black glass. His decor, subtle fear by way of accented red lights. Today's topics: how vaccines can make you gay, the pedo-lizard people in the Federal Reserve, and are atheists worse than democrats?

Now, however, Sam Stephens slips off script, narrating the live footage of a car burning on the eastern spur of the Jersey turnpike.

"And you see, folks, that's a false flag if I've ever seen one. You know how you can tell? See, it's the pixels. The pixels don't line up right. If you look—and see how we're watching this from a helicopter with, uh, limited perspective? Very convenient that the freeway's almost empty. No wide shots. Okay, if you squint—just go ahead, everyone, and squint—you can see the little imperfections where the software doesn't get the fire right and the flames go all—I dunno what the technical term is—retarded? Can I say that? Or have the thought police marked that word verboten? My floor director's nodding his head. But, folks, the thing is..."

Three cameras, tight on Sam Stephens, all controlled by remotes on his desk. There is no floor director; the last one quit after being paid in exposure. No producer nor script supervisor. There is makeup, however, done by Sam's precise hand. And if the cameras could see beneath the ominous black desk, they would catch the glitter of his OPI nail polish, his paisley yoga pants, and how nice his legs feel, all sleek and compressed.

IT GOES on across the country: a subtle release. Dots on a great grid, following their targets, waiting for approval to disconnect. In a few days they will be home, greeted by annoyed spouses, missed appointments, kids who don't understand that "I can't talk about my job" is both for their protection and legally binding.

36

BOSTON

FRIDAY - NOON

IN CASES WHERE DEATH IS DEEMED UNNATURAL, AN AUTOPSY IS ordered. In cases where an autodidact induces telekinetic powers, secrecy is paramount. Preferring not to leave an exploratory autopsy to the Boston medical examiner, Dr. Munson takes a red-eye. The Department of Defense's Armed Forces Medical Examiner System dispatches a forensic pathologist from Dover Air Force Base to assist. The two arrive simultaneously. On paper, the Boston medical examiner remains in charge. In practice, he is led to the next room, where he watches via video and offers occasional thoughts over the intercom, some followed, some not.

A standard autopsy table is a sight to behold. Stainless steel, brushed to a polish, with short, uniform lines. This one is L-shaped and raised with three perforated dissection grids that allow for easy cleanup of fluids. Twelve hours after Roger leapt out a window, the first incision is made. He is a cool thirty-nine degrees. The L-shaped table also allows the pathologists to work efficiently, one dissecting while the other collects and records. It is an emotionless affair; the human body is an organic machine, and machines, even in their abuses, are mostly unsurprising to those who disassemble them. Still, there are moments that call for the camera, a laptop, and a consultation with specialists that requires encryption.

There is only one intrusion: a federal agent in a well-fitted suit, stopping by, just before lunch.

The Boston medical examiner is acquainted with the Code of Massachusetts Regulations Title 505, which governs the handling of remains and the disclosure of autopsy reports. He is not, however, familiar with the U.S. Code Title 59 Chapter 23. In fact, he understands little on the memorandum of understanding in front of him now, just the implication, summed up at the bottom: *Notwithstanding the above, any disclosure of the listed topics, whether accidental or intentional, verbal or written, is a federal crime punishable under all applicable laws.*

The agent is polite, his face a noetic mask. Yet it is just that, the medical examiner suspects, a mask, one that leaves him unsettled. He signs the document quickly and the federal agent thanks him. He does not leave a copy of the memorandum behind.

As ROGER FENTON lies spread out in pieces, his curiosities placed in labeled containers, six floors above, two hands connect with a friendly squeeze.

"You did a fine thing, Commander," Carruthers says and releases the officer's hand. "Your city owes you a debt of gratitude."

Roger's mens corpus left Commander Harrington out in the halls with a concussion, two broken ribs, and a shattered collarbone. Despite this, Harrington managed to regroup with the second SWAT team and intercept Roger—his physical body— when he backtracked into the stairs. Following him into the labyrinth of air conditioners and water heaters, Harrington was the last to see Roger alive.

"Hell, it's nice of you to say that," Harrington says, squirming. "Truth is, I don't feel like much of anything. It's all kind of fuzzy."

"You will, in time," Carruthers says. "I know of a few necks you saved. Are you comfortable?"

"Well, I suppose. The TV's busted, and the Wi-Fi keeps crashing. But if I get bored, I get to press the morphine button. Then it's like sitting on the beach in Bermuda, minus the wife."

"They'll be letting her visit soon, I'm told. They just need to make sure there weren't any lingering effects from the gas."

Harrington cocks his head. "Gas?"

"That's what the suspect deployed in the hotel room. The booby trap."

"I... I'm not sure I follow."

"The doctor didn't go over it? It's right here, in the chart." Carruthers takes the medical papers from the clipboard at the base of the bed and passes them to Harrington. "Aerosolized DMT and a stimulant as well. You didn't wonder how he managed to hold off your team?"

Harrington squints at the chart. "He... gassed us?"

"Well, sure, but y'all put up a good fight."

Michaels taps the door, steps in. "How's he doing?"

"Comfortable," Carruthers says. "Still a bit groggy. Commander, this is my partner, Michaels. Michaels—"

"We met last night," Michaels says.

This draws further bewilderment. "We did?"

"The doctor didn't mention the gas," Carruthers says quietly yet just loud enough.

"Oh? Oh! Geez, this must be quite the trip then, huh?" Michaels takes the medical chart. "You're in safe hands for the comedown. And good news, they'll let you have visitors soon. I think I saw your wife out in the lobby."

"That reminds me," Carruthers says and swaps clipboards with Michaels. "Since this is an ongoing investigation, we need to get your signature. Just a formality, before they'll let you have visitors. Down at the bottom."

Harrington's eyes bounce from Carruthers to the clipboard on the tray before him, then to Michaels, who passes him a pen, and back to the forms. It's all happening fast. "I really should have the union rep present."

"We can call him," Michaels says. "Attwell, right? Said he'll be here, first thing on Monday."

"Monday?"

"He's fishing in Vermont," Carruthers says.

"But if you want to wait, I'm sure your wife'll understand," Michaels says. "In the meantime, maybe they have some books?"

"We don't want you signing anything you're not comfortable with—"

"Hell, give me that," the commander says. "This isn't my first time tangoing with the feds. Here." He scrawls his name at the bottom of each page, giving it a cursory glance. Michaels makes a note to have someone follow up by phone.

"Say, is it true? What they're saying on the news? That we caught the God's Breath Killer and that van fire down in Jersey's a false flag?"

Carruthers furrows her brow. "Where'd you hear that?"

"*The Straight Shot*, with Sam Stephens," Harrington says. "Before the Wi-Fi died."

Michaels rubs his chin. "Well, in a year where funding plummeted and every agency is scaling back, I suppose it's possible that the government would devote threadbare resources to staging a Hollywood production over a single man. I mean, Sam Stephens has been predicting the rapture for, what, five years now?"

"Ten," Carruthers says.

"Right. So yeah, I mean, anything's possible."

Outside, Michaels tears up Harrington's original chart and drops it into the hazardous-waste chute. A Foundation-revised chart now hangs at the foot of the bed. Harrington never noticed the switch. "And that's the last of the primaries."

"God, I feel dirty," Carruthers says, feeding the vending machine enough change for a Diet Coke.

"Sometimes the best way to beat the conspiracy is to lean into it."

"It helps if you're part of it," she says and takes a sip.

"The foundation of civilization is a presumption of security. It's like oxygen. People with it don't think about it. People without it, that's all they want."

"Tell me something: how'd they pull off the Newark distraction so fast?"

"Staging and stock footage, I presume. Leak it to a hungry local network. A bullet-ridden van bursting into flames goes a long way in the ratings war."

They walk down the hall, passing the nurse's station. "What about the witness?"

"What witness?"

"CNN had a guy saying he watched it all go down."

Michaels shrugs. "Some people say anything to get on TV."

Outside, Michaels hails a taxi while Carruthers pulls out her phone. "I'll see you back at the hotel," she says and orders an Uber.

"You know, you might as well put a homing beacon on your neck," Michaels says and motions to the phone.

"After what I've seen, I'm sure there's a few on me. You enjoy your taxi. Say hi to the nineties."

HE PASSES the elevator ride by ranking the worst hangovers he's had. Paris most likely. Or perhaps Spokane. He'd drank heavily in both places, one to enhance the experience, one to forget he was there. He casts a wary eye at the security camera, wondering, *How much had Nox seen?*

The long halls of the Hyatt stretch on, dimly lit. His feet ache, his tongue tastes like paste, and for the past hour he has simultaneously wanted to crawl into bed and start knocking back more bourbon. A hangover is a form of withdrawal; this he knows. It's the body craving the very poison it is trying to purge.

A tough investigation isn't so different.

Weeks to months, spiked by the dopamine flow of discovery and the surge of adrenaline. And now, the long calm, the paperwork, the reviews that precede the closure of a case. Soon, hundreds of hours of closed-door testimony and empaneled committees. Real life isn't kicking in a door and chasing a suspect through Chinatown. Real life is a week in Wyoming, tracking a grad student and burying your own shit. Real life is getting signed NDAs, even if it means printing them in braille.

And now he stands at her door once again. What also stands there is a housekeeping cart propping it open. Caitlyn's room is empty. A young maid turns down the sheets.

"Uh, excuse me, is the guest in?" Michaels asks.

The maid shrugs. Michaels looks behind the door. There, just as it was hours ago: the braille NDA, unsigned, unopened.

Downstairs, the hangover parts just long enough for Michaels to use his badge to cut to the front of the registration line.

"Caitlyn," the desk agent repeats, tapping the keys. "G-R-E-Y. Hmm. Says here she checked out around nine. Wait, was she..."

"Blind, yeah."

"Visually impaired," the desk agent says. "That's the polite term. Yes, I remember her. Manuel took her to the cab."

"Wait, she's gone?"

"Ah, you're Michaels. She dictated a note for you. I'll print you a copy."

Michaels takes the paper, still warm and stinking of ink, and reads it by the fountain.

Dear Michaels,

I spent the night thinking about what you said: "Seeing the world... then not." I'm tired of traveling with closed eyes. I can't see the world, not anymore, but that doesn't mean I can't be a part of it. I'm going to hear it and smell it and feel it. The first step, then, is just that: a step. The rest will fall into place. Thanks for helping me close out the past.

Sincerely,

Caitlyn Grey
P.S. It's a big and beautiful world. Don't be a stranger.

He folds the letter and puts it in his jacket pocket, close to his heart. He could text her, true. He will have to follow up soon. But for now, he lets her have her journey.

He imagines her at Logan, listening to the announcements of departing flights. He can almost see the crowds and the chaos and the destinations, all bringing a smile to his lips.

37

SOUTH STATION
BOSTON - 3:00 P.M., EST

MICHAELS IS RIGHT ABOUT ONE THING: CAITLYN IS LISTENING. NOT TO airport announcements but for her departing train.

This stone and metal atrium bustles with humanity. She can feel it past her fingertips, like a bird skimming the surface of the water. To her left: the earthy, bold scent of fresh-brewed coffee. To her right: the chirp of a gift shop register as trinkets are scanned. All around: baggage wheels rattling on the marble floor.

"Ma'am, can I help you?" asks a cordial voice before her. "I don't mean to presume, but you look like you could use assistance."

As Caitlyn's vision worsened and her dependence on her cane grew, she knew there would be days when she needed to rely upon strangers. Blind or not, it is always a leap.

In Jakarta, at fifteen, a taxi driver took her for a forty-minute ride to a destination only five blocks away. In India, she caught a hotel clerk hiding in her room after he pretended to leave. And at home, in San Francisco, a lady at a workshop for disabled entrepreneurs insisted on driving her home. Caitlyn wasn't bothered when the lady tried to kiss her goodnight on her front porch; she is straight—*mostly*—and she told the lady as much. When Mrs.

Bakshi let herself in the next day to switch out air filters, she found the lady inside, jewelry in hand. She ran off, taking her mother's necklace and the last of Caitlyn's trust.

"Ma'am, if you're catching a train, I'm happy to escort you there," the voice says. "I work for the MBTA."

"That's just what an ax murderer would say," Caitlyn says and aims her smile in the voice's direction. "But I don't hear any screaming, so it must be a small ax."

There is a soft chuckle and Caitlyn redirects her smile. "I'm afraid they only trust public servants with a walkie-talkie."

Time to leap. Caitlyn tucks the cane under her arm. She shifts her backpack and offers an elbow to the nameless voice. "Thank you."

They walk through the station, Caitlyn counting the steps and noting the sounds. Someone to her right is zipping up a bag. A baby crying in a stroller behind her. Beneath her feet, the tactile paving guides her along, first down stairs, then along a platform where the air is laced with oils and exhaust and warmed by the friction of metal.

"Platform seven," the voice says. "Here's your train car. I'm going to help you step on it. Then we'll talk to the conductor. Ready?"

The ground gives way to rubber warning strips. Then, with a light step, she is on the train. A faint tickle underfoot as the floor buzzes with idling motors.

"Ma'am, this is your conductor, Julia," the voice says. "She's to your right."

"Welcome aboard," Julia says. "You're traveling with us to Chicago, right?"

"I am, Julia," Caitlyn says. She likes the woman's voice. A friendly drawl, Southern perhaps. *Wonder how far she's traveled*.

"Well, if I could just get a look at your e-ticket to confirm?"

Caitlyn triple-clicks her phone's side button. The voice assistant reads the contents of the digital wallet as she swipes through. Credit cards, a gift voucher for Sephora, Amtrak E-Pass. A beep as Julia scans the e-ticket.

"And there we go, Ms. Grey. I'll take you to your roomette now and get you settled in. Is this your first time traveling America by rail?"

Caitlyn's cheeks flush as she answers. "It is."

"Is there anything else you'll need to make this a cozy trip?"

"One thing," Caitlyn says. "Would you describe what my room looks like?"

AT 6:30 P.M., to a packed crowd in the Marriot's Grand Ballroom, Dr. Francis Linamore delivers the keynote speech, opening the 44th Annual Conference of the Society of Clinical Neuropsychology. Two hundred attendees rise to their feet in applause; at his call for greater funding of bold research; for a return to patient-centered treatment; and to his pledge to fight the dopamine pirates, those software profiteers who embed addictive triggers in social media and hijack the mind. Equally important: they laugh at his jokes.

"What did the teenager say when oxygen hooked up with magnesium?" A pause. "Oh... Em... Gee."

In the back, past the overflow, Carruthers whispers to Michaels, "I don't get it."

"Oxygen is O on the periodic table," he whispers. "Magnesium is Mg. OMG."

"We should pistol-whip him."

They duck out before the speech wraps up and catch dinner downstairs, at the same restaurant Roger stood outside last night. If Michaels squints, he can almost see Roger leering, an angry ghost, born back when the world was slower and his whole future lay ahead.

"You know, we've been retracing the last six months of Roger's life," Carruthers says and looks up from the files. "The thing that gets me is how focused he was. It's like he found God."

"He thought he had," Michaels says. "You saw the autopsy. His temporal lobe was swollen. His whole brain was lesioned like pizza. In another six months, he would've been in a wheelchair."

"That's what bugs me. We've got agents in Missouri interviewing his ex-wife and all she's saying is what a loser he turned out to be. Guy couldn't fight his way out of a wet paper bag. So, what, he sits on this for three decades, then snaps? Starts googling everyone that wronged him?"

"You're looking for closure?"

"I'm looking for a trigger."

"Dunno if we'll find it. At least not enough to wrap a bow around. Here's a guy who helped prevent an escape and wound up getting gassed. And, to make it a real suck sandwich, he's allergic to a compound in the gas. I feel bad for Roger—I do."

The waiter stops by. Michaels considers ordering a bourbon but settles on sparkling water. He leans in when she's gone. "You remember when those Chechen separatists took over that Moscow opera house?"

"It was a theater, and yeah, I remember it well."

"Few hundred hostages, and what, a few dozen terrorists? What'd the Russians do?"

"They gassed the whole place," Carruthers says.

"That's right. Pumped it in through the vents. Over a hundred dead. Terrorists and hostages—it didn't matter. Why is that?"

"Spetsnaz tactics," Carruthers says. "To show that Russia doesn't bow to aggression. The response was the message."

"And so was Roger's. Beyond that, who knows what his end game was? A manifesto? Maybe we'll find one, maybe not. Sometimes it's a trigger and sometimes it's a fuse. Roger's was lit long ago, and it took decades to burn."

As MICHAELS and Carruthers dig into dessert, across town, in the cool autopsy suite, Dr. Munson lowers his thermos, his fourth coffee since arriving. As the senior pathologist, he believes it important to impart lessons, and he favors the Socratic method of his mentors.

"What do you make of this?" he asks the junior pathologist, pointing to where Roger's neck is peeled back, draped across his face like a rolled-up sleeve. His cervical spine is exposed, bone jutting out from a pink blossom of tissue.

"I was going to ask you the same thing," the junior pathologist says, bending close to the autopsy table. There are muscle striations, small but patterned.

"Yes, but I asked first."

"Well, the decedent shows severe trauma consistent with a fall of near terminal velocity. There are clear impact wounds from the tree branches. Secondary impact was the concrete slope. He exsanguinated into the gutter."

"That's what the police report says."

"And it's what the body shows."

"Does it?" Dr. Munson uses the forceps to move a layer of tissue. "What's the second cervical vertebra called?"

"The axis."

"Yes, but what's the nickname?"

"The hangman's vertebra"

"And why is that?"

"Because a good hangman needed to understand physics," he says. "Drop height, in particular. They're severing the spinal cord between the first and second vertebrae. Internal decapitation."

"What else can cause that?"

"Whiplash. A car accident. Any hyperextension that exerts sufficient force at the base of the skull."

"And is that what we see here?"

"Well, the wounds are mostly planar," he says, "indicating one direction of impact. And there's the hangman's fracture. The decedent leapt to his death, probably hit branches, slowing his fall—"

"Probably? Do you see any trauma on the face or neck consistent with blunt impact?"

"The incised wound along the left side of his face, and the fracture to the skull."

"Compare that to the right femoral abrasions. There's clear trauma, even trace bark that penetrated his sweatpants. Same with his hand. You can see the splinters embedded here."

"Is it possible his neck caught in a branch and fractured? It's happened before."

"Possible, yes. But thirteen floors and a sudden stop? Total decapitation would be assured. But there're no external signs of contact with wood above his shoulders."

The junior pathologist steps back, tilting his head. "Impact with the asphalt wouldn't cause circumferential wounding."

"There you go. Imagine we just met this man. Shoulders up, what do the wounds tell us?"

He clears his throat, tries to clear his mind. The word "autopsy" comes from Latin and means *to see for yourself*. Not always easy with hours over the same sack of meat. A deep breath, then: "Dissection of the neck reveals extensive, circumferential intramuscular strain, specifically, the left platysma, omohyoid, sternomastoid, and sternohyoid muscles."

"Stick your hand in his neck block," Dr. Munson says. "Go on, test it."

So the junior pathologist does. Gets his hand in through Roger's jawbone, fingers the back of the skull.

"What do you feel when you nod his head?"

"Crunching," the junior pathologist says, rotating the skull. "First and second vertebrae jiggle about. Huh..."

Dr. Munson grins. "You've seen this before."

"Little over a year ago. A babysitter on base claimed she found an infant unresponsive. There were no visible bruises, but the autopsy revealed trauma. She'd gotten tired of the boy, gave him a throttle. Kids are resilient, but even they have limits."

"And how did she throttle the poor child?"

"From behind, hands around his throat. Just like—my god."

"So you see?" Dr. Munson says. "These facial abrasions, the planar fracturing of skull, those were made by blunt contact with glass. You can see little shards. But that wasn't what killed him. This man was killed—throttled, as you say. *Then* he was thrown through the glass. He was dead before he hit the ground."

38

AMTRAK, LAKE SHORE LIMITED
FRIDAY - 7:30 P.M.

CAITLYN FINISHES HER TEA AND PLACES THE CUP ON THE TABLE. THE day's final rays stretch through her window and fall warm upon her face. They're outside Albany now, train bound for places with great names: Schenectady and Utica and then on to Syracuse. In her mind's eye, pastoral lands pass by, green and undulating beneath a gentle breeze. Small towns, a church spire perhaps. Or water towers or grain silos soon to be filled.

"Caitlyn, it's Julia," says the voice to her left. "How was your supper?"

"Wonderful, thank you." And that isn't a lie. The herbed chicken and lemongrass fried rice was a pleasant surprise. The shaved fennel salad as well. Even the panbrioche had a flaky crust that reminded Caitlyn of her mother's cooking, back when they sailed the Mediterranean, the sea beneath them and the turquoise horizon ahead.

"I'm glad to hear that," Julia says. "Well, your room is ready. The bed's set up. The sheets are turned down. You're welcome to stay in the dining car, of course. They'll be serving refreshments until ten. Or if you want, I'm happy to walk you to your room."

Caitlyn senses the sun setting, warmth leaving the window,

conversations quieting. "I suppose it's the same view in both places. I'll tuck in."

"Most do after sundown."

"But I think I'll make my own way back, thank you."

Caitlyn takes each of the ninety-four steps slow. Feels the sway of the train underfoot. Listens to the groan of metals, the hum of great and powerful gears. The mental map she has built is a long cylinder of vibrating silver. Cold glass, pimpled with strong bolts. Doors edged in rubber that moan when opened. Everything resists, and she finds moving through the train to be a fun challenge.

In her roomette, she finds her toiletry kit on the sink, brushes her teeth, and slips into a pair of cozy pants. She traces the edge of the bed. Pulls herself up and onto the mattress. Synthetic fabric scratches her ankles, and she imagines material with all the personality of a dead possum. Still, this is home for her journey west. Better get comfortable.

She pulls her legs into the half-lotus position. Finds her phone and opens the web browser. "Bookmarks," the assistant announces as she slides her finger across the screen. "Reading list. Ad blocker. Search bar."

Caitlyn cues up dictation with a double click of the *volume down* key. "Image search," she says. "Boston. Hyatt Regency. Downtown."

The phone pulses twice, indicating a successful search. She lays it beside her. Focuses on the rumbling of the train. Lets her mind relax. Counting down now, she closes her eyes. Ten... nine... eight...

It's hours before she sleeps.

DR. FRANCIS LINAMORE, sober, smiles as he rides the elevator up to his floor. He thinks of calling his sponsor, to tell the old man he has found something better than the peaty taste of Laphroaig and the inner fire that follows. He has found professional recognition.

Imposter syndrome—the fear of being publicly called out for failure, for being named a scholarly fraud—has never felt further away. When the grand ballroom displayed his name: *Keynote Speaker*; when the deputy editor of *The Lancet* introduced Francis as "esteemed"; and only now—jacket pocket fattened with business cards—has the decades-long roar of doubt faded to a place abstract and mute.

Perhaps he'll call his wife. She has stuck with him through two relapses; she deserves to share his joy. But it's 4:00 a.m. in London. She also deserves to sleep. Flowers then.

As the elevator rises, he scrolls through a boutique florist, settles on a luxury bouquet called Black Diamond Kiss. It is a wholly inappropriate explosion of calla lilies wreathed with roses a soft shade of peach. Blue lisianthus adds a dash of sophistication.

As he unlocks his room door, he upgrades the vase to something called a Crystal Dream. He closes the door, turns the light on, and reaches for his wallet, ready to hit *BUY*.

The order never goes through.

There is a flicker, a faint click as the bedside lamp brightens. Then the room falls to dim amber, long shadows dripping with whispers. Dr. Francis Linamore feels a shiver born of a primal unquiet that has lain dormant for years. Now, roused by instinct, he knows with a sharp specificity that the breath upon the back of his neck is cold and hungry and in this room he is no longer alone.

"DAD?" PJ says from an island between worlds. "Dad, wake up."

The soft edges of Neel Patel's dream give way to the haze of the hotel room, the distant hum of Boston. His contacts are out and everything's fuzzy. The bedside clock blinks a blurry 3:44 a.m. and the wakeup call isn't for another two hours. This had better be important.

"What's up, Peej? You having a bad dream?"

"Dad, there's a leak in the ceiling."

"A leak?"

Neel snatches his glasses from the base of the lamp. He turns on the light.

And he gasps.

PJ rubs his eyes as the light scours the darkness. It isn't his son that loosens Neel's lungs; it's the wet crimson smear running down the boy's face. Neel's cry shakes every muscle in the boy, drives him backward against the bed. Upon his son's pillow: a wet halo of red growing with each *drip, drip, drip*.

Neel's eyes rise to the ceiling, to the glistening blood. He shoots his hands out, grabbing his son, covering the boy's eyes, sweeping him up into his arms, and rushing out into the hall, screams following them in the shattered silence of the night.

[PART 4]

Deep vengeance is the daughter of deep silence.

— Vittorio Alfieri

39

WIPING SLEEP FROM HER EYES, CARRUTHERS OPENS THE DOOR TO FIND Michaels, pale and puffy and clutching two cups of coffee.

"Take this," he says. "I'll brief you on the way."

She forces the last of the black liquid down as they arrive at the Marriott. Dawn, just an eastern smolder, and yet the hotel is lit up like Christmas. News teams jostling for position. Cops shouting not to enter or idle on the street. Few listen.

"Parasites," says the cop that greets them. "They got here before the first responders. We caught one of them in the hall shooting video *Nightcrawler* style."

"Did they disturb the scene?" Michaels asks as they cross the lobby.

"Not that I know. If it was me who'd caught 'em, well, they'd be in cuffs, nursing a thumpin'."

To make a point of it, he gives a cameraman a shove as they pass.

"I worked violent crimes for a stretch, and I've never seen anything like this. Hope you've got a strong stomach."

Half the hotel is awake. The night staff stretched to keep order. Two guests, a man and his son, sit wrapped in blankets, being interviewed.

"That bad, huh?" Carruthers asks.

The officer holds the elevator. "Forensics is bringing in buckets."

Michaels presses 15. "How many witnesses?"

"Firm numbers?" The officer clicks his tongue. "Maybe a dozen at least. Victim's still pouring in through the ceiling. Say, is this connected to that thing at the InterGlobal?"

"Too early to tell," Michaels says and catches Carruthers's nervous glance off the elevator mirror.

"Well, the force is leery with all that's going on. Here we are."

Line up twelve pint glasses and fill them to the brim. That's how much blood the average body contains. The oxidization of hemoglobin's iron molecules gives it the distinct metallic smell. A sickening sweet redolent of salt and iron and threats of infection. Buried deep in evolutionary instinct, pathogen avoidance tightens the bowels and loosens the will, stress-related chemosignals scream, *Run, run, run!*

"Christ," Carruthers says as they step under the police tape that blocks off the hall.

"Clean suits and rain boots are here," the officer says and points to a setup area by the ice machine. "End of the line for me."

MICHAELS SQUEEZES his hand and counts down from five. This lessens the shaking but doesn't end it.

Outside the restaurant, the morning fog has turned to drizzle. The gold dome of the state house stands shadowed and wet. Inside, lonely drunks and a few Saturday early birds sip coffee and poke at their meals.

Michaels forces the eggs down but pushes the bacon aside. Pink meat, too close to what he's seen. Carruthers returns from the restroom looking older, like she'd entered Francis's room and come out hollowed. He supposes they both have. His face off the diner's wet window is that of a stranger.

"That was the British embassy," Carruthers says. "Naturally, they're sympathetic to our investigation, but they're notifying Dr. Linamore's next of kin within the hour."

"Of course," Michaels says.

"If he'd kept his U.S. citizenship after Clearwater, I dunno, maybe we could've suppressed it."

"No, it's too late." Michaels pushes another slice of bacon aside. "This, plus the incident at the InterGlobal... too many clustered events."

"No more disinformation?"

"I'm sure there'll be plenty. Foundation's probably pulling YouTube clips and blaming it on a pit bull. Still, there's no way to contain this."

Carruthers exhales. "How the hell did we blow this?"

"I blew it. Focused on a lone wolf theory when clearly it's not. Roger had help, a partner. Someone from the program. Remember what Dr. Chase said? The subjects needed to previsualize the location."

"Like a wingman?"

Michaels closes his eyes. In the far reaches of his mind, there is that curious image: Roger, rattling cross-country, the RV filled with maps and gospel CDs. His neighbors had said Roger found God, a trait common in TBI. When the dorsolateral prefrontal cortex develops lesions, cognitive flexibility plummets and religious conviction rises.

But maybe God had found Roger.

"What if Roger was the spotter?" Michaels asks. "His journal entries were missing pages. What if they weren't for him? So we caught onto Roger, cornered him, and what's there to do? Why keep someone alive who might talk? Why not just break his neck, throw him out the window?"

"Through the window," Carruthers says. "That was thick glass. Takes a lot of force to break it." She taps the diner window with her fork. "Just like in San Francisco. Christ, it could be here, right now."

At this, they both stiffen. The damp morning beyond oozes

shimmering hints, as if every wet shadow and sun-lit nook might sharpen and start running their way.

"We've had round-the-clock surveillance on the subjects," Carruthers says. "We know when they eat and sleep, what they jack off to. It's... exhaustive. The only one we're missing is Zara Eisler, and no one's seen her since the AOL days."

Worse than that, Michaels thinks. The Foundation is scraping facial recognition from video at every friendly airport, train station, and border crossing. Not a single hit. If Zara is out there, if she is involved, it's from so far beyond the modern world it might as well be from a cave in Tibet.

"So here's what we know," Michaels says. "It's sticking to the pattern. It knows we're involved. And it doesn't care because this murder was brazen."

"Murder, by definition, is between humans," Carruthers says. "Whatever butchered Linamore, there's no humanity there."

Michaels closes his eyes. The halls of his mind stretch out, labyrinthian and rambling. Doors, marked with prime numbers, endless and locked. One answer behind infinite handles left to test. Yes. His eyes snap open. The only way he knows to bring lab-like conditions to this investigation... is to bring this investigation to a lab.

"Chase said he could test them," Michaels says. "Right now, our best asset—our *only* asset—is on her way to Chicago and we're searching for something we can't even see. We need a new plan of attack,"

"You've got an idea?"

"Half a plan, maybe a little less. I need you to track down Caitlyn. I'm going to get Dr. Chase."

"We're bringing him in?"

"We're bringing them all in."

40

WITH THE COOPERATION OF NINE FEDERAL AND STATE AGENCIES, Operation: Alumni Reunion is executed simultaneously in six states at 11:30 a.m. EST on the second Saturday of May.

In Keene, New Hampshire, while stepping out to walk her half chow Muffin, Maggie Neuhaus watches the Spectrum cable installers break into a sprint. They run like athletes. The bulge beneath their overalls is not a uniform but slim protective armor. She is too shocked to notice the unmarked sedans, now flashing their lights.

She processes it all: the men in overalls, now shouting, "Freeze! Don't move!"; the curious cars now crowding her cul-de-sac; the chirp of the birds taking flight.

"Neuhaus," the closest Spectrum man says. Those aren't tools strapped to his belt. "Margret Neuhaus, please come with us."

"I'm sorry, but what is this regarding?" she asks in her best church voice. "And who are you people?"

Badges and warrants answer her two questions. A third simply slips out, "My husband's away on business, so who will watch my dog?"

"We'll have that taken care of," Agent Alvarado says and takes Muffin's leash. Maggie had bought the dog for protection, yet it never barked or snarled. Instead, it licks Alvarado's hand and turns in playful circles.

AT THE BUNS Away Bakery in Savannah, Georgia, during a lull in the lunch rush, Lucy Oates-Deanna shrieks as three customers suddenly stand up from their tables. Two walk toward her like synchronized assassins. The third locks the door. They pull out glistening metal—not guns but badges—and as she flees out the rear, she finds a fourth stepping in from the back door.

IN WEATHERFORD, Oklahoma, as Patricia Whitehead finishes her brunch of yogurt, berries, and granola, she smiles at the Home Depot refrigerator men. Perhaps now they can upgrade the cafeteria's machines. They talk to the day nurse, holding out gold credentials. They turn to her, moving quickly.

"Ah, you're back!" she says, and this time they aren't smiling.

IN EUGENE, Oregon, Jamal Munday swallows the last of his 7-Eleven sandwich and waves off a pigeon. Birds carry diseases. Worse, they carry messages in their optical processors. Those capture everything for the spies that control them.

No they don't, he thinks and squeezes his neck. *Jamal, you're just having a moment*.

As he cuts through the park, Jamal previews this morning's drama: there is a new busker outside the Whole Foods. Doesn't that fool know this is his spot? Ill omens for a fight. The clouds are odd, the pigeons suspicious, and the echoes behind his eyes are rattling about, dropping fishhooks into his gray matter. *Plop, plop, plop*.

Keep it together, he tells himself and senses a tilt to the street. There are cars and people, and often Jamal spots the bots in this simulation. Sometimes it takes a firm slap to knock order back into his world. Today, not so. The tilt becomes a tumble. And the man in his spot isn't a busker; he is One of Them.

Jamal's stomach tightens. *Be cool. Be cool. Be… shit.*

And there is Another One, now crossing the street. Nano-optic eyes lock on Jamal.

Spies, bots, birds. Now the fishhooks are dredging his brain. Jamal winces, standing right there in the middle of the street.

Spies, bots, birds. Stuck in a loop. Spies, bots, birds.

"Jamal Munday?" the spy asks and pulls gold out of his coat. "Please come with us."

Spies, bots, birds. Three spies. Three pigeons, pecking at a sandwich. Three is a trinity of tactical advantage.

"Shh," Jamal says and draws a triangle in the air. "So the government wants my assistance again?"

"Er… yes," one of the spies says. He looks confused. His firmware must be outdated.

"Very well, let me get my suit."

Jamal's right cross knocks the spy off his feet. His partner lunges for Jamal's arm, but a kick to the balls stops him, drops him to his knees.

Five minutes later, Jamal, now naked and screaming, tries to climb the chain-link fence that separates the bike path from the Willamette River. Only one person, a jogger, witnesses the men with their gloved hands prying Jamal from the fence and stuffing him in the van. And the jogger thinks, *Good. One less wacko on the street.*

In Boulder, Colorado, Martin Peck senses the void in his bed where Kylie, a graduate student—not *his* student, no, no, of course not—is no longer sleeping. He isn't dreaming but resting while watching his apartment from a thousand feet up. Curious, all those dark cars converging at the carport. Then, when the door unlocks, when he hears Kylie say, "Yeah, so let's see your warrant," Peck snaps awake.

This is it. They've found the video, no doubt. He tries to think, *When did I last clear my Internet history? Best to just go out the window.*

Peck is halfway through when he feels the stampeding of feet on the shag carpet. Something shatters, a bottle of rum or maybe his bong. A glance back. The feds are pouring in.

"Peck!" one of them shouts. "Peck! Dammit, he went out the west window. Suspect is in tighty-whities and socks. See if you can intercept. Over."

Intercept him they do. Peck makes it as far as the second dumpster before the agents swarm him. He puts his hands over his head, drops to his knees. "I want to speak to my attorney. His name is—"

"Stow it, Peck," one of the agents says. "Now get up before you scare the kids."

In Seattle, Washington, Felix Mayer whistles in the locker room, changing into his work clothes after a long night at the casino. Now, a long day ahead. Containers of Chinese snacks bound for Costco are held up at inspection. Good, he is driving the forklift. Even better, being dockside in such lovely weather. Best of all, some physical labor to let his mind rest.

Then he senses he is no longer alone. Shoes, boots, feet moving quickly on locker room tiles. Felix sighs, turns to the men too well-dressed to be from the union or management. Dressed up like bad news. So which casino finally wised up to his racket? They aren't Native American, so perhaps the Atlantis in Nassau. Or the Russians that run the back rooms at Borgata.

"Mr. Mayer?" the suit on the right asks as he closes the gap. "You need to come with... shit."

Felix puts his hand to his temple, closes his eyes, does his best Professor X impression. A low-pressure rumble. The locker beside the agent rattles and snaps open with enough force it could drive the man's nose deep into his skull. Today, it just gives him a nudge on the shoulder.

Felix opens his eyes, shrugs. "Rusty pipes."

He turns. He runs. He makes it three paces before the Taser drops him to the floor.

ARIZONA, the home studio of the Straight Shooter Sam Stephens, where the hour is always "the Hour of Power to the People," the host himself streaming to his morning audience. Today's topic: Progressives' War Tactics to Seed Universities with Marxist-Lenin Doctrine. The video evidence: a mohawked young woman hassling a seventy-eight-year-old man in a red cap, calling him a race traitor.

"So, and this is where it gets me, folks, this is where it's just downright shameful that in America, our forefathers—oh, and now she's trying to take his hat too. Would you look at that? A veteran and—bless you for your service, sir—see this is what we're up against, folks, when the looney left has nothing better to do than accost elderly service men and women. Oh, and now she's following him to his car. This wouldn't happen in an open-carry state—no, sir—or any state of sanity, folks. This is the Leninist left on full display. Look at that."

What Sam Stephens isn't looking at, what he doesn't see, is the little icon in the corner of the server: *NO INTERNET CONNECTION.* He speaks through it all: the Wi-Fi light turning from green to yellow; the pause of the chat room commentary; the video downgrading from 4K to HD to 480p, then stopping altogether.

Only when he sees the shadows approaching—men in unmarked jackets pouring in through the laundry room door—does he realize this video isn't his most pressing topic.

"Folks, friends, breaking news here. We've finally done it. Looks like the deep state has sent its agents of oppression to… Sir, this is private property and as a sovereign journalist I am ordering —stay off the gosh-darn floor! This is a news studio!"

The news floor is thirty feet of converted garage and easily crossed. They present him with a warrant and a badge. Sam, red-faced and pounding the desk, makes clear his disagreement to an audience of none.

"I reject this tyranny!" he shouts to Cameras 1, 2, and 3. "I beseech my viewers right now: take up arms! God bless us, the great storm has finally arrived!"

Millions of viewers, many with bunkers and ammunition and the Sam Stephens brand of Freedom Rations. Some might even heed his call to arms. Instead, tuning in now, they see the following:

This account has been removed for violating the terms of service.

SHE RESTS her head against the cool window, soaking up the train's vibrations, a soothing hum in her bones. Last night she got the best sleep of her life. And today, dawn reached into her roomette, a gentle touch on her shoulders, telling her, *All will be okay.*

Four more hours. Caitlyn imagines Chicago and all it will present. The wind off the lake. The elevated train. The buzz of humanity off glass and steel towers.

She saw a picture of the Cloud Gate long ago, that great metal bean melding heaven and earth into a single, reflective reality. Sure, she can't see it now—not without a quiet place to park her body—but she doesn't want to experience it that way. Better to reach out and feel the sculpture, solid and imperfect and real.

And of course, there is food. Living off delivery has dulled her taste buds. Now they are awakening, frantic and ravenous. Where to start? Perhaps at Au Cheval with its famous burgers. Or Kai Zan, with its Japanese *omakase* cuisine. And she can't miss Pequod's Pizza, where the deep dish is crusted with caramelized cheese. If she does nothing more than eat her way across Chicago, this will be the perfect vacation.

A whoosh a few hundred feet off. The rattle of a low-flying helicopter and a shift in vibrations. The train is beginning to slow.

"I didn't hear the announcement," a passenger says.

Caitlyn places her hand against the arm rest. The engine is weakening. A faint din overtakes the dining car. Whispers. Someone's phone clicks as a picture is snapped.

"What are the police doing here?"

"Those look like federal agents—"

"You think we're in danger?"

A lump forms, the warmth of her morning tea now replaced by a cold fear.

Okay, deep breath, count down from ten. Get cozy. Go for a look. Nine, eight, seven...

The din becomes a low mumble. Work boots on the dining car floor. *Six, five, four...*

She balls her fists, then relaxes. Here's the tingle that precedes the blink. *Remember the train last night, the walk down the moonlit aisles. Three, two...*

"Caitlyn, I'm sorry to wake you," Julia says. "I'm afraid there's some folks who need you to come with them."

One.

She sees it all in warm sunrise hues: a grab bag of Illinois State Troopers and FBI jackets. One face, familiar, only a few feet off and closing.

Carruthers reaches out and places a hand on Caitlyn's shoulder. She squeezes. Color drains from the world, the curtain falls, and now Caitlyn is back in her body.

"Special Agent Carruthers," Caitlyn says and gives the woman's hand a pat. "Am I being detained?"

OF THE CLEARWATER COHORT, two are deceased and one is still missing. At least according to the records.

Beneath a pair of birch trees at the Sunset Memorial Park in Twin Falls, Idaho, the remains of Cynthia Nesbit are exhumed.

The coffin hisses as five years of putrefaction meets daylight and air. Michaels studies the video stream from forty-one thousand feet, just east of the Blue Ridge Mountains. Rapid DNA confirms a match. One more checkmark on his tablet.

That leaves two: Zara Eisler and Tae Hwan Kim.

Eisler, still a ghost; a signature-scraping algorithm turned up her passport number at a Cartagena guest house back when Clinton was in his second term. After that, nothing. The Department of State lists 165 known American deaths in Colombia during those early dot-com years. Other possibilities: a robbery, a roadside accident, another anonymous body in an overseas morgue.

And still the itch persists.

Tae Hwan Kim, then, in South Korea. The only itch Michaels can scratch. The Korean authorities have been dragging their feet. Time to turn up the pressure with someone he trusts.

"Brad, it's Michaels," he says into the phone. "Got your passport handy? Good. How soon can you get packed?"

OPERATION ALUMNI WEEKEND
For Authorized Eyes Only - Penalty 18 U.S. Code § 798

S1. KIM, Tae Hwan
Status: Deceased
Location: Gyeongju, South Korea
Assigned to: Lee, Brad

S2. EISLER, Zara
Status: Missing
Location: Unknown
Assigned to: Maddox & Anand

S3. JENSEN, Theodore
Status: Incapacitated
Location: Central City, Iowa
Assigned to: Carruthers & Michaels

S4. NESBIT, Cynthia
Status: Deceased
Location: Twin Falls, Idaho
Assigned to: N/A

S5. MAYER, Felix
Status: Alive
Location: Seattle, Washington
Assigned to: Pendergast & Kang

S6. MUNDAY, Jamal

Status: Alive
Location: Eugene, Oregon
Assigned to: Lowe & Romero

S7. NUEHOUSE, Margret
Status: Alive
Location: Keene, New Hampshire
Assigned to: Alvarado & Fong

S8. OATES-DEANNA, Lucille
Status: Alive
Location: Savannah, Georgia
Assigned to: Flick & Dunning

S9. PECK, Martin
Status: Alive
Location: Boulder, Colorado
Assigned to: Crouch & Konrath

S10. STEPHENS, Sam
Status: Alive
Location: Scottsdale, Arizona
Assigned to: Kensington & Faye

S11. WHITEHEAD, Patricia
Status: Alive
Location: Weatherford, Oklahoma
Assigned to: Berrong & Kruger

LOCATION: REDACTED
MONDAY – 6 A.M., PST

TWENTY MILES NORTH OF LAKE TAHOE, ALPENGLOW BLEEDS ACROSS the Sierra peaks. Goldenrod follows, a promise of dawn. Here, in the late spring, granite crags scratch the clouds and leave cerulean wounds through which the last stars shine. They shine on the shadowed trucks now rumbling down miles of unmarked road, twisting through brambled canyons. They shine off the warm hoods, sleek metal and chrome.

The U.S. government owns nearly 770,000 empty buildings, hundreds kept in a state of suspension in case of nuclear war. Of those, fourteen are classified beyond top secret.

Here, near the California-Nevada border, one site groans from the depths of the canyon, this slumbering concrete titan waking from decades of quiet.

The orders have been given; the convoy follows. All-terrain tires and V8 engines ferry electricians and plumbers and engineers. Past rusty fences chained for decades. Through snowmelt warming with dawn's ginger reflections. Beneath pillars of spruce and cedar and oak where moss gently sways in the slipstream of trucks.

By sunrise the first crates are cracked open. And he is watching.

Here, where the road ends at the concrete maw of the mountain, Dr. Robert Chase looks up at the facility. Dust is stirred by the circling trucks, and pine fills his nose. Woodpeckers clatter as day breaks. Details he has forgotten in the march of the decades.

"Dr. Chase." The lead engineer waves him to the great metal doors that lead into the mountain. An old magnetic card reader, pockmarked and rusted, lies on its side. A new biometric reader is being screwed into place. "We'll have the basic amenities up and running by 1200. Warm water by 1600. Sir, welcome to Clearwater Canyon."

No, he thinks. *Welcome back.*

Below, buzzing currents give life to dormant wiring and lights. Bulb by bulb, the long hallway blinks awake. Signs and painted lines emerge. *RESTRICTED LAB AHEAD - NO UNAUTHORIZED PERSONNEL.* Startled from its nest, a rat runs past a long-abandoned guard desk, little nails going *clickity click.*

It takes Dr. Chase a moment to realize why the halls look wrong. It isn't his memory; there is a visual difference. The bulbs have been switched over to LEDs. Gone is the incandescent glow, replaced by this new surgical white.

Hot water within hours. Refrigeration, AC, even high-speed Internet. Rusty pipes rumble overhead, and to Chase, they sound not unlike the first time he heard the human circulatory system: *lub dub, lub dub.*

Chase is not surprised to find the restricted wing open. The blast doors are long gone. Perhaps repurposed to build a fighter jet. Perhaps sold for scrap. What surprises him is the fear.

Here is the test chamber, this concrete arena where their ambition met failure. Nearly forty million dollars. He had been the most promising post-doc his department had produced. His letters of recommendation were penned by advisors to Reagan and Bush. Some still circle the highest strata of politics and academia and cutting-edge research. None ever return his correspondence.

He leans against the rail. From the catwalk, looking down on the moldering terraces, he can almost see the shadows of the equipment: the tape drives, the deprivation pods, the observation deck with its mirrored glass. Squinting, he can see the fossilized past. His colleagues' careers had exploded while his own festered in darkness, classified and denied.

Thirty years. And now, with the noises behind him, technicians and electricians, the engineers hauling crates of equipment, the shape of tomorrow taking place today, Dr. Robert Chase squeezes the cold metal railing as a smile tugs at his lips.

42

RENO

TUESDAY, 1:00 P.M., PST

THE MOUNTAINS COME INTO VIEW, ALL HIGH DESERT AND SNOWCAPS. Then the tires touch tarmac as the jet hums to a stop. Michaels thanks the pilots and steps down onto the runway, bracing against the conifer breeze off the Sierras.

There, at the edge of the hanger, is Carruthers. She leads him to an SUV, a black thing of government inspiration. The driver opens the door.

"Don't expect the welcome committee," Carruthers says. "Everyone's been working nonstop to get the site up and running."

"We're all in a hustle," Michaels says. "Good to see you."

"Not all of us arrived on a private jet."

"No helicopter?" Michaels asks the driver.

"Winds off the canyon make landing tricky," the driver says and gestures to the door. "Now, if you don't mind."

The driver doesn't ask where they are going. Just gets in and drives. In this shifting economy, the Foundation has turned to recruiting private military contractors for entry-level jobs. They are cheap, follow orders, and have the personality of cork.

Michaels opens his tablet, checks the schedule. "Have the scientists arrived?"

"Most last night," Carruthers says. "A few trickling in this morning."

"And the subjects?"

"They're coming shortly."

"Are they cooperating?"

"Who? The subjects or the scientists?"

"Both."

Carruthers says, "We've compartmentalized the scientists, but they're clever. They figured out why they're here and there's a fair bit of excitement. As for the test subjects, well, we detained them courtesy of the National Emergencies Act. They're as friendly as expected."

"And how's Caitlyn?"

Carruthers hesitates. "We are not her favorite people right now."

The SUV stops for the airport security gate. The driver flashes a badge, the guard checks the paperwork, and that is that. A moment later, they're merging onto the northbound 580.

"Level with me," Carruthers says. "This plan, you really think it'll work?"

"Chase does," Michaels says. "So I think it just might."

"There's a lot of space between might work and will."

"Yeah, and there's a lot of Linamore's blood on our hands," Michaels says. "This thing isn't playing by the rules."

"We didn't kill him. We did our best with what we were given."

"So does a toilet. Our best wasn't good enough." He squeezes his hand. "What are you really worried about?"

Carruthers says nothing. Studies the passing highway, Reno giving way to subdivisions and high desert, sagebrush and pine. "Thirty years ago the government fried half these people's brains. Now we're rounding them up under sealed warrants?"

"For a short series of tests."

"To the place they tried to escape."

"And they did escape," Michaels says. "With a sizable settlement—"

"Not that sizable—"

"Seven figures is sizable. And a contract promise: never to project again."

To this, Carruthers says nothing.

"Denise, you've seen their files. They show clear signs of decoherence, far beyond good luck. Hell, look at these MRIs. Tell me those look normal. Some are just as bad as Roger. A few'll be in Depends, drinking liquid meals by the next decade."

"You're not incorrect," Carruthers says. "It's just... Have you thought this through? Where this could be headed? What I mean is, what's the difference between this and what Dr. Chase did?"

"The difference, Denise, is that we catch the killer. We send him—or her, whatever—to the deepest, darkest black site. What was done to Linamore and the others, that is evil. And that evil is out there, unpunished. There's no place we can go that it can't come for us, now or next year. So yeah, I've thought it through. It ends with that thing in a box or us on a slab."

Carruthers lets her disapproval hang there, heavy and festering in the silence. The SUV enters the Sierras, where crags rise to greet the sky in a majesty of leaf and rock. Beyond looms Clearwater Canyon, those cold halls now buzzing with life.

43

CLEARWATER
TUESDAY – 2:30 P.M., PST

Clattering gravel rouses Michaels from sleep. Here they are, the SUV stopping before a fence, a thick chain, and a sign:

WARNING!
SUPERFUND SITE - TOXIC MATERIALS PRESENT
NO ENTRY OR EXIT.

Not as dramatic as the sign at Area 51 with its bullet holes and warnings of force. Still, it has its own functional charm.

Rattling down six miles of winding, wet Sierra roads, Michaels thinks back to the photograph from Newell's storage locker. Eight men, three women, by a stream in the late afternoon light. There's the stream now, just to the left of the bridge they are crossing. And the picnic bench, rotted and swallowed by decades of brambles. Finches scatter at their passing.

Michaels senses the activity before he sees it. Vehicles circled up, loadmasters directing forklifts and pushcarts, wheels kicking up dust in the afternoon light. Beyond it is the mouth of the facility: colossal doors built into the side of the mountain.

"Welcome to Clearwater Canyon," Chase says.

He leads them into the yawning cavern, the clack of his

crutches echoing beneath the arched girders of this cathedral to metal and stone. It strikes Michaels as a marvel of engineering. To Carruthers, it looks like hubris.

"This facility was started when Kennedy was in office," Chase says. "Built to withstand a direct nuclear strike. Even then, the government knew there was no winning a nuke fight. Tomorrow's wars would need to be surgical. Which is why they funded my research when all others balked."

Chase stops at the service elevator. The shaft is open, a forty-five-degree slope where track lighting descends into darkness. A lift wide enough to accommodate three cars at least. Michaels bends down, touching scuff marks from forklifts and the splintered remains of a pallet.

"Are we on schedule?" he asks, swaying as the elevator begins a tilted descent.

"I'm afraid my time in the private sector has rubbed off on me," Chase says. "We're ahead by roughly a day."

"So that's why the uniforms are grumpy," Carruthers says.

"I have little patience for military time. I've called in more favors than I'm owed to procure the needed equipment. So have others."

"And your team?" Michaels asks. "How do they feel?"

In the slow descent, the shaft paints Chase in bands of white and red. "They understand the necessity of this research. The magnitude of what—"

"It isn't research," Michaels says. "It's an interrogation."

"Like a lineup," Carruthers adds.

"Surely you see this as more than that, Agents. It could be—"

"What I see," Michaels says, "is you made something that leapt the lab walls. This is a containment in a controlled environment, Dr. Chase, nothing more."

The air grows cooler. Glancing back, Michaels sees the slant of light a hundred feet up.

"I admit, I am an opportunist," Chase says. "But also an optimist. The first patients treated with penicillin were burn victims from a fire that claimed five hundred lives. Science is an engine of prosperity, but often tragedy comes first."

"That's a noble position to have," Carruthers says, "when it's your science. How'd it turn out for Professor Moore, Francis Linamore, Teddy fucking Jensen?"

"Yes, and how'd it turn out for poor Bridget Driscoll?"

"Who's that?" Michaels asks.

"The first death due to automobile," Chase says. "The car was moving at five miles per hour. Poor Bridget was too awestruck to step aside."

"So the slow-moving get crushed," Carruthers says. "That's your hot take?"

Chase sighs. "Try to think bigger, Special Agent. The car has brought us commerce and freedom and connection. A vast web of roads, even here to this mountain. Imagine if we gave that up because of Bridget Driscoll." Chase's eyes fall to Michaels's hand. "Tell me, Agent Michaels, how long have you had your tic?"

He squeezes his hand. Damn, was he flapping unconsciously? "Since your case fell into my lap, Doc, but that's not the point—"

"With respect, it is *entirely* the point. Mirror neurons often misprocess stress chemosignals. You favor order, consistent colors, find certain numbers pleasing, yes? And yet you hide your hand because you are more than misfiring neurons. Some cannot hide, Agent. Some minds are hindered by the failings of flesh. Imagine our loss if science had not given Stephen Hawking a voice. Language led us to consciousness. Now consciousness can lead us to freedom. Isn't that worth pursuing while we can?"

Michaels finds his composure, forces himself to meet the doctor's gaze. "We're not here to change the world. We're here to clean up your mess."

Chase braces himself against the elevator rail. "I had hoped we could do both."

"Then I'm sorry to disappoint you."

With a clank, the elevator stops. Carruthers opens the swing gate, gestures to Chase. *After you.* They follow him into a cavernous chamber. "When you called me, I cashed in every favor I was owed. This is the beating heart of Clearwater."

Beating indeed. The room opens up into a concrete lab in the throes of resurrection. Sleek medical machines are plugged in and daisy-chained to each other. Pane by pane, one-way glass is being installed. Close by, a bank of monitors displays cameras coming online. Clearwater is picking back up, bolstered by thirty years of new technology.

"Agent Michaels, Special Agent Carruthers," Chase says, "allow me to introduce the head of research, Dr. Carolyn Locke."

Chase places his hand on Dr. Locke's shoulder. She is a small woman with eyes like fire opals and a smile brimming with elan. Michaels recognizes her from the jacket flap of her best-selling book, *Dark Matter, Dark Minds: Our Post-Conscious Future.* Carruthers envisions her rowing in the predawn light.

"Carolyn, we were just discussing Bridget Driscoll and the automobile on our way down."

"Ah, did Bob give you the penicillin pitch?" She shakes their hands. "He's been doing that since I was his research assistant."

"And now look at you," Chase says. "Head of your own lab at Johns Hopkins. I like to think our time together was formative."

"I'm sure you do."

Chase's glasses flash. "Well, I'll leave you three to touch base while I see to the deliverables."

They watch Chase shuffle off, talking to technicians and pointing with his crutch. "He's something, isn't he?" Dr. Locke says. "So, Agents, I've been briefed on what you need: positive proof of the ability to project with an estimate of the most recent decoherence."

"And you can do that?" Michaels asks. "Dr. Chase said it was possible."

"I'm sure he promised as much," she says, her voice lowering. Michaels senses frustration behind the sidelong glances she shoots across the lab. "Truthfully, the last voice I ever thought I'd hear at 2:00 a.m. was Bob Chase. I didn't think anything would surprise me until I said 'maybe,' and fifteen minutes later a helicopter was on my lawn. When I arrived, I put it together: we made the God's Breath Killer."

"Can you identify them?"

"With today's tech, yes, in theory."

"In theory?" Carruthers asks.

"I've spent the morning studying Roger's autopsy. Specifically, the regions of his brain that redistributed due to DZ3-induced decoherence. Since he's expired, we can't get a proper neuroimage, but we can with the... What do we call them now? Suspects?"

"People of interest," Carruthers says.

"Potentials," Michaels adds.

"Right, potentials. Using next-gen magnetoencephalography— MEG-II scans—we'll run them through a series of exercises and measure the responses. We'll compare those to the results from the project thirty years ago."

"What results?" Carruthers asks. "Wasn't that data lost?"

"It was," Michaels says. "Dr. Locke has an eidetic memory. She can memorize anything. It was in her book."

"Well, it's more of a mnemonic trick, optimized for my synaptic disposition. I'm afraid I don't do well with music. My son jokes that every time I hear a song it's the first time."

"Okay, pause," Carruthers says. "You remember scans from three decades ago?"

"I've had to re-memorize them," she says. "The brain requires upkeep. Some people watch a favorite movie again and again. I review my life. As to your potentials, yes, the team and I are finalizing a test to rank psychokinetic strength and recent neural activity."

"And this requires their cooperation?" Michaels asks.

"It makes it easier." A smile. "I'm told you have someone outside the program, an anchor subject?"

"We do," Carruthers says. "Though she might not be in the best of moods."

"Oh, and why is that?"

"YOU SEND federal agents to detain me on a train," Caitlyn says, "in front of everyone. You fly me across the country. No one tells me where I am, why I'm here. I didn't even get a phone call. It's been three days—I think—and now you're asking for my help?"

Michaels nods at each statement and tries to lean back. The chair doesn't budge. It is bolted to the floor of the conference room, which is, he realizes, an interrogation chamber decorated with chalkboards, a mirror, and fake potted plants.

"Yeah, Caitlyn, that's what we're asking."

"Give me your hand." She reaches across the table. For a moment he doesn't know what to do. "Your hand." He lets her find it. She leans closer, feels her way up his elbow, to his shoulder, to his face. She touches his cheek.

Then she slaps him.

Not hard, but hard enough. A wet crack in the quiet of the room. Michaels rubs his stinging face.

"You deserve that," Caitlyn says.

"Yeah, I do."

"They put a bag over my head. Like some terrorist."

"They weren't supposed to do that, Caitlyn. Not to you."

"Well, they did."

"I'll have words with them, I promise."

"And where are we? I tried to blink, but…" She taps her head. "I can't do it because I don't know what to visualize. Every time I try to leave, it's just… static."

The first try had been a minor inconvenience, a buzzing inside her mind and a brief glimpse of her apartment, the walls collapsing to ashen mud. The second time she tried to blink, glass rattled behind her eyes. She saw a glimpse of her family's boat, anchored in the Red Sea off the Egyptian shores. Then it melted to ochre. The third and final time she had envisioned Angkor Wat, dawn crawling across the serene faces of stone. The faces had screamed; the stone cracked and crumbled. And Caitlyn found herself nursing a migraine that lasted for hours.

"Yeah, that's by design, I'm afraid," Michaels says.

"Design?"

"Most of the facility is basically a Faraday cage. Poured concrete with mesh wiring. Like an MRI room, except bigger. No cell phones or radio signals, and no blinking outside an amplified test chamber."

"Why would someone build a—*wait*. We're at the place, Clearwater."

Silence follows the name.

"We are," Michaels says.

She taps her fingers on the table. Her eyes narrow. A reflex habit? She isn't looking at him, yet it's like she is boring a hole through him. Guilty conscience.

"What's really happening?" she asks.

Michaels takes a deep breath. Then he tells her. About Roger's neck, broken before he went through the glass. About Dr. Linamore, and how the killer made it last for an hour. About the three men and four women in accommodations just like Caitlyn's.

"Accommodations? This isn't an Airbnb, Michaels. This is detainment."

"It's an imperfect solution to a very unique problem." He steeples his hands to keep them from shaking. Taps to five while thinking of primes. How much can he tell her before the knowledge puts her in danger? "Caitlyn, my supervisor's daily briefing goes to the desk of the Deputy Director of National Intelligence. This… unique problem constitutes a threat growing exponentially worse. The minute my supervisor doubts containment, I'll be sidelined and they'll take over."

"Take over? What does that even mean?"

"It means… Okay, there are places, black sites, far beyond any laws or accounting. Oubliettes on old oil rigs, off grid in international waters. They have one purpose: to squeeze every ounce of information from those that end up there."

"You've seen these places?"

"No. But I've seen where the tracks end."

And a little more. The years spent by families on useless investigations to find their missing. No closure, never. All the money, all the Freedom of Information Act requests, all the lawsuits buy are an endless maze of false hopes and false flags designed to break the soul. He knows this. He might have even planted a few.

"So all of the test subjects are here?" Caitlyn asks. "In the facility?"

"Most," Michaels says. "We're still tracking one down. And Brad's in Korea, checking on another."

"And one of them was working with Roger?"

"They had to be."

"Why?"

"Roger was communicating through a mail-forwarding service. He was financed by someone with means greater than his. He had lockers stocked with DZ3 within thirty miles of crime sites. But most of all: the nature of the wounds. SWAT was roughed up, bruises and a few broken bones. But the murders were more primal, more... well, you know."

Caitlyn bites her lip. A bitter truth she had bet against. "In the hotel, I could see him. I figured maybe it was because I surprised him. Damn, I fumbled, didn't I?"

"No, not at all. There's no script for this. My mandate is ICC: investigate, contain, control. Caitlyn, we've contained what we can. We need your help with the others."

"And if I say no?"

"I'll cut you loose, personally. I'll even take you to the airport. But, Caitlyn, you're on radars other than mine. Powerful people know your name, your skill. You'll be offered things, consultancy. In time, those offers might turn into demands."

"You people," Caitlyn says. "A week ago you sat in my living room, laughing. Now you want me to walk into a lab with a killer? All because I went to a diner."

"It's been a weird kind of week." He leans in, asks, "Can I hold your hand?"

She tilts her head. Then she lays her right hand out on the cold table, palm up. He takes it in his.

"I'm sorry. In my head I can simulate a dozen ways to solve a problem. I can balance them out, optimizing. But when it comes to people, my mind gets all gummed up."

"That's because you're using the wrong part."

He feels his heart racing. "In Boston, I should've come with you, back to your room. That was dumb of me."

She smirks, little crescents forming above her freckled cheeks. "No, Michaels, it was kind of sweet that you didn't."

KTX SEOUL TO BUSAN, SOUTH KOREA
THURSDAY - 7:30 A.M., KST

SIX YEARS SINCE HE LEFT SOUTH KOREA. IT MIGHT AS WELL BE SIXTY. The country builds fast and moves faster. Returning to this peninsula feels like stepping back into the future. Next-gen wireless is everywhere, even here, deep in the countryside, where lush valleys and farmlands rush past. From the KTX bullet train, he watches explosions of pink and white petals dotting the railways and roads. At three hundred kilometers per hour, the foreground is a pastel blur.

Brad Lee returns to the file before him. Under pressure, the Korean embassy in DC finally forwarded all their records of Tae Hwan Kim. Here it is, the story of a life on old photocopied paper.

Born to a Korean father and an American mother, Tae Hwan enjoyed dual citizenship. He could cross regularly into the U.S., and he had, attending middle school in Arizona, high school in Seoul, and one year of college in Phoenix until he volunteered for Clearwater.

As a Korean male, he was required to enlist in military service. After Clearwater, Tae Hwan faced a choice: give up his ancestral citizenship or spend two years serving in the Korean armed forces. Seeing what America could do to its own, perhaps Tae Hwan had pinned his future on Korea. Not a bad plan. While the

U.S. was divided over the Clinton impeachment, Korea was united in building a digital tomorrow. Tae Hwan arrived as Korea joined the ranks of developed nations.

At twenty-four, Tae Hwan was older than most conscripts. A small solace in Confucian culture where age means respect. Still, he must have been worried. He was a *gyopo*—a Korean from outside Korea—and in Brad's experience from being stationed in Pyeongtaek, gyopos got the short end of both sticks. Korea treated you like family when it wanted something; it treated you as an outsider when it wanted to dismiss you.

Tae Hwan's emails to his half brother laid out a similar fear. The Korea of the mid-nineties was a fledgling democracy. The shadows of dictatorship still loomed. Conscript abuse was a near certainty. Long hours, beatings, the occasional male rape, none were unheard of. It was said that the universities made the men into global thinkers, but military service made those boys into men. Tae Hwan's emails harbored deep skepticism of such claims.

Brad's own service had come to an end near his twelve-month mark. Competitive by nature, he looked forward to intramural weekend for months. While closing in on his company's obstacle course record, he found a fresh nest of wasps at the top of the confidence climb. He discovered two things. He was deathly allergic to their venom. And that when the military no longer needs you, it shows you the door.

Tae Hwan made it further. The files show a young man quickly ascending to leadership positions. Though the English translation is imperfect, there is a trajectory. Tae Hwan kept his head down, kept focused.

Then, the collapse.

The building was a flat-slab structure sans crossbeams, built in the hasty push to modernize Seoul before the 1988 Summer Olympics. A perfect storm of hubris, nepotism, and crony capitalism forced the department store to be erected in record time. Design limits were ignored and a fifth floor was added. To the owner, the Sampoong Department Store was to be Seoul's response to Fifth Avenue, its own mall of tomorrow. Once open, nearly forty thousand shoppers flooded the building daily, up escalators and stairs, across floors where load-bearing columns had been reduced to maximize retail space, past the storefronts and stalls of vendors hawking wears, all participants in this gleaming arena of commerce.

In April 1995, the first cracks appeared. The owner did nothing. Three months later, on June 29, the top floor began to sag. A few senior executives fled the building. Shortly before dinner, the structure collapsed in a series of thunderclaps. The dust was visible for miles. Until September 11th, it was the worst building collapse in history. And it hadn't been brought down by planes.

Over five hundred lives were compacted, remains nearly impossible to identify. Tae Hwan was among them. It had been his first day off in months and he was shopping for a girlfriend no one had met.

Bad luck, Brad thinks as the bullet train begins to slow. Out the window, the tea plantations that had given the landscape soft curves are now fading behind the rise of large apartment buildings, sandstone and ivory mega-communities with the charm of cinder blocks. It is here, in the southern city of Gyeongju, that Brad is set to meet Tae Hwan Kim's half brother.

And to pay his respect to Tae Hwan's remains.

[45]

CLEARWATER

WEDNESDAY - 3:30 P.M., PST

INSOLENT PRICK, MICHAELS THINKS AS THE MAN ACROSS FROM HIM leans back and a smirk splits his face.

"It tickles your noodle, don't it?" Sam Stephens says. "I mean, sure, it explains a thing or two: me, knowing all about you and this little operation."

Without the blazer made from an American flag, without his green screen and patriotic videos, Sam Stephens is just your average boomer, wide at the chest and soft in the sides. Behind his black desk, he towered, all ammo and camo. Here, in this interview room, he is all gin blossoms and bad tan.

"So what all do you know?" Carruthers asks. "About this little operation?"

Sam points at her. "Ah, nice try. You think I'm going to tip my hand, G-man?"

"You sure like to talk about the God's Breath Killer," Michaels says.

"Yeah, and y'all sure try to muddy public discourse."

"But you gave it that name," Carruthers says. "That was you online, posting over five hundred comments."

"Branding's important."

"You like the attention?"

"I like the money. Advertising keeps the lights on. News is expensive these days."

"That's what you call your show?" Michaels asks. "News?"

"Sure, just like you call this keeping the peace."

"I thought you were a friend of law enforcement," Carruthers says. "Blue Lives Matter."

Sam smiles. "I like law enforcement. I like the ones I can see at town halls and church. The ones I know by name. Never trust a hog that won't eat from your trough."

"That's a good expression," Michaels says to Carruthers. "How did it go? Never trust—"

"I didn't kill 'em," Sam says. "And I know that's what the killer would say, but I didn't."

Michaels opens his mouth but thinks better of it. Carruthers told him with big personalities it's best to give space and silence and let their noise fill it in.

"And, I suppose, if I had a guest in my studio, this would be where I'd let them keep talking," Sam says and scratches at a scuff on the metal table. "Thirty years. You believe I put this dent here with just the power of my thought?"

"What makes you think we're here to discuss a homicide?" Carruthers asks.

"A homicide, singular?" Sam smiles, tilting his head. "You know, you make the same mistake most smart people do: you assume everyone's dumber. I know, 'cause I make it too. See, I've been through Clearwater, took the ride, got the shirt. I know what the government's capable of covering up and what it ain't and how it'd try to throw sand in our eye. When God's Breath made the news the first thing I did was dig. I gave the 'Frisco lawyer a call, fed his ex a story about being old law school pals, and boom, the broad spilled the beans."

Michaels balls his feet. Tries to keep his face flat. It's not just the man's arrogance but the word 'Frisco. No one from the bay ever calls it that.

"Now, I know I'm not the killer. But I also know there's only a dozen people on Earth able to do what God's Breath did. Best to keep all the clowns under one tent, right? So logically, I'd round us all up."

Carruthers asks, "Have you projected since you signed the terms of your settlement?"

Sam closes his eyes. Hums. A moment of beautiful silence. Then he slams his hand on the table. "Hell yes I have! You think any of us gave up that gift? That's fire coming to the savage. That's gunpowder, baby. And the airplane and the Internet all rolled into one."

"You're admitting to breaking the terms of a classified government contract?" Michaels asks.

"And you're admitting the government classified a contract?" Sam replies. "That's convenient. Could I see said contract so I can verify which clause I'm in breach of?"

"You signed the thing," Carruthers says. "You know full well what was in it."

"Yeah, and I know you full well," Sam says, eyes probing Carruthers up and down. "You're the kind of woman a man wants when he really wants another man."

Carruthers blinks, steadies her nerves against his words. She's heard worse. This is his pigpen, and he enjoys being down in the mud. *Don't give him the pleasure.*

Sam takes off his glasses. "Look, I'm just saving y'all some time. However many of us you've got here, that's how many broke that contract. Now take me away in cuffs." He holds out his wrists.

Michaels asks, "How many times have you projected?"

"How many hairs you got on your head?"

"Why did you project?"

"Have some fun. Maybe see what our commander in thief is tweeting on the john."

"When and where was the last time you projected?"

"Eaglebrook School in Massachusetts on, oh… nine days ago?"

"Eaglebrook," Carruthers repeats. "That's a boy's school."

"Good deduction, Detective. It is, and it ain't what you think. My son was giving a speech for model UN. I was supposed to be there but got stuck at a rally. Better than Zoom."

"I bet he appreciated it," Michaels says.

"No, he pretty much hates me, but that's fifteen for you. Kids say they want to be left alone. Then when you do, they say you were never around. Look, are we through here? There's HBO in my cell and I never finished *Game of Thrones*."

"Here's some homework," Michaels says and slides him a questionnaire as thick as his thumb. "Save us more time."

"And why would I do that?"

"So the tests don't hurt as much," Michaels says and gives the big man a wink. For a brief moment, the Straight Shooter looks unsettled. "And, Sam, don't make us shut off your TV."

Outside, in the hallway, Carruthers leans in. "These tests aren't distressing or painful or—"

"No, not all," Michaels says. "But he doesn't know that."

[46]

GYEONGJU, SOUTH KOREA
THURSDAY - 9:30 A.M., KST

"CALL ME TOM, PLEASE," THE MAN AT THE SINGYEONGJU TRAIN station says. "It's my English name. Tom, like Tom Cruise."

Tae Hwan's half brother is not how Brad imagined. Then again, few things in Korea are. When Wolf Blitzer and his guest entertainers bloviate about affairs half a world away, it is easy to assume South Koreans live with the fear American media peddles. Nuclear tensions, viral outbreaks, raging dictators. Yet few things are more speculative than American news, a fact Brad is beginning to understand.

Still, when this full-blooded Korean man with a George Clooney beard and a poet-chic fashion pulls up in a McLaren 570GT, Brad admits he is privately surprised.

"Agent Lee, is it?" Tom asks.

"Yes, nice to meet you, Tom," Brad says. He isn't sure whether to shake hands or bow. Tom makes the choice for him, extending a hand and giving Brad's palm a solid squeeze. "You choose that name yourself?"

"I did. *Top Gun* was most popular when I was at American university. Is nice, when you name yourself. Like a—how would I say?—fresh identity."

"Yeah, I can be Brad Pitt. Sounds good."

Tom laughs. If it isn't sincere, at least the effort is. "Can I take you to lunch? There's an excellent American restaurant not far away."

"No thank you. I ate on the train." It has not occurred to Brad to come all the way to Korea to eat the food of his home country. A flash of his paternal Korean grandparents on a family trip to Paris, complaining they couldn't find noodles and kimbap. "Tom, if you don't mind, I have to wait until my colleague arrives from Busan."

"From Busan? Are more investigators coming?"

"No, she's a professor at the university."

"Ah, very impressive," Tom says and takes out a cigarette. It surprises Brad how many people still smoke in this peninsula. Maybe vapes didn't make the leap across the Pacific. "This, uh, professor, what is her—how do you say?—specialty?"

"Forensic anthropology," Brad says. "She's a remains-recovery specialist."

"Ah, very good," Tom says.

There it is again, the same scripted sincerity that had masked Tom's laughter. And when he takes a drag, Brad wonders, *Was his hand trembling before?*

DR. DANA PARK pauses to rest against the trunk of a camphor tree. The sky is a vanilla wash, more clouds than light. Spring hues dance in her black hair. Ahead of them, the forest opens to reveal the rolling lumps of overgrown grass. Burial mounds.

"Need to catch the breath?" Tom asks and stops where the trail meets the slope.

"No, just my bearings," Dr. Park says and turns to study the hill. They are deep in the Gyeongju Kim family burial plots, a long rise on the side of a scraggy hill a half hour's drive from the train station. As the eldest son, Tom has the duty of maintaining this burial site. This Tom tells them as they hike up the old path. And he has been derelict in his duties, he says, picking old twigs off the trail and pulling the occasional weed.

"Can I carry that for you?" Brad asks as Dr. Park places her large backpack against a rock.

"That would be lovely, thanks. Just try not to drop it."

Brad swaps his rucksack to the other shoulder and hefts Dr. Park's backpack. A flash, and he is back in boot camp, a MOLLE strapped to his back and sixty pounds of nonsense filling up every liter. Dr. Park isn't more than a hundred pounds. How the hell is she humping the hill with this weight on her back?

She inspects the trees, the foliage, the dirt, and the rocks. Every now and then, she pauses to turn around and take in the blooming woods. She reminds Brad of Michaels in her attention to detail, and although they have been hiking for an hour, he finds himself falling into his usual romantic reveries. What music might they have at their wedding? What would they name their kids? Will she take his name, or maybe he could be progressive and take hers? They could combine it. They could...

Every five minutes Dr. Park speaks to Tom in Korean and the two banter. Brad's Korean has languished, frozen around middle school when he gave it up altogether. He processes their conversation with a short delay. Tom's Korean is quick, guttural, punctuated with the occasional sigh and the sucking of air through his teeth. Dr. Park's is soft. Brad senses a bit of an accent—Australian, or Kiwi perhaps—peeking out at times. This goes on as they walk. Then Dr. Park turns to Brad and says, "I asked about the wild boars out here. He said he hasn't seen any."

And that is that.

The top of the trail now, where the hills flatten into a bramble plateau. Gingko blooms in yellow explosions. Late cherry blossoms flutter in the warm breeze, snow-dusting the spring grass.

"Wow," Brad says, rendered nearly silent by this place of rest. "This is something else."

"Korea is, ah, very old country," Tom says. "Funerary rites are important. This has been family land for many generations."

Dr. Park speaks in Korean. Tom gestures toward the far side of the plateau. There are more mounds there, five or six feet high, twenty feet in diameter. Some are adorned with stone markers. Some are not. To Brad, there is a shadow of familiarity in such a place. It whispers of reverence that transcends cultures and geography. This is where memory rests.

And it is a puzzle too, one he doesn't know how to approach. For this he is glad the embassy put him in touch with Dr. Park, even if his back is sore from her pack.

"You can put it down here," Dr. Park says and gestures to a mound near the forest's edge. "Tom, this is your brother's grave, Kim Tae Hwan, yes?"

Tom nods and fishes out another cigarette. He spots some weeds at the base of a mound. Rolls up his sleeves and starts pulling. Wipes dust from his ancestors' stone markers.

All the while, Dr. Park unzips her rucksack and lays out the pieces. Brad tries to mentally assemble her tools. First it is a radar gun, then a weed whacker. With the snap of a long rod, it becomes a metal detector. Now wheels click into place and it is some rolling device with a mount for a smartphone.

"I can't tell if you're going to cut the grass or search for bottle caps," Brad says. *God, you sound dumb when you try to sound funny.* Dr. Park, with her PhD and mid-calf hiking boots, her visiting fellowship. What could a thirty-year-old CBI agent say that could charm her? *Be professional. Stop falling in love with every woman that smiles your way.*

"It's HD GPR," she says. "High-density ground-penetrating radar. It's... Well, it does what the name says."

"Oh, is that like LiDAR?"

"Actually, it's quite different. But when they're used in tandem, you could map out a whole city, aboveground features and below."

She begins rolling the device in a slow line, like a lawnmower.

Ten meters, turns, then back ten meters. Ten meters, turns, then forward.

"I saw LiDAR at a trade show," Brad says. "They had it on this little drone you could throw into the air and it'd fly right through an open window. They had an attachment for a Taser, but I s'pose you could even put a gun on it."

"Some of the most revolutionary tech in the history of our species and men want to weaponize it."

"Yeah," Brad says. "I thought it was pretty tasteless too."

The corners of her lips hint at a smile. "Ever been to Myanmar?"

"Just last year on Google Earth."

"We mapped the new temples at Bagan, buildings totally unknown. Used just a tractor and HD GPR kits. I have a colleague in Yemen who's using this to find ordnances dropped in the war. In a few years, we'll probably be digging up all kinds of discoveries: lost subway tunnels, Roman villages, Neanderthal graves. But I'll tell you this, Agent Lee: we won't be finding anything here."

She stops pushing the device and lets it settle near the base of the mound.

"Come again?"

She holds out her smartphone. The screen is a full-color cloud, shades of blue, red, and green. With a touch, she rotates the image, and Brad realizes he is looking at something like a 3D ultrasound.

"We won't find anything here," she repeats, "because there's nothing here to find. This isn't a grave."

"What do you mean?"

"I mean Kim Tae Hwan isn't buried here. No one is."

Deep in Brad's mind, he has always entertained this possibility. Investigators are taught not to assume past evidence is perfect. Still, he had relegated the doubts to a dark corner, the place where assumptions went to be forgotten.

"Look at those graves." She points to a pair of mounds by a

maple. "As the body decays and the coffin rots, the mounds form an indentation—a pocket collapse. See?"

Brad has to squint, but when she says "pocket" it all becomes clear. Not a space where something is, but where something was. A sagging of the earth. Now that he knows what topography to look for, he spots it upon other burial mounds.

But not this one.

"Earlier, I asked him if he was present for his brother's funeral, and he said he was the only one. He…" She pauses.

"Shit, where is he?" Brad asks, scanning the empty plateau. No puffs of cigarette smoke at the tree line. No crunching of twigs as Tom clears a few graves. "Did Tom just pull a runner?"

Dr. Park is already on the move and damn she moves fast. A few strides and she's at the edge of the trail. There, they can see the distant shape of Tom running down the weedy path, stumbling, falling, then getting up to run downhill some more.

Brad, paralyzed by confusion. Then his brain screams, *Chase him!*

Dr. Park grabs him, gesturing, *Wait.* She's already dialing, pressing the phone to her ear.

"He's getting away!"

"We're in a peninsula with water on three sides and the DMZ to the north. Tom's not going anywhere." Then, into her phone, "Agent Moon, badge fifty-nine delta three." A pause as she eyes Brad and lets his mind catch up with her words. "Operator, I need a detention on foreign soil. South Korea, I pre-flagged his name this morning." Another sidelong glance at Brad. "No, the *other* one. Yes. Good. He's heading to an orange McLaren, parked near Geogok-ro, in Oryu-ri. Yes, Gyeongsangbuk-do. Ping my location. Have the police detain him until we arrive."

She hangs up. Looks at Brad. His lips make little gasps as he connects the dots.

"What?"

"You… You work for the Foundation?"

"Don't be ridiculous. We both know there's no such thing." She begins disassembling her HD GPR scanner. "Don't we?"

"Who the heck are you?" Brad stammers.

"Me?" She considers the question as if it has never been asked. "I'm a research geek with unique funding and a few friends in common. Come, help me pack this up."

47

CLEARWATER
WEDNESDAY - 6:00 P.M., PST

NINE HUNDRED FEET BELOW THE SURFACE, THE CLEARWATER SUITES rival Singapore and Hong Kong in their cost per square foot. They are fully contained living quarters, capable of housing families through Armageddon. A bathroom, a shower, living spaces separate from the bedroom. Lighting is ample. The color temperature synchronizes to the time of the day. There is an exit at each end of the suite; one leads to the outer hallways, the other leads in deeper, to a central chamber, a series of communal rooms and recreational facilities and a library whose shelves are now empty.

The doors to the outer halls remain locked, always.

When the common room unlocks, the first to step out are those who have made peace with their confinement. The others, those who know nothing of the murders—or claim to—linger in their suites like animals, hesitant to venture beyond the metal doors.

"Holy smokes, it's skinny Felix himself," says Sam Stephens, striding across the common room to meet his old friend. "Not so skinny anymore, amigo."

Felix's gaze traces Sam's bulky frame. A smirk tells Sam all he needs to know: the feeling is mutual.

"The Straight Shooter," Felix says. "What ever will your listeners do now that their mad dog is muzzled?"

Sam shrugs. "I was getting tired of that hustle anyway. Maybe I'll run for office."

"God help us."

They hug, slapping each other's shoulders and squeezing tight.

"Look at you," Sam says. "Doing well for yourself?"

"Well enough. Until the feds dragged me in. So… you do it?"

Sam paces. "Can't say that I did. Course, I'm not broken up about it either."

Felix rifles through the kitchenette cupboards. Dry goods. Health food. Damn, no liquor. "I got the best sleep of my life after they told me why we were here."

"And why would that be?" asks a voice emerging from an adjacent suite.

"Martin Peck," Felix says, eyeing the scholar with a smirk. "Last time we all bunked up, we were chasing tail in Bangkok."

"Indeed, we were," Peck says. "Technically, I believe Sam ended up chasing head."

"A nice surprise on the government's dime," Sam says. "How are you these days, Pecker?"

Peck sinks into the couch, feet up on the coffee table. "Older, none the wiser." He eyes Felix. "You dodged my question. Why would you sleep well if you're suspected of murder?"

Felix walks the perimeter of the common room, a dog checking the fence. "Because I didn't murder anyone, you Mr. Bean-looking creep. I thought this was a tax pinch."

Another door, another voice joining. "What about you?" asks Maggie Neuhaus, inspecting the communal DVD collection. Pixar flicks, a few dozen documentaries. Nothing beyond PG-13.

"Me?" Felix asks.

"No, Peck," she says. "You were always saying how you'd make the program pay."

"And they did pay," Peck says. "For my masters and PhD."

Sam points a stubby finger at Peck. "You used to read those stories in group."

"'And what rough beast, its hour come round at last,'" Felix recites. "'Slouches towards Bethlehem to be born?' Spooky stuff."

"Yeats's words, not my own," Peck says. "You think I'd whack some quacks and not hit a bank? I drive a fucking Yaris."

"Not if you wanted to stay above suspicion," Maggie says.

"This is pathetic, all of you," says a new voice in the fray. "You nu-nu-know how y'all sound?" Lucy lingers by her suite door, one hand on her gray braids.

"We nu-nu-know how you do, Lucy," Sam says. "Nice to ca-ca-catch up."

"Samuel, it's an engineering miracle they squeezed your ego down here," Maggie says. "Lucy, c'mere dear."

"Still painting these days, Margret?" Sam asks. "I meant to catch your latest show but I don't live near a Goodwill."

A middle finger from Maggie, then no more. She and Lucy find a quiet corner by the stationary bikes.

"Lucy is right," says a voice by the refrigerator. With shaking hands, Patricia Whitehead fishes out a bottle of water. "We sound like a bunch of old farts, wheezing over the bill at Denny's."

"I bet she's the one," Peck says to Felix and points at Patricia. "You remember how strong she was?"

Felix nods. "Bent one of the pods right in half."

"That's right," Patricia says, her left hand slipping against the plastic bottle cap. "And I didn't see straight for a month." She puts the bottle in the crook of her arm, twists, fumbles.

A tan hand takes it from her. Jamal Munday, shaven and clear-eyed. He opens it, passes it back to Patricia.

She continues. "I also remember when Felix broke Dr. Chow's arm."

"Check your memory," Felix says. "That was Dr. Moore's arm. And Teddy did it, not me."

"Teddy!" Sam shouts at the remaining three suites, all shut. He bangs on the first door. "Where are you, kiddo? C'mon out." Bangs on the second door. "Teddy?" Third door. "Oh... hello."

"Teddy won't be joining us," Caitlyn says, using her cane and left hand to feel her way into the common room. Sam waves his palm before her face, but Caitlyn simply looks off at a distant nothing as she traces her way along the wall and over to the sofa.

"Who the hell are you?" Felix asks.

"Someone who shares your skill and predicament, but not your past," she says. "I'm Caitlyn. I wasn't part of this program. I wasn't lied to, denied, forced to participate past my consent."

"Oh, so you've read our files," Maggie says. "Lovely."

"Enlighten us," Peck says. "How'd you become decoherent without the DZ3 lobotomy?"

"A brain lesion," Caitlyn says. "I went blind and gained second sight."

"Wow, that's, uh… That's some deep irony and all," Sam says, drawing close, closer now. So close she can smell his salty musk. "So how'd you wind up here with these losers?"

"She's the specialist," Maggie says. "The fed lady mentioned her. That's you, right?"

"That's right," Caitlyn says.

"So wu-wu-why won't Teddy be ju-ju-joining us?" Lucy asks.

"Bet he's living the Rio life." Felix laughs. "Knee deep in pu—"

"Teddy's in a coma," Caitlyn says. "He's all but brain dead."

The coffee pot fills in the silence, burbling and hissing.

"Damn," Sam mutters. "Teddy was…"

"He was one of the good ones," Patricia says, voice cracking.

"And you saw this?" Peck asks. "Figuratively speaking."

"I sat by his bed," Caitlyn says. "I spoke to his mother as the machines breathed for him. He's gone, and so are half the scientists who gutted your minds."

"Maybe his mind," Felix says. "But not mine. Everything's hunky-dory, upstairs and down."

"Oh please," Maggie says. "You don't wake up, confused, sheets wet 'cause you spent weeks walking outside your skin?"

A pop to Caitlyn's right, then a hissing drip. Jamal nurses his hand, a crushed soda can in it. Caitlyn listens to the *ssss-plop-ssss* as Jamal sucks on his fingers. What she can't hear, what she can only sense, are the glances that pass among the cohort. Silence speaking loudly.

"Sons of bu-bu-bitches," Lucy says. "I tried to get treatment for my stu-stu-stutter at the VA. I was denied because I had bu-bu-been dishonorably discharged. Government put an ODPMC in my file. You know what that do-do-do... You know what that means?"

"Why don't you tell us?" Felix says. "Go on."

"It's su-su—"

"It's a discharge, Section 8," Peck says. "'Other designated physical or mental conditions.' They put one in my file too."

"Bastards flagged me for desertion," Sam adds. "Really helps with the red-state cred."

"But you did desert," Patricia says.

"Yeah. But I went back."

"Speaking of co-co-coming back, who are we missing? These numbers don't—"

"Add up?" Felix asks. "No, they don't. Where's Tae Hwan?"

"And Zara," Patricia says. "And what's her name... Cynthia?"

"Nesbit," Peck says. "Cyndi Nesbit. She's gone."

"Gone?" Felix asks. "Like dead? How do you know?"

"Trust me on this."

"We're locked up without due process," Sam says. "And one of us has been offing our former benefactors. Trust is in short supply, amigo."

"Peck, you and Nesbit were close, like this," Felix says and crosses his fingers. "Y'all had a thing, didn't you?"

"We were friends." Peck sighs. "We had common interests, literature and poetry."

"What about common enemies?" Sam asks. "Maybe it was a team effort. You and Nesbit and that Roger fellow, all taking turns. The feds tell y'all Roger was the guide? That's what I figured."

"Well, it wasn't Cyndi," Peck says. "Because I helped her die five years ago."

Another wave of silence settles across the common room. Then: "What do you mu-mu-mean?" Lucy asks. "Helped her du-du-die?"

Peck finds a stool at the edge of the kitchenette. He runs his fingers along the countertop. Caitlyn senses him licking his lips, weighing his words.

"You remember those migraines? Like there was glass behind your eyes you could never dig out?"

"Remember?" Patricia laughs. "It's a good day if I don't get one before lunch. I'm in assisted living. Just so I don't have to drive to the hospital for an IV."

"Yeah, well, Cyndi had those, bad," Peck says. "She was self-medicating. Fentanyl, morphine, you name it. See, she was sprouting a tumor as big as a fist, right behind her eyes. Thing is, it wasn't going to be fatal. It was just going to consume her, bit by bit, until nothing recognizable remained. Cyndi wanted to die but she didn't want to go alone. She visited me, and, well, then I visited her. Not physically but... enough to ease her passing. So I know it ain't Cyndi Nesbit. I watched her draw her last breath and her eyes glaze over. Hell, I called it in so her body wouldn't rot."

Maggie swallows. "We're all going extinct. If we don't do it, something worse will."

"Speak for yourself," Felix says. "I'm going to live to be a hundred at least."

"Why wu-wu-one hundred?"

"Because that's when the president writes you a birthday card," Felix says. "Then I'll write one back and we'll team up to blow this whole operation out of the water. That's the plan, Mr. President and me."

"Or Mu-Mu-Madam President."

Sam scoffs. "Now you're just being silly."

• • •

THE BANK of monitors displays every visible angle: the common area, the recreation rooms, even inside the refrigerators and out from the webcams. Terabytes of live audio and video in perfect sync. Thirty years ago they used reel-to-reel tapes and had to reuse every fifth spool. Now it is all saved to a server, a nineteen-inch 42u rack that sits in the corner, whisper quiet.

Michaels accepts the incoming video from Caitlyn's suite. Her door is closed, and she is sitting down at a desk. "One second," she says.

The original plan called for total Internet isolation, a digital detox. Carruthers had pointed out that restricting Internet usage would restrict information that might implicate the guilty party. Michaels reluctantly agreed. Within each suite is a computer connected to the world in browse-only mode.

He assumed configuring Caitlyn's computer would be a challenge. Not so. JAWS software provides screen-reading, and assistive mode allows her to navigate the OS through function keys. Her hand almost never touches the mouse. He notices she keeps her right ear turned toward the speakers, listening as the voice assistant announces every field and entry.

"It says you're there," Caitlyn says as the video feed crystalizes.

"Hey, how are you holding up?" Michaels asks.

"Well, I feel like Jane Goodall when she first met the apes. They tolerate me, but they don't know what to think."

"That's not a bad spot to be in, I suppose. Did they say anything we should be aware of?"

"Isn't your software scraping the conversations, making little transcripts?"

"Text is a lossy medium. Better to hear it from a friendly face."

"They're complaining the shower smells funny."

"We'll see that's fixed ASAP," Michaels says, and he means it. Demonstrating immediate responses to feedback builds trust.

"Now, for places to start combing, I'd consider Jamal and Lucy."

"Really?" This surprises him. "I pegged Sam and Felix as fron-trunners. Peck too, since he's admitted to blinking."

"Obvious choices, right? And they've all profited. But that got me thinking: why ruin a good thing? I built my travel company on word of mouth. They're the same. They're not looking for a big score but a slow boil."

"You think it could be Lucy?"

"Lucy's stutter is different. It's... How should I say? Like her mind and her mouth can't quite sync up. When I blink for too long, the return is jarring. Things don't fit back in place."

"What about Jamal?"

"Watch the video from earlier, in the common room, maybe two hours ago. Jamal crushed a soda in his hand. It was an acci-dent, but I've had bleed-through where actions I did while blinking carried over."

"Like a reflex?"

"More like an echo. How you twitch yourself awake at night. And if you crushed someone's heart—"

"Your hand might make that same motion. That's really help-ful, Caitlyn. Thank you."

"Well, that's what I'm here for, right?"

"Your insights, and your sense of humor."

She smiles. But it's not the same. Formal, wounded.

"Can we get you anything?"

"You can get me out of here."

"I was thinking like specialty foods or an extra pillow? We're sending out for supplies in an hour."

"Michaels, I'll be honest, I don't think you're going to find any goodwill with this group. All the pizza parties and cupcakes won't solve it. They're pissed."

As they should be. He wants to tell her he regrets this situation and all that came before it. He regrets not trusting her sooner. This grotesque change, from a supervisor to a friend and now some sort of jailor. More than anything, he hopes they can be peers.

That soon this will be an ordeal they can laugh at over drinks, like they had.

"Michaels, are you there?" On-screen, she tilts her head back to the right, trying to read the silence.

"I need to sign off. Let's check back in at six."

"You know where to find me."

Then she is gone, the screen a dark nothing, her voice an echo in his mind: *You know where to find me. You know where to find me.*

48

CLEARWATER

THURSDAY - 7:45 A.M., PST

HE RUNS HIS PALM ALONG THE RAILING, CARESSING THE COOL METAL. Below, eight pods sit in a circular configuration, smooth and near sensuous in their curves. There is a saying about government spending: it expands to fit whatever hole it seeks to fill. Then it keeps expanding.

For thirty years, Robert Chase, MD, PhD, has been accountable to shareholders, angel investors, speculators, foreign entrepreneurs, regulators, boards and boards of sniveling directors. All the while he has been running. From the shadow that clouded his post-doc years. From the rumors even a classified project couldn't contain. From the holes on his CV—1988 to 1993—that simply read, *Director of Research*. Holes filled by the whispers of his enemies.

And he has many.

As any researcher learns, the more one innovates, the more one has to overturn. Ceilings aren't shattered without chipping away at foundations. Mentors professionally passed. The old growth is burned to give room for new seeds of ideas. Yet humans are fickle, wary of change. Ask a man in the midst of an economic boom and he'll say the sky's the limit. Ask him again in a recession and he'll claim the sky is falling. Humans can't tell what part of the wave they're riding, the crest or the trough. To Chase, the base measurement of progress is the decade. Anything less is just statistical noise.

So three decades it is, then, to measure this moment. Here, from his vantage point on the catwalks, humanity has come far. The old test chamber is once again humming. These tanks have evolved into sleek pieces of science and art. Integrated, curved screens display internal temperatures, float gasses, and thermal video. When they are connected wirelessly to biomedical devices, the possibilities are endless. The mute could find a voice, the frail a new way to run. How many minds like Hawking had been lost to sick bodies? Where could the species be if its thoughts were unshackled?

"Almost done, Dr. Chase," a technician shouts from below. There, closet-sized cooling fans had once whirred, desperate to keep low-resolution brain sensors from overheating. Now whisper-quiet hardware feeds the MEG-II scanners, integrated into the pods. Screens, once black and green, now vibrantly render brain layers in sub-millisecond time. What took months to install is now like upgrading a car stereo.

"The meeting starts in a few minutes, sir," his assistant says, breaking Chase's reverie. "Sir?"

The doctor turns to him, a pallid man with a military tag and a pocket full of pens. *ANDERS, M*, reads his military tag. Goodness how young he is. Had Chase's own team been so smooth-faced?

"Sir, they're waiting for you."

Let them wait, he thinks and turns his gaze back to the test chamber as it all comes together. He's waited three decades. They can wait a few minutes longer.

AT A QUARTER PAST EIGHT, the facility is cleared of all nonessential personnel. In attendance: Dr. Chase and the five remaining Clearwater researchers. On the investigative side: Michaels and Carruthers.

Michaels had suspected Chase's former colleagues would be hesitant, perhaps even hostile. Over the past seventy-two hours they have surprised him, trading handshakes and hugs and a great many professional compliments.

From the photograph in Newell's locker, the living are still recognizable. Wrinkles have grown from the corners of their eyes. Hairlines have receded. If there is a single, universal change, it is the appearance of gray. And yet, as they talk across the table and reflect on career trajectories—running a bio-medical supplier, advising a startup, volunteering for Doctors Without Borders—it is, Michaels thinks, as if the years in between have been one life, the time underground another. A life they are falling back into with the familiarity of hometown streets.

The collegial banter fades as Dr. Locke taps on the table.

"Clearwater was a moonshot project," she says. "And we can all remember where we were when we landed on the moon. There were great minds among us, and great minds still at this table. I don't say that as an aggrandizement. I say that out of respect for our colleagues who aren't here. Minds taken from us, from the scientific community, far too early and far too cruelly to go unanswered. Make no mistake, our work contributed to that loss. These consequences weigh heavily on me. If they didn't weigh on you, this table would be empty. But it isn't. And with your help, we can bring their killer to justice."

"Here here," Dr. Ibrihim says and raps on the table. He is big-shouldered, one of the few men from the photo who's kept a full head of hair.

"The profile Agent Michaels has provided us," Dr. Locke says, passing out papers, "along with the in-scene descriptions from Caitlyn, suggests the killer is able to decohere, forming a fully fluid mens corpus unbound by their autobiographical mind. Dr. Chase and I have ranked the past occurrences, but this is working from memory. Do you see any discrepancies?"

Murmurs as the scientists leaf through the handouts. The clicking of pens. "I'd put Teddy up higher," Dr. Chow says.

"Teddy's in a PVS," Chase says. "Tae Hwan and Cynthia are deceased. Zara has been off the grid since the mid-nineties. Those potentials in bold are what we're working with."

"Then let's bump up Felix," Dr. Tannen says. "He was able to form a vaporous telepresence. Didn't he give himself extra fingers?"

"True," Dr. Chow says. "But Lucy was able to create a light-refracting projection. Minus her legs."

"Technically they all were," Dr. Locke says. "But your point is Lucy was first past the post."

"This brings up an interesting divergence," Dr. Ibrihim says. "Are we analyzing based upon their ability at the program's termination? Or potential trajectory?"

"Both," Dr. Locke says.

The conversation goes on as such, the scientists circling names and questioning semantics. Carruthers tilts her notepad toward Michaels. *Academics* is written in blue. Michaels smiles but feels the growing urge to twitch his hands. He'll need to step in. The researchers are debating the difference between "likely" and "high probability."

"What we need," Michaels says, "and what Dr. Locke states you can provide, is biological proof. Who most recently deco-hered? Who could cause this kind of damage?"

Michaels taps his tablet. The TV screen isn't off; it's just displaying a black slide. Now still frames. Indentations on a linoleum floor. A video of the diner window shattering. X-rays of broken bones. An autopsy photo of—

"Enough," Dr. Chow says. "You've made your point."

"No, I'm afraid I haven't," Michaels says. "The point of justice is that it applies to us all. The point of the law is that it works. That point has not been made. Not to whoever did this. Dr. Locke —yes or no—can your team help us?"

"It should be possible, yes."

Carruthers asks what the others are thinking. "How?"

"We can spend all day speculating, but the one thing we know, definitively, is that there is a price for decoherence. Neurotrauma occurs in exponential proportion to mental force exerted over time and distance. To fuel the mens corpus, the mind consumes itself."

"Younger brains are more resilient," Dr. Tannen adds.

"Correct. The prefrontal cortex isn't fully wired until the mid-twenties. Our youngest subjects showed the fastest growth at the cost of demyelination. Their neurons unraveled. There was a genetic component we tried to identify, but forgive me, this was before 23andMe. What we can do—what we can demonstrate—is a baseline level of capability. We use MEG-II scans and run the subjects through stress tests. We compare pre and post brain activity with known trajectories."

"You want to give them brain damage," Carruthers says, "to see how much brain damage they gave themselves?"

"I want to help find a killer, Special Agent. This is no different than an allergy test. Prick the skin, measure the response."

"Or a polygraph," Dr. Chow says, "accurate to the neuron. Unbeatable."

"And we'll have a friendly to assist," Chase says. "Caitlyn will be our control."

"So we're sending her in with a potential killer," Carruthers says, "and hoping they'll play nice?"

"We have countermeasures," Chase says. "Audio and physical stimulation. And sedatives. Dr. Chow's new pods and biosuits allow for remote activation."

"Propofol," Dr. Chow says. "No different than when you get your wisdom teeth removed. The doses are titrated."

Chase continues. "And any deviant neural activity will correspond to the suspect. We pinpoint them, sedate them."

"Yeah, we wouldn't want to gas them," Carruthers says.

"What happened to officer Fenton was unconscionable," Dr. Locke says. "And unpredictable. I will atone for it before God. But if there's a sliver of good, it's that his ailment helped us understand the variables that caused Gulf War syndrome."

"I'm sure Roger was pleased to assist," Carruthers says.

"Special Agent Carruthers," Chase says, "if there's something on your mind, speak freely."

She clicks her pen. "I just... I think we're losing the plot here. Michaels, I do. We're talking about testing brains and probing neurons."

"True," Michaels says. "Is that different than using DNA to place a subject at the scene of a crime?"

"DNA shows probability."

"So does this. If my gun is missing a slug and there's a victim with one in its head, that's probability. If it matched, you'd arrest me. Those people down there? Their minds are the weapons. We just need to measure the caliber."

"This is way past the edge of the map," she says. "I'm not comfortable here."

Chase's chair squeaks as he sits down. "That is a good thing, Special Agent. It means you respect the power."

"Eduardo Alvarez," Michaels says. "Argentina, 1892."

Carruthers squints. "What?"

"You didn't study him at Quantico?"

"That was twenty-six years ago."

"In 1892, Inspector Alvarez got the first murder conviction using fingerprints. A mother. She slit her kids' throats and then her own to escape suspicion. That these ridges on a finger could connect someone to a crime was totally untested. Until then. We can wax about historical hindsight, but the fact remains that Inspector Alvarez had to choose: let fear of the future paralyze him or embrace a new science and bring justice for the dead."

"It's not paralysis—it's prudence." She taps the handout. "These are mental exercises, not absolutes."

"Neither is a police lineup. But it's a tool we still use."

"Show of hands," Chase says and searches the faces at the table. "How many have full faith in Dr. Locke's methodology?"

One by one, everyone with a career in research raises their hand.

"Unequivocally," Dr. Chow says.

49

GYEONGJU, SOUTH KOREA
THURSDAY - 9 P.M., KST

"YOU HAVE EXPERIENCE WITH INTERROGATIONS?" DR. PARK ASKS AND drains the last of her tea. She drops the paper cup in the recycling bin.

Brad stifles a yawn. "Uh, yeah. Actually, I kicked this whole thing off in a room just like that."

"Good. They'll bring him in soon."

If Dr. Park is impressed, she hides it well. His words slide right off her, like rain against a statue. And why wouldn't they? The whole day has played out just as she said it would. The backhoes arrived at the gravesite before they'd hit the freeway. Within three hours, Tae Hwan's grave was exhumed.

As for his half brother, Tom, the Korean police caught him twenty kilometers up the Seoul-to-Busan freeway, walking after his McLaren spun out. The KPD passed him off to the KCIA, who kept him in detention for Dr. Park. She surprised Brad yet again when she identified herself as a badged member of Interpol's narcotics force. Koreans take a dim view of substance abuse beyond alcohol, she had said. This bought them time to let Tom sweat. When they arrived, the KCIA pointed out Tom was technically a dual citizen.

And now, hours after he had been pulled off the highway,

crying, the high-angle video feed shows Tom being led into the interview room, sweating and ready to crack.

She turns to Brad. "You're up."

He stands up. She doesn't. "Wait, you're not coming in?"

"I spent four years building this cover and I'm up for tenure review in a month. I'm not risking my assignment for yours. For all Tom knows, you called this in."

"What if he speaks Korean?"

"Then make him speak English. This isn't California. Ball a fist, raise a hand. He probably expects to get roughed up."

"I'm not really comfortable, like, beating him or—"

"That's fine. Just don't tell him that, okay?"

"Okay."

"If you need something, just whisper." She holds out an earpiece with a hair-thin transmitter. Damn, Korea really does have all the toys. "Turn around."

Dr. Park snakes the clear wire around his left ear and thumbs the driver into his canal. Goosebumps. Whoever she is, she's fascinating. An expert forensic anthropologist. Fast-acting in a pinch. Earlier, she drove stick, shifting like they were in the Le Mans. It doesn't hurt that she has a jawline as sharp as an oaken frame. Why does he always mistake attention for interest?

"Go get your confession, Agent Lee."

Thirty seconds later, the interview door closes behind him. "Mr. Thomas Kim," Brad says, dropping an octave. He slides a chair up to the desk. "You have been a bit loose with the truth."

Something hardens in Tom's eyes. "You," he says. "You don't have jurisdiction here. I don't have to talk to you."

"Our governments have an extradition treaty," Brad says. "And as far as I can tell, you've been receiving survivor benefits from your brother, courtesy of two countries. That's fraud, Tom. And when it happens across borders, it's called international fraud. We pulled Tae Hwan's casket. There's no body. You've spent twenty-seven years tending to an empty grave."

"I don't know anything about that."

"The U.S. embassy says you do." Brad slides a folder to Tom. "That's your signature, your family stamp right there. You filed a Foreign Death of an American Citizen report. "

"I never opened the coffin. How would I know he wasn't inside it?"

"I see your English has improved."

Tom shrugs. Brad scoots in. Close enough to smell the sweat off Tom after hours in custody. He thinks, *WWCD? What would Carruthers do?*

"Tom, come on. I know brothers can be a pain in the ass. Mine sure was. He made me do his homework, all the way through high school. He got into CalTech on the grades I earned. Now he's a manager at some big German conglomerate. Married, lives in the EU, and summers in Greece. Last time we met up, he lectured me about hard work paying off. Like he earned every cent. Brothers suck. But you know, they're family too, so what can you do?"

Brad leans back. It had all just come out. And it was the truth. Every word.

"Was… Was that, like, to build trust or something?" Tom laughs. "I grew up in the States. I own a condo in Westwood. That's some second-rate cop-drama stuff. It's cute. Tell me, do you really think my country will extradite me over an alleged social security scam?"

Keep it together. "No, maybe not." A pause, then: "Of course, they'd cooperate with a murder investigation. Multiple. Especially if you received financial assistance in exchange for a false cover."

"Murder," Tom says, and the laugh seems forced now. "That's absurd."

"Is it? Because I'd like you to meet someone. Dr. Francis Linamore."

Brad slaps a photo down on the table. Tom studies it, mind trying to piece it together. How it had once been human. And how a human could be reduced to such broken matter.

"Oops, bad pic. Here's a better one. Newell Sacks."

"I... I don't want to see that—"

Another photo on the table. The broken tiles of the San Francisco diner. The broken skull of the lawyer.

"Dang, how about this angle?" Another photo. Santa Rosa. Professor Moore, his office painted red from arterial spray.

"Stop!" Tom cries. "I'm going to be sick!"

"You're going to be more than that, Tom. If Tae Hwan had anything to do with this—and you offered him even one helpful word—they'll see you tried as an accomplice on American soil. Death penalty, Tom. Let that sink in."

Tom, stifling wet gasps now, trying to look away. "You're stretching the leash," Dr. Park says over the earpiece. "Now pull it back in."

Brad hands Tom a tissue and waits. The waterworks subside. Then, with a deep breath, it all comes out.

"My brother is dead, okay?"

"Bullshit, Tom."

"It's true. He died twice. And you're right: his grave has been empty. Tae Hwan was in the collapse, but he made it out. He said his girlfriend *saved* him. He came here to visit, but not like this. He was... I could see right through him. I could feel him when he spoke."

"Like a ghost?"

Tom nods. "He was still alive, just distant. And he said you people would come looking for him. One day or another. That you had done things and he would never be free and this was his chance. So we buried him. I never saw our father cry so hard. Korean funerals last for three days and I've carried his secret for every hour since."

"Tom, when did you see Tae Hwan?"

"Never. Only a voice or a touch. When our father died, Tae Hawn visited and said, '아버지는 형님이 자랑스러우실 꺼예요.'"

Brad slowly translates. "Our father—"

"'Dad would be proud of you.'"

Brad sits back. This is all too much, too weird. A breath, some balance.

"You said he died twice. Explain."

"He sent letters with money orders. Instructions on how to deposit them. Then they all stopped. The letters, the money, the midnight whispers. I knew then his paranoia was right. Maybe you people had finally caught him."

"When was this? The date, or the place the letters came from, anything?"

"I don't remember," Tom says. "But if you take me home, I will show you his last words."

50

CLEARWATER
THURSDAY - 10:00 A.M., PST

WITH A DEEP RUMBLE, THE HALLS UNDER CLEARWATER CANYON COME alive with the pounding of feet moving to stations. There is no guard at Roger's old desk. The security is automatic now, keypads and overrides replaced by biometric recognition. Cheap hardware by government standards, all procured off the shelf.

In the front of the observation booth, Dr. Chase perches like a cat in its favorite sunbeam. He doesn't smile, at least not outwardly. Such displays are, in his opinion, reserved for moments of triumph. What is unfolding now is no such moment. Rather, it is an opportunity, and opportunities require strategic thinking. No time for smiles. Not yet.

"Shall we begin calibrating the tests?" Dr. Locke asks as she powers on a bank of monitors. To her left, the wide window looks down upon the test chamber. "Robert, I'll need your voice authorization."

There is a hesitation, a procedural sigh where even the walls seem to hold their breath. The screen on Chase's tablet flashes a prompt. The spectrogram reads flat. Then...

"Authorized, commence test calibration. Challenge green."

"Response alpha," chirps the tablet, far more pleasant than the sibilant speakers of old. So it begins. The deep unlocking of pipes.

The flicker of screens. The pod doors rising open, like hands to the sun. A place for everyone, and everyone in their place.

Dr. Locke, supervising the bank of monitors, directing the assistants.

Dr. Chow, checking the status of her pods.

Dr. Beane, synchronizing a pushcart of wireless medical sensors.

Dr. Tannen, readying a station of kettlebell weights and gel pressure cubes.

Dr. Ibrihim, calibrating the cameras and microphones to balanced recording levels.

Dr. Chase, finding it all marvelous to behold. What took a dozen full-timers and another two dozen lab assistants is now half automated by machine-learning AI. The humans are truly the assistants.

"Dr. Chase, we're prepping in the control subject," Dr. Locke says. "This may take a moment, if you'd like to sit."

"No," he says. "I prefer to stand."

THREE FLOORS BELOW, there is a shower, a bench, and a series of lockers. Atop the waiting room door, the timer counts down. It all strikes Michaels as a bit theatrical.

"What's that noise?" Caitlyn asks, her right hand touching the edge of the wall and following the rail.

"The door will unlock in under a minute," he says. "I imagine it's going to be a bit loud. They're basically bank vaults."

"Ah, that explains the earbuds." She thumbs the wires hanging around her neck. Silicone-molded earbuds on a cable leash. "Just tell me the skivvies aren't pink."

She is wearing a drysuit, a thing of form-fitting neoprene and latex. It looks comfortable to his eye, but he tries not to stare. Like a kid catching a glance of his summer crush in her bikini.

"No, it's black," Michaels says, adding, "It looks rather badass."

"Yeah, that's me, badass and totally not nervous." She gives him the A-okay sign.

"Don't be. You're just calibrating the tests. They need a baseline."

"Like a vanilla ice cream? Start there, then go to funky monkey or bacon and toffee."

"Trust me, Caitlyn, you're anything but vanilla."

A pensive smile. "I always pegged myself as mint chocolate chip."

"Pistachio," Michaels says. "If my personality was a flavor."

"Okay, let's pretend you never said that."

The timer hits zero. A low buzz and the clattering of locks. As the door opens, Michaels raises a hand over his eyes. Caitlyn feels the change, the dim glow becoming a bright, sterile sheen off metal and plastic. It hits her cheeks like a desert wind.

"Jesus," he says and gives her elbow a squeeze. "It's like the floor of a coliseum."

He leads her out, through the doorway, into the test chamber. His eyes rise to take in the concrete terraces, the lights, the catwalks. Cameras and sensors and microphones, all mounted on trusses. Above, the one-way mirrors wrap around a third of the room, steeply angled with enough space for observers to look down. A flash in his mind: an amoeba on a microscope slide.

Before them, spread out in a flower petal formation, are the pods. Eight white ovoids, near seamless, both futuristic and archaic. White, fused metal and plastic, splayed open to reveal blue lights and shimmering shadows.

He tells Caitlyn each and every detail before him. He helps her run a hand over her pod. As the assistant wheels a cart out, Michaels itemizes each tool upon it.

"A swim cap, not pink. A pair of darkened goggles. A few towels. There's a shaving razor."

"What for?"

"We have to install a blood monitor," Anders, the assistant, says. "I'm going to unzip your biosuit down to your right shoulder. Is that okay?"

Caitlyn nods. The young man shaves Caitlyn's tricep.

"Here comes the alcohol wipe. And in a moment you'll feel some pressure, and—done."

The click lasts half a second. There is pressure. Then there is a tan puck on her arm the size of a few quarters.

"Not bad," Caitlyn says. "You've got a gentle touch, Doc."

"Oh, I'm not a doctor," Anders says. "Not yet. We'll be done here in a moment."

He attaches an IV line to the sensor, threads it through the biosuit to a bag. Michaels eyes the label as it slides into a zippered pocket. *Propofol.*

"What color are the towels?" Caitlyn asks.

"Green," Michaels says. "All of them."

"Ah, that's a good sign," Caitlyn says. "You know that story about Van Halen and how they demanded bowls of M&Ms backstage, with all the brown ones taken out? People thought they were just picky. But really, it was how they ensured the venue read the contract and did the rigging safely. When they found brown M&Ms backstage, they knew to double-check everything."

"So you asked for green towels," Michaels says. "Clever."

There is a click from above, then a short crackle. Dr. Locke's voice booms through the chamber. "Caitlyn, we're almost ready here in the control booth. How are you feeling, hon?"

"Good, I guess."

"We'll have you comfy here in a moment. Can you feel the rim of the pod, just to your right? Good. Now, the pod's at a slight incline, thirty degrees. It'll be like climbing into a big La-Z-Boy. There's handles to help you in. There you go."

The smooth rim ends and then there is nothing. Or rather, what feels like nothing. A void. And yet, something pushes back against her fingers.

"That's a bio-plastic membrane inside," Dr. Locke says. "Six times less dense than air. When it's fully inflated, the sensation's like floating."

"I thought these used water," Michaels says.

"Most do," Dr. Locke says. "But this is less intrusive, more hygienic. Just lean onto the surface, Caitlyn. It'll mold to your shape."

Bathed in blue light, Caitlyn lies back. The plastic shimmers, a thread-wrapped fog, or a cloud somehow stitched together. It is impossible to see its edges, yet sure enough, when Caitlyn moves, she is embraced by the mist.

She asks, "Does this look as weird as it feels?"

"You have no idea."

"The membrane will adjust to your body temperature," Dr. Locke says. "Just try to get comfortable. In the meantime, Dr. Beane's going to take over."

Caitlyn traces the edges of the pod. Feels the T-shaped top where the side opens. Sensors the size of golf balls. She continues following the top of the pod, the sides. Eight feet long by five feet wide and a few feet deep. Just enough to feel that it isn't quite enough.

"Hi, Caitlyn," says a voice to her right. Southern, friendly, a hint of coffee with too much sugar. "Dr. Beane here. We met earlier. How's your pod feel? Not too tight, I hope."

"Not so far."

"Good. Now let's sync your biosuit up with the MEG-II scanner. We'll be monitoring a whole host of functions. Don't be afraid to talk to us, tell us how you're feeling, okay?"

"Okay."

A body shifting to her left, fingers tapping a tablet. Then warmth as hands near her. The membrane jiggles. "There we go," Dr. Beane says. "Got a nice, steady heartbeat. Great respiration. Caitlyn, would you squeeze your hands and feet and hold your breath for ten seconds? Starting now, and ten, nine, eight…"

Thousands of vibrations along the suit, haptic motors, like fingers playing piano up and down her skin.

"… two and one. Release," Dr. Beane says. "I hope that didn't tickle."

"No, it sure didn't," Caitlyn says. But it was almost sensual.

"Let's fit your MEG-II cap on. If you'll just lay still, face up."

A squeak to Caitlyn's left as the cart is pulled over. Dr. Beane's hands on her forehead, brushing hair back. Other senses: the snap of stretching rubber, a tightening from nape to forehead, now the squeeze on her crown.

"You'll feel some pressure as we connect the SQUIDs to your cap."

"Squids?"

"Superconducting quantum interference device," Dr. Beane says, and sure enough there are a series of button-like clicks as sensors snap into sockets. "SQUIDs detect magnetic activity at the neural level. They let us get a look upstairs." He taps her forehead.

"Ah, good luck," Caitlyn says. "It's mostly cobwebs."

"I very much doubt that. Now let's connect your earbuds. You'll hear some humming, then silence, perhaps a slight delay when—"

A heavy blanket envelopes her, a field of infinite quiet. Then a low thrumming, hissing, rising. Is that the sound of her blood?

"There we go. How's that, Caitlyn?"

"Good," Caitlyn says. "Wow, that's really clear."

"It's a pure audio feed, from my mic to your ear. We'll connect the others momentarily. First let's train your mic to filter nonverbal input. It's amazing how noisy our bodies are. My gut is like the 1812 Overture. Okay, repeat after me: wave, vintage, eastern, gentle sir…"

"Wave," Caitlyn says and licks her lips. The doctor is right: there are countless micro-sounds. Creaking teeth, booming veins, a rattle with each breath. "Eastern… gentle sir."

"Good. One more pass and here we go. Yosemite, Milton, nodding, discombobulate, cellar door—"

Caitlyn repeats them all, careful not to make little P-pops with her lips.

"Great. Can you cough for me?"

Caitlyn coughs. Or at least she tries to. There is nothing. She tries again.

"That's good, Caitlyn. The filter's working. Neat, isn't it?"

"Yeah." She snaps her finger next to her ear. Nothing. She touches her cap. A mohawk of sensors and wires join a central, braided ribbon, connected to the tank behind her.

"It can be disorienting at first, but you'll settle in quick. In the meantime, try not to bang your head. Those sensors are worth more than a Ferrari."

Caitlyn takes a deep breath, lets the cool air fill her lungs. She is the focus of a great many eyes. Is this how divers feel, exploring the dark scars of the Mariana Trench? Or astronauts and Mission Control? Frightening, yes, but tinged with addiction. She can imagine signing up for this, one small step at a time.

"Caitlyn, this is Dr. Locke. We're about ready to begin. Do you have any questions for us?"

"When I'm inside, will you see me?"

"We have infrared cameras inside your pod, as well as 3D mapping. We can read your lips, see when you're smiling or if you're distressed. Someone will be watching you at all times for signs of discomfort. I see you've had an MRI recently?"

"About two years ago."

"Well, this should be familiar."

"So I need to stay still?"

"Not at all. Just relax in whatever position's comfortable. Once closed, the membrane will pressurize and temperature-match your body. Are you ready?"

Another deep breath. Or rather, she thinks about it. Tells her body, *Breathe*. But did it follow the command? Hard to tell. She touches her chest, feels the rise and fall. "Should we do a count-down, or...?"

"We can. Would you like that?"

"It's always been helpful."

"Okay, let's give Caitlyn a countdown. Sixty seconds, starting on my mark. Here we go. Mark sixty... fifty-nine..."

MICHAELS LEANS AGAINST THE GLASS, watching the test chamber below. Such organization. Five lead researchers, a half dozen technicians, two government agents, and one supervising scientist. A symphony requires perfect coordination, and this is as close to synchronization as he's ever seen. Here, in these halls of iron and stone, as the pod swallows Caitlyn with a confident click, Michaels understands how Dr. Chase had fallen in love with this lab.

"Thirty-three... thirty-two... thirty-one..."

Michaels stops at the monitoring station. There, on nine screens in a three-by-three configuration, is Caitlyn in cool greens and blues of infrared. Dr. Ibrihim maximizes the video feed so Caitlyn takes up all nine screens.

"She's getting comfortable," he says. "You know this setup would have been useful a few decades back."

"What did you use then?"

"Boom mics and big-ass video cameras. Half the time they shorted. These subjects put out a lot of electromagnetic radiation. When they interact, it can cascade, like a feedback loop."

"Comms quiet please," Dr. Locke says. "Ten seconds."

"Status report," Chase says.

Dr. Beane: "MEG-II is online."

Dr. Chow: "Membrane and pod are temperature-synced."

Dr. Ibrihim: "Audio and video are flawless. We're talking zero interference."

Dr. Tannen: "Blind sites are synched, both local and remote."

Dr. Locke: "Subject's heart rate is rising. Biosuit's registering perspiration."

Dr. Beane leans in. "MEG's registering excitement in the left amygdala." His screens display gray wrinkles and bone, a topographical map of the mind. Two tiny walnuts in the temporal lobes bloom purple, sending out fractal branches that ignite further neon blossoms.

"Fear?" Carruthers asks.

"Unclear. But with the rising heart rate..."

The video feed: Caitlyn's eyes twitching beneath the lids. Hands curling into tight balls. "Is that normal?" Michaels asks.

"'Normal' is an adjective that won't see much use today," Dr. Ibrihim says. "But judging by her pulse, blood pressure, and the MEG scans... I'd say it's within range for someone about to have a panic attack."

51

GREAT WAVES IN THE DARKNESS. SLOSHING WATER, NOW TOSSING HER against the edge of the pod. The cords, the biosuit, the equipment: all submerged. Churning cold drags Caitlyn down into the bottom, where the walls narrow and squeeze.

Water. Salt water.

Okay, be realistic. Something has gone wrong.

Salt water slaps at her chest, her neck, now her chin and her ears. Where is the rescue? Are they getting crowbars? Are they striking the pod and prying it open?

Rising water. *Just need to buy some time. Hold your breath. Survive.*

Now a voice, burbling, "Caitlyn, sweetie, can you hear me?"

There is light. Red and green, bobbing across the murky surface. Caitlyn reaches out, seizes the plastic rectangle.

"Caitlyn?" it hisses. "I need you to answer me."

That voice. She knows it.

"Daddy?" she says and presses the *talk* button. The radio warbles and squawks. The walls groan, old fiberglass and metal. Something falls with a *ker-plunk* and she sees water slap the port window. "Daddy, what's happening?"

"We've had an accident, honey, okay? We're taking on water."

"I was..." Where? Someplace else, someplace different. "I think I was dreaming."

"No time for that, Caitlyn. I need you to listen."

Time. She had been in a different time. A feeling, impossible, that these moments are laid over each other, entwined. No, she is here, now, in this sinking boat.

"Caitlyn, listen to me, okay? Can you do that?"

"I can... I'm so scared but I'll try..."

"That's my girl. Now, I need you to look to your right. What do you see?"

"I... It's so dark."

"Use your hands."

"There's a hose. It's metal. I can feel it on my fingers. Why's it so dark?"

"We lost power. The boat's capsized and we're underwater. Now, I think the surge knocked you out of bed and that's the shower hose, so you're in the head and that's good. You know why?"

"Why?"

"Because you're just a short swim from the V-berth. There's the bed, the forward hatch above it. You climb out through it, okay?"

"What about you? Where's Mom?"

"One thing at a time. We'll be right behind you. Caitlyn, honey, we've practiced for moments like this, remember?"

"Yes, I... I remember."

"Of course you do. Breath in, breath out. Deep breath, then dive. This is our home. You can swim it blind, right?"

"Right."

"Radio me once you're topside. Now go. Swim!"

A breath. She lets it fill her chest. Down to where her ribs met her gut. Everything glistens. Exhale. Now, the deep breath. Now, the dive.

She feels her way through the water, past the edge of the bath-room door, and now confusion. Something in the way. She feels ridges, slats, a knob. A cabinet, yes. In the accident, it must have come open. She pushes the door back, squirms past it. The sea water stings her eyes, a chemical sheen, cooking oil and kerosene and the contents of their kitchen all roiling together.

Right hand pulling her forward, legs kicking, brushing up against... against what? A plant? No plants on the boat, only herbs. Too stringy to be basil or rosemary or—

Another sensation: four short little sticks, soft and curved and ending in–

Fingernails, Caitlyn realizes. A hand, a wrist, a thin band around it.

Mom, she almost screams but forces her lips to stay sealed. She squeezes her mother's hand but it doesn't squeeze back. *Can't stay, losing air, but where?* The V-berth, the plan. *Get air, then come back for Mom.*

Caitlyn kicks and wriggles and swims into the cabin. Smacks into the base of the bed. She knows every inch of the boat, but not at this tilt. Up, up, a pocket of air, thank God! She wheezes, gulping in sharp lungfuls.

Then she reaches back into the liquid. Feels until she feels the unmistakable shape of a body. Long hair, thin neck. Caitlyn grabs a fistful of shirt fabric and tugs.

Nothing.

She ducks into the inky water, wraps her hands beneath her mother's waist. Feels the soft flesh, grips her hips, and pulls... Pulls... *Pulls!*

Still nothing.

Now kicking and twisting and pushing off the angled floor, all her muscles screaming and her lungs heaving and little fireworks bursting at the edge of her vision. *Pop, pop, pop.*

Stone-heavy, her mother lies beneath the water, impossible to move.

Caitlyn can pull no more. She swims back up, into the bedroom, into the shrinking air pocket, eyes burning with tears.

Her father's voice comes in over the groaning of wood. Caitlyn squeezes the *talk* button, sobs. "It's Mom... She's stuck in the cabin. She's not moving, Dad. I can't get her out."

From the cold static, there is a broken cry, then radio silence. It occurs to her in this darkness her father's heart has just shattered. She has known them only as parents, but to each other they were more. Then, in a crackle, the walkie-talkie buzzes to life.

"Caitlyn, listen, focus, okay?" She senses the words are for him as much as for her. Adults are no different than kids; they just have more practice. "You're in the V-berth, right? Can you look up and see the hatch?"

"It's... maybe ten feet away."

"Swim up to it, sweetie. Climb through it and up onto deck."

There is no way to swim up to it; it is not up but over. The boat is full tilt now, an inch of the hatch under the waterline. Behind it, the dim flicker of stars and the red flash of the boat's safety lights.

Crawling, climbing, onto the swampy bed. The mattress slides off like a wet scab and sheets tangle her feet. Now reaching, stretching, fingers so desperate and cold, and then she grasps the latch and she unlocks it from the inside and—

It doesn't budge. Instead of opening upward and sliding, the hatch rattles against an impossible firmness. Impossible because there shouldn't be anything there. She has climbed out this way dozens of times.

No, try again. Up, onto the bed, jiggle the latch and push the hatch and—

Still blocked.

"Caitlyn, honey, tell me you're topside." In the sloshing din lit by the blinking light, she can almost see the obstruction.

"Dad, there's something blocking it. I can't get out."

Radio silence. Seconds that feel like a decade. Then: "Okay, can... can you get back the way you came? Do you see a safe way to—"

A pause. The crackling of static, then a real cracking. The ship lurches. Caitlyn stumbles into the wall. The waterline sloshes to the right, then comes cresting back. *Breathe now.* The wave rises over her, drops. Gasping, spitting, she climbs back onto the bed. Two feet of air. The water is over the starboard window; the way back is a churning morass.

"Caitlyn, honey, are you there?"

"I'm here. Dad, I'm really scared." The most honest words she has said to her father in weeks. Why did it take a tragedy to get them talking again?

"I am too, honey," he says. "Now listen: remember when you were little and we'd go for walks in our dreams? You called them staycations. We'd stay at home and revisit a vacation place. And remember how I made you promise never to do that without me?"

"Dad, I don't understand—"

"Just listen, please! We walked on the water in Boracay. We watched the first snow cover Fuji..."

An old door, forgotten and bricked over, now flung open in her subconscious. She can see those nocturnal wanderings. They hold the crystalline clarity no dream keeps past dawn. Sharp, even years later. But why now, why here?

"And those weren't dreams, honey. We were there."

"I don't... I don't understand—"

"Just trust me, okay?" Frustration in his voice. "We'll get you out of there. Now focus on my voice. Like we did years ago. Ready?"

She places the walkie-talkie at the edge of the shelf. Instinctually, she knows what is coming. Six inches below, the black water rises, rises.

"Ten... nine... eight..."

Caitlyn closes her eyes.

"Seven... six... five..."

She focuses on her breath. Ignores the cracking hull, the

shrinking darkness. Lets the seconds stretch out, each doubling in length.

"Four... three... two..."

There is a shimmer, a sheen that peels from the world. The air pocket collapses until all she sees is a curtain of woven snow, each stitch a distinct place. Caitlyn senses that she now stands before the totality of space and time. That she is, somehow, looking at *all*. What the mind can only perceive as static, cosmic and endless, vibrating and alive.

"One... and zero. Caitlyn, you can step out now. We're ready to begin."

The voice, that isn't her father but one she has forgotten, one she now remembers. A person of science and technology and—

Caitlyn raises her hands. These aren't the grubby fingers of a sixteen-year-old girl; she sees that now. These are her hands and a decade has passed. Her wrists and forearms bear scars and tattoos and a curious wrinkle or two, fossils in flesh of the years since her final night in that boat.

Caitlyn sits up. A sudden tug, like a guitar string plucked hard, vibrating in several places at once. She hadn't clenched her muscles, arched her back. She had simply blinked herself up.

"Oh wow," she says as the static parts. This is darkness, but it isn't wet. The walls are tilted, lined not with portholes but sensors and lenses. And her body. It lies below her, not upon a soaked mattress but embraced by a tissue-thin membrane. A picture of slumbering comfort.

"Caitlyn, this is Dr. Beane. The MEG's showing us you're fully decoherent. Just try to relax. This might be more intense than you're used to—"

"No kidding."

Her voice is different, enveloping. She reminds herself her lips didn't actually move. They are still, sealed, three feet below.

"So we'll be describing a location. We'd like you to visit this place. One moment while we cue it up."

Looking down now, upon herself—her *physical* self. Her

hands, her feet, her slender legs that end in painted nails. Shocking blues and molten golds, colors beyond human perception. An amplifier, that's what they called the test chamber, this blind site. No one mentioned how high it went. And she realizes that if she focuses, she can see the cells of her skin. Harder still, and she can see the very molecules of the air.

[52]

CLEARWATER

THURSDAY - 11:00 A.M., PST

DR. IBRIHIM'S GLASSES SHIMMER AS HE PUSHES THEM UP. OVER HIS shoulder, Michaels studies the MEG-II readout, a brain pulsing tendrils of red, orange, and pink. Visual. Tactical. Spatial. Like a plane's cockpit flying through the aurora borealis.

"Were all your test subjects like this?" Michaels asks.

"We used different imaging back then," Dr. Ibrihim says. "Maybe it's on par for our subjects. All of them, simultaneously. But on their own? No way."

"You've never seen this?"

"Oh I've seen this. We ran DMT tests at UCSF. Watched subjects' brains build entirely new neural routes. Took months. Caitlyn's doing that on her own."

"How is this possible?"

He shrugs. "You tell me, Agent. You found her."

In the test chamber, a technician wheels over a metal cart. Three rows of objects are laid out. The top row: photographs mounted on black paper. The bottom two: kettlebell weights and gel pressure cubes.

Dr. Tannen leans up to her mic. "Caitlyn, we're going to start by measuring distance and spatial reconstruction. We're going to describe the destination. I would like you to project your mens corpus there. Blink there, as you say."

The screen shows her brain settling down. Oranges and yellows subsumed by cool greens and blues.

"Robert, are you catching this?" Dr. Beane asks. Chase nods. Whatever the meaning, it is lost on Michaels. He is an observer, watching a sport and still learning the rules.

In the chamber, Dr. Tannen swipes her tablet, dimming the lights. A projector mounted to the catwalk beams a pattern onto the floor. To Michaels, it looks like a QR code, but with a series of shapes instead of blocks.

"Challenge Amber," Dr. Tannen says over the mic.

Dr. Chow cues up an audio file. A voice, gender neutral, no inflections. "Challenge Amber. Row one: circle, circle, triangle, star, triangle, square, square. Row two..."

It's reading the symbols, Michaels realizes. Left to right, top to bottom. Helicopters have a big H with a circle for a landing pad. This is—

A flash on Dr. Ibrihim's MEG-II scans. Bright reds and deep purples. The text: *DECOHERENCE DETECTED!*

"... triangle, circle, square. Row three..."

Dr. Chow asks, "Jesus, you think she's already here?"

Rubber soles squeaking, Dr. Locke paces between the MEG-II scans and the video stream from inside the pod. She pushes her glasses up. "It's an error. She couldn't—"

The video of the test chamber stutters, skips. Pixels flicker in horizontal lines. Clusters here, inverted rows there. A distortion unfolds in the center of the concrete chamber.

And then it is gone.

"Eight seconds," Dr. Tannen says. "That's going to be a tough time to beat."

"And look at that, a partial mens corpus," Dr. Locke says. "You can see her if you look away."

Michaels tries, but there's nothing in the chamber. "No, look away, Agent," Dr. Locke adds. "Don't just rotate your neck. There."

As Michaels turns, there it is: a shimmer. Like heat on the highway or fog in a sunbeam. An arm, a head, a body standing over the card and studying the photographs. Gone when he turns back. He shivers, every hair on his neck rising straight up.

"What's the MEG show?" Dr. Locke asks.

"Low excitement," Dr. Ibrihim says. "She's barely pumping the gas."

"Can she talk?" Carruthers asks.

"She can try, but don't expect much to—"

"So this is where we're going?" comes the voice. Caitlyn, in clarity that can almost split atoms. Intimate and enveloping. Carruthers spins and looks over her shoulder. Michaels wipes the back of his neck.

Dr. Beane leans into the mic. "Uh, hold for a moment, Caitlyn."

"It's quantum harmonics, Agents," Dr. Chow says. "The aural decay from a higher dimensional source. If it sounds like it's coming from inside your head, that's because it is."

"So she can hear us?" Michaels asks.

"In the traditional sense, she can't hear or see anything. Her mens corpus has no eardrums, no eyes. It's a projection, no more a body than the Mona Lisa is a woman."

"But she can listen?"

"With enough practice she can do whatever she wants. A fully decoherent mind can shed its physical form entirely."

"And you've seen this?" Carruthers asks.

"Glimpsed it on the horizon." Dr. Chow turns to the agents. "Why do you think the program was shuttered?"

"I see no reason not to give the girl a challenge," Chase says. "Dr. Locke, begin spatial apperception."

Fingers, now sliding across the touchscreen, activating an audio file. "Challenge one: spatial apperception."

. . .

CAITLYN, trying to keep her mind on a leash. Trying to fight the absolute awe.

Flashes of her fingernails, the hyper clarity of the chipped polish where cuticles meet skin. If she squints, she can see the fissures and ridges where the polish didn't settle flat, like flying over vast canyons with infinite zoom. No Saturday night edible has ever done this.

Had her brain saved an exact map of the nail as she ran her fingers over it? Even squinting, that act is fallacious. She has no eyelids, just the lingering habit held by her mind.

"Challenge one: spatial apperception," says the androgynous voice. "Task: identify photo labeled target A. Time: thirty seconds."

The voice continues. Caitlyn doesn't need repeat instructions. She is already studying the photograph on the black paper. A nondescript warehouse, old and forlorn. Metal beams, dusty air. Where great machines slumber and rest.

"Should I go here?" Caitlyn asks.

There is a pause, then Dr. Beane's voice in her ear and every corner of existence. "Yes, if you can, that would be—"

Caitlyn focuses on the photo: that dusty warehouse, frozen in time. It expands, blooms out, swallowing her in a blink.

And now she is there.

"Good. Take your time."

"Done," she says. There is no answer. Clearwater is far away, hundreds of miles. This warehouse is somewhere in the American Southwest. A golden glimpse through the broken windows: red mesas and high desert thick with sage blooming purple.

"Challenge two: interpolate new target. Identify object not pictured. Color: silver. Size..."

Caitlyn spots a silver train car sitting on the far side of the warehouse. She doesn't turn, doesn't move. She just blinks and then she is there.

The train car is old, mid-eighties, decommissioned. As the instructions continue, she knows this is her target. "Some game of hide-and-seek," she says. A few resting pigeons flutter and take flight.

"Challenge three: spatial apperception. Task: identify target B. Time: thirty seconds."

No need to walk up the train car steps. In a burst of rusted metal, she is simply inside. There, atop a thin metal pole at the center of a table, is a plastic cube with pictures inside. A new addition. There are still footprints on the dusty floor.

"Challenge four: reconstruction. Task: identify next target. Time: two minutes."

Caitlyn circles the plastic cube, a picture on each side like a museum display. Six close-up shots, each distinct.

Scattered driftwood.

A pile of anchors.

A dark cave at the edge of a beach.

A torn piece of a topographical map.

A charcoal sketch of towering sea cliffs.

Three rocks surrounded by water.

Two minutes, huh? Caitlyn assembles the model in her mind, starting with the topographical map. The lines, the curve of ridges. Simple shapes, gracefully swaying, now filling in with rock and erosion. Sand and seawater, waves in motion. Cold currents threshing against jagged jetties. The ocean spray, and now the tan hues of foam flung into bitter winds.

And the anchors. Barnacled husks of curved iron. Hundreds of anchors loom in the shallows, forming a tidal break of metal decay.

Now Caitlyn is here, wherever this truly is. She senses human feet rarely tread upon this long wash of sand. North, a dark cave yawns with the thundering ocean. East, swallows nest among the crags, swooping and chirping. High above, fog-swaddled cliffs.

"Challenge five: structural breach. Task: identify and enter non-described location north-northwest. Time: two minutes."

Caitlyn studies the endless sand and fog, like the very mists of memory itself. Non-described location? There had been six images. The anchors, the driftwood, the cave. The cliffs and the maps gave her directions. That leaves—

The three rocks off the shore, to her left. Jagged knuckles spotted white and rising from the waves like a fist.

She is there now, standing on these rocks. The white spots are gulls, thousands of them, the stones humming with song. Beyond the rocks, she sees it: a lighthouse perched upon a damp scratch of land.

"Ninety seconds."

As fast as she saw the lighthouse, she is now at its base. Stone and metal rise into the murk where blackbirds circle the lightroom. Caitlyn paces around the tower. On the far side, she finds a door, a chain barring the way. No need to knock. She can peek through the cracks and that's enough to pass through.

"Forty-five seconds."

Inside, corroded stairs twist upward. Lichen blooms in ochre and emerald. At the top, where a great Fresnel lens once took up the whole lightroom, there is only a simple television. Beneath it, a VCR and a sputtering generator. The TV is tuned to static. A tape protrudes from the VCR, waiting and labeled *PLAY ME*.

Caitlyn grew up in the golden days of DVD and the dawn of streaming. Still, she remembers VHS tapes from her schools abroad, which often made do with patchwork electronics.

"Challenge six: object manipulation. Task: acquire next target. Time: sixty seconds."

Caitlyn studies the tape. Object manipulation, that's a new one. She reaches out. A single finger, hesitating, flickering. *Now push.*

Her hand passes through the VHS tape.

Second try. *Focus.* She draws a deep breath. Thousands of miles away, her body does the same. *Focus. Now push.*

The VHS tape rattles. Again, her hand slides through plastic.

"Thirty seconds."

You can do this. You've always known you can do more. Look at you.

Look. You're seeing with eyes that are blind. You can push with a hand that's not there.

The world sharpens, colors without names radiating, lines defined and electric. And when she pushes—

The tape slides into the VCR. The whirring of spools. Static parts, and a title card reads, *Final Challenge. Task: Old Headline. Time: 5 mins.*

A series of images: a metal bull, ready to charge; a wrought-iron fence with a statue of a man in armor; a stone eagle, talon grasping at branches; shadows and light moving down a brownstone facade.

That first image, familiar, but from where? A snippet of news lodged deep in her subconscious.

The images loop, twice more. Then the tape rewinds and is ejected, awaiting another push into the VCR. But the lightroom is empty.

Three thousand nine hundred and sixty-eight miles to the southeast as the particle flies, Caitlyn looks out at the sleek bronze that forms the Charging Bull, a statue meant to inspire tenacity and often branded a symbol of Wall Street consumption.

Then another statue, two thousand feet away. Giovanni da Verrazzano, with his armor and pauldrons. Five hundred years ago he sailed these shores and met with the natives. Four years later, in the Caribbean, he was killed and consumed. Today his metal gaze falls on the grass of the Battery, Manhattan's southern tip at the edge of the Hudson. Boats slice across the windy waters Giovanni once knew.

"Four minutes."

Business to handle. Her task: old headline. Now where to start?

There. By the benches. Several people are reading newspapers. *The Wall Street Journal. The Post. The Daily News.* A young woman, legs crossed and lost in concentration, sips coffee as she skims the business section of *The New York Times.* Nice, Caitlyn thinks, to see print sticking around. More than many things she's lost, she misses the feel of newspaper between her fingers.

But none of those headlines are old.

"Three minutes."

Caitlyn scans the park. Other possibilities: students and textbooks, a couple with Kindles, and a woman with a poodle and *The New Yorker*. All current.

"Two minutes."

Then she spots him. He is older, mid-fifties, a bag of walnuts in his hand. Every now and then, he flings a few to the grass where a scurry of squirrels steal from each other. On his bench: a stack of clipped photocopies.

Caitlyn is beside him now. His head turns ever so slightly at her arrival. He looks at her—through her—then shivers. Now back to his squirrels.

"One minute."

She takes one look at the photocopies on the bench. That is all she needs to see; this is the objective.

Then she just sits. Takes in the world. The kids playing, laughing, chasing each other. A young couple in their active wear, jogging past the glimmering waters. How nice would it be to stand here? To visit this very spot and feel the wind in her hair, the breeze against her skin. Someday. Someday soon. And then—

"Test completed."

Then it is gone. The paper and the park and all of Manhattan. The curtain falls from all angles, subsuming her vision until only darkness remains.

An alarm rings in her ears, harsh. Haptic motors vibrate her biosuit. She touches plastic at her sides, all around her. Stretching out, her fingers fall on the dimpled edges of—what's this?—the pod, yes, its bumpy sensors.

Caitlyn is back.

. . .

IN THE OBSERVATION ROOM, all eyes are on Dr. Beane as he speaks. "Sorry for the alarm, Caitlyn, but it helps keep subjects from wandering too far. If you weren't able to complete all the tasks, that's perfectly fine. Frankly, we—"

"'Mayor Plans Party to Mark New Subway Stop,'" she says over the speaker. "That was the headline."

Michaels notes the total pause on the scientists. Someone scoffs. Then a quick scramble. A lab technician hands a tablet to Dr. Beane, cued up to a PDF with the newspaper. There it is: 11/21/1983. The very words she'd just said.

"Uh, Caitlyn, that's correct," Dr. Beane says. "Would you, uh, please hold while I confer with my colleagues?" Dr. Beane mutes the mic. "Well, there we have it. A perfect score."

Applause and a few guffaws and a half dozen voices all clamoring to be heard. Dr. Ibrihim mutters, "No fucking way." Someone actually pumps their fist. To Carruthers, it's like they just won the Oscars. Michaels even finds himself swept up in the moment.

Dr. Locke has to raise her hands. "Folks, folks, I know this is exciting—"

"Exciting?" Dr. Beane says. "Her measurements are flawless. This validates thirty years of speculation."

"This doesn't just validate it," Dr. Ibrihim cuts in. "This opens entire new paths."

"And you remember that nonlocal mind model Francis was working on?" Dr. Chow says. "He was on to something. We just didn't have the tools." She turns to Chase. "Robert, I could redesign the pods to—"

"Ladies and gentlemen," Michaels says. "I'm happy for you, truly. Can these results help us?"

"Agent Michaels," Dr. Locke says, "these results could help change the world."

"We're not here to change the world, Dr. Locke. We're here to catch a killer. Can we do that?"

"With Caitlyn's cooperation, we can do anything."

DAEGU, SOUTH KOREA
FRIDAY - 2:30 A.M., KST

FROM A MILE AWAY, THE CINDERBLOCK GRID OF THE LOTTE CASTLE apartments lightens the nightline of industrial Daegu. As they drive closer, Brad realizes the apartments are multiple towers, skinny and numbered, like dominos stacked in a row.

Dr. Park says something to Tom in Korean, rousing him from his slumber in the back seat. Tom nods to a building, huge numerals painted on the side: *104*.

As Dr. Park guides the car into the parking lot, Tom grumbles. When Dr. Park responds, he shakes his head and sucks air in through his teeth. *Ah, shibal*, the Korean equivalent of "fuck." Echoes now, of Brad's grandfather, muttering that curse while merging onto the freeway, thinking that because Brad's parents spoke English at home, Brad hadn't picked up Korean slang from his brother.

"Tom Cruise, you still bitter?" Brad asks, eyeing their passenger in the back seat. Post-interrogation, Tom has clammed up, refusing to speak English for the hour-long drive.

"He asked if I could take off his handcuffs," Dr. Park says, "in case his neighbors see him. I told him no."

"Should have thought of that before you left us up the mountain, Mr. Cruise."

Tom barks a few words in Korean; several Brad recognizes. "Son of a bitch," literally. Tom calls this American the deformed offspring of a dog.

No neighbors notice as they perp walk Tom through the lobby, into the elevator, and then down the hall of the eighteenth floor. The lock on his apartment door is a digital keypad. Dr. Park presses her tablet to the sensor. A green blink, deadbolts sliding, then she pushes it open. Motion sensors activate the lights.

"Sit him on the couch," she says, removing her shoes.

The apartment is stunning. Three bedrooms. Granite counter tops. An LG TV that takes up most of the wall.

"Wow," Brad says. "They must pay English teachers well to afford a place like this."

"I'm not an English teacher," Tom spits. "I own twenty schools."

"English schools?"

"And Chinese and math."

"Well, I must have missed your updated résumé," Brad says and deposits Tom on the leather sofa.

Another exchange of words to Dr. Park. Tom deflates again, nods toward a spare bedroom. "Keep him close," Dr. Park says. "I'm going to check the closet. Tom, you better not be wasting our time."

Dr. Park leaves the two men alone in the living room, where the silence is deafening. Brad paces, studying the layout, pleasantly surprised. From the outside, Lotte Castle is ostentatious, a filing cabinet gussied up like a theme park and failing at both. The inside, however, is ultra-modern. Looking out the window, down eighteen floors, Brad sees a playground and a community pool and other buildings like this. The homes of hundreds of families.

"Agent Lee," Dr. Park says, carrying a wooden box.

She places the box on the granite countertop that divides the kitchen and living room. Empties it out. Envelopes, most a similar shape with the familiar red-white-blue trim of air mail. Inside:

carbon paper receipts for international money orders. One thousand dollars each order, grouped in tens or twenties.

Brad lays them out, arranges them by date from 1997 to 2012. Then they end.

Back-of-the-napkin math: a few million dollars over fifteen years. Some of the dates are clustered; some leave gaps of six months at least.

Dr. Park begins photographing each and every receipt, front and back. "Tae Hwan was smart. Keeping the money orders small meant less scrutiny. Turn it over."

No return address. No name. Just the markings of faded stamps, postal codes and distant places. *Camboge. Lombok. Cartagena, Colombia.*

"Looks like Tae Hwan got around too," Brad says.

Tom, rising, takes a step away from the couch and pivots to the floor-to-ceiling window that looks out onto the dark lattice of building 108. And the courtyard below.

And now Tom is running, hands cuffed behind his back, gathering speed as he screams. He braces his body for the window and the fall and the concrete embrace eighteen floors down. Headfirst, he throws himself into the double-paned glass—

And rebounds off, hard.

Tom hits the wood floor with a meaty *thwap*, lights out.

"Jesus," Brad says. "Did Tom just try to kill himself?"

"Yes, of course he did," Dr. Park says.

Brad rolls the unconscious man onto his side so he can breathe. There's a welt already forming. The window bears a matching smudge, the dusting of Tom's hair product.

"Leave him," Dr. Park says. "I just got a pattern match on these locations."

"What if he wakes up and tries again?"

Dr. Park considers it. "You're right."

Five minutes and one rung doorbell later, a pair of neighbors are seated on Tom's sofa, blinking off sleep and nodding respectfully as Dr. Park gives them instructions. One of them keeps looking at Brad. "I am sorry," the man says and gives Brad a deep bow. Then Dr. Park is up, the wood box and its contents under one arm, her tablet in her other hand.

"I told them Tom got drunk and assaulted a foreigner," she whispers. "The police are on the way. But we have to leave, now."

"Why now?"

"Because it's a hundred kilometers to Busan."

Out in the hallway, he stops her by the elevator. "Why are we going to Busan? And hey." He puts his hand over the elevator panel. "I appreciate your help, but look, this is my investigation."

Dr. Park smiles. The smile of a mother about to explain something to a child. The coy smile of insight. And in it Brad sees everything, what he has come to suspect yet fears to hear.

"Agent Lee, respectfully," she says, "this has never been your investigation."

[54]

CLEARWATER
THURSDAY - NOON, PST

To Caitlyn, it is just a twenty-pound kettlebell in the overhead press.

To the observation room, the kettlebell is floating on a ribbon of light. While the scientists confer, Michaels, Carruthers, and Dr. Tannen watch the video feed of the test chamber.

"If she's not using muscle fibers," Carruthers says, "why can't she just lift the whole cart?"

"She probably can," Dr. Tannen says, "if she truly exerts."

"So is it a Jedi thing, like the Force? Or a Buddhist thing, or what?"

"A bit of both, I suppose. Here, look." Dr. Tannen points to Caitlyn's MEG-II scan. A section lit up in oranges and reds. "When tasked with visualizing something, the dorsal and ventral pathways excite. The premotor cortex—say, hand-eye coordination—would be less stimulated. In Caitlyn, it's all harmonizing, see?" She pinches and zooms in on a fold where purples and deep blues connect to the oranges and reds, like tributaries in rivers, ever-flowing back into each other. A kaleidoscope of neuronal activity that makes up Caitlyn's very thoughts, her reality in real time.

"And in English?" Carruthers says.

"To her brain, there's no difference between mental and physical tasks," Michaels says.

"Yes. Yes, that's quite correct."

"But how," Carruthers says. "How do they do that?"

"The kinetic force that determines a bullet's path begins in the chamber," Dr. Tannen says, "when the hammer strikes the primer and the bullet is fired. Even that word—'fired'—denotes a reaction that gives the slug force. A bullet exists in one place yet contains the power to propel itself beyond. The decoherent mind is not dissimilar."

"What's the heaviest someone's manipulated?" Michaels asks.

"I'm afraid my memory isn't as good as Dr. Locke's. But you should be aware, Agent, that what's happening now is far more impressive than simple strength."

"Which is?"

"Seeing when you're blind. Moreover, seeing oneself. That young woman down there perceives her hands in two states. One, a direct correlation to the physical movements. The other, a subjective ideal, a projection in the very sense of the word. And that logic implies halls of thought I'm not ready to explore."

"Why not?" Carruthers asks.

"Such concepts challenge our definition of consciousness. Where our self begins and ends. How porous reality is. That's the realm of philosophy, perhaps even the divine."

Beneath his notebook, Michaels's fingers crave release, begging to flap. The loop that had begun in Florida weeks ago, still in full spin. The momentary relief found in Boston, a distant dream.

"Folks," Dr. Chase says. The huddle is over, and the team heads back to their stations. "We've reached quorum. It's time to begin."

THREE FLOORS BELOW, seven people sit on a bench that has not felt their warmth in three decades. Their arms are shaved. Their graying hair is up, held in place by plastic clips. Miles of sensors and wires thread their biosuits, fabric tight in places.

"Anyone else's banana hammock crushing their junk?" Sam Stephens asks.

A few low-key chuckles. Locker room nerves before the big game.

"It's not your junk that's the problem," Maggie says. "It's everything else."

"The man has us back in detention," Sam says. "And you're making fun of my weight. That's cold, Margaret."

"No, Samuel," Maggie says, "I'm saying you're too egotistical."

"And you're too fat," Peck adds.

Sam shrugs. "Well, at least I ain't a killer."

"Yet here you are with them just the same," Patricia says, winking.

"Hey, speak for yourself," Sam says. "I know my rights. And my lawyer knows how to kick in a few teeth. You'll see. I've got a dead man's switch. Any minute now and I'll be out of here."

"Do you get a plus one?" Felix asks, adding, "Old buddy, old pal."

Sam squeezes Felix's shoulder. "Sure enough, amigo, just don't do me in. 'Cause I know it was you."

Grinning, Felix draws a line across his throat.

"There's nu-nu-nothing funny about this," Lucy says.

"It's a rhetorical performance," Felix says. "I'm all out of feed-back cards."

"Just do what they say," Jamal mumbles and scratches his ear. "Just do what they say."

"Jamal's right," Patricia says. "We're angry, but let's not make this any worse."

"Worse?" Peck laughs. "I've spent thirty years trying to forget this place, thank you very much. It's like moving back in with your parents. Except you sued them and won."

"The Pecker has a point," Felix says. "What happened when

we played nice? They ignored us. But when we rattled the cages—"

"No," Lucy says. "I du-du-don't want to hear this."

"Then mute your hearing aid, Tinker Bell, 'cause here it comes," Felix says. "Like before, the only way out is to make it too costly to keep us."

Maggie cocks her head. "We stage another revolt?"

"What I'm saying is—"

There is a click, then the sound of a klaxon, unheard for thirty years yet instantly recognized. With a deep groan of hinges and motors, the door opens.

"Holy shit," Felix finds himself saying. His thoughts of revolt come to a halt. Now, he is looking upon the test chamber, bathed in light. A familiar structure with new furnishings.

"Upgrades, heh heh," Jamal mutters, his left shoulder twitching.

One by one, they step into the test chamber, turning to study the changes. No spinning tape drives. No green glow of cathode-ray screens. Everything's new and thin, sleek and silent.

There is a faint breeze, Felix senses, passing by his right shoulder. A shimmer, out of the corner of his eyes. "I don't think we're alone." Only Jamal hears him.

Then the hum of a microphone fills the chamber. Their attention is pulled upward, to the catwalks and dispassionate glass.

"All of you now returning to this place, you have my sincere gratitude," speaks the voice over the PA.

"Chase," Peck spits. "Of course he's weaseled his way into this."

"I have no doubt that you harbor ill feelings toward me, toward the program. For that, I can only ask for something I'm not worthy of: your trust. I would ask you to trust us to get to the bottom of this investigation. The easier we can make it, the smoother it will go, and the sooner we'll be on our way."

Sam smirks. Dr. Chase is using "we" to cast himself among the detained. A tactic Sam learned from his days of talk radio. While

the doctor drones on, Sam scans the room. The sensory deprivation pods, curved metal and plastic. The pipes above are gone,
and that is a welcome sight; no sprinklers to gas them with. The
carts hold weights and gel cubes and he notices the twenty-pound
kettlebell is askew.

And a damp breeze, just a breath to his left. Every hair on his
neck rises. The certainty that eyes are upon them, within the very
chamber. And he knows why. One of the pods is already closed.

"... can be assured you will be financially compensated per the
agreement—er, settlement, ahem—as per the terms of—"

"Hey, Dr. Mengele," Sam shouts, staring up and into the
mirror. He knows Dr. Chase always stands right at the edge. Right
where he can look down upon them. "Are we going to do this or
what?"

ON THE OTHER side of the glass, Chase's cheeks flush warm. Thirty
years of regret yet the words fall from his tongue, clumsy and
dumb. Things the lawyers had instructed him never to do: never
apologize, never beg forgiveness. To do so is to admit culpability.
Let the bureaucracy deflect. Chase wants them to know—to truly
understand—none of this is as he intended. If only they would
listen.

And yet, a dark part feels fury at their petulant glares. Don't
they know what greatness is locked in their heads? Humanity put
foot on the moon thanks to those who built rockets. Thanks to
those who put the "we" before "me." Where would the species be
without its pioneers? Still living in caves and flinching at shadows. Still limping along. How dare these gifted few mock the fire
he ignited in their minds. How dare—

*No, no, put it aside, Bob. Acknowledge the intrusive thought. Then
move on.* What had he said, all those years ago? *Let's make distance
a thing of the past.*

Chase clears his throat, steps back from the mirror, and turns
to Dr. Locke. A sigh. "Let us begin."

• • •

MICHAELS'S HEART rate quickens to match pace with the lab. This ballet of sharp minds and sharp machines, researchers swiping screens and directing assistants.

Dr. Chase confers with Dr. Locke at the monitoring station. Dr. Ibrihim instructs the subjects to climb into the pods. There's Dr. Beane and his assistants below, synchronizing the biosuits and wireless IVs. And Dr. Chow confirming all MEG-II scanners are running. Lab techs pass off tablets to each other, to their supervisors for authorizations. To Michaels, it's a front-row seat to the launch of tomorrow.

"Elephant in the room," Carruthers says, leaning in. "Say we ID the suspect. What then? Think they'll comply?"

"Plugged into a pod with the full power of this blind site?" Michaels shakes his head. "No, they won't come quietly."

"So how are we planning the takedown?"

Michaels activates his tablet. On-screen, a full reading of each pod. Pod 5 now, a video feed. Patricia Whitehead, settling onto the membrane.

"With the push of a button," Michaels says and presses a red field. *ACTIVATE SEDATIVE?*

"So instead of gassing the lab we hit them individually?" Carruthers asks.

"Better tactics through science."

"Yeah, that's one way to look at it. Another is that we're in dark territory."

"Denise, I just want to smoke out a monster."

"And thirty years ago everyone here just wanted to change the world." She stands up.

"Where you going?"

"To the surface. To stretch my legs and listen to some crickets. Humans aren't meant to be below ground."

She leaves Michaels to the screens and video feeds: seven faces, eyes closed and still. Dark brains on the MEG-II scans.

Dormant. A flicker here, a spark there. Now wakening, one by one. The visual systems of the occipital lobe. The sensory cortex in the parietal lobe. The almond-shaped clusters of the amygdalae—the fear centers—deep within the temporal lobes.

Gray folds send fractal blasts outward. Sparks become strands, chain lightning. Then a thick webwork refracting back, weaving vibrant threads before Michaels's eyes as decoherent minds come online.

"Well, they're in," Dr. Ibrihim says.

"That was fast," Dr. Chow says.

"It could be neural pathways responding to taught stimulus," Dr. Tannen says. "Like riding a bike after years away."

"Or they've been busy projecting?" Michaels says.

"Impossible to make a ruling one way or the other," Dr. Locke says. "Every brain is different. Take Felix here." She enlarges his MEG-II scan until it fills three monitors. "He was one of the younger subjects, twenty-one at the time. Notice the redistribution of mass, away from the prefrontal cortex? Male brains aren't fully developed until age twenty-five."

"The prefrontal cortex controls impulse," Michaels says. "If his shrunk, could he have impulses to kill?"

"Sure," Dr. Locke says. "Or to gamble."

On the far corner of the screen, a red circle turns green. The scientists stiffen, shoulders going rigid. Dr. Beane clicks off his microphone, turns to the group. "Our first subject is ready. Here we go."

MAGGIE NEUHAUS, in the deep dark. Now Maggie in the sky. Maggie, telling herself, *Don't panic. Think back. You've done this before. Now do this once more. Your whole life has been running from this place. Now look it in the face. Breathe deep. Nothing to fear. Nothing to see. Nothing to be but...*

Calm. Calm.

A voice. Old and familiar. "Margaret, you remember the drill,

I'm sure. We'll drop the white noise here in a second. We've got cameras inside, so nod when you're ready."

Maggie gives a weak nod of her chin. Then another, stronger. She is ready. To put this place behind her. To prove that the only part of Clearwater that lives in the darkness is the part of her that still clings to this gift.

Then what? *Live your life*, she tells herself. Fifty-seven is still young... *ish*. She has her health. Still has enough of her mind. And a bank account too. Wise investments over the years. Years? What year is it? The present. The president. Is he the mumbler? The buffoon? No, no, there is the other. Then... when? When had she eaten last? The past it is—was—will be muddy, murky. Hard to recall. This fog, when had it come? Lack of certainty, lack of clarity, everything now jumbled together. She needs to clear her mind. Clear her... water. Yes, Clearwater. She is here, in this place. Her mind is now open and she can see forever.

CAITLYN HAS LONG WONDERED, how does she appear when blinking to a new place? Is it a burst of light? A sudden pop? Does she gracefully fade, like an old polaroid coming into existence?

It turns out it is all that and more.

Like an origami box, the space before her unfolds, and now there is a figure momentarily made of stars. With a shimmer, the air clears and here comes her form. Bones first, a layer of muscle, then skin, all coalescing into this homely woman at the far end of fifty.

"Oh, it's you again," Maggie says. "You can see me."

"I can," Caitlyn says.

Maggie nods. "Well, I suppose that makes sense."

"It does?"

Maggie strolls around the test chamber. She runs a hand over a gel block. Gives a metal top a quick spin. "Tell me, dear, what color is my hair?"

"Your hair? Chestnut, I'd say. Streaks of blonde in it."

"Mmm, that's nice to hear. I've been gray for a decade. Funny, isn't it? What we bring and what we leave behind."

"Sometimes I wonder, how much of this is really me?"

"As much as you want. Or as little."

As she says this, Caitlyn catches a few wrinkles fading in and out at the corners of her eyes.

The click of a microphone. Dr. Beane's voice, straight into Caitlyn's mind. "Caitlyn, we're feeding the first subject her challenges now. We'll have you act as observer. Connecting the audio feed—"

"—photo labeled target A. Time: thirty seconds."

Maggie is already walking over to the table. She lifts the photo, looks back at Caitlyn. "I suppose I might see you there."

And then she is gone. To the cameras, to the observation booth, to Michaels and all the others, the picture drifts and comes to a rest on the table, askew.

Maggie is right. Caitlyn does see her there. First in bright vibrating lines at the warehouse, then wispy atop the lighthouse, and finally a vague shade at the windy edge of Battery Park.

NINE HUNDRED FEET above the cold chamber where eight minds are entangled across higher dimensions, Carruthers steps out into the noon light of the Sierras. A few black SUVs parked at the mouth of the facility. A pair of guards, smoking and chatting. With a shrill cry that echoes off the canyon, a shadow passes overhead.

A golden eagle. Wings easily six feet wide, gliding on a current past the rimrock and brambles. The size of the bird humbles her.

Then another cry. A second golden eagle, smaller, a fledgling with messy feathers, its wings flapping and working hard to keep up. It weaves in and out of the air current, lacking the grace of the elder bird, yet still trying.

Carruthers could stand here forever, watching them circle the rocks and the trees, the sun rendering their wingtips into glistening shards. A cry, and they dive beyond the pines, gone.

She takes out her phone, finds her message from last week. Saves it to drafts and types out a new one.

Jade,

   Your mother is stubborn and imperfect but she loves you. And she is proud of you. Of your accomplishments. Of your fierce independence. Of the woman you're becoming and the woman you already are.

   Yes, I'm sad you're not going to Berkeley but I'll get over it. I haven't been around much lately. I am so very sorry. I owe you a better past but that's something I can't change. Would you let me work on our future? Whatever direction you chose and wherever you go, I'd like to be present and cheering you on.

   Love,

   Denise, a/k/a Other Mom

It takes all her courage to hit *send*. And she does. Then she waits. For the little blue bar to fill and the *swoosh* of confirmation. It never comes.

SEND MESSAGE FAILED - NO SERVICE. RETRY?

The nearest road is miles away. The nearest cell tower, probably further. Carruthers puts the phone back in her pocket. Breathes in five minutes' worth of crystalline breeze. Then heads back in, down the lift and down the halls to where the air is damp and charged and the concrete drips with ambition.

BUSAN, SOUTH KOREA
FRIDAY - 4:30 A.M., KST

THE KOREAN WORD FOR BUTTERFLY IS *NABI*, AND THE NABI PC ROOM is a colorful cavern of tech on the second floor of the Busan Intercity Bus Station. Behind the crackle of digital gunfire and the clattering of keyboards, behind the spice of hot ramen and an occasional cigarette smoked on the sly, sits the only secure, third-party connection to the Trans-Pacific Express cable, seventeen thousand miles of submarine fiber that connects East Asia to the North American west coast.

Dr. Park leads Brad past chairs filled with screen-glazed teens and vitamin D deficiencies. She presses her Busan University faculty card to the reader at a door marked *WATER CLOSET - OUT OF SERVICE*.

There is no bathroom behind this door, and the sanctorum within is far larger than a closet. Shielding prevents all radio signals from entering or exiting.

"Sit to my right and don't say a word unless he talks to you," Dr. Park says. She powers on the computer and pulls her hair back into a ponytail, then waits.

"So who is he?" Brad asks, struggling with the speed at which Dr. Park works and thinks. While they'd floored it to Busan, Dr.

Park had gone quiet, brown eyes darting about the dark lanes. He had asked questions and she had answered with silence.

"He is my boss," she says as the webcam starts up. "Your boss as well."

"He works for the CBI?"

"Don't be silly. I ran a parallel investigation to your Agent Michaels's. What we've just uncovered—"

A flash on-screen. The icon indicates an encrypted connection. Brad spots himself on the edge of the video feed, small and nervous, a passenger in a car no longer under his control.

The other end of the connection comes into view. The man is so ordinary he could have stepped out of a casual menswear catalogue. His lips are thin, his hair combed and fashionably graying. But his eyes, those are the eyes of a soldier. Brad met men like him on base. Mercenaries who accomplished tasks with surgical precision and came from units that didn't exist.

"I'm looking at your last report now," Nox says, eyes flicking to a tablet in hand. "What else do I need to know?"

"An update, sir," Dr. Park says. "On the Kim Tae Hwan case. It overlaps with another investigation, possibly multiple."

The coordinator puts his tablet down and stares straight into the screen. Brad can feel those eyes searching him. Christ, they cut right into him. Then they return to Dr. Park.

"I'm listening."

"Kim Tae Hwan didn't die in the Sampoong collapse. Brad here—Agent Lee—he helped us uncover that. We exhumed the grave. It's empty. Tae Hwan's half brother, Tom, filed a false death certificate. Tae Hwan used the confusion to make a clean break."

"You discovered this?" Nox asks, those turquoise eyes back on Brad.

"Yes, sir," he says. "But I mean, to be totally fair, it was a team effort. See, Dr. Park, she—"

"Explain the overlap," Nox says, turning back to Dr. Park.

"My second field assignment should be in front of you. I was in Bali, interning with the embassy, assisting local law with cross-border fraud."

"You're referring to this robbery in Jakarta?"

"Yes, as well as others. Lombok, Siem Reap, Colombia, probably a dozen more. They all had the same MO. Someone with knowledge of bank security, able to walk in and out during daylight hours. Most of all, total familiarity with CIA deposit boxes. Our profile predicted a team, right? North Korean money launderers, maybe Chinese hackers. They only hit black ops petty cash, and never the same place twice."

Brad fidgets, struggling to follow the words coming from the petite scholar beside him. At some point her accent changed.

"Kim Tae Hwan was sending money orders to his half brother. The pattern fits. It's not perfect, but within a three-month variation in similar regions. They scouted agency accounts, long enough to find the cash deposit schedule. Then they hit them."

"You've said 'they' twice now."

"Tae Hwan met someone. And according to his brother, it was someone who shared a similar skill, someone who saved him. I think you see where I'm going with this."

"I do," the man says. "Without a body, we need DNA."

"Already done," she says. "I scooped Tom's toothbrush and comb. I'll send them to the local lab now." A flash in Brad's mind: Dr. Park emerging from Tom's bathroom before they left. Had she been zipping her purse?

"Good," Nox says.

And still, Brad shifts, sensing a connection at the edge of his thoughts. A cold case from over a decade. A dead man with deep knowledge of banks. Test subjects in the high Sierras. How the hell does this all fit together?

Then his spine bristles, his neck shivers, and the words simply burst past his lips.

"No fucking way."

[56]

CLEARWATER

THURSDAY – 2:00 P.M., PST

THEY CALL HER THE BASELINE, BUT CAITLYN FEELS LIKE A PUNCHLINE. Blind girl visually confirms that Subject 3 is able to lift a seven-pound kettlebell. Check. Blind girl witnesses Subject 4 unable to project his way into a lighthouse. Check. Blind girl watches Subject 5 squeeze a gel cube so hard it bursts its mylar container. Check.

And now, Subject 6 stands at the center of the chamber, a kettlebell in each hand, pumping up and down, up and down.

"I can go all day," Sam Stephens says with a wink. "I'm curious: you ever try screwing like this?"

Caitlyn blinks. "Screwing?"

"Well yeah, the sideways no pants dance."

"No, Mr. Stephens, I can't say I have. Now, can you—"

"Think about it: it's the perfect birth control. No hormones, no messy cleanup. I tried to talk Lucy into it but she's not into dudes. But does it matter, out of body? So what do you say?"

"I would say that's literally the worst pickup attempt I've ever heard."

"Eh, give me some time. I can do worse."

"I don't doubt it."

Thump. He drops the kettlebell on the table. "Okay, I'm done. If you change your mind..." He tilts his head, gestures two thumbs toward his pod.

Caitlyn can't help but laugh. God, he is repulsive.

And then he is gone. She's alone now, one subject left. Tired too. Not physically but deeper, a disconnection from her body, like being stuck in an airplane for too long.

"Caitlyn, we'll have the last subject out in a moment," comes Dr. Beane's voice in her ear. "We're just having a—"

Static screams from the speakers.

IN THE OBSERVATION ROOM, a dozen alarms flash across a dozen screens. Michaels turns to the closest monitor, Dr. Ibrihim's. He is pinching and zooming in on Patricia Whitehead. "What the hell just happened?"

"She's coding," Dr. Tannen says and enlarges the display. "Shit shit shit." The cool hue of an ultraviolet video feed inside the pod: Patricia Whitehead, twisting and turning and thrashing about. Her lips make little gasps, a fish flopping on the hot deck of a boat. Her hands slap the air.

"Christ, what did we do?" Chase asks Dr. Beane. "Is it neurological or myocardial?"

"Both," Dr. Beane says. "And we haven't even started her test."

"It's not a stroke," Dr. Chow shouts.

"Well what do you call that?" Dr. Ibrihim points to the MEG-II scan. A supernova of colors. Blues and violets, reds and oranges. The very shape of the brain itself is shifting, splitting in places.

"I don't know," Dr. Chow says, her hands on her cheeks.

"Eileen, it's your device. Handle it."

On-screen, the slate wall that forms the shadow of the skullcap snaps. A burst, and the once-orderly contours of the human brain become an abstract mess of fractures and fading colors turning darker, darker, darker.

For a moment both brief and awful, Dr. Chow realizes that

what she is looking at, what the scans show in fractious clips, is something that has no earthly business being inside a living brain.

It is a hand. And it is squeezing.

The computer screams, *FLATLINE!* One of the technicians screams as well. The video feed is a flickering mess. Patricia Whitehead, sinking into the deflating, frothy membrane.

The cameras aimed into the test chamber catch every angle: the pod blowing open, the lid crashing down, the hiss of gas and the flood of gore.

What the cameras do not capture—except in a blur of twisting pixels and a shimmer of darkness—is what leaps out of Patricia's pod and lands on the concrete with a snarl.

Caitlyn has seen it before. Nearly two weeks ago, and every night since in the dark halls of her mind. This prowling, stalking, spastically walking thing of shadow and claw. Silver drips from hollow eye sockets. Sharp fingers curl. Its frame is gaunt, tall, both human and simian. Form unfurling, the dhimoni rises.

Then, without pause, it leaps into another pod.

A scream. The terrible rending of metal. The pod bulges and buckles and crimson froths from its seams.

In the observation room, Michaels struggles to keep up. Another alarm shrieks as techs dart from station to station.

"Who is it?" Michaels asks. "Who's doing this?"

"I don't know," Dr. Beane says. The MEG-II scan shows a brain in the throes of purples and reds. "Is it Peck?"

"No, it can't be Peck," Dr. Ibrihim says. "He's asystole —flatlining."

"Someone's killing them," Michaels says. "Who's projecting right now?"

Dr. Ibrihim turns his tablet toward Michaels. Four brains lit up on the MEG-II scans. Now five. "Who isn't?"

. . .

TO THE CAMERAS, to the viewers above, the test chamber is awash in flying metal and falling sparks. Water, thick with viscera, burps and slides from Peck's pod.

To Caitlyn, this is the return of her nightmare. The dhimoni splits the pod in two, sending broken husks bouncing to the edge of the test chamber.

Eyes smoldering silver, it races toward a third pod.

Do something. Do what? It's killing them. Do anything!

Feet bounding and cracking concrete, the dhimoni closes in on Pod 3. With a swipe it sends a medical cart tumbling. Then its world shifts.

It finds itself flung, rolling, tackled by the most curious of things. A woman, Caitlyn, both small and fast. The dhimoni's shadow form recondenses, and then it is back on its feet.

"Step aside," it hisses, voice both youthful and ancient. "This isn't your fight." The speakers hum as feedback rises and a light bursts overhead.

Caitlyn doesn't recall talking but the words leave her lips all the same. Instinct made verbal. "I'm making it my fight."

The dhimoni grins. There is a face, a flicker of something human beneath. "You'll regret—"

The best way to win is to strike first. Her father told her this once. Outside a ring, there's no such thing as a clean fight.

Caitlyn pushes the medical cart with all her focus. Its wheels flip and spin, and eighty pounds of stainless steel wipes the grin off that creature's face.

Then it is gone. Just like that. Shadows bloom and fade as a black mist suffuses the room, like ash in the wind.

That's it? No, it can't be. Caitlyn scans the test chamber, the two shattered pods, the lights showering sparks. The shadows, swinging, racing, moving along the wall just past her vision.

A low rumble. A thundercrack. The shadows collapse upon her.

No, right behind her.

Caitlyn feels the blow, not as a physical pain, but as a sudden tug. She has been grabbed, yanked, flung from behind, and now she is tumbling into—

The spare cart of weights topples. Her vision dims to a little sphere. She is on the floor now, and her hands, she can see right through them.

Running now, gathering speed, the dhimoni lets loose a howl, then leaps into Pod 3.

"STATUS REPORT!" Dr. Locke shouts over the screaming alarms. "Vitals, talk to me!"

"We're losing Pod 3!" Dr. Ibrihim says. "Christ, she's being ripped apart."

"Chase!" Michaels shouts. "How bad is this?"

Dr. Chase opens his mouth. No words come out. Instead, he gives a slight shake of the head, then turns back to his screens.

"Chase, answer me."

"I don't know, I don't know. It could be Felix or Sam or it could be Caitlyn."

"You don't know?"

"We need time to analyze for aberrant patterns."

"Dr. Locke," Michaels says. "Pull them out."

"No!" Chase says. "We'll lose all this data."

"We are losing lives! Dr. Locke, get them out of there!"

"Listen. Listen to me," Chase says. "Whoever's doing this, in their mind is the very key to harnessing this phenomenon. Think of that! We need to isolate them, systematically. This is frightening, I know, but think of all we stand upon—"

"Enough." Michaels grabs his tablet, logs in, and cues up his control app. He finds the emergency shutdown field. Action 1: *AUDIO INTERRUPT*.

He presses the button. The countdown begins. Thirty seconds. *OVERRIDE Y/N?* He presses it again.

. . .

CAITLYN, watching from a far distant place as the test chamber gives way to shadows. *No, not now.* She is drowning again. Splashing about the darkness. Yet this darkness is different; there are edges and bumps and the flexible cushion of a—

Membrane. She is in the pod. Alarms engulfing her, an audio assault. Sirens and whistles and a click-clack that cleaves her concentration like knives in her mind.

The earbuds. *They're trying to pull you out.*

"Why?"

Doesn't matter. Do what you can. Save them.

Caitlyn tugs the earbuds free. Flings them into the shadows. Takes a deep breath. No time to count down. Just step out.

"Where?"

Right there. You know how to do this.

"No. I can't stop it. It's too much. Too strong."

You're stronger than you know. Now go. Get yourself out of here. That's my girl.

BLISS, yes. This exquisite engine—the human heart—beats in the palm of its hand.

And now, with a twist, its music comes to an end. Sinking claws into a soft mind. Neurons firing as memories collapse.

Now she is silent, that last spark of life surging, fighting, flickering no more. Maggie Neuhaus lies still, a quiet wreck.

They call it the Breath of God. And this pleases it, yes, though it's not a breath but a storm. And God, after all, what is God but retribution and wrath?

Kill, kill, yes. This it *must* do. Must make them suffer and pay. It sends the plastic halves of the pod flying. Sends Maggie's remains rolling across this wretched temple of science.

And here, with grating annoyance, it sees vestiges of its old life. There they stand in defiance, luminous and weak.

"If you want to get them," Sam Stephens says, "you go through me."

Another voice enters the fray, form unfolding. "No, you go through us," Felix says.

And another.

"This ends here," Caitlyn says, blinking in beside them.

It curses them with lips dry and diseased. A wheeze leaves its throat. Bounding now, racing toward them, claws extending. With a swipe, it flings a chair into the air. Then it is gone.

And now it is there, twenty feet up. It catches the chair and sends it toward Felix. Thirty pounds of government metal, spinning and sharp.

Felix, in its path. Then he is a foot to its right. The chair clatters past him—

—but the edge nicks Caitlyn, sends her stumbling. Sam catches her with a firm touch.

A flash between them. Caitlyn, in the boat, looking down at her face as the waters surge forth. And Sam, in this very room, three decades younger. Dr. Chase in his face: "All right, Samuel, let's see the world."

The memory vanishes and Sam is helping her up. "Stop holding onto your body. In your skin, you're just a blind girl. Here, you're so much more."

"Head's up," Felix says, and then he blinks behind the charging dhimoni. He grabs a handful of shadows—the creature's twisting leg—and he tugs and he tears. Black mist sloughs off, tarlike and taut. "Dammit, help me wrangle this demon."

The dhimoni turns and slashes, claws cleaving air, feral and fast. Felix drives a knee into the creature's gaunt back. They hit the floor, splitting concrete and rattling the room.

The dhimoni screams, eyes burning silver, dark contrails lashing behind it. And its hand, that claw rises up, higher, readies a downstroke on Felix and—

A palm seizes its spindly wrist. A body follows, unfolding from nothing. Jamal Munday, shadows settling around him like volcanic ash. He stands there, stands tall and proud, no twitch to his body, just eyes focused and fierce. Caitlyn senses the dim outline of great wings behind him.

"Gentlemen," Jamal says with a nod to his old cohort. He pins the dhimoni's wrist in a tight grip. "This will be enough, monster."

A crack to Caitlyn's left. Lucy, eyes made of pure light. She says nothing, just hovers two feet off the ground. Her legs are a dress of gray ribbons.

The dhimoni screams at Jamal, thrashing and slashing.

"You know, I was certain it was you," Sam says to Felix. "Glad to be wrong for once."

"Yeah, well, I wasn't so sure either," Felix says. "So who the hell is it?"

"Pain and anger," Jamal says. "This thing is human no more."

"Enough with its pain," Lucy says without stuttering. "Time to put it down. Jamal, ready?"

He nods. The dhimoni twists and tugs. A pulse as their ethereal forms entangle. A power outlet spits smoke, plastic melting. The lights grow brighter, brighter—

A black flash. Then the dhimoni is behind Jamal, claws sinking into his arm, tearing through muscle and bone. No blood, only a flicker of displacement. When Jamal's arm coalesces, the creature is loose.

"Little help, please," Felix says, racing headlong to catch it.

Sam and Lucy and Caitlyn all seize a piece of the beast, holding and pinning. Sharp and wet and shimmering with fury, it is in there, a body beneath the cloak of darkness. Caitlyn can sense —can *see*—thin arms and cool skin.

A rip, and the dhimoni sheds the shadows like torn clothes. A naked form, mottled and withered, takes three feeble steps. Then darkness snaps back, swaddling it in black mist.

Felix says, "Was that—"

The dhimoni bursts. The test chamber flickers as bulbs rain sparks and glass. Pitch black now.

"Oh hell no," Sam says. "You ain't the only one who's learned a few new—"

He lurches, clutching his chest.

"Sam?" Felix asks.

A fissure opens up, stretching from Sam's navel to neck. A static glow, as if every atom is cindering. Caitlyn finds herself awestruck, sensing that what she is seeing is the full memory of a human life—a soul—now rising to luminous mist.

Sam's mens corpus collapses. A second later, his physical body hits the floor. The top half.

"The pods!" Lucy shouts. "Keep it away from our bodies!"

Felix and Jamal vanish, swirling mist in their wake. Lucy lets out a gurgle, stumbles.

Jamal tears the shrieking beast out of Lucy's pod. Felix seizes its wrists. Caitlyn assists. Writhing, squealing. Pulses of light, great arcs of energy as their mental bodies entangle.

"Are you okay?" Jamal asks.

"Just a bu-bu-bit short of breath," she says. "Bastard was crushing my throat."

"We can't fight it," Felix says. "We need to exhaust it."

"How?" Caitlyn asks.

"Run its battery down. All this energy has a cost on its mind."

"Gu-gu-get it out of here."

"Where?" Jamal asks, dodging a slash.

"Far away from our b-b-bodies!"

"Leave that to me," Caitlyn says and latches onto the writhing shadow. Thin arms and taut skin. Like reaching into a puddle of oil and finding a forest of bones. Now what? Visualize it. Where? The teal waters off Crete, the snows of Kilimanjaro, the—

Concrete walls dissolve to blue sky. The ducts twist and stretch to form a cool horizon. Caitlyn isn't running but tumbling now, from forty-one thousand feet. This is where the Learjet passed a week ago, over eastern Tennessee.

Entangled and spinning, limbs and legs. Caitlyn clutches the thrashing dhimoni as the air whooshes and they fall, fall, fall, fast through a cold, open sky.

A flash of transference, a memory between them. A young Dr. Chase, looking down as he closes the pod. Caitlyn, looking up at the boat's hatch from below.

Now the twisting sky. The dhimoni digs thin fingers into her shoulder. Hisses into her ear, "Let... go..."

She screams back, "You're coming with me!"

A blink, and rushing wind becomes rumbling water. Iguazú Falls blurs past them now, a million gallons of power. Tumbling, into the mist. Down, into the churning currents. Caitlyn squeezes, holds firm as they near the cold valley. The dhimoni pivots, tries to break free. She digs her fingers in, deeper still, peeling shadow free to reveal lesioned skin.

In threshing rocks and glistening foam, the waterfall comes to a thundering end.

And still she holds on. Through churning currents, nothing but bubbles and darkness. She focuses her mind in the blink of an eye.

The roiling water freezes into a desert of ice. Spraying mist, and an explosion of snow signals their arrival upon the shadow of Everest. Rolling, head over foot, down the eastern slope of the crown of the world.

To the climbers braving the spring thaw, it looks like a far-off avalanche is forming. To Caitlyn, it is the answer to another question: could she pull this monster through blink after blink? Turns out she can. What she lacks in strength she makes up for with tenacity and a deep well of experiences.

Careening toward an icy ravine, Caitlyn visualizes their next destination. Perhaps she'll drop the dhimoni into the fires of Kīlauea. Or take it deep into the Mariana Trench. Maybe the crushing depths—

A sudden tug, 7481 miles in a violent blast. Chest vibrating now, fingers all over her body, hands—

Whose hands? *Not yours. Where? You're in the pod. Your biosuit's shaking. They're trying to pull you out. Trying to bring you back to—*

Caitlyn tears the neoprene and latex open. Unzips. The haptic motors pulse inside fabric, but she's out now—she's out. *Blink. Do it. Five... four... three... two—*

Back to the test chamber, back in the slushing red mess. Electric currents, hissing and spitting. Lights swinging from the trusses above.

"Smart girl," Felix says, materializing beside her. "You unplugged yours as well."

"I almost had him," Caitlyn says, steadying herself against the tilt of blink after blink. "I took him far away."

"Yeah, you did. I tried to keep up, but damn, you move fast."

A crack as Lucy appears beside them. "These idiots are going to be the death of us."

"Okay, circle up," Felix says. "I'm checking on Jamal."

Caitlyn and Lucy put their backs to each other, static passing between them. They scan the dark walls, the catwalk, the pods.

"Have you ever seen this thing before?" Caitlyn asks.

"No," Lucy says. "But I wasn't as talented as the others."

Felix is at Jamal's pod when it opens. A hiss, a weak push. Jamal waves a limp wrist in their direction. "What a curious thing," he says. "I dreamt we escaped and grew old."

He collapses to the floor, the back of his head a raw hollow.

A deep clang as his pod spins, tugging tubes and cords and rolling end over end.

A convergence of shadows. A crack. The dhimoni skitters up the walls.

"Keep it away from our pods, dammit," Lucy says. "We're sleeping ducks."

Up on the catwalks, the dhimoni turns to face them. A human hint behind a mask of decay. Eyes, one green and one blue, dripping silver smoke. Teeth behind lips stretching into a cruel sneer.

Caitlyn searches for something, anything. A kettlebell. Perfect.

A memory: cricket practice in Chennai when she was thirteen.

Do her muscles remember? Her mind probably does. Time to find out. *Coil your body, lean back, now spin and… Release!*

The dhimoni is skittering down the wall when the kettlebell catches it mid-strafe. A burst of shadows and the echo of a shriek. For a moment the kettlebell hangs there, embedded in the concrete. Then, with a boom, it falls to the floor.

"Did we get it?" Lucy asks. "Do you think—"

A low rumble. Shadows congeal. With a crack, it is back, bounding toward them, warping and shifting. To the left, now feinting right. Shouting and claws extending and—

Caitlyn grabs the heaviest kettlebell. Feels it rise. Then feels it fall from her grip. No, through her fingers.

Her hand is transparent.

"Do you… Do you feel that?" Felix asks. The chamber tilts to the left. Caitlyn steadies herself against the table, hand pushing against it. Then sliding through.

"Something's happening," Lucy says.

Little curtains unravel in the corner of Caitlyn's vision. Black velvet, billowing.

And still the dhimoni comes.

"THAT'S ONE DOSE," Dr. Beane says and turns to Dr. Locke. The screen reads, *SEDATIVE ADMINISTERED.*

"Another," Dr. Locke says. "Do it."

"Carol, we don't know how they'll react," Dr. Tannen says.

"They're tearing each other apart," Dr. Locke says. "That's the reaction. Now hit them again!"

"Dr. Chase?" Dr. Beane asks. "Sir?"

The stoic man stares at the chaos, trying to read it all. MEG-II scans show three brains in a full cascade. Five more in terminal states. He reaches out, tenderly touches the colors of Caitlyn's brain. "It's a thing of beauty, is it not? So much potential, from such an unlikely place."

The chamber beyond the glass is a pit of shattered tech and

sputtering lights. A tempest of metal and plastic, shimmering ribbons, and wet echoes.

"Chase!" Michaels shouts. "We need your override!"

And Chase just watches, still as a statue from the outside, inwardly retreating behind the walls of his mental castle, beholding his creations now coming undone.

"Goddammit, Bob," Dr. Locke says. In one swift motion she grabs the tablet from Dr. Beane, slaps Chase's finger to the scanner. *OVERRIDE: ADMINISTER ADDITIONAL SEDATIVE? Y/N.*

She hits *YES* as many times as she can.

"DAMN, THEY'RE GONNA..." Felix says, his voice dropping two octaves.

Caitlyn leans against a shattered pod. No, no, not now. "Pull the IV," she says from a deep, distant place. The sparks fall like dead leaves. How has the air gotten so thick?

She closes her eyes. Lets the darkness embrace her. Curtains of hard plastic and soft membrane.

She is in the pod now. Why? The IV puck. Left arm. *Pull it out. Do it.* A deep pinch as the port tears free from her vein. A smell: rust, copper, a wet penny under her nose. Blood pooling in her elbow ditch.

Now what? Rest. *So tired. No. Step out. Five, four... Five, four, three... Five, four, three, two, one—*

Back to the test chamber. Falling cinders, and the air redolent of burned circuits. Her heartbeat slowing. *Lub... dub... lub... dub.* There's the dhimoni, moving faster. Lucy's limp hand hanging out from her broken pod.

Caitlyn fights an entire battle just to rise to her knees. She brushes away strands of black fabric at the corners of her vision. *Walk, dammit!* Left foot, right foot, left. The instructions are clear but the body is slow. Everything's vicious and tilting.

Felix locks eyes with her, mutters, "Hell of a way to go."

Then he is gone, tugged back into his pod.

"No!" Caitlyn cries, watching it all unfold.

The dhimoni, running, not to her but past her. To Felix. To his pod.

With a crunch of metal and plastic, the beast drives itself into the tank. Pipes buckle and rupture, hissing gas. A deep moan from within. Like a can beneath a boot, the pod collapses.

Caitlyn tries to steel her mind against it: the fingers between the cracks, the red spray. It takes fifty-thousand pounds per square inch to bend stainless steel.

But it takes far less to break glass.

With a hard pivot, the dhimoni sends the pod soaring—a bloody crumple flipping end over end—up, up, and into the observation booth. From a yawning well of her mind, Caitlyn watches as the dispassionate glass is simply obliterated.

CARRUTHERS SPRAYS A SMOLDERING CONSOLE WITH A FIRE extinguisher. Alarms scream for attention while Michaels pulls glass from his cheek. Pipes hiss the last of their steam. Moaning, a technician helps Dr. Locke to her feet. Dr. Chow nurses a broken arm.

Where Felix's pod has come to a stop lies a twisted mess in a reddening lab coat. On it, Michaels finds no pulse, no face. Only a name tag that reads, *TANNEN, SIAN*.

"We need to get out of here," Dr. Chow shouts. "Everyone, to the surface, now!"

"We need to sedate them," Dr. Locke says. "They'll tear this whole place apart."

"There is no *them*, only *her*," Dr. Ibrihim says, struggling out from under his toppled desk. "How can we sedate her when our systems are fucked?"

Dr. Locke can't find the words. Her face says it all: they haven't prepared for this.

"Chase, give me a hand," Michaels says. He pushes two monitors off Dr. Ibrihim while Chase untangles cables. "Grab his shoulders and pull, now." Michaels slides the desk to the side. Crutches wobbling, Chase wraps his arms beneath Dr. Ibrihim. A tug, a scream, and the man comes loose. His legs are still there; that's the good news.

"How bad is it?" Dr. Ibrihim asks. "I'm afraid to look down."

"It's a compound fracture," Michaels says. "You won't be rollerblading anytime soon, but you'll be—"

Dr. Ibrihim is yanked right out of their arms. Pulled ten feet away and into the twisted pod. There is a single note, a yelp from the darkness. Then a terrible crunch.

Michaels stands there, frozen, trying to understand what he's just seen. He goes for his sidearm. "No," Carruthers says. "Run, now."

A low rumble saturates the air. The voice arrives from all sides, a guttural grinding, like glass in a blender. "Now comes the judgment of all wicked beings."

Dr. Ibrihim's broken body is flung from the pod. Slides to a wet stop at Dr. Locke's feet.

"Be penitent and kneel," speaks the voice. "Or cry out and hide. Death comes for you all."

Before them: a shimmer of air. Flooring buckles beneath invisible feet. Incisions open up along a table as unseen claws split metal.

Behind them: a blast of cool air, an open door. Carruthers, turning the manual wheel, waving them into the halls.

Dr. Beane falls to his knees. "Please. Be merciful. We didn't mean—"

From a sidelong glance, Michaels sees the shimmer seize the doctor's face. Then the doctor's pleas become shrieks.

Michaels finds the fire alarm. Brings the butt of his pistol down on the glass. *Crack!* A fizzle from the sprinklers, the spray of dirty water. Droplets suffuse the observation room.

He can see it now, the shape of a gaunt figure thrashing Dr. Beane. Wishes he could scrub it from his mind. He raises his Glock, aims for center mass, squeezes the trigger. Hears the gunshots, like thunder. Doesn't hear the pop of Dr. Beane's skull.

The hollow-point slugs hit the wet silhouette and exit in twisting angles. And that is it. Nothing. Not even a scratch.

Carruthers grabs Michaels, pulls him out through the door. Chase clatters ahead, down the hall.

There is only so much to be seen before the mind walls itself off. Michaels can feel his own sanity starting to crack. Catches fleeting glimpses as they race down the halls.

Dr. Chow, lifted into the air, twisted by nothing. Dr. Chow, now in pieces. Dr. Locke, crawling across the damp floor and out into the hall. Dr. Locke, peeled like a weed from wet soil.

"We can't leave them," Michaels says.

"And we can't save them," Carruthers says. "Go!"

They near the elevator, Chase hobbling, pushed on by Carruthers. He hits the *lift* button. The elevator rumbles.

Michaels pries the shaft door open. There it is, far, far above: the elevator, safety lights descending the angled shaft, too steep to climb. No time.

This cold hallway, then. Three hundred feet of metal and concrete. Two doors wide open, one at each end. Enough distance to watch death approach.

They check their sidearms.

"How many shots you get off?" Carruthers asks.

"Six. They might as well be spitballs."

"Yeah, well, at least spitballs stick to your skin. Here it comes."

The far end of the hall: a slim, wispy figure. Michaels raises his Glock, tilts his head. At a sidelong angle, he can see two flickering eyes.

Then it is down on its hands and knees. Running, racing, skittering up the wall. Along the ceiling. Closer and closer—

Michaels focuses on a pipe. *CAUTION: THERMAL VENTING.* Two shots—ricochets, *pling-plinging.* Two more, one deep enough to unleash a sizzling blast. The stink of rotten eggs and a spray of deep heat.

As the form moves through the steam, Michaels switches to his Taser. Takes aim and discharges.

The Axon Taser 7 uses compressed nitrogen to fire two wired probes at almost two hundred feet per second to a range of twenty-five feet. The battery delivers fifty thousand volts at twenty-six watts, overloading an attacker's nervous system. Enough to stop a bear.

The prongs sink into the mist, sparks erupting. A scream, unlike anything Michaels has ever heard. The air itself wails. Wires hover, humming and clicking. *Tic tic tic tic tic—*

Then the scream fades. Turns to a cackle. The probes drop to the ground.

"Did... Did you really think that would work?" laughs a voice. Close. Closer...

A pulse, and now Michaels feels burning cold strike his face. His left ear goes, *Eeeeeeeeeeeee*. He tastes metal, realizing that his trachea is being squeezed—impossibly—from inside his neck. Like choking on ice.

"You've sought to chase me," says the reeking voice upon him. Damp metal, air before a great storm. "And now our paths collapse. What did you hope to achieve?"

"Jus... tice..." Michaels says, the vise tightening beneath his jaw. A gasp flies past his lips. Then he spits a mouthful of blood.

Droplets, passing through the air. Droplets, vaporizing into red mist. And a few ruby droplets, now sliding down the contours of a sneering, gaunt face.

"Why have you quit?" he asks from the shadows.

A wet groan as the hull splinters and cracks. Water sloshes over her shoulder, swallowing her. She sees nothing.

"I can't do it, Dad," Caitlyn says. "It's too hard. Everything's dark and I'm lost."

"No, sweetie, you're not lost. You're right where you need to be."

"I couldn't save Mom."

"We never could."

"I can't save myself."

Another deep shudder. Bitter oils on her lips. Churning salt water pours in, the full might of the ocean upon this shattering boat.

"But, sweetie, don't you see? You did save yourself. How do you think you got out?"

She opens her mouth but the water is there. She coughs, spits. *Got* out? And where is the walkie-talkie? The room is flooded; the radio must be underwater. Then another thought: so how is he talking to her?

"There you go," her father says. "You've been free for a decade. You *did* save yourself."

"But... what about you?"

A subtle change in his voice. Recognizable only from sixteen years of traveling together. This is the sound of her father smiling as he speaks. "Sweetie, I've been gone for a long time. Now go. Your eyes are open. Just step through the curtain."

The wet darkness parts at her touch. Fiberglass and water and the flash of a red emergency light. She is above, on the foredeck now, just left of the hatch. There's the obstruction, where the jib has come loose from the halyard and wrapped around the edge of the hatch. All she has to do is pull the fabric loose.

And that's what she does.

Then she slides the hatch open. Down there, sinking into the murky depths, is her body, sixteen years old and sun-kissed. Braided hair, souvenirs from their stay in Seychelles. Funny, these details time swallowed.

Caitlyn reaches down, takes the body—*her* body—by the shoulders. She pulls herself up, out through the hatch. Almost free.

But something is stuck. A tangle of bedsheets, tight around her ankles. Caitlyn lays her physical body along the lip of the hatch. How to get the rest of her out?

The answer is so simple she almost laughs. She had moved up onto the deck. *Now go back below.*

Six feet in a blink. Down in the bedroom now, she's looking up at the hatch, at her bruised legs hanging through. *Unwrap the sheets. Good. Now push from below. Gentle, gentle.*

Lifting, she feels an odd strain, deep behind her eyes. Glass forming, growing, sliding, and severing.

Up now. She hoists her body onto the deck. And now she is looking down on herself—her physical body—wet and unconscious.

"Wake up!" she says, but she doesn't move. "Wake up!"

Why not? *Because it's not then-you. It's now-you.* How hasn't she noticed? This body below her has undercut hair, black at the roots and blonde on the tips. Arms, pale and tattooed. Skin that hasn't felt the African sun in years.

Caitlyn pushes the hatch aside and now there is light. Sterile bulbs swinging from cables. Shadows across concrete walls. An overturned pod. And—*oh God*—still-fresh blood on the walls of the observation room.

Gunshots. Far-off echoes, unmistakable. She's heard that sound a lot this past week.

Think. Focus. You saved yourself. Time to rescue the others.

Caitlyn blinks into the observation room, a voyeur into this abattoir of pain. Broken bodies, broken machines. She puts them in a numb part of her mind. *See, but move on.*

More gunshots. The hiss of gas down a hall. She can see it. She is there.

Hot fog sprays from a broken pipe. A shadow cackles beyond. The dhimoni gripping, lifting Michaels, asking, "What did you truly hope to achieve?"

Michaels mumbles, spits red. A clawed hand rises to pry open his face.

She blinks into the dark creature now, hands digging into shadows. It drops Michaels, writhes and twists and throws itself against the walls. She feels skin, feels flesh within. Feels muscles tensing and brittle bones beneath. A scream, deep inside this shroud of darkness, and a surge of light wipes all thoughts from their minds.

CARRUTHERS GRABS MICHAELS, pulls him away. There is something else there, a second shape, feminine and furious, wrapped not in darkness but stars.

And then a deep pulse. A wave of static surges down the hall. The bulbs burst—*pop, pop, pop!*—and leave only damp ozone and thunder. For one second, an afterglow remains: two forms, twisting in an upside-down dance.

Then comes the fade as the facility rattles and yawns and falls into darkness.

[PART 5]

When the time comes, let loose a tiger and a devil; but wait for the time with the tiger and the devil chained—not shown—yet always ready.

— Charles Dickens, *A Tale of Two Cities*

58

PLUMAS COUNTY, CALIFORNIA
THURSDAY - 3:00 P.M., PST

THE BERGMAN FAMILY VAN IS A NEARLY NEW ELECTRIC, UPGRADED TO a long-range battery. With less than seven hundred miles on the digital odometer, it still smells factory fresh. At seventy-seven percent charged, it sputters and shuts down. Cursing, he guides it to the shoulder.

Here, on the side of Highway 284, he tells himself he should be able to fix this. He has a degree in IT; he's a mid-level manager. And yet, after fifteen minutes of leafing through the manual and staring under the hood, he finally gives up.

"Hon, I don't think it's like the olden days," his wife says, leaning out the window. "You can't just get in there with a wrench."

"No, I know that," he says, yet there's a compulsion to solve it. Or, at the least, to look the part. He puts his hands on his hips and studies the van's battery. "I swear I'm going to robopark this damn thing up Elon's ass."

"Language, honey."

"And it's autopark, Dad," his son says.

"Good to know."

"So, like, my phone's totally busted," his daughter adds.

"Not my fault. Told you to charge it before we left."

"Yeah, and I did," his daughter says, elongating the last vowel. "Mom, is yours even working?"

His wife shakes her head. "Keeps restarting."

"You know, I bet this is 'cause we're near a secret alien facility," his son says. "There's *tons* of them out here."

"You're an alien facility," his daughter says.

"What does that even mean?"

"It means you're from planet weirdo," she says, "because you're adopted."

"Dad, is that true?"

"Yes, it's true," he says. "But we love you anyway. Okay, there's a car coming. Everyone, just... act human."

He steps out onto the shoulder. He puts on his best holiday smile, despite the fact that this holiday has been a weeklong headache. The rafting trip was nonstop mosquitos. The Airbnb was little more than a hovel. And now the Bergman family van has died on this godforsaken road. At least the crags provide some afternoon shade.

A parade of black SUVs dots the horizon. Chevy Suburbans, gas guzzlers fueled by dead dinosaurs, not some bundle of Chinese batteries. Lucky for them.

Waving, he watches them approach.

Waving, he feels them rumbling closer and closer.

One and two and now nearly a dozen. They don't slow down, don't even acknowledge his presence. Then he stops waving and his feet do the thinking. He steps off the road and back onto the shoulder.

The Suburbans blow past, no hint of slowing. Black paint jobs, black plates, and black tinted windows. Shadows on the highway, engines roaring off rocks, screaming deeper into the mountains.

59

CLEARWATER
THURSDAY - 3:00 P.M., PST

So this is it, he thinks. The big adios. A cracked neck, then cut to black. But shouldn't there be more time before the mind goes offline? Five minutes for brain death.

"Are you... Are you okay?" Carruthers asks. "There you are. You're okay. I'm okay. Christ, we're all right."

She helps Michaels to his feet. He feels... What does he feel? Alive. And damn sore too. His jaw clicks and his neck tingles. One of his molars wiggles loose.

"Where'd it go?" he asks the darkness. "Where is it?"

"I don't know. But my flashlight and phone are both fried. Yours?"

Michaels tries them. The flashlight: no good. His smartphone: nothing. Wait. A cool rectangle, then an Apple logo. Loading...

"So that was a cascade?" Michaels asks.

"Indeed," Chase says. "And why we've had to contain them inside this mountain."

"Like an EMP, really. Half the facility's probably fried."

Carruthers asks, "How come your phone's working?"

"Shielded," Michaels says and taps the case.

"You spooks get all the good toys."

"Without a signal, it's just a bad flashlight."

The light guides them, five feet at a time down the hissing, dark hall.

"I think I saw Caitlyn," Carruthers says. "For just a brief second."

"Yeah," Michaels says. "I think I did too."

"You get a look at it? The... dhimoni?"

Michaels shrugs, then realizes Carruthers can't see the gesture. "Sort of."

"And?"

"A few minutes ago I was being throttled by thin air. Now I'm stuck twenty floors below with a wicked headache. I don't know what to think."

"Because you're in shock," Chase says. "It takes the body a half second to produce adrenaline, far longer to metabolize it."

They make their way to the far end of the hallway, light guiding them step by step. Michaels winces. The taste of blood in the back of his throat. Damn, his molar is about to pop out.

"Stay here, Doc," he says.

They stop before the observation room. Gone is the hum and the buzz. Only a deep, earthen silence from beyond light's reach. The air, salty and smoky and sticking to the lips. The drip-dripping beyond becomes a sloshing at their feet.

Carruthers pries open the door. In the darkness, Michaels hears her swallowing, suppressing a gag. "God Almighty," she says. "They're in pieces."

60

When the locked doors to the lower levels are opened, it is not by Michaels's hand. Still, he recognizes their tools. They carry portable batteries with enough juice to reboot the consoles. They carry magnetically shielded tablets. Acetylene torches spark in the dark, cutting through doors that don't unlock. They wear no standard uniforms, only tactical black that might trickle down to the military in another ten years.

"Shit," Michaels whispers.

"What?" Carruthers asks. "That's the welcome wagon, right?"

"Yeah, maybe," Michaels says, though he senses this wagon comes at a high cost.

"Agent Michaels," says someone he hasn't met in person in years. "I was curious: would we find you in one place or several?"

Without asking for permission, Foundation agents check Carruthers and Michaels for injuries. Others slap battery-powered LEDs on the walls, turning the observation room into a shimmering, blue crypt. A few are already bagging and tagging. Cameras flash in the shadows, glimpses of the slaughter.

Coordinator Nox steps over a red lump, trailed by an ensemble of techs. "I am delighted that you've staved off harm. Remarkable, truly."

"He's good," one of the med techs tells Nox. "Some bruising around the throat, glass patterns. She's got a few facial abrasions. Their blood sugar's low."

"Someone fetch them a Snickers."

"Sir," Michaels says. "I'm grateful. We are all grateful for your assistance. I just… I didn't request any of this, so I'm having a little trouble understanding—"

"Why we're here? Yes, that must be confusing. Come, it's time we coordinate stories."

They follow Nox into the dark hall. Down, taking a left toward the offices. At the junction, two escorts stop Carruthers with a hand on her shoulder.

"Sir," Michaels says. "Special Agent Carruthers is a valuable partner—"

"Yes, your contributions have been most useful," Nox says and stares at Carruthers. "We'll see to your compensation. Your country thanks you."

"Sir," Michaels repeats, and this time it's his hand on the coordinator's shoulder. "She's been with my investigation since the start."

Nox turns his eyes on Michaels. As turquoise as the sea, and far colder.

"It's not your investigation anymore," he says. "Now, if you still wish to contribute, I suggest you follow me. And do keep your mouth shut. It's your least useful feature."

The coordinator is off, leaving Michaels with a choice: stay with Carruthers and whatever end comes to their involvement or go deeper, following the coordinator into the light-spattered halls.

"Go," Carruthers mouths and seals his path with a nod. Further it is.

MICHAELS HAS STOOD on both sides of this one-way mirror. There, in the interview room, listening to subjects. And here, on this side, conferring with scientists. Dead now, so many dead.

But not her.

Temporary lights dot the walls, cold orbs taped to concrete. Dim illumination, but it doesn't matter to the woman on the gurney. Caitlyn lies strapped to a stretcher; airport-grade headphones encase her ears. Every thirty seconds she twitches and spasms.

"What are you doing to her?" Michaels demands. He makes it halfway to the door between rooms when the guards stop him.

"Sit down, Michaels," Nox says.

"I prefer to stand, sir."

"I wasn't asking."

A deep breath. Then Michaels complies. The room is small, thick with the sweat of men twenty floors underground. Salt and nylon and airplane-grade coffee.

"What the hell are you doing to her?"

"Caitlyn is coming out of sedation," Nox says. "Once she regains consciousness—if her mind isn't fried—the sonic restraint will prevent decoherence. Blinking, as she calls it. It's a form of protection."

"Yeah, 'cause it looks more like torture. What's next, waterboarding?"

"We have more surgical methods, if need be."

"What needs might those be, sir?"

"The security of our nation."

"So how does torturing a blind woman achieve that?"

"Because she isn't," a voice adds. Dr. Chase closes the door, stains beneath his armpits, hair greasy. A wobbly man who just ran a forced marathon.

"Isn't what?" Michaels asks.

"She isn't blind," Chase says and slides a tablet over.

Michaels studies the MEG-II scans. Two rows. The top labeled *VISUALLY IMPAIRED*. The bottom labeled *GREY, CAITLYN*. Today's date is on it.

Chase says, "Caitlyn's medical records show a steady decline in visual apperception over the past decade. Yet she has no ocular malformations. Her rods and cones are functional. Her optic nerves are healthy. Dr. Beane brought this to my attention during the test. Physiologically, Caitlyn is perfectly capable of seeing."

"Well, that's just not possible. You mean she's lying?"

"No, not quite. One thing is preventing her vision, and it's here, a form of cortical blindness."

Michaels follows the doc's yellow fingernail across the tablet, from the top row of the brain scan to the bottom. Comparing, he spots differences but they don't click into place, not yet. Then Chase taps his own temple.

"Her records attribute visual degradation to intracranial lesioning following a sailing accident. I have no doubt she sincerely believes this. However, I've seen such patterning before. It's a direct result of decoherence. In a sense, she's bricked over the windows to keep her house safe."

"That makes no sense," Michaels says. "Why would she do that?"

"She didn't," Chase says. "Not consciously. In an open environment, the decoherent mind consumes other systems. It's too much stimulus. You've seen the scans. Roger, Teddy, everyone we tested today. Even if they never intentionally projected, on a subconscious level they could never stop. But Caitlyn, her mind used these lesions to protect itself. Her cortical blindness, her agoraphobia, her ability, they're all interrelated. By inhibiting the conscious processing of vision, her brain found equilibrium. If she were to abstain from blinking, these lesions would shrink. In theory, her vision could return. But if she continues…"

Michaels, reeling. "So what, her ability is an accident?"

"No, no, Agent Michaels, quite the opposite in fact."

Coordinator Nox leans forward. Now it's his turn to slide Michaels a tablet. "How far into Caitlyn's past have you looked?"

Michaels swipes through her dossier. The same documents he pulled from the FBI, CA.GOV, Social Security, ICE, and more. Ten years of information, ordered by date. There are new pages now: a passport at age twelve, a class photo from Zurich International

School, one from a yearbook where a preschool-age Caitlyn smiles with her classmates in Bolivia.

"So?"

Nox folds his hands. "Why can a young woman achieve what took Dr. Chase years and forty million dollars to discover?"

"We screened hundreds of candidates," Chase adds. "I've always maintained that there is a genetic component to this. The neuroplasticity of youth and a predisposition of the mind."

"Yeah, but you can't control for that," Michaels says.

"You're right," Chase says. "But she did."

"The point of an investigation," Nox cuts in, "is to uncover the truth through the accumulation of facts. You brought us facts which uncovered connections. That woman in the next room is able to project for one simple reason: she's the daughter of Zara Eisler and Tae Hwan Kim."

Dead silence. Then Michaels scoffs. "That's not possible. Tae Hwan—"

"Died, in 1995?" Nox asks. "Except he didn't. He paid his brother to cover it up. Special Agent Lee exhumed the tomb. It's just worms and air."

A flash in Michaels's mind. Tae Hwan's face, young and youthful. Is there a shadow of him on Caitlyn? No, no, it's impossible. It is—

"Epigenetics was hardly a whisper when we started Clearwater," Chase says. "Now it's the next genomic frontier. In utero exposure to decoherence would provide a powerful imprint. Zara and Tae Hwan could walk, but Caitlyn can fly."

"Yeah, hold on," Michaels says. Tries to process it all but the pieces aren't fitting. "Her parents died a decade ago in—what was it?—Kenya. This doesn't connect."

"Tae Hwan and Zara went off grid in the mid-nineties," Nox says. "When they resurfaced, they were Jason and Terry, just two Americans in a diaspora of millions. In Switzerland Terry worked as a customs broker. In Romania, Jason was a financial consultant. They flew under the radar, lived like proper expats, even filed taxes. But our algorithms picked up a pattern. The CIA keeps cash reserves for black ops in dummy accounts abroad, and someone kept making withdrawals. Fifty grand here, one hundred grand there. Small enough not to trigger an audit but enough to be missed. The case went cold a decade back. Each location, without fail, was somewhere Caitlyn lived."

"So you're postulating that her parents were, what, some kind of psychic Bonnie and Clyde?"

"That's one way to put it," Nox says. "Or perhaps they were trying to buy their daughter a better future. Their life insurance policy was a ruse, a trust set up in Macao and laundered through her uncle."

"Money and proximity," Michaels says. "It's a specious connection, at best."

"And there's DNA," Nox says with a smile. "We pulled hairs on intake. Caitlyn's a genetic match to Tae Hwan's half brother, Tom. He's her uncle."

Michaels's palms dampen, begging to twitch. He squeezes them against his knees. "Okay, so assuming this is true, it's financial fraud. Inadvertent. That's IRS stuff. No reason to hold her like this."

"We're not holding her for fraud," Nox says. "We're holding her for murder."

Michaels opens his mouth but only a puff of warm air comes out. He swallows to wet his tongue. "Whose murder?"

"Look around you. This investigation has cost more lives than it was tasked with saving."

"But that's not Caitlyn's fault. She—"

"Yes, she tried to warn you," Nox says. "Curious thing, isn't it? The daughter of two test subjects embeds herself in the investigation, gains access to every target, and now we're left with a dozen body bags."

"Robert, you saw her assist us," Michaels says. "You can't be serious."

"What I saw were brain scans," Chase says, tapping the screen.

"Here, during the bulk of the test. And here, during the last episode. Lit up, see? Like the Fourth of July."

"No." Michaels shoves the tablet away. "This doesn't prove she murdered people."

"It proves she was exerting enough force to," Nox says. "That was the goal of this test, wasn't it? It proves she's a weapon."

Chase taps the tablet again. "The mics picked this up during peak neural activity."

It's a video clip, the feed from inside Caitlyn's pod. She's tugging out her earbuds, whispering, "No. I can't stop it. It's too much. Too strong." Her eyes are closed.

Michaels asks, "You think she just snapped and went on a rampage?"

"No, no, of course not," Chase says. "That sweet girl in there never would. But something inside her—call it a genetic echo or a bifurcated subconscious—it could do things she never would."

"Like a dissociative identity? No way."

"A mens corpus is dissociative by definition. Our subjects manifested half-formed bodies and crawled down walls—"

"*Your* subjects. Not Caitlyn. She's not capable of that kind of violence."

"That girl is stronger than all our subjects combined," Chase says. "Her mind should be ruined. Yet it found harmony, one sense stepping aside for another."

Another flash. The first time Michaels truly believed Caitlyn. When she located Roger, in a dummy room one floor below. When she returned to the plane with a gasp and began bleeding from her eyes.

"You think she was working with Roger?"

"Someone was," Nox says. "A self-medicating paranoid schizophrenic? It wouldn't take much to set him off. A few well-placed whispers, some tasks, a sense of righteous purpose. Then cut him loose when the walls tighten."

"No, I don't buy it," Michaels says. "It doesn't track. It doesn't feel right."

"Feel?" Nox asks. "When does Michaels default to feelings? Did she win you over with that elevator ride? Pause, Agent. Take a breath. Stop thinking with your dick and—"

Michaels winds up and socks the coordinator. Right in his smug fucking face. Doesn't even think, just swings tight and fast.

Then they're both on the floor, Michaels beneath an agent, two more pouring in.

Nox, knocked against the one-way mirror, wipes his bloody nose with his sleeve. "Get him out of here! Find a broom closet and stuff him inside."

Michaels hears the click of the door behind him and the floor slides beneath. He tries to walk but the agents aren't having it. They drag him out, into the hallway, away from Caitlyn and that room. He squeezes his right hand, then lets it twitch wildly.

[61]

A MESS, THIS WHOLE OPERATION. NOX WIPES A SPECK OF BLOOD FROM his shoe.

Robert Chase offers him a handkerchief, the man's arm wobbling against the crutch. Nox takes it, takes a moment to consider what's salvageable. He watched the investigation unfold from a distant place. Steeled himself for a full clear. But now, here in the trenches, there might be a few moves left to make.

"Your work has caused a lot of problems, Dr. Chase. Tell me: do you still think you can make distance a thing of the past?"

"I did," Chase says. "Once." He takes the handkerchief, folds it, then drops it in the trash.

"I'm going topside to make some calls. Walk with me, Doc. Pitch me. I'm curious what you might do with unlimited funding."

With the elevator disabled, the hike to the surface takes twenty minutes and four hundred steps. It is the longest climb of Robert Chase's life. By the time they make it to the surface, he is glistening and parched. Nox simply listened, a good sign to Chase after decades of begging boardrooms and long nights writing grants.

Daylight now, and a convoy of black SUVs parked at the facility's doors. An operations technician hands Nox a sat phone. Before answering, he cups it and bores those green eyes into Chase.

"Understand this: we are not some venture fund you can milk for your mortgage. Results are expected. Are we clear, Dr. Chase?"

Chase stifles the excitement, the joy, the sweet little victory that has eluded him for decades. He gives his new benefactor a solemn nod, nothing more.

Nox says, "Welcome to the Foundation."

CARRUTHERS CRUSHES THE BOTTLED WATER AND DROPS IT IN THE BIN. Michaels wipes his forehead. Without AC, the facility is fast becoming a sweat lodge. Doesn't help when they're crammed into Peck's former suite.

"Detained by an agency that doesn't exist," Carruthers says. "This will be a fun one to fill out on the time card."

"You'll be fine," Michaels says. "The Foundation hasn't gotten this far without a few friends in the Bureau. They'll probably bump back your retirement, if you ask."

Carruthers shakes her head. "They've been showing me the door for a while. I doubt there's enough interagency goodwill to pump those brakes."

"I never asked you why."

"Why what?"

"Your retirement, Denise. You're eligible, but it's not mandatory until fifty-seven."

"I thought you read my file."

"May have skimmed a few parts."

Carruthers taps Peck's computer. Nothing. Not even a flicker. "Remember that college admissions scandal? Those families that greased hands to get their kids into Ivy Leagues?"

"Of course."

"One of our ASACs was involved. I made the arrest. Turns out feds hate the perp walk too."

Michaels rubs his throbbing jaw. Tries not to smile at that image.

"And it also turns out former feds can still apply pressure. Look the other way, just forget this email. You know me—that's not in my DNA. What's funny is, it wasn't even my case. I was just brought in to lighten the load. Just like this."

"The Foundation is always scouting consultants. That's how they got me."

"I'll stick to my paperwork."

"Then what? After the paperwork, I mean."

Carruthers considers it. A soft smile tugs at the corners of her lips. "Make a phone call, mend some fences, tell my daughter I'm sorry. Maybe take her on a vacation. Someplace warm."

"A vacation sounds nice." And he thinks that's about as likely as Nox bringing them some cake.

"You think we'll get the big picture?" Carruthers asks. "All the loose ends, tied together?"

"Someone will. In a room, some subcommittee hearing way above my pay grade. They'll lay it all out, thirty-odd years. What we caught was a glimpse."

"No way Caitlyn did this," Carruthers says. "Not on her own."

"I don't even know what she's capable of." Michaels sighs. "Roger was feeding someone locations. That's all we know."

"Yeah, and someone was feeding Roger enough ketamine to kill a horse."

Michaels smiles. Funny expression. To kill a horse.

Then his hand goes into full-on spasms. He squeezes it. A chill slithers up his neck.

Carruthers tilts her head. "You okay?"

"Wait, just... just shut up, Denise."

"Excuse me?"

Stammering, fingers dancing, his eyes dart about the room,

left, right, left. Thoughts popping, neuronal connections retracing pathways backward through time, and he mumbles, "Not much you can do when they go lame."

"Michaels, you really put the 'special' in special agent."

"To kill a horse," he says.

A thousand threads in his head now, a tenuous decision: which one to tug? Memories of sights and sounds, snippets of conversations half heard. To access a memory is to alter the memory, so which thought to retrace? The tank? Delicate webs glistening with dew. Barn? He wants—no, he needs—these random firings of disparate facts. Confluence, yes. Roger? The obscure clarifies for the span of a blink. Think. Redistribution? It is close now, so close he can taste it on the tip of his tongue, like metal, like glass, like a white powdery substance that can be snorted or vaporized or shot. Horses. Shot. Not with a gun but a bolt pistol.

A flash of Mrs. Jensen, in her kitchen. "Long day," she had said. "Had to put a horse down. Not much you can do when they go lame."

Michaels speaks each word slowly, deliberately. "Vetalar was in Roger's tank, along with LSD. That's the homebrew recipe for DZ3."

"We've established that. And Roger got the formula from McNare."

"The formula. But not the Vetalar. Those doses were too high for any street dealer."

"So he had a hookup at a lab or a veterinarian."

"Or a veterinarian," Michaels says. "At a horse sanctuary."

Carruthers blinks. She purses her lips, about to protest the logic, but pulls back at the last second.

Michaels says, "Every test subject showed redistribution of brain mass, right? The longer they're gone, the stronger they get, the more the mind devours itself."

Carruthers senses where this is going. She closes her eyes. "No."

"And what do they lose? Their perception of self. If you were decoherent for years—if you were in a coma—would you even look human?"

She shivers, feels her back tighten. Threshold moment. Everything screams, *Step back. Don't open this door*. "You think Teddy blinked so much he put himself in a coma?"

"Maybe. Or maybe it's the other way around."

"Christ, if this is true, we were standing right next to him. Why not just rip us to shreds?"

"And draw our attention? No. He needed to turn down the heat. And Mrs. Jensen, she practically handed us Roger. She gave us that tip—"

"And the RV. If Roger wanted to hit Linamore, why torch his own truck? Just leave it."

"Because he didn't. Because the fire was started inside, not to conceal but reveal."

"And then we rounded everyone up. Brought them all back here—"

"To the one place Teddy knew better than any other."

A canyon of silence between them. Then an explosion of motion. Carruthers, at the door, pounding. Michaels, on his tablet, opening files. "I'm locked out of the investigation," he says.

"What does that mean?"

"Best-case scenario, I'm under active suspension."

A click at the door. A young face with a gumdrop neck jutting out from a tactical suit. Their driver from Reno. "Hainsely, right?" Michaels asks.

The man shakes his head. "Barnes. Operations Technology."

"Barnes, that's it," Michaels says. "Listen, I know you have orders, but we need to talk to Coordinator Nox. You need to escort us to him. It's urgent."

Barnes holds up a hand—*hold tight*—and taps his tablet. Michaels waits. Had he detected a panhandle twang to the young man's voice? Barnes is new. In another twelve months the elocution training will rub all regional hints away. Maybe there's an angle to play.

"Good news: you're free to go," Barnes says. "Follow me to the surface. Don't wander."

FOUR HUNDRED STEPS LATER, the long, late-afternoon sun of the High Sierras falls upon their sweaty faces. The facility is once again being mothballed. Metal covers are screwed over outlets. Outside, three Suburbans idle in the gravel lot. Empty.

"He's not here," Michaels says. "Where is he?"

"You're an investigator," Barnes says and takes a puff off an e-cigarette. "Start investigating the tire tracks."

A pair of op techs chuckle and head back inside.

"When did they leave?" Carruthers asks. "Minutes? An hour? It's urgent—"

"Yeah, urgent, you already said that. And the coordinator said y'all can hitch a ride home."

"Barnes, I know you're just following orders," Michaels says. "I get that. But they're still at risk and we need your help."

Barnes nods, blows out a chemical cloud. "Not my circus, not my monkeys."

Then he heads back toward the facility. He makes it three feet.

When properly executed, a rear naked choke uses lateral vascular restraint to block the left and right carotid arteries. Regardless of size, the result is cerebral ischemia and a loss of consciousness in seconds. Barnes barely has his fingers in the crook of Carruthers's elbow when hypoxia hits. Then his arms fall limp and his knees buckle. Gently, tenderly, she lowers him to the ground.

"Get his keys and his phone," she says, motioning with her chin. "We'll take his car and call Nox from the road."

Michaels pulls himself from his stupor, jumps into action. He finds a key fob, a Foundation-issued smartphone and tablet. He finds a service pistol, ejects the magazine, and flings the gun into a pile of snowmelt. He gives the fob to Carruthers. "You drive."

"We need to go, now," Carruthers says. "He's going to be up any—"

"Ahhhhhhhh!" Barnes screams as he snaps up and claws at his throat. It takes him five seconds to come back online, to understand he isn't dying. Then he is on his feet, 230 pounds rushing the SUV. He hits the driver's side door as it closes, goes for his gun, but finds an empty holster. So he finds a rock and strikes the SUV as it executes a three-point turn.

The window shatters on the second hit, and now it is Barnes who is grabbing at Carruthers. He finds her arm, finds the steering wheel, then finds the SUV taking a sharp turn. He slides down the running board and tumbles into the scrub brush.

"Is he okay?" Carruthers asks. "Tell me he didn't go under."

In the rearview mirror: Barnes, limping behind a cloud of dust. "I'll send him a card," Michaels says. "He was just following orders."

"Lot of that going around."

"Yeah, well, you're not wrong," Michaels says. "Let's hope he keeps his phone charged."

The lock screen is a picture of Barnes's wife and it requires a biometric key. Still, Michaels knows there is a flaw the OS hasn't patched. In addition to 911, all Foundation phones are preset with emergency contacts. Press the power and volume buttons together and—bingo!

"Gate's locked," Carruthers says as they race toward the access gate. A chain and a lock and it pops off with a strong nudge. The chain whips back and lashes a long scratch down the hood.

"Damn deer," Carruthers says. "Can you believe the deer did that? Jumped right out and left just as quick."

With a skid, the gravel gives way to smooth road, Highway 284.

"East or west?"

"They'll be taking Caitlyn to the nearest airfield," Michaels says. "Reno. Head east."

Carruthers hits the gas. For a heavy truck, this Suburban has some kick.

On the phone: emergency contacts. Michaels recognizes the first one as it dials. A buzz, then: "Thank you for calling Wong's Fine Chinese Dining. We are currently—"

"Operator," Michaels says. Then again: "Operator."

A long pause. A hiss. High above, satellites and cell phone towers are coordinating handshakes to secure a connection. The only way to intercept this call is if someone is flying a drone with a Stingray and scouring the mountains. Or—

"This is an emergency in progress," Michaels says. "There is an imminent attack. I repeat: an imminent terror threat on a civilian center with military-grade weapons. Operator."

"What the hell?" Carruthers says.

Michaels cups the receiver. "Say the right words into a secure line and it's auto-flagged. Even classified, it leaves a record. One of the downsides of piggybacking on an NSA satellite."

"Operator speaking. Confirm voice identification."

"This is Field Agent Michaels, badge ID seven, seven, three, beta, zulu. I'm using an op tech's commandeered phone due to emergency. I need—"

"Voice identification doesn't match the registered device. Be advised, you're in possession of a restricted—"

"Listen to me," Michaels says. "I know you've got scripted responses on the screen. I cut my teeth in field support."

Michaels can see it: the computer monitor reflected in the trainee's glasses. The otherwise dim room at Kray Mesa. The live scan going speech-to-text, offering scripted responses while he opens a drawer.

"Hell, you're probably reaching for the handbook, right? Trying to figure out protocol for a field agent on a nonauthorized phone. What's it say? Keep me talking while you run a trace and wipe the device?"

"Ummm." The operator clears his throat, leaves silence on the other end. That answers that.

"I'll save you the bandwidth," Michaels says. "We're on 284 south to 70, Reno-bound. Now, you've got my badge number, right? I need to be patched through to my coordinator. Surname: N-O-X. He's likely in a convoy headed to Reno airport. He and his passengers are in danger. I repeat: they are in immediate danger."

More silence. Then the voice finds its breath. "Can you clarify?"

"Not without beyond top secret authorization. Have you signed your lifetime NDA?"

"Uh, I'm not sure—"

"You'd know if you had."

"Sir... Agent, I appreciate the urgency. I just... I can't do this."

A whoosh and the scent of redwood through the shattered window. Carruthers overtakes a lumber truck rattling with logs. All around, shadows on mountains and the promise of dusk.

"No, you're not *supposed* to," Michaels says. "Hell, if I were on your end, I'd say the same thing. But technically, you can do this. He's in your system. You've got my profile in front of you. Look under 'direct manager.' That's him, right there. N-O-X. So you need to choose: follow the rules or keep that man safe. We both know this call's being logged, so lock in your choice."

A long pause. The gulp of a dry throat on the other side of the phone. "Okay, just hold on a moment. I've... I've never done this before."

Michaels almost smiles. Carruthers overtakes a Prius. "We're a bit short on time here. Just transfer this call to his mobile line."

"No, I mean... I've never transferred a call before. It's... This is my first day on desk and..." The voice cracks. "I'm kind of freaking out."

Carruthers glances at Michaels, mouths, *Everything okay?*

Michaels rubs his temples. "Well, I can promise you one thing: every call from now on will be a breeze."

INTERSTATE 395 OUTSIDE RENO
THURSDAY - 5:00 PM, PST

DUSK PAINTING PEAVINE MOUNTAIN IN GILDED HUES. SHADOWS creeping up folded slopes. Reno, just starting to sparkle. Twenty-one miles from Michaels and Carruthers, a convoy of black SUVs crests the northern edge of the Biggest Little City in the World.

In the lead vehicle, Coordinator Nox drafts a summary of the day's events. At 2000 PST he will send a video briefing to the Joint Chiefs of Staff. His assessment contains a table of costs and losses, including the loss of life and requisite cover stories and compensation. He estimates this week's failure at 7.8 million. He believes he can reduce it to five due to clear evidence the subjects breached the terms of their 1993 contract. If their next of kin resist, if push comes to shove, he can seize all goods acquired in violation of the settlement. The cameras had captured every interview, admissions and all. And where there isn't audio, there are video algorithms that can near perfectly read lips.

Privately, when the stress of his job robs his senses of joy, Nox retreats into his mind. He finds solace in poems and the precise click of his mechanical watch. He runs mental simulations.

An unmanned combat air vehicle can exceed fifteen million dollars per unit after development costs. They require a ground crew and eight thousand pounds of fuel to keep it circling and strike-ready. They are loud and easily tracked and as surgical as a sledgehammer. For every terrorist taken out by a Hellfire missile, there are entire weddings wiped off the sand.

Today's implications: no need for strike teams if the agents can be anywhere in the field, no need for secure lines if the conversations occur in a higher dimension. Data collection from anywhere on earth. No costly refueling. The Foundation could be what Nox has always wanted: nimble, precise, nonexistent. The young woman has shown him this potential.

Nox clicks his tablet. Work to be done. Now, to get his benefactors on board. He cues up the videos of the lab massacre. Earlier, he had streamed it live on his flight. Now, he is able to admire it, to take a more critical eye. He highlights a few juicy clips, adds kinetic measurements, snips in some audio from the autopsy in Boston. Just a taste.

If his benefactors want more, they'll have to write a blank check. Until then, better keep this weapon and her creator off grid. There are foggy miles of Alaskan waters where she is headed. If the higher-ups say no, well, a lot of things can happen offshore.

THREE CARS BACK, pressed against the windows, Robert Chase counts his good fortune. The casino lights of Reno glisten in the distance, but he has already won. His poor colleagues, all dead, bags in an unmarked truck. He is saddened, yes. So much suffering and death have come from Clearwater's halls.

And yet, if he is honest, if he catalogues the true depth of his heart, he finds himself giddy again, almost grinning. This should come with great shame, he tells himself, this new beginning. Shouldn't survivor's guilt show up soon? It probably will.

His colleagues paid upon the altar of knowledge; they knew the risk. The true shame, he tells himself, is they will never see the future they founded.

. . . .

ONE CAR AWAY, Caitlyn lies strapped to a gurney, trapped in a sea of noise and sensation. She is beta testing a new restraint, on loan from DARPA. The size of a straightjacket with headphones and boots, the Confinement Submission System is a cruel marvel. A random sample of music plays in disparate modulations, intervals rising and falling. Volume swings between twenty and eighty decibels.

When the jacket's sensors detect a decrease in heart rate, the motors squeeze, mimicking any sensation from a hug to convulsions. When applied to one side, the feeling is like rolling. The boots are the latest accessory. Tight around the toes and ankles, they deliver mild shocks when patterns become predictable. The mind, after all, is the ultimate problem-solving machine. To gain a subject's cooperation, it needs to be broken.

Caitlyn Grey, now swaddled in sound. First the Ramones singing about how they don't want to be buried in the Pet Semetary. Cut to Coolio asking, "Why are we too blind to see that the ones we hurt are…" Then Beethoven, the ninth, third overture. When she hears this, she thinks of her mom and now her feet are cramping and she can't itch them and what is that noise? Is that her voice? Is she screaming? Is she thrashing at the leather straps and crying out for someone to end it, end it, end it all, please please please?

Then, it does. Darkness. Her veil of shadows. Hands, reaching out, and if she can just lift the curtain, she can see beyond and—

Three Dog Night. A bullfrog named Jeremiah. An old friend. *Only you don't have friends, do you? You have clients you keep at phone distance and an octogenarian neighbor who pities your existence. No one is coming because you've kept everyone away, and all the bullfrogs and straight shooters and sons of guns won't save you now.*

AT NINETY MILES PER HOUR, Carruthers brings the Suburban zooming past a slow-moving Civic. Reno, on the horizon. The first sign of the city.

Ear warm, Michaels listens as the call connects. Then the coordinator's voice: "Nox speaking."

The operator says, "Sir, I'm sorry, but—"

Michaels cuts in: "Nox, it's Michaels. Listen to me: you've made a mistake. It's not Caitlyn. It's Teddy. Teddy Jensen—"

"Michaels?" For the first time in years, genuine frustration in the man's voice. "How'd you get an op tech's phone? Ah, emergency call. Well, consider this the formal end to your involvement—"

"Sir, goddammit, just listen—"

"No, you listen. You've displayed reckless behavior. Your judgment is suspect."

"It's not Caitlyn, you arrogant prick!"

"Good day."

Click. The line goes dead. Just Michaels and the operator, who says, "I'm in deep shit, aren't I?"

"We all are," Michaels says and hangs up.

"So what do we do now?" Carruthers asks, passing a truck. "The only phone we've got is locked. Are pay phones still a thing?"

Michaels studies the dashboard. Like all Foundation vehicles, this one has a police scanner. He activates the phone's emergency call. "Let's put the scanner to work." Dialing... dialing...

Connected. "Washoe County 911, please state your emergency."

Breathe deep. Speak fast. "Oh God, I need to report a child abduction in progress. A group of black SUVs heading to Reno. They said they were taking her to the airport. A description? Yes, he's Caucasian, late forties, silver hair. They're armed... He said something about QAnon. What? Yes, of course I'll stay on the line."

Best performance of his life.

Carruthers takes her eyes off the road for a quick glance. They are as wide as he's ever seen them. Grinning, she shakes her head. "You are making my retirement exciting."

Michaels adjusts the police scanner, presses *search*. It cycles through channels, static mostly, then: "All units in Reno, 10-35 alert, be on the lookout for a possible 427 in progress. Vehicle description is incoming."

Then the dispatcher, into his ear: "Sir, can you describe the vehicle and suspects in detail?"

"I sure can. Ready?"

[64]
LINN COUNTY, IOWA
THURSDAY - 7:15 P.M., CST

THE GREAT QUARTER HORSES AND STALLIONS, THE APPALOOSAS AND thoroughbreds, these beasts of speed and swift motion, now stir as the spring gloaming recedes. They run through the evening misting as a cold wind picks up, whipping across the field, scattering the herd and sending sparrows crying into flight.

In a dark bedroom of the Jensen farmhouse, machines keep a steady rhythm. Serenity in this music, she thinks. The hiss that breathes for her son.

Theodore Jonah Jensen came into this world bright-eyed and smiling. He had hardly cried. And when she held him, she marveled over his tiny fingers and little nails, all so perfectly formed, counting them again and again. And she marveled at his potential. So much possibility. He could be anything. He could have been anything.

And now she squeezes her son's ragged hand. Dry, even with daily moisturizing. He consumes over five thousand calories via a feeding tube and still he consumes himself. At forty-eight, Teddy has collapsed back into a second infancy. But what he has lost in body he has gained in spirit.

"There, there, my child," she says as his hand squeezes back. She has long ago given up hope for an awakening. She knows these spasms and tics for what they are: reflex firings of systems going dormant. Like a summer home at season's end, Theodore Jonah Jensen, her only son, her only family, is shutting down room by room.

She lowers her head in prayer. She is grateful, yes, but she is also burdened. She feels every minute of her seven decades. She wants to ask God for another miracle, to see her son's eyes clear and bright, just once more. She knows such a request is greedy. God has given her boy a gift in the form of a curse. God has brought him back from the realm of the dead.

Now comes the miracle.

A creaking of floorboards, a shifting wind. She feels the presence of her son—the breath of God himself—and now a cold finger wipes tears from her cheek.

"Again? So soon?" she whispers. "Very well. Let us begin."

With a groan, she wheels his bed across the room. The dialysis machine goes on pause. She disconnects the liquid feed from the PEG tube that delivers nutrition directly into his stomach. She clamps off the tube, tapes it to his abdomen. She wipes the discharge with a gentle hand.

In the bathroom stands a walk-in tub, rubber straps ready to embrace him. She pauses his bedside ventilator and switches the endotracheal tube to the portable. A reflexive gurgle. Weak lungs fluttering like butterflies in a sack. She slings the portable ventilator over her right shoulder. Then Susan Jensen lifts her son. He weighs fifty-eight pounds, half the weight of the foals she has helped birth.

Gentle, gentle. Laying him now upon rubber netting above the tub. The muscles in his neck have long since atrophied, causing his head to loll and bump against the rim. A low rumble suffuses the air. The tiles creak.

"Forgive me, angel," she says. There will be a bruise; she can see its shadow forming now. Tenderly, she places his hands at his side. Then she presses the button and the water begins.

The walk-in tub is stained a mustard shade from the salt that gives him buoyancy and the fluids that he leaks. No amount of scrubbing has cleaned it. There is a lesson here, she supposes. That what began decades ago still taints today.

One foot of water. She can feel his gaze forming. Just a matter of time.

"Be patient, my sweet. We are so very close."

The tub groans and buckles. Two feet of water. It is upon his skin now, rising through the rubber net. A trickle of blood bubbles from his nostril.

"Be patient," she says and wipes it. "All good things come to those who wait."

The tub is full now, the water at level. Teddy's body floats, cradled in liquid, braced by the net. His head rests upon floral towels. Wiping wispy hairs aside, she places a pair of headphones over his ears. A damp washcloth over his eyes.

Then she opens a folder. There are photographs, some printed and some clipped from magazines. Vibrant colors and old newspaper gray. Descriptions handwritten in fountain pen ink.

"Dr. Eileen Chow?" she asks, studying the printout from the company website. A low rumble. A breath of wind. The picture slowly splits down the middle.

"Dr. Sian Tannen?" Another tear, this time into pieces. She proffers a smile. "Dr. Carloyn Locke—"

Another rip, a whole stack.

"Dr. Miguel Beane—"

And another.

"Dr. David Ibrihim—"

And the room flutters with shredded paper. Great confetti. Faces and names and accomplishments, torn and snowing upon mother and son.

"Dr. Robert Chase?" she asks.

The tub rumbles. The water seems to flash-boil. Then, the roar. It comes from all around her, a cold voice. It penetrates her, a blade within static. She knows that voice, can never forget it. It is the voice of her son, the voice of an angel.

She smiles and says, "Now make him suffer."

[65]
RENO, NEVADA
THURSDAY - 5:20 PM, PST

WHEN THE SHERIFF'S CRUISER PULLS UP BESIDE THE LEAD VEHICLE, THE coordinator feels a pang of annoyance. Local law, while well-meaning, are often nosy. It has been months since he has needed to pull rank. Bad day to resume.

Then, when the second cruiser pulls up, annoyance becomes frustration. A roadblock at the intersection ahead. How? Never mind. He deduces it at once: Michaels. Emergency or not, Nox makes a mental note to have IT disable all outgoing calls from locked Foundation phones.

"Sir, what should I do?" the driver asks. One hundred feet ahead, patrol cars converge in roadblock formation. Guns being drawn and spike strips deployed. "Sir?"

"Pull us over, nice and slow," Nox says. "Let's parley with the locals."

Five minutes later and the air is still thick with dissent. "This will be a lot easier if y'all consent to a vehicle search," the sheriff says. He is an officious man, Nox muses. Rudimentary. He passes his fingers over his handcuffs in attempt at intimidation. Nox isn't having it.

"As I've said, that's just not possible." Nox ensures his hands are where the sheriff can see them. Cops. Their default setting is distrust and they work their way up. "What we have in the truck is DoD property, and we—"

"Have jurisdiction. Yeah, you said that." The sheriff turns the coordinator's credentials over while passing drivers rubberneck. A rare sight: six federal vehicles pulled over by a half dozen state cruisers.

"Call the verification number," Nox says. "There, on the back of my badge."

"I'll be back. You wait right there, that's what." He points to the curb.

"It's your show, Sheriff," Nox calls out and thinks, *For now*.

While his credentials hit the system, bouncing from state to federal databases and back, the coordinator studies the names, the badge numbers. Nox has an excellent memory, not like Michaels, but better than most. If the cops decide to posture and stretch their authority—and some always do—he'll make a few calls. Better it doesn't come to that, but if it does—

Glinting metal clears that thought. The sun off the side mirror of a speeding Suburban. An op tech vehicle, engine purring.

The Suburban comes to a screeching halt as several cops wave the driver out. Hands over gun holsters, close to brandishing. When the passenger door opens, Nox clenches his teeth.

"Listen to me now!" Michaels shouts, his badge in one hand and his tablet in the other. "Let me through. I need to talk to him!"

Confused, the cops grunt and bark orders. Nox considers letting it all play out. It would be amusing to see Michaels in cuffs. Perhaps they might deploy a K9.

"… not Caitlyn. It's Teddy! Teddy Jensen!"

As the cops hold him back, it is Dr. Chase, hobbling through the fray, that catches the coordinator's eye. "How do you know?" Chase asks. "How can you be sure?"

Nox sighs. Time to intervene before the madness spreads.

"The longer they decohere, the higher the cost," Michaels says, "the less of their body remains. It's not Caitlyn. It's Teddy."

"Think about it," Carruthers says. "He has intimate knowledge of the facility. He's the only one left."

"Dr. Chase," Nox says, "Agent Michaels has exceeded his short leash and is now—"

"Wait!" Chase says, eyes studying the highway, searching for some answer beyond. "If he's comatose, if his insular cortex is corrupted... his sense of self would be shattered. He'd be locked out. He'd need another, not just a spotter but someone to induce decoherence and guide—"

"His mother," Carruthers says.

Chase hesitates, still staring at the asphalt.

"Dr. Chase, you wanted to weaponize the mind," Michaels says. "What if Teddy beat you to it?"

"Does he know Reno?" Carruthers asks. "Would Teddy have any memory of this place?"

Chase swallows. Looks them dead in the eyes. "Like his own backyard. They all did. This was our first major blind site."

A low, subsonic pulse, over a block away. And something else. In the evening glow, it is almost unnoticeable. Just a dark ribbon stretching beneath the flickering streetlights. But Michaels sees it. So does Dr. Chase.

Then, a crack. Warm asphalt buckles under pressure. Something shimmers on the pavement. Something slinks through the heat.

"Carruthers," Michaels says. "Get Dr. Chase out of here."

At the head of the roadblock, where the state troopers' cars meet the black SUVs, a single side mirror shatters. Five feet closer, a state trooper cries out, pirouettes, and bounces off a guard rail.

"Carruthers—"

"I see it."

"Get him out of here!"

"Already on it."

The hood of a police car folds inward. But nothing is there.

Four metal fissures split down the side of an SUV, nails rending steel and aluminum. And nothing is there.

A Foundation agent is flung up and over the SUV he stood guarding, his black glasses spinning in the cool breeze. Still, nothing is there.

The state troopers shout, raise weapons, scan the road for assailants. The Foundation agents aren't faring much better. "Sniper!" someone shouts. Calm becomes confusion with a rumble of fear.

The mind is not a muscle, yet it still depends on twitch reflex. Ancestral genetics have embedded primal instructions modern humans rarely touch. A flinch at the shape of a snake. The shadow of a skittering spider. Instinctive avoidance from the scent of a gangrenous wound.

There is no such reflex for what is coming.

It takes great trauma to cross the canyon of the unthinkable. Michaels had crossed it this afternoon. Coordinator Nox will, too, if he lives to see tomorrow.

For now, all he can say is, "That's not... She's not... She shouldn't be here."

"Because that's not her, sir," Michaels says. "Now which truck is she in?"

The lead SUV's driver-side door is ripped off its hinges. Sent sailing into the middle of the road.

"Teddy wants Dr. Chase," Michaels continues. "And Caitlyn is the only thing that can stop him. You want to live? Create a distraction. Send every vehicle in a different direction. That'll buy us time."

"Time for what?"

"Time to take down the farm. Now go, and give the orders."

Nox points to a van. Michaels makes it to the passenger side as an SUV's rear doors explode. Teddy isn't happy with the empty package. The other four SUVs scream into motion, splitting off in different directions.

Finger indentations form on another SUV's fender. Wheels spin against asphalt, kicking up white smoke. Then the hood is torn open, the windshield peeled from its seams.

"Go!" Michaels shouts to his van driver, a junior agent named Frank. "Get us back to Clearwater, now!"

Nimble hands slam the gearshift into reverse. Frank spins the wheel. Michaels steadies himself, climbs into the back. The van is a rolling ER, enough machinery to make an ambulance feel outdated. Cabinets rattle with vials and trauma supplies.

"You can't be here," the med tech says, but Michaels pushes his way past. There, on the stretcher, restrained and pacified, lies Caitlyn. Hot fury gets the better of him. His hands wrap around the med tech's neck.

"Take this off her before I throw you out the back."

The med tech unfastens restraints and unclasps headphones. The mouthguard comes out last, and with it Caitlyn lets out a scream.

"I'm here. It's Michaels. Caitlyn, I'm here, okay? Are you all right?"

"No," she says, feeling the world around her. The metal rail of the stretcher. His sleeve. The bench and the knee of the med tech and the loose restraints. "Why? Why did you do this to me?"

She balls her fists and strikes him, again and again. He deserves it, he tells himself. For failing. For losing so many lives. For not seeing the truth. And for letting this happen to her.

"I'm so sorry," he says. "It was my boss. They thought you were the killer."

"What? How could they think that?"

No, tell her later. It's not fair to lay it all on her now. And another part of him wonders, *Will it ever be?*

"Caitlyn, they were wrong. I was wrong. We thought we could contain this, control it, but we can't."

A screech of brakes, a thundering crunch. Something alongside the van razes metal and dents the side.

"Are we in a car? Was that an accident?"

Michaels looks up front. The van's doing seventy down an industrial parkway. Frank, shooting nervous glances back. "I think it just tried to ram us."

"Get us onto the freeway. Next on-ramp." Michaels turns back to the medic. "Is she okay? Did you drug her?"

"No, we just restrained—"

A low hum. A flicker. The sense that something cold has just passed overhead.

Two lanes adjacent, a black SUV swerves hard right. Michaels sees it before his own driver does. The agent in the parallel SUV, his hands off the wheel, clutching his collar. Fighting nothing. Squeezing to free his throat and—

The SUV rebounds off a parked car, fishtails hard left. Michaels grabs Frank's wheel, jerks it right. The out-of-control SUV passes within inches of their hood. Through its shattered back window, a sickening sight: one agent, back folded across the seat and moaning in pain. The driver, still fighting an invisible force. Trying to steer with his knees as his fingers bend the wrong way.

In a clash of metal and glass, the SUV rides the median and tumbles, end over end. The van shoots past.

"There, the on-ramp!" Michaels points.

"It's a red light."

"So use the sirens!"

The van screams through the intersection, wheels chattering over the rumble strips, medicine cabinet clanging open.

"Medic, what's your name?"

"Mansour."

"Mansour, congratulations." Michaels pushes him into the front seat. "You're Frank's navigator."

"What's going on?"

"There's an invisible monster coming for us and she's the only one that can stop it." The words leave his lips, easy as that. Funny how sane it now sounds. "Get us away before it peels this van open. Go!"

Fumbling with his tablet, Mansour squawks the megaphone and shouts at cars.

Michaels squeezes Caitlyn's hand, settles in beside her.

"It's bad, isn't it?" she asks. "Where are we now?"

"Leaving Reno. And yeah, it's not looking too good."

"I think it's Teddy," she says. "He's doing this. God, he's so confused."

"It is. How'd you know?"

"In the lab, our memories got entangled. I could feel his pain. I've never felt anything like that before."

A familiar rumble passes beneath the car. Then smooth acceleration. They're on the highway now.

"Caitlyn, we're going to have Iowa SWAT storm the farm. Until then, I need a favor."

Caitlyn's head drifts to one side, her eyes crossing his gaze, then beyond. A brief flash of Dr. Chase's prognosis: *If she were to abstain from blinking, these lesions would shrink. But if she continues...*

It isn't the question he fears but the cost of the answer.

"Say it," Caitlyn says.

"Can you hold Teddy off?"

THREE MILES SOUTHWEST, a black SUV careens down Mill Street and blows through the intersection at Kietzke Lane. Sirens blaring, the driver swerves around a skateboarder with earbuds who crosses traffic without looking. Six inches left and she'd be in the grill.

"Careful now," Coordinator Nox says, looking up from his tablet. His screen displays a map of Reno and the southern bulge of Washoe County. GPS-III signals from M-code satellites pinpoint the convoys with centimeter precision. It will be years before this tech hits smartphones. Now, Nox tracks the convoys, which scatter across the map like shrapnel.

"How's it looking, sir?" the driver asks. He is a first-year, must be nervous; he usually doesn't converse upstream.

"See that medical center up ahead?"

"Yes, sir. The one across from the park?"

"Good. Take a left after the park."

The driver pushes the accelerator. "You think, uh, maybe he won't find us if he's never been here?"

"I don't know how it all works. But let's hope this makes it harder."

Nox studies the screen. Which SUV had taken Dr. Chase? Number one is crippled, back with the cops. Number three has come to a stop by an on-ramp and is facing the wrong way. Not good. Three vehicles remain, all at different parts of the city. And then there's Michaels and the weapon in the medical van.

And Theodore Jensen, out there. Time to take out that problem, fast.

THE CALL COMES in at 7:37 p.m. An emergency channel, straight to Linn County SWAT. In less than three minutes, the captain is briefing his team while his assistant coordinates with County Rural Electric. Exigent circumstances, the belief that harm is imminent, allows them to forgo all warrants for the moment.

By road, it is thirty-four minutes to the Jensen farmstead. But only eight minutes by helicopter.

The Bell 412 and the pilot come courtesy of the Iowa Department of Homeland Security and Emergency Management. At 7:45 p.m., they lift off, screaming west, six SWAT operators listening as Undersheriff Acosta briefs them en route, shouting over the hum of the engine and the drumming of his heart.

66

DOWNTOWN RENO, THE NEON BABYLON, HOME TO TWO HUNDRED thousand souls. Here, the glimmer of chance still holds court. Unable to compete with the spectacle of Las Vegas, these casinos trade on nostalgia and price-conscious dreams while the Sierras promise of crystalline lakes.

Now, black machinery careens toward the city center, 355 horsepower and tinted windows. She drives tight, fighting the desire to overcompensate for the turns. It has been years since Carruthers trained at the Precision Obstacle Course at Quantico, but it's all coming back. Preempt the obstructions. Feel your center of gravity. Steer, brake, accelerate, but only one at a time.

"That was close," Dr. Chase says as a motorcyclist swerves and gives them the finger. "That was too close."

"You want to live, Doc, we need some skin in the game. Tell me, how can we lose him?"

"I don't know if we can."

"Then can we shake him?"

"Maybe. Moving objects were difficult for our subjects. Some were able to project themselves into planes. As long as he can't see us, we have a chance—"

Carruthers swerves around a dark truck that blows through a

red light. The wheels stutter and lean. The truck is a black SUV, a Suburban like theirs, all scratched metal and cracked glass. Spinning, the SUV comes to a stop on its side in a parking lot.

Carruthers and Chase share a look: not good. She hits the accelerator, three tons of aluminum picking up speed.

Just not as quickly as the neurons in Teddy Jensen's head.

When Chase glances at the wreck, he senses his prize pupil glaring back. Thirty years of history, lab-forged and cold. For a sunset flicker he can see the silhouette of something inhuman—something post-human—glaring across the road, across a thousand miles, across canyons of time.

"He sees us," Chase whispers. "God help us. He—"

The wrecked Suburban's side door bursts from its hinges.

Three cars back, the roof of a Honda Accord collapses under invisible feet.

Two cars back, a Mini Cooper's hood compresses and the engine hits the pavement in a crescendo of metal.

One car back, the driver of a Hyundai Sonata feels a deep chill and reaches for the heater. A second later, every window explodes as the air pressurizes in a low-frequency boom.

A heavy presence strikes the rear of Carruthers's SUV—a sudden tug—and for a half second the front wheels leave the road. Then the rear door is torn open—torn right off—and sent spinning into traffic.

Carruthers's ears pop as she spots a flicker in the rearview mirror. A fine mist coalescing, two eyes of steaming silver.

"Hello, Doctor Chase—"

Carruthers eyes the shimmer, then slams the brakes and spins the wheel. The weight shifts. A damp chill moistens her cheek, tumbles past her.

As the SUV fishtails around the corner of Park and onto Kuenzil, the passengers of Bus 18 feel a thump pass beneath them.

"Oh Lord, we just clipped a cyclist," a woman cries, clutching her Pomeranian to her chest. The bus screeches to a hard stop, the passengers scanning out the left window while the dog looks to the right. It perceives what the others only feel as a breeze.

A man-thing, both youthful and ancient. Its scents: salt water and shit and organs at the edge of collapse. Fingers, stretching out into claws. Eyes, eyes, two unblinking eyes that turn to the little dog and see.

The man-thing puts a finger with too many joints to its lips. Makes the same gesture Master does to be silent. The Pomeranian's instinct is to bark, to act as generations of breeding compel it to do. Instead, it cocks its head in wonder, lets the piss dribble down its legs and onto its owner. Its mighty bark leaves its lips as a whimper.

Then the bus windows explode. The Pomeranian's eyes follow the shape, which is running first on two legs, now on all fours, tearing through the air.

IT COMES NOW. For the flesh and bones that flee inside metal. For those that help and those that stand in the way. He will kneel, this man that plays God. Yes, he will bend his knee, and then it will be torn from its socket.

And her voice, clear and commanding. Mother must be followed, yes. Mother's word is law. "End it, Teddy, my dear," she says from all around. "Make him suffer!"

Teddy, yes. It has a name. It has a purpose.

"Doctor Robert Chase," Mother says. "Age: sixty-three. Hair: brown and gray. Eyes: blue. Weight: 220 pounds. He is the enemy. He is unworthy. Make him pay for his sins. Do it now! Doctor Robert Chase. Age: sixty-three. Hair…"

It focuses on the black SUV, the correct SUV. Then it is there. On this hood, this metal carapace, these great and terrible feet digging in. Its hand: these can be claws now, yes, sharp little tools. It can rend skin but first it must peel metal. *Do it.*

With a clang, it pulls the hood free from the body. Sees the engine sputtering heat. Hoists the hood up and brings it down on the glass. The woman driving jerks the wheel—left, right, left—and it wobbles, yes it does, but its balance is strong. It drives the hood through the glass. Then, with a dark hand, it peels the windshield right off.

Nowhere left to go, it muses. This rolling box is a coffin. It sees inside, focusing, pouring its shape into the back seat. Beside him now, so close it can smell sweat. It focuses, digs deep into memory and brings forth its once beautiful form. This god-doctor sees it, sees the molted humanity.

"Teddy, my God…"

And now it sees something pleasing on that old, wrinkled face.

Awe. And more, yes, the very thing it has craved for so long.

It sees fear in the eyes of its maker.

Then a luminous flash, and it sees them no more.

CAITLYN, chasing his voice across a fracturing landscape, plains of static, half-formed skylines and mountains, cities of veiled windows.

"Intersection of Ballpark and East 2nd Street," Michaels says. "There's—"

She sees them. Green signs, white text. Buildings bursting from the static, blooming into hard focus.

"—a stadium and a neon sign that says Freight House District."

Here it is, the ballpark, a thing of modern brick and green metal. There they are, the roads unrolling. Cars whizzing by, sirens crying and—

"Look for a black SUV. It's a Chevy Suburban, uh, probably damaged and—"

It all slams into view. The Chevy, under assault. The dhimoni, in the back seat, its arm raised to strike. Robert Chase, helpless and cowering.

Caitlyn Grey lies in the back of the medical van, her body speeding toward Clearwater Canyon at ninety-one miles per hour.

Her mens corpus moves faster. It crosses twenty-four miles in fifty milliseconds, the time it takes a neuron to fire one impulse. One point seven million miles per hour.

Even a dhimoni can't shrug off that impact.

Carruthers and Chase are rocked by a luminous surge passing through the car, wiping away the silver form of Teddy, wiping away their vision and all spatial perception. Then the world crashes back into place. The road, the humming traffic, the rubber against pavement. The Suburban fishtails, Carruthers regaining control.

Caitlyn sees none of this. She sees only the thing in her arms, silver-eyed and furious, raking her with desperate claws, digging fingers deep into her mind.

"Come on out, Teddy," Caitlyn cries, and the curtains embrace them. "You're with me now."

67

FAR TO THE EAST, WHERE THE AFRICAN WATERS MEET THE DARKENING sky, Saturn rises, soon to be pursued by the moon.

She climbs out of the boat's cabin and into the cockpit. Hands him a hot cup of tea, the last of their leaves from Sri Lanka. Savors the steamy notes of citrus and honey against the crisp evening wind. This sailboat, their cozy home for several years. The wide world ahead.

"How's she looking?" her mother asks. The sea, always a she.

"Clear skies and calm waters," her father says and sips the tea. To the west, lavender glass suffuses the line between heaven and earth. Blue hour soon, and black to follow.

Caitlyn never knew them as anything but her parents. Now, looking at them, she is awed by their youth. Forever in their forties here, in this living memory, the horizon ahead.

"Mom," Caitlyn says. "Dad."

Her mother turns to her, looks at her, looks through her. Then stifles a yawn. Gives her husband's hand a squeeze. "Don't stay up too late."

Her mother, Terry, so slender and graceful. Linen dress, loose and billowing. And it occurs to Caitlyn, as her mother descends below deck and the stern lights flicker, that this moment, this image, is the last memory of them she has.

The explosion hits below the cockpit and splits the hull almost in two. It doesn't stop the boat but cleaves it, slamming the halves port side, tilting the mast near vertical and dragging the ruins across fuel-slick waters.

Her father, at the helm only a moment ago, is now nowhere to be seen. The cockpit is a fast-collapsing wreck, waters foaming and swirling and swallowing the stern.

No, no, not again. Can she change this? Perhaps she can rescue her mother.

Below deck, the kitchen lists, water pouring through shelving and gushing out the oven. Caitlyn's bunk, the cozy bed with its lee cloth and little lamp. All the nights she read in that very nook. And here she is now, sun-kissed and young.

But she's not alone.

Something is throttling her body, her physical body. A shadow straddles her, spindly fingers wound tight around her throat.

Teddy's dhimoni.

She hits him in a furious surge, ten years of momentum that fries the boat's circuits and blows out the engine. The walls splinter and fray. Dark sea surges in, embracing them as she clings to his shadow-wrapped skin and—

Death.

Now Death stares down, backlit by morning. Death, ensconced in stained glass and lead, a shroud-wrapped reaper of souls. His companions, Pestilence, Famine, and War, surround him mid-charge, weapons outstretched. Hymns fill the air.

This is hallowed ground, this Iowa chapel full of Baptist song. Parishioners clapping and swaying, loud with the power of the spirit. Saints and prophets and biblical terrors, all proudly stand in their colored glass windows.

But not him.

Teddy Jensen, rosy-cheeked with thinning red hair, lurches back from the rear pew and collapses. He hits the ground hard, convulsing. Lips quivering, he slaps at the empty air as if batting away flies.

And Caitlyn.

These are her hands wrapped around his neck. These are Caitlyn's fingers dug deep into his mind. *Do it! Reach deeper and squeeeeeeeeeeeeze!*

No...

She lets him go. The parishioners swarm this seizing man. Teddy's pupils dilate, rods and cones consuming the light that streams in through the stained glass, through the shadow-wrapped reaper, this visage of Death etched here forever among Teddy's last waking thoughts.

A SPEEDING VAN, five miles off the northbound 70, pushing ninety. Caitlyn, waking up with a scream. She squeezes Michaels's wrist, braces against the stretcher. Her breath returns in waves.

"Whatever you're doing, it's working. Caitlyn, listen to me: you've bought us some time. Do you think you can buy us some more?"

"I don't know," she says. "I'm losing sense of time. I think I made Teddy. I think maybe we both made each other."

"Damn, you're really bleeding." Michaels dabs at her eyes with a wet wipe. "The SWAT team is hitting the farm. County's coordinating a power cut. We just need to hold him off."

The van rattles and swerves. Caitlyn clutches his hand as rocks bounce in the wheel well.

"That's Clearwater property," Mansour shouts from the front seat. "Jesus, she's got acute haemolacria?"

"What's that?" Caitlyn asks.

"It means you're bleeding from your eyes," Mansour says. "I'm coming back."

Stretching on gloves, Mansour pushes his way into the back as Michaels starts to climb up front.

"Wait." Caitlyn tugs at Michaels's hand. "I don't know if I can find my way back. Guide me."

"Okay."

Through the windshield: the lonely gravel road winds past spruces and pines, deep into the shadowed canyons. Michaels opens his mouth and Caitlyn counts down.

ONE THOUSAND FIVE hundred and eleven miles away, the Bell 412's four-blade rotors thunder low over the golden-green hills. The boys and girls of Iowa State's Joint Task Force are clipping in the last of their tactical gear. A full loadout. Not how they thought they'd be spending Thursday night.

On the horizon: the Jensen farmhouse, its faded barn and near endless meadows. Room for horses to run in the glimmering dusk. There they go now, spooked by the roaring twin engines.

Undersheriff Acosta, to the SWAT team: "Power's cut, but the farm's still on solar and battery. If they didn't know we're coming, they do now." Then, to the pilot: "How about just past the hoop house?"

The pilot brings the helicopter to a hover east of the farmhouse. The hoop house plastic billows in the downwash. Tail wagging, a three-legged dog circles and barks.

Rope hits the earth, followed by boots. The SWAT team has practiced fast-roping from a bird, and their best time for six operators is twenty-nine seconds. Tonight, they unload in twenty-two.

They run fast and low, shadows in the amber dust. An old pickup blocks the pantry. The only way in is through the front. The porch it is. A no-knock raid, full flashbangs at the ready. Officer Marco, on breach, draws back the ram.

Then the door opens.

The first shot catches Marco mid-swing, sixteen pellets of number one buckshot. The hard body armor stops most of it, but from ten feet back, the spread is wide and the damage deep. By the time he lands in the bush, his neck and face are peppered rubies. By the time he pulls his glasses off, he is already in shock.

"Shots fired! Shots fired!"

The second and third blasts come in rapid succession. Gaping holes punch out the doorframe. The fourth catches Sergeant Andrews squatting and knocks him on his ass. He crawls to the other side of a porch pillar, hands scouring his face, his chest. Hot pellets rattle in Kevlar and clatter to the gravel.

"I'm okay," he says, over the radio. "Vest took the bulk of it. God, the bitch probably broke half my ribs."

Nearby, Marco's head lolls to the right, his breath a frothy hiss through his neck. He reaches out, sputters something that nobody hears.

Return fire pockmarks the porch, blows out half the door. Inside, a voice, a woman crying out, "They're at the porch, Teddy! Make them pay! Make them suffer and scream!"

Nox IGNORES the siren as the SUV cuts through downtown Reno traffic. He ignores the skid of the tire, the shout of the motorists. What has his full attention are the sounds coming in through the radio. In the space of a breath, the channel becomes a chaotic refrain. There is gunfire, scattered, then a concussive blast. There is static, a persistent hiss.

"This is Coordinator Nox. Do you copy?"

"Uh, this is Acosta. Hold one moment."

Hold? Nox clenches his jaw. More static on the line. This is it, where it all goes pear-shaped fifteen hundred miles away. He's running out of plays to make.

EMPTY OF SWAT, the Bell 412 weighs almost seven thousand pounds. As it suddenly buckles and dips, the pilot nearly breaks his wrist trying to keep the bird level. As the window cracks and pops, he banks it to the left.

"Ground fire! We're taking ground fire!" he shouts, yet he sees no muzzle flashes, hears no pling of bullets breaching the cockpit.

The helicopter spins. Sunset and sky, then tree line and earth. Warnings scream, "Impact! Impact!" And in that spin, the pilot thinks the impossible: there's something crawling up the window and tearing off the blades.

The sown earth embraces the helicopter in plastic and damp strawberries. The hoop house entangles, PVC piping and clear plastic sheets. In a sputtering tumble, the metal bird comes apart.

Fifty feet away, Sergeant Andrews beholds the nightmare. Each breath tinged with the sharp focus of adrenaline. Yet this is impossible; this makes no sense.

The helicopter, rolling to rest in a tangle of plastic and metal. His team, running for cover or being picked off one by one.

And by what? Nothing is there. Yet he can sense it all around. A whirling dervish in the corners of his eyes. Violence without form.

A teammate breaks cover and runs for the tractor, slides beneath. Then he's tugged right out and flung aside.

Something among the dust, yes, a growling presence, spectral and cruel. Teddy, draped in silver and smoke, stalks the crawling officer across the grass he once played upon. The cop catches a shimmer, a sharp hulking form. And Teddy thinks, *Maybe I'll flay this intruder. Peel his skin from his body, make it dance for his friends.*

Then Mother's command from inside the house: "Teddy! Finish this! Finish it now!"

In the corner of his eye, Andrews senses a subsonic collapse, a flash that will haunt him for years, will pull him from sleep and bring him screaming into the night. A shriveled man-thing, wet and sickly, floating in the air and dripping with wires.

Then it is gone, leaving only the cries of his teammates.

Now MOVING through Mother's house, pockmarked with bullets. To the bedroom, where she reloads her shotgun. Where the tape player carries her amplified commandments over copper wire, out through headphone drivers, then into his ears and deep into his mind. There, it undergoes another conversion, piercing consciousness and suffusing all thoughts.

"Doctor Robert Chase. Age: sixty-three. Hair: brown and gray. Eyes—"

It comes into focus, each piece at a time. The road, the car, the neon lights. Some arrive instantly, etched with laser-like precision. Others are soft and hazy, glimpses amidst a billowing static-laced curtain.

Curtains, damn. She's done a number on him. He can still taste Caitlyn's echo. She'll be joining him soon, in his permanent twilight. When this is over, she'll serve him or scream.

But until then, yes, Dr. Chase. Flesh to finish. Here it is, the speeding black truck. A blight of bright lights and nighttime crowds pouring forth. Here he is, the maker, cowering in the back seat.

Time to strike. His head or his heart? Something else, yes. *Make the suffering last.* His liver.

Do it. Do it now. Rip and rend and show him his own guts.

"Not so fast," says a voice beside him. And again her hand is on his, luminous and strong.

IN THE DEEP test chamber of the Clearwater lab. No time for a countdown. Michaels, holding watch with Mansour as Caitlyn lies in the one functioning pod. There is enough equipment here to use, but not enough to use safely. The biosuit shows her vitals all over the map. Respiration: low. Neural activity: high. Michaels hopes she's under, hopes she knows where she's going.

A low-frequency boom answers that question.

CARRUTHERS SENSES THE EXPANSION, more than two people here in the SUV. Lights flickering, and now the low hum. All she can do is hold her breath. All she can do is accept that death is behind her as she blows through the intersection.

"Talk to me, Doc," she says. "How you doing?"

"It feels," Chase says, "like angels fighting over my soul."

"Yeah, well, you're not half wrong. Now promise me one thing: if Caitlyn gets you out of this you'll—"

To Carruthers's left: the glint of chrome off a dusty grill. The driver's side window explodes.

The horizon is sideways now, sliding. Sparks and pavement spatter the interior. Shielding his face, Chase blocks the screaming metal, the embers scorching his hair. *Hold on.* It's slowing, slowing. *Now check yourself.*

With a rattling groan, the Suburban comes to a stop on the sidewalk, facing the wrong way. The city bus that struck them has fishtailed, clipped a row of parked cars. Pedestrians hurry over, quick to help. They pull him out, wiping away glass and telling Chase to sit here, by this parking meter, that he is in shock, that he's just been hit by a bus. Clips of dialogue heard from a distance.

"Shit, man, you must've been going ninety."

"Idiot's lucky to be alive."

"—came out of nowhere."

Robert Chase feels the world stabilize. Pushes aside the pedestrians and stumbles back to the SUV. He gets his crutches. Has to get her out too, has to help—

"Carruthers, c'mon. We've got to go."

Carruthers responds, just not in words he can understand. Her face lies in her folded arms, resting on the steering wheel. The airbag never deployed. She hears the doctor, knows he is nearby, just past the wet crimson wall. *Damn, I made a mess of my face.* She lets out a low, muffled sound—"Go, run"—and wills her right hand to wave the doctor off.

Then comes the warmth and the silence as Denise Carruthers bleeds out and dies among a crowd she can no longer see.

MICHAELS DIPS the bandage in water and dabs at Caitlyn's face. Crimson threads leak from her eyes as the open pod air steams in cool ribbons. Warnings on all screens.

"How's she doing?" Michaels asks.

Wide-eyed, Mansour studies her vitals. "I... I don't know."

"You're a physician, right? Tell me if she's okay or if I should pull her out."

"No, I don't think she's okay," Mansour says. "Not at all. And if you pull her out now, the shock might stop her heart."

CHASE FLEES THE SCENE.

Perhaps those who pulled him from the wreckage could have stopped him, but their eyes rise skyward. There is a pulse, and every light on the block flickers and dims. In the darkness between buildings, where neon subsides, two shapes flash.

A woman, half formed out of silver mist. And something that resembles death. Both locked in a furious dance.

Hobbling past the valet, Chase pushes through the oaken doors of the Silver Legacy Resort Casino. Past the gambling masses, curious faces turning from their slot machines, amused at the latest entertainment spat up from Reno's streets. A drunk, perhaps. Or an overstimulated tourist. Two Mai Tai-plied retirees raise cocktails in Chase's direction.

Then a row of slot machines bursts into pieces. Screams mix with the rattle of coins. Some scatter. Some fill their pockets. Most don't notice the amber flooring crack beneath bending shadows and light.

The security cameras capture it all: the looting crowds, the pixel distortions warping across the lobby. Flickering pulses that bloom and congeal, forcing the camera to refocus.

On a bank of video monitors, in an unlisted floor above, the shift boss points it out. Wavy lines, like old cable channels, scrambled and inverted. The artifacts part and separate and the junior tech says, "No way that's in the lens. We're tracking it from multiple cameras."

There are two artifacts now, both far apart. One seems to be losing clarity. The other grows by the broken slots.

The shift boss swallows. "Are... Are those footprints?"

The junior tech leans close, breath steaming the screen. He rubs his eyes, tries to wipe away the odd afterimage that sticks in his mind.

A shimmering woman, falling to her knees. Static gushing from hollow eyes.

And the shift boss asks, "Where'd it go?"

There are 488 cameras in the Silver Legacy Resort Casino. To save data, most activate on motion. Floor two: a long set of indentations forming in real time. Floor three: a door blown from its hinges. The fourth-floor stairwell: a man limping up, taking the steps two at a time.

Out into the parking garage now, where the camera captures the man's frantic scramble.

"Christ, we've got a situation in the garage, top floor," the shift boss says into the walkie-talkie. "Can we get... The hell?"

He lets go of the talk button. Squints at the screen.

The artifacts return, first static then something black. Smoke billowing in backward. Impossible, he thinks, and realizes that between the stuttering jerks, he can see a half formed young man, feet drifting off the ground.

SUSAN JENSEN FIRES the last of the number one buckshot and falls back to the bedroom. She leaves the shotgun on the floor and barricades herself in. The old couch, her rocking chair, Teddy's medical bed. They all go against the door and the windows, just like she's practiced.

Then she retreats into the bathroom.

Her Smith & Wesson Model 610 revolver holds six .40-caliber

cartridges. She has four speed loaders in her pockets, full and ready. Five boxes by the sink. More than enough for these pigs.

This is her house they have violated. Her boy will protect her; her boy always has. For now she needs a clean line of sight.

She scoots a dresser to the bathroom door, keeps the walk-in tub to her right. The waters are roiling, Teddy's skin salt-crusted and steaming. She senses a shimmer, candescent and warm.

"Don't wait, honey! You make him pay! Make them all suffer for their sins!"

THE HIGHEST BUILDING in Reno is a dispassionate wall of black windows and white concrete lit up in green like the money it covets. Thirty-eight floors of the Silver Legacy Resort Casino look down on this parking garage roof, silent witness to a doctor's final run.

"You're out of room, Doctor Chase. All out of space." The voice comes from everywhere. Off the walls, the scattered cars, the cool mountain air.

Chase spins. "Teddy? Is that you?"

"You don't recognize your star pupil?"

"It's been thirty years, my boy. Don't take it personal."

There he is, in the middle of the lot. Fifty feet away and floating.

And here he is now, unfolding right in front of Chase. The old man gasps and falls back on his ass. Teddy grins.

"It's hard not to take it personal," Teddy says. "When you look at yourself, you look in the mirror. When I want to see my face, I look down on a husk."

"What happened to you was unconscionable. We had no intention of harming anyone."

"And yet you did."

"Yes, I did," Chase says. "But you did as well. I warned you what could happen if you weren't careful. What you've become, this is your making as well."

"You played Prometheus, then you backed out. You gave us fire, Dr. Chase. Then you made us stay cold."

"I gave you my life's work!" Chase shouts. "And you turned it against me! If I could fix this, I would. But I can't. You forgot your humanity. This twisted thing you've become, I've had no part in this."

A ding at the elevator, a din of voices. "Freeze!" Two security guards rush out, pausing, staring up at this floating mens corpus. A young man, eyes molten silver, body draped in mist.

In the time it takes them to blink, Teddy warps across one hundred feet of lot and flips a BMW into them. A crunch of bones, the squeal of a car alarm, and the elevator doors buckle in. Then, just the hissing of coolant, the dripping of oil.

"Gods," Chase says.

Beneath Teddy's translucent skin flicker different faces. A cold skull. A shriveled, sick man. A smooth form, some ideal between youth and decay. And the dhimoni, that reaper, always vibrating at the edge of his form. Teddy's feet touch the concrete, forming cracks. He takes a step toward Chase. Another.

"It takes so much concentration to make myself visible," Teddy says and waves his hands. "When I first showed my splendor to Roger, I had to rest for a month. But I want you to see the face of your judgment. See me, as I pull your heart from your chest."

A step closer.

"They call me the Breath of God, don't they? It's a bit much."

Another step. Closer and closer.

"I'm not the breath of anything," he says. "But I am a god."

Closer.

"No, you're not," says a voice at the edge of the lot. Caitlyn. "You are no god, Teddy."

Chase can't see her—not directly—but he feels her hand on his shoulder, pushing him aside. He catches a flicker: luminous steam out the side of his vision. Senses warmth passing on his left.

Wait for it, she tells herself. *You've got one shot. Just focus and wait.*

"You were a victim, Teddy, yes. But now you're a freak, a mistake, a bad day at the lab."

Teddy roars. He is the dhimoni now; he is death. He is shriveled and youthful and all things at once. How dare this girl spew insolence at his glory!

He pounces upon her, fingers stretching into hooks at her throat, and he will tear every last strand of her matter apart now, yes. He will unweave her mind until she is drooling and simple. "When I'm done with the doctor, you will weep at how I ruin your flesh."

She stares him straight in the eyes. *Wait for it.* "This is your last chance, Teddy. You're trapped. You've got nowhere to go."

Teddy cackles. Behind his lips, rows of teeth lead into a maw without end. He says, "I can go everywhere."

Sorrow crosses Caitlyn's face. But only a flicker.

Wait for it.

"No, Teddy, I can go everywhere," Caitlyn says, and her eyes harden before closing. "But you still live with your mom."

And in a blink, she is gone.

THERE ARE over one hundred thousand miles of myelin-sheathed neurons in the brain, one hundred trillion synaptic connections. When Teddy understands Caitlyn's words, his alpha motor neurons—the fastest neurons in a human body—fire in rapid succession, tearing him back across fifteen hundred miles of America. Across the great swaths of violet-bloom desert he had wandered in his dreams. Over the Salt Lake. Through Ogden, its brown brick buildings and suburban sprawls. Past winding freeways where cars and trucks ply the pavement like the electrical signals in his mind, from the axon tips, across the synaptic gap, to the dendrites of the next neuron, a dance from node to node, state to state, memory to memory.

Fast, yes, Teddy moves as fast as he ever has. Across southern Wyoming now, Elk Mountain against the pink dusk. Over the prairies and plains of Nebraska, spring green giving way to summer gold. Past rusty railroads and cracked byways and wastelands like the fallow fields of his mind.

Faster now, yes. Yet he sees her ahead. *No, faster.* He feels the weight of the dhimoni, all that he's broken. The halls and the floors, the flesh and the bone. Feels the great heft of his fury. *No, no.* And he is turbulent now, dragging, and he cannot keep up with her. *No, no, no!* He cannot keep up.

Teddy arrives back at his house just in time to see this: Caitlyn, here, in his bathroom, seizing Mother's hand and wrenching it to the right. Away from the bedroom and the police and the chaos down the hall. Aiming her heirloom revolver at the tub, now squeezing and—

A lone crack of thunder.

Mrs. Jensen lets out a shrill cry when she sees what she's done. Her boy, bobbing in the reddening waters. The leaking tub. The machines crying out. *Flatline!*

Impossible. She had been aiming at the door, yet now...

"No, no, baby, please. Sweetie, wake up. Please don't leave me alone."

Caitlyn steels herself for what may come next. Teddy's body, in this crimson bath. Teddy's *mens corpus*, arriving a half second too late. He isn't wrapped in shadows. Nor is he shriveled and sick. He is just the young boy from the files, eighteen and clear-eyed, his whole life ahead. Caitlyn senses that a small part of Teddy has always been there, locked behind old doors in a house of his mind with too many rooms.

Teddy meets her gaze, opens his mouth to say something, but only static pours forth. Then he is gone and the lights flicker and brighten.

"Please don't leave me, baby. Please."

It is Caitlyn's turn to depart. Susan Jensen senses the emptiness that follows. Guilt, but only for a moment. There are boots stomping down the hallway, radios squawking tactical violence. She can hear them ordering her to come out with her hands up.

Hands. She squeezes her son's hand one final time, lets him sink into the warm, ruby depths.

Then she puts the gun in her mouth and squeezes the trigger.

THERE IS a sense that something has happened, a reckoning at the edge of perception. And still, he holds his breath. Dr. Robert Chase, on the parking garage roof, on stage. The focus of curious eyes behind the green-lit windows of this citadel of chance. He waits for his death.

But death does not come.

Only a voice, enveloping and warm.

"It's over, Doctor."

"Caitlyn?" he asks, and he catches a glimmer each time he turns. A form, sun-kissed and luminous, eyes of bright dawn. "Why? Why save me? I don't deserve this."

"Maybe not," she says, her warm lips against his ears. "So be worthy of it."

"Caitlyn?" he asks again and again, turning, sensing that this lot is finally empty.

68

CLEARWATER

COORDINATOR NOX FINDS MICHAELS SITTING BENEATH A BLOOMING cottonwood at the mouth of Clearwater. A med tech checks him for injuries but he waves the man off. Weapons drawn, the op techs storm the facility.

"Word from Iowa is the farmhouse went quiet," Nox says. He has a few cuts on his face and a spot of dried blood on his collar. Michaels tries not to notice. "Nary a peep since Mrs. Jensen plugged her son."

Michaels chews a toothpick, one of his last.

"Well, whatever you did, it worked."

"I didn't do anything. I just asked her for help."

"Asset management is a skill. Not an easy one either." A pause. "She is still inside, yes?"

Michaels holds up his tablet. Vital signs read *ALL FLAT*. Neural activity, respiration, pulse. "She's gone."

Nox sighs. "I am sorry to hear that. The nation owes her a debt of gratitude."

"They'll never know her name."

"No," Nox says. "Of course not. So much wasted potential, all around us. Perhaps we can salvage something."

He waits for Michaels to talk, but it never comes. The man

without emotions, now in mourning. A truck pulls up, then another. Barnes is among the cleanup crew. He gives Michaels a sour look but Nox waves him off.

"Well, Reno's a mess," Nox says. "We'll suppress it, but it needs a deft touch. We can use you there, Agent Michaels."

"I'm sure you could."

It's only now that the coordinator notices Michaels's badge and ID sitting nearby, next to a gun. "Take a few weeks to ruminate. We all think about walking, from time to time."

Michaels meets those turquoise eyes. "What keeps you here?"

Nox considers the question. There is a softening, something like nostalgia at the edge of his lips. He bends down, brushes away dirt, and finds a perfectly smooth stone.

"The potential. It's never perfect, but neither are we."

"Chase said the same thing."

"Way of the world," Nox says and sends the stone skipping across the dark eddies at the edge of the river. "Last week, some twelve-year-old hacker nearly brought down Air Force One. Last month, a grad student in Austin used CRISPR to mix coronavirus and Alzheimer's. And yes, three decades ago, Clearwater jumped from this lab. There is the future. Then there's everyone else, trying to catch up. Our ancestors harnessed fire and broke skulls with stones. We take that warmth and those stones and we build civilization."

"But why us?" Michaels asks. "Why does the Foundation get this?"

"Don't get too philosophical, Michaels. It's a muddy road."

"Humor me."

"When I go before the subcommittees and the grand juries and the Joint Chiefs of Staff, I tell them it's for our protection and the moral right of our nation."

Michaels scoffs. "Please."

"What it really comes down to is this: better we've got the fire and the others do not."

Barnes walks over. Whispers into the coordinator's ear. Hands him the radio. Nox listens to the other end. That flat line that splits his thin lips, almost unreadable. Almost. But not entirely. A flash of fury, a spark come and gone. Then calm and his green eyes turn to Michaels as he gives Barnes the radio.

"It seems that Ms. Grey's pod is empty," Nox says. "There's no body down there. Where is she?"

"You tell me." Michaels shrugs. "Like I said, she's gone."

Then he is up and off. He unlocks an SUV and opens the driver's side door.

A hand falls on his shoulder. Barnes, two other op techs. They check the vehicle as the coordinator looks on. Open the trunk, lift a canvas bag, shine lights into the spare tire compartment, but it's—

"Empty, sir," Barnes says.

The coordinator locks eyes with Michaels. Then he gives a slight nod. Michaels climbs into the SUV, turns the key, and drives off down the dirt road. The stars are rising and a thin band of daylight clings to the western horizon, pierced by these shadowed peaks that know decades of horror.

Michaels drives on, forward, and doesn't look back.

[PART 6]

You know the future is happening when you start feeling scared.

— Graffiti on an interstate billboard

69

THE EVENTS OF EARLY MAY IN RENO MAKE THE NEWS AS FAR AS Beijing.

Officially, an experimental fighter jet out of Nellis ran into trouble with its onboard AI. Thirty miles northwest of Reno, an EMP was accidentally deployed. The Air Force is proud to report that the electrical grid held up during the unscheduled stress test. Many of the city's lights and cameras, however, need to be upgraded. A Department of Energy grant is covering the cost.

Unrelated is the car chase that ended on the steps of the Silver Legacy Resort Casino. The suspect, a middle-aged Hispanic male on an expired visa, is being held by ICE, pending transfer to Arizona on a charge of statutory rape. The federal agent who intervened and lost her life is a decorated FBI agent months from early retirement. She was in Reno on vacation.

In early June, Sam Stephens is found dead in a motel in Pattaya, Thailand. There is no note, but viewers familiar with his episodes of manic depression are mostly unsurprised. A video uploaded by a fresh YouTube account shows a dark go-go bar off Walking Street. And Sam, drunk, carousing for cocaine and lady boys. His most ardent listeners maintain the video is a deepfake, a false flag to distract people from the fact that the Bilderberg Group is planning a coup via a shadow clause in the constitution.

In July, a website run by Sam Stephen's attorney releases years of sworn testimony from Sam about government experiments. Within a week, seven other websites claim to have similar files. Overwhelmed, WikiLeaks publishes them all. Twenty-one thousand pages of transcripts are downloaded 1,300,000 times and fully read by ninety-seven people.

No minds are changed.

IT TAKES three threats of litigation, two grand juries, and a charge of child pornography filed and dropped against one of their own for the Iowa State SWAT to come to the collective understanding that what happened at the Jensen farm was due to a buildup of carbon monoxide in the helicopter's ventilation system. A parallel investigation uncovers mistakes in the aircraft's maintenance log. Further examination reveals the existence of toxic black mold.

Among the catalogue of items found at the Jensen farm is a key to a post office box in Coggon, Iowa, where letters from Roger continue to arrive in the weeks after his death. They bear postal codes from two re-mailing services, one in Fort Worth, the other in Lexington. The letters promise endless supplication and worship and praise for the meaning now given to his life in service of a new god, one he met thirty years ago when he first saw him crawl out of a pod.

Teddy's tumor-riddled brain is weighed, photographed, and shipped off under armed escort. His body as well.

Seven gallons of DZ3 are found in an empty horse stall, alongside a half kilogram of Vetalar, stockpiled over years. Hanging from a nail, like an old family recipe, is the exact process to make DZ3, handwritten. Flecks of blood confirm the match to William McNare.

Bodies are returned to families in staggered increments during the summer. In all cases, the next of kin are told that their parent or spouse or sibling had perished while on classified work abroad. They are given stories of bravery, vague on details but high on heroism. Stories that tell the completion of lives. A research breakthrough on malarial drugs tested in Zaire, then a bus accident on the drive home. Or the unlocking of new neural pathways in coma patients at a clinic in Belize. Then a heart attack in their sleep. In each case, the stories are corroborated and seem believable, as if they are carefully designed for the listener, to fill some need.

By September every test subject from Clearwater is cremated or buried.

Or so the families believe.

THE PAPERWORK LASTS FOR MONTHS, and Michaels finds himself looking at their faces often. He imagines Roger in his RV, careening across the country. The desperate Mrs. Jensen. And Teddy, lost between worlds. His body, a fifty-pound anchor. His brain turning on itself, consuming the human parts to fuel the dhimoni.

He feels little enmity toward him now, mostly pity.

In the van, Caitlyn had said they might have created each other, Teddy and her. So when Michaels lays out the dates, it clicks into place. Ten years ago, at a church in Iowa, a man had a stroke. Half a world away, on the very same day, a boat sank off the dark Kenyan waters. It hurts his head to think about it, so mostly he doesn't.

August finds him in St. Louis, where the postal worker grumbles and hands him a bin of mail. At home, after throwing out dead houseplants and opening the windows, Michaels sorts through five months of mail, mostly junk.

Tucked inside a National Geographic Travel Expeditions brochure is a single-spaced typed page.

Ninety days since I last blinked. A new personal best. Last night I saw my first planet. Saturn rising, just like how my parents taught me to navigate at night. One point of light, that's all you need.

Dr. Chase mentioned entanglement and I think I get it now. Teddy and I, we are binary stars. Sometimes I see him in my sleep. He no longer scares me.

I never thanked you for the warning. Maybe someday I can? This world is big and beautiful and I hope you'll agree there's room for us both.

Written in pen, at the bottom, in a scrawl that portends improvement:

Happy Travels,
  Caitlyn Grey

A SILENT CURTAIN has descended over the farm and the meadows. The hoop house lies in tatters, the strawberries long since rotted and dry. The horses have all been sent elsewhere, to run with warm winds in far open fields. The three-legged dog hobbles with them.

At night, when the humidity seems so thick the air might cry, when the crickets hold their song and the old barn groans as the breeze stirs up, on some such nights the local kids—drunk or stoned or simply looking to scare each other—sneak onto the property. There, where the air feels electric and the world fades, a few swear they can hear the echoing hiss of machines breathing deep in the farmhouse.

[70]

UNIVERSITY OF VIRGINIA
NOVEMBER - 10:00 A.M., EST

LATE AUTUMN, THE CAMPUS COLLECTIVELY LIMPING TOWARD THE Thanksgiving break. The turkey and family and a much-needed intermission.

Michaels finds her easily; she looks like her mother. Except the eyes. Those must have come from the donor.

He buys her a chai latte and they sit in the warmth of a heat lamp while the rain pours down in silver sheets. He had hoped she would ask questions. About her mother, Denise, and the short time they worked together. Perhaps how she had died. He doesn't like talking but he tries to paint a picture his partner—his first and only partner—would have wanted her daughter to know.

"Mostly, what I guess I'm here to say is, I'm sorry. She would still be here if she hadn't helped my investigation. And that your mother was proud of you. She had hoped to get to know you more, when she retired."

Jade says, "Yeah, well, we'll never know, will we?" She thumbs her chai latte and wipes a smudge off her legal textbook. "God, we would've driven each other nuts."

Michaels nods and sips his coffee. "Yeah, we did too," he says. "But Denise was one of the good ones. Which reminds me..."

He takes out a plastic evidence bag. Carruthers's cell phone. He slides it to Jade.

"There's a few messages on there she meant to send you. Her passcode's your birthday."

Something softens in Jade's eyes. Nineteen years old, Michaels thinks. He has to reach far back just to remember himself then. He had burned with convictions. Jade seems suffused with wise calm.

She places the phone in her backpack. "Maybe you can stop by sometime," she says, "Like, to tell me more about the FBI."

"I'm just a civilian. I never worked for the Bureau."

"Oh. That's too bad. You know, I never told her this, but the reason I chose UVA is 'cause it's a feeder for Quantico. I just... I didn't want her to think I was following her path, you know?"

"I think maybe she knew," he says, and it's a lie, but it leaves his lips with a smile because it brings one to this young woman's face. "And that she was proud of you, whatever path you took. Parents cast long shadows."

"Yeah. Well, I need to get to class."

A handshake that turns into a soft hug. Then Jade Carruthers-Letova walks off and joins her friends in the sea of young minds, eager to learn, eager to move into a future that can't come soon enough.

Michaels finishes his coffee and places it in the recycling. He moves slower these days. His hands tremble less. He can't recall the last time he counted primes. On his way out, he stops at a table where two men wear hoodies and jeans.

"You know, you fellas stick out like tits on a wall," he says.

The men exchange practiced glances. They're too well-groomed for any campus. "I'm sorry, do we know you?"

"You should. That's my dossier right there." He taps on the edge of metal and glass, a tablet sticking out beneath a newspaper. "You've been tailing me since the airport. Friendly advice: it never takes four hours to read *USA Today*."

One man stammers and clears his throat. The other glances away. "There's been a mistake."

"Fair enough. See you at the hearing."

Then Michaels walks off, leaving the two to lean in and whisper, to raise a hidden mic to their lips and leave their meals uneaten as they resume shadowing him from fifty yards back.

[71]

WASHINGTON DC
NOVEMBER - 3:00 P.M., EST

THE SELECT COMMITTEE ON SPECIAL INVESTIGATIONS AND
Foundation Review—a committee that does not exist—meets in a
nondescript conference room at the edge of the Capitol Building.
In the echoing, marble halls, Michaels spots a familiar face. Brad
Lee, formerly of the CBI, flanked by a stunning Asian woman.
Both are dressed in their D.C. best. Michaels senses a closeness to
their stance, the way her perfume has joined his cologne, a hint
that tells him they dressed in the same hotel room.

"I don't know what to call you," Brad says. "Michaels? I think
of Agent Michaels, but I mean, you're not."

"Call me Mike," he says and adds, "Field Agent Lee."

"Hey, that's Field Agent Trainee."

"You'll advance fast."

Brad nods, but there's something pained on his face.

"Relax, I've been where you are. I know what's coming.
They've got you testifying about how I mismanaged the investi-
gation, let it all go sideways, right? They need to blame someone.
Who better than someone stepping out the door?"

Brad opens his mouth but Michaels shushes him. In the marble
halls, it almost sounds like a shout.

"Don't lie," Michaels says. "Not yet. Save them, like bullets. Every hearing needs a villain. Today, it's my turn."

Brad nods and offers him a smile and then says no more.

THEY ARRIVE in order of importance. The witnesses and the panel and several coordinators, Nox and others whom Michaels has never met. Then Senator Marks, Congresswoman Chatterjee, and Judge Maberry, who was called in from the golf course on his only day off.

Michaels doesn't dispute the findings. He resigned months ago and the punishment is mostly symbolic. For all the Foundation's secrecy, there is a recording courtesy of the NSA that proves his negligence didn't lead to treason or enable a terrorist attack. He tried to warn Nox what was coming for Reno.

Still, the punishment stings. The computer screen shows eight years of service, his name next to twenty-three solved cases, twenty-eight thousand hours worked, over sixty a week. And with a click, his name and record are reduced to an encrypted file, purged just like that. Time to start building a life.

"You know, you could probably have avoided this if you hadn't helped her escape," Judge Maberry says.

"But I didn't."

"And you didn't stop her either," Congresswoman Chatterjee says. "A weapon we built."

"That's true."

"So why don't you just tell us how she did it, son?" Senator Marks croaks in his Kentucky drawl. "How's it you let a blind girl get up out of there? What'd you do? Carry her out or something?"

"Maybe," Michaels says. "Or maybe she carried herself."

Silence. Then a chuckle. A few more joining in. "Now, son, even with this hoopla, that's just plain silly."

Michaels smiles. "You're right. It is."

THERE IS A BOAT AT REST NEAR A PINK CORAL BEACH WHERE THE
mangroves claw at the edge of the water. The boat is forty-seven
feet long and in remarkable shape for its age. Its hull has spent a
decade without feeling the sea. It is for this reason the owner has
decided to sell it at a discount, even though the buyer did not
haggle. She could have, and the owner wanted her to. Haggling is
common in this part of the world. And although he was born far
from these shores, this is where he has ended up, where he will
spend his sunset years, now that his retirement is financed.

Still, he is a man and a sailor at heart. Old sailors never quit
the sea. So the old man and the boat spend these cloudless months
edging their way ever closer to the water. He senses the weight of
her impending voyage with each finished task. The hull is now
clean, the electrical systems working. They have upgraded the
sails and the masts. When a new satellite navigation system
arrives, the old sailor helps her install it and afterward she cooks
him a dinner of curried tiger prawns and dumplings and seaweed
salad.

She shares little of herself, her journey, how she came to these
equatorial shores. Most here are leaving something behind. He

likes to close his eyes and listen; he can hear the world in her voice.

And now rain clouds the horizon. The turquoise waters are churning with the breeze. A stranger walks down the beach and the old sailor shouts, "Myra, you've got a visitor."

She doesn't hear the old sailor. There is a radio blaring as the dock sways with the dancing tide. She doesn't hear the visitor's footsteps, the wobbling of old wood. Doesn't seem to notice his tan, his hair a little longer now, his face less rutted from lies.

Myra, it's what the locals call her. To him, she almost looks the part. Her hair is lightened by the equatorial sun, and her left arm bears a new colorful tattoo. He wonders, *How long has it been since she last blinked?* And he also wonders if she's happy. He hopes that she is.

And then, perhaps unexpectedly, or perhaps sensing his presence, she answers it for him. She wipes her face with a towel, turns around, and smiles when it's him that she sees.

EPILOGUE
LOCATION: REDACTED

IT BEGINS AGAIN, DEEP IN A PLACE OF CRASHING WATER AND METAL, where the light comes from diodes and the walls are fresh concrete. Where oxygen is pumped in through labyrinthian tubes. Where the filters break down the bitter salt in the air. It happens when skin is peeled back and dead nerves are exposed. When fibrous webs are pressed between conductive glass sheets. It happens as brains are bathed in chemicals, their engorged folds mapped and compared. As currents charge through lattices of dead neurons, as questions are asked and answers are sought.

Here, on wave-battered pylons, miles from the shore, shivers are common, the air whispers often, and in these shadowy halls, the lights always blink.

ACKNOWLEDGMENTS

Much of *Blind Site* is deeply fictional, but the people who helped shape it are not.

Thanks to Clay Stafford and the Killer Nashville team for their generous support of this project at a time when it most needed nurturing. Additional thanks to Bryan Robinson and the Jimmy Loftin Memorial Scholarship, which made key research possible.

On the tactical side, my sincere thanks to Matt Espenshade, retired FBI Assistant Special Agent in Charge. My gratitude to the friendly folks at the FBI's amazing IPPAU, including Public Affairs Officer Angela Bell and Special Agent Jeff Heinze, who let me throw some ridiculous questions their way and returned thoughtful, sincere answers. Additional thanks to the San Jose State University Department of Justice Studies and the men and women of law enforcement who gave their time generously to answer this writer's far-fetched questions. And thank you to my doppelgänger brother from another mother and father, Texas badass Andrew van Wey. Sorry to commandeer our name.

On the medical side, I'm grateful for the perspectives of Jennifer Dornbush and Dr. Bradley Harper, both of whom answered my grotesque questions without flinching and let me follow them around the halls of Killer Nashville without calling for security.

Some of Michaels's paranoia and practice was formed by Kevin Mitnick and Robert Vamosi's excellent book *The Art of Invisibility: The World's Most Famous Hacker Teaches You How to Be Safe in the Age of Big Brother and Big Data*. Additionally, Judy Melinek and T.J. Mitchell's book *Working Stiff: 2 Years, 262 Bodies and the Making of a Medical Examiner* is a gruesomely beautiful work and a must-read for anyone curious about what happens in the autopsy suite. For an insightful trip into the brain's inner workings, be sure to pick up Michael Pollan's wonderful book *How to Change Your Mind: What the New Science of Psychedelics Teaches Us About Consciousness, Dying, Addiction, Depression, and Transcendence*.

My deepest thanks to the following creatives: Nick Taylor, the peninsula's best writer of baseball noir and an all-around fantastic educator; Paul Douglass and Ryan Skinnell, for their thoughtful feedback. Jim Thompson and Mark Schwartz helped develop this project when it was a far different creature with far different claws. Thank you.

Poor Bodie Dykstra has suffered my countless malapropisms with grace and deserves a huge shout out. Tom Jordan narrated the audiobook and it's a total home run. Thanks to Phillip Kim for correcting my atrocious Korean. And big love to the Reddit community on r/blind, who tolerated my questions, enriched my perspective, and infused Caitlyn with grace, strength, and a depth of experience.

All that I got right is due to the fine people above. All that I fumbled is on me.

The technology used to create Dr. Robert Chase's decoherence is fictional. Yet much of our progress in science and medicine has come from those we have treated unfairly, often without their consent. We owe it to our future to acknowledge our past.

Thank you to my family and friends who have had to deal with my random questions. A writer spends most of their time alone. With support and love they rarely feel lonely. I never have.

To my wife, Marissa. We fell in love through stories and adventures, both fictional and lived. My time with you has been the greatest adventure of all. Thank you, truly.

And to my readers, you've made it this far. In an age of infinite distractions, you chose to spend your time with my words. You are why I do this, why I keep on writing. Thank you.

Andrew Van Wey
    April 5th, 2021

ABOUT THE AUTHOR

ANDREW VAN WEY was born in Palo Alto, California, spent part of his childhood in New England, lived abroad for almost a decade, and currently resides in Northern California with his wife and their Old English Sheepdog, Daenerys.

As a child of the late 80's and early 90's, Andrew fondly remembers a time when cell phones were the size of bricks, a good scare could be found in a stack of torn Stephen King books, and a sleepover was best spent scaring friends with low-budget horror on VHS.

When he's not writing Andrew can probably be found mountain biking or playing video games (if time permits). He loves teaching, traveling, and geeking out about D&D and new technology. He considers bacon and eggs to be a perfectly acceptable meal at all times of day, and tattoos to be high art.

For special offers and new releases, please sign up for his newsletter at andrewvanwey.com

- instagram.com/heydrew
- facebook.com/andrewvanwey
- goodreads.com/andrewvanwey
- bookbub.com/authors/andrew-van-wey
- amazon.com/author/andrewvanwey
- twitter.com/andrewvanwey

CPSIA information can be obtained
at www.ICGtesting.com
Printed in the USA
LVHW030623220921
698416LV00003B/159